THE IMPERIALIST
A NOVEL OF THE HAWAIIAN REVOLUTION
KURT HANSON

For Rosalyn and Audrey

PROLOGUE

Hawaii, 1887.

"If you gentleman would, on behalf of your respective countries, be so kind as to take possession of my kingdom until such time as events return to normal, we would consider this a great act of friendship."

The King made his request, and for perhaps the first time ever six assembled diplomats could think of nothing to say. They shifted uncomfortably on the balls of their feet in the royal reception hall of the Iolani Palace as the King anxiously anticipated a response. One of them opened his mouth as if to speak, but words would not come. Five of them broke protocol and stole questioning glances at the American minister to the Hawaiian kingdom. As discreetly as possible, he shrugged his shoulders and turned up his palms.

"Gentlemen, please!" his majesty, King Kalakaua demanded of the diplomats, spraying gin-scented saliva in his desperation. "Armed men are roaming the streets. A private army of traitors has risen up to destroy us. Surely you, representatives of the great powers of the world will assert yourselves in this crisis!"

"Your majesty, if I may," the British minister broke the ambassadorial silence.

"Ah, our emissary from Queen Victoria. Please, speak."

The Brit didn't know quite where to start, but he was sure that there was no precedent for a collection of powers that occasionally went to war against each other to spontaneously come together to form a protectorate over a wayside Polynesian kingdom. Even if such a thing were permitted by his government, he couldn't imagine including the German minister, who stood next to him, stinking of beer and pickled herring.

"Yes, well, Your Majesty…What you suggest, that is, that sort of thing, well…it simply isn't done."

"Why not?"

"It just isn't."

The king was now quite desperate, not to mention a little drunk. He paced back and forth in his quasi-military royal regalia. The diplomats eyed the four Royal Guards standing at attention behind the King. They were so large. After another turn, the King simply kept walking out of the hall, muttering an unintelligible series of vowels as he left. The Royal Guard followed. The diplomats, not having been officially dismissed, waited another confused moment until again the British diplomat spoke.

"Well, then, gentlemen, I suppose we should show ourselves out."

Once outside the palace they could see a throng of well-dressed protestors in a procession on the street beyond the gates. The crowd followed a wagon carrying two bound men, one of whom was the King's Prime Minister.

"Oh, my," the American and British ministers said in unison.

The Japanese minister looked closely at the crowd, which he estimated at over one hundred, and commented on its collective complexion. "All white."

"Yes," the American concurred. "I suppose they are."

"They seem to be headed toward the wharf," the British minister said.

"Following them might be advisable, at a safe distance, of course."

"Indeed." The little clump of diplomats left their carriages at the palace and followed the throng on foot. Immediately outside the palace gates a company of soldiers from the Honolulu Rifles—the private army that had the King in such a state—stood at attention, bayonets at the ready. As the diplomats caught up with the crowd, they saw more clearly the Prime Minister and his grown son sitting in a wagon, hands bound behind their backs, looking very much like condemned men.

At the wharf another crowd was already assembled around some scaffolding that had been pulled to the center of the dock, evidently as a makeshift gallows. The two nooses hanging from the crossbar made it difficult to draw any other conclusion.

"Hang 'em! Hang 'em both!" shouted a very angry old man, elegantly dressed in his frock coat and top hat.

"I know that fellow," said the American. "He goes to my church."

"I take it he's better behaved there?" asked the Brit.

"Yes, actually. He leads our prayers."

The wagon halted in front of the scaffold and the forlorn prisoners looked miserably at the dangling ropes that awaited their necks.

"String 'em up!" the cries began again. The mob's blood lust seemed to grow as the prisoners blanched. They wanted them dead.

"Well, this seems to have gotten out of hand." Lorrin Thurston sidled up to the diplomats, obviously enjoying the chaos.

"You might want to do something about this, Thurston. Your mob is about to hang the prime minister," the America minister said.

"So I see," he said with a nonchalance the diplomats found disturbing. Thurston, dressed in a business suit, walked through the crowd, ascended the scaffold, and calmly hauled down the nooses to the great disappointment of the crowd. He spoke directly to the prisoners in a low voice, but the bound men answered his questions animatedly. Thurston signaled a group of private soldiers to approach. Moments later the soldiers escorted the prisoners on ship to the accompaniment of disappointed catcalls from the mob. Thurston watched from the scaffold to see that the prisoners made it safely down the gangway. That done, he returned to the diplomats.

"I gave them the choice of standing trial here or taking a ride on this lovely boat to San Francisco. They chose the latter."

5

"And what would they be charged with if they were foolish enough to stay?"

"Treason, same as the King."

"Treason? My God, have you overthrown the monarchy?"

"Lovely idea, but, alas, no." He was interrupted by the sound of another company of troops marching past, toward the Palace. "We're simply modifying things a bit. The King is a corrupt drunkard, and his despotic debauchery has gone on quite long enough."

"Then you have overthrown him. He believes you mean to kill him."

Thurston paused. "You've been to see him?"

"Yes this morning. He offered his kingdom to us for safekeeping."

"Safekeeping, you say?" Thurston seemed to enjoy the absurdity of it. He smiled as another company of private soldiers marched passed, their bayonets gleaming in the sun.

CHAPTER ONE

Seattle, 1892

The twentieth century was only eight years away, and the world was definitely getting smaller. People were coming and going to and from the furthest reaches of the earth, with boatloads of nasty little people of every imaginable hew arriving in American cities every day. It seemed important to make sure everyone behaved themselves. Accordingly, the congregation of Seattle's Methodist Episcopal Church eagerly anticipated Reverend Jacob Steele's talk on his travels through the world and encounters with naked heathens as he taught them what they were doing wrong.

First, the midday reception—a chance for the congregation to socialize with the Great Missionary, himself. Christopher Jones, having survived four years of Christian scholarship, had been treated to Reverend Steele's talks before. The man was an exhilarating speaker, but Christopher had a belly full of 'evangelize the world' talk at seminary. Somewhere along the line he decided the world was probably just fine, but of course he felt guilty for thinking so. His fiancée, Lydia, who had her own purposes, insisted they attend the event.

Something was amiss. Christopher watched from the side of the hall as the Reverend, at the front, alternately chatted warmly with the parishioners who stopped by, then not so warmly he turned his attention to other members of his own party. The Reverend's wife held what looked like a telegram, the contents of which obviously gave them both some distress. The local pastor, Reverend Bemis, clearly wanted to help but seemed limited in his ability to do so. Reverend Steele asked questions and Reverend Bemis shrugged his shoulders, looked around the hall, scratched his chin, then his bald pate, none of which seemed to help. Steele looked elsewhere for answers, but was interrupted by another parishioner, Christopher's beloved Lydia. Christopher was not at all surprised to see that she had worked her way into the amorphous flock of parishioners floating around Reverend Steele—her pretty face generally gained her entree wherever she wanted to go—but he was impressed by her ability to sustain her conversation with the guests of honor beyond simple pleasantries.

Swimming in the social chatter, Lydia was in her element as much as Christopher was not, conversing with people he neither knew nor cared about. He could see that she had ingratiated herself with the honored guests, who now seemed to be consulting her on the contents of the vexing telegram. Mrs. Steele produced the document and pointed out part of its contents to Lydia. Reverend Bemis, evidently off the hook, stopped scratching things and rejoined the conversation. Lydia pointed across the hall to Christopher, who waved toward them a bit awkwardly. They waved back, smiling, nodding their heads and narrowing their eyes in scrutiny as they listened to Lydia speak. Christopher thought perhaps he should join them, but Lydia subtly yet firmly instructed him not to with an almost imperceptible tilt of head and arch of brow.

Lydia took her leave of the group, but not before the Reverend and his wife thanked her warmly for whatever service she had rendered them. The Reverend Bemis just looked relieved. Again, they smiled and waved at Christopher.

"What was that all about?" he asked Lydia as she returned.

"Oh, nothing really. We can discuss it later," she said as she walked off to chat with another group of friends.

Christopher was about to follow when a babbling intrusion interrupted his thoughts. Lydia's mother, apropos of nothing, guided him to a seat and started in about how she suffered when her family first made the trek across the country to the Northwest as homesteaders thirty years earlier. You would have thought she had guided Lewis and Clark while carrying a cross on her back. He tried to act like he was actually listening, but his curiosity at Lydia's operation nagged at him almost as loudly as Lydia's mother. As the woman replenished her wind with a long breath he knew he would not escape anytime soon, so he sat and pretended to listen.

The afternoon passed into evening, and giddy chatter gave way to the solemn and serious considerations owf the sermon in this hallowed sanctuary. Something about the transition from the afternoon's amiable socializing, with the movement of bodies bustling about sharing news and gossip, to the same group sitting in this sanctuary, suddenly still and focused, lent energy to the atmosphere. The afternoon had been, in a way, foreplay, and now they were ready to take it all in. At least these were among the guilty little half-thoughts streaming through Christopher's brain as Lydia's slender body was pressed against him in the crowded pew. He turned slightly to look at her. She gently pushed his hand away when he ran a finger through a ringlet of light brown hair, which Christopher found so lovely when she let it fall about her shoulders, but she usually kept severely pulled back and done up in the style of the day, often hidden under a scarf or some sort of bonnet. So no touching, evidently, but he could still look at her pretty face, with her high cheek bones and green eyes that Christopher found captivating. He was far more interested in Lydia than the evening's speaker. Unlike the rest of the congregation, he had a pretty clear idea of what Reverend Steele was going to say, having endured the heavy air of missionary Congregationalism at college for the past four years. He had attended countless sermons and prayer meetings from which Protestant congregations were sending young missionary couples off to some remote corner of the planet to brave dangers unknown as they converted various dark heathens to Christianity.

The Reverends Steele and Bemis ascended the dais, the former taking a seat as the latter began a long introduction. When the squatty Reverend Bemis finally gave way and Reverend Steele rose to the lectern, he impressed the congregation before he had even spoken a word. He was a tall, imposing man with a shock of silver hair and flowing white beard. His manner was kindly, yet intense, as he surveyed the congregation before him. When he spoke, he surprised them with not so much a sermon as a love song to the Anglo-Saxon Protestant—*to them*.

"The restless surge of energy evident in white America's westward penetration of virgin lands over the past hundred years," he began, "foretells magnificent possibilities for our future. This new nation, so young and strong, yet wise in the ways of wealth and government, must assume her right and true position as leader of the civilized world." Spreading his arms and closing his eyes he intoned, "This will be but the consummation of a movement as old as civilization."

His words elicited a warm smile from Lydia, as she glanced at Christopher to share the moment. Just a passing glance, but as he was less enthralled with the speech than the rest, he allowed his mind to linger over images of her face, how much he liked to look at her, how painfully pretty she was to him. He was jarred out of this reverie by the Reverend's emphatic insistence upon America's mission as a higher race. "In the superior vigor of our people there is affirmation of Mr. Darwin's favorite theory of natural selection, which would seem to indicate that the world's history thus far has been simply preparatory for *our* future." He paused, allowing the concept time to resonate before delving a little more deeply into current racial theory. "There is abundant reason to believe that the Anglo-Saxon race is to be, is indeed already becoming, more effective here than in Great Britain. The marked superiority of this race is due, in large measure, to its highly mixed origin. It is a general rule, now almost universally admitted by ethnologists, that the mixed races of mankind are superior to the pure ones. Among modern races, the most conspicuous example is afforded by the Anglo-Saxons. There is here a new commingling of races; the largest injections of foreign blood are substantially the same elements that constituted the original Anglo-Saxon admixture, so the general type will be preserved while at the same time it is strengthened through the mixture of other strains." Several of the ladies in the congregation caught their breath at the implications of all this mingling, and the Reverend—aware that he was traversing dangerous, if tantalizing, territory—moved quickly on.

Lydia, a bit red in the cheeks at all this talk of interbreeding, looked to Christopher as if to confirm that she had heard what she thought she heard. He took her hand in his as he returned his gaze toward the speaker. His mind wandered off again as the Reverend drew toward the culmination of Anglo-Saxon responsibilities. "Another marked characteristic of the Anglo-Saxon is what may be called an instinct or genius for colonizing. His unequaled energy, his indomitable perseverance, and his personal independence, made him a pioneer. Charles Dickens once said that the typical American would hesitate to enter heaven unless assured that he could go farther west." The congregation's laughter released some of the pent-up tension that had developed in the earlier part of his talk. Encouraged by their response, Reverend Steele steamed toward his conclusion. "What is the significance of such facts?" he resumed. "These tendencies enfold the future; they are the mighty alphabet with which God writes his prophecies. May we not, by a careful laying together of the letters, spell out something of his meaning? It seems to me that God is training the Anglo-Saxon race for an hour sure to come in the world's future. Heretofore there has always been in the history of the world a comparatively unoccupied land westward, into which the crowded countries of the East have poured their surplus populations. But the widening waves of migration, which millenniums ago rolled east and west from the valley of the Euphrates, meet today on our Pacific coast. It appears

11

there are no more new worlds. The unoccupied arable lands of the earth are limited, and will soon be taken. The time is coming when the pressure of population on the means of subsistence will be felt here as it is now felt in Europe and Asia. The world will enter upon a new stage of its history—*the final competition of races, for which the Anglo-Saxon has been schooled.*"

The congregation, riveted by this racial drama, sat rapt. Christopher, concerned with other things, stared at his knees wondering how he could, once again, misunderstand Lydia's glance when he held her hand. She gave his fingers the dismissive squeeze before she withdrew her hand from his. He knew it, the dismissal, too well; it was the same gentle but firm demarcation of boundary she had offered him so many times before. The rebuffs were agonizing to him, but she did not seem to notice, and probably would not sympathize if she had. He had committed himself to her for all his life, yet these small intimacies were denied him. So he asked why from time to time, and she would casually dispatch his question in a way that should have told him how completely unimportant to her were such things, if only he had ears to hear it. Instead he listened to her words, which were, "there will be plenty of time for that later." Those words, which were for her a perfunctory postponement of an unpleasant subject, were for him encouragement, a promise of future happiness, even bliss. As the missionary's talk reached its climax, Christopher permitted himself to imagine a kiss, and he easily drifted into a prolonged carnal fantasy. She was gentle in all things, leaving him to imagine the graceful way she might lean her head back and part her lips as they tenderly...

"Oh, Christopher, it's perfect for you!" Lydia's cheeks were flushed.

"Me? What?" he said, shaken from his romantic daydream.

"And it would satisfy that yearning for travel you're always speaking of. You'll see all China!"

Before he could answer, or rather ask what they were talking about, the Reverend Steele, smiling from ear to ear, had bounded down the aisle and into the pews, and practically lifted Christopher right out of his seat as he grabbed him lustily, joyfully, and welcomed him to The Cause.

"Cause?" said a perplexed Christopher, as the crowd bustled around him.

"Saving heathens, yes! *God's Cause!*" bellowed the pastor, supremely happy to welcome a new missionary to the fight. Rev. Steele finished the oration standing in the middle of the congregation, his right arm firmly wrapped around a shocked and disoriented Christopher, his left hand thrusting the King James Bible into the air. "Nothing can save the inferior race but a ready and pliant assimilation. Whether the feebler and more abject races are going to be regenerated and raised up is a question readily answerable by all of you who witnessed the brave and valiant devotion of this man as he makes his commitment before all of you to be God's agent to the East. *Onward Christian soldiers!*"

The congregation burst into song around the old missionary and the new. The minister spoke for a while after that, but Christopher didn't hear any of it. There was a prayer, which the newest missionary was asked to lead. Christopher said something, but he wasn't entirely aware what it was, which he followed with an "Amen," and then the room settled into the cacophonous murmur that follows such occasions. Filing by, people patted him on the back or stopped briefly to congratulate him on his new mission and wedding. The last part surprised him, although at this point he was nearly past the point of surprise at anything. "Wedding?" he turned to Lydia.

"We can't go China without getting married first," she responded. "Missionaries are *always* married—you know that."

"Oh," was all he could think to say.

"Yes, indeed" interrupted Reverend Steele, now flanked by his smiling wife. "I'll perform the ceremony myself tomorrow. We'll make it part of the evening services."

"Tomorrow?" Christopher asked.

"Yes, of course. We'll be leaving on ship a few days after that.

After we spoke this afternoon I knew you two would be the perfect replacement for the other couple."

"What other couple?" Christopher asked, but the Reverend was already on his way through the crowd, occupied in conversation.

"I'll tell you about it later," Lydia answered for the absent Reverend. "Wear your good suit, Christopher," she said as she picked up the little bag of note papers she carried everywhere. "I'll see you tomorrow at the wedding." And with that she was off, as if she had said nothing particularly important. Christopher wanted to ask her what had happened, how she seemed to know about some "other couple," and just what had she been talking to the Reverend and his wife about that afternoon. These questions seemed urgent just then, but she was gone, just like the life he had been planning when he woke up that morning.

Nor would Christopher be allowed another chance to speak with Lydia before they were to be wed the following day. She needed to get away from Christopher, and the thousand questions she knew he would have, until they were safely married. Social events fell in clumps, and Lydia collected them as profitably as possible. She wrote about them for the *Seattle Star*—not so much as a reporter, but as a partygoer with a note pad. She wrote long, detailed, and painfully descriptive articles on every wedding, party, or flower show she could possibly attend, and submitted them to the society editor, who would usually print only the first paragraph, disregarding the rest. Unfortunately, she was paid by the line. Worse, she was growing tired of it. In a port city like Seattle, where prostitutes and loggers established social trends, writing about 'society' was pretentious at best. Still, the progressive elements of the city strove to create some semblance of civilization amid the beer and chewing tobacco, and Lydia believed herself a part of that movement.

Lydia was off to make one more attempt to change the world,

and get published for it, before marrying and leaving for China. Mostly, she just needed to avoid Christopher and all of his questions until the wedding.

A presentation by the Knights of Labor at the home of Mrs. Kenworthy was as good an escape as any. In the Widow Kenworthy's large frame house at the corner of Fifth and Union, next to the wooden building absurdly called the University of Washington, Seattle's reform movements found a home—every damn one of them. Mary Kenworthy, it seemed, discriminated against no movement that promised change: if you were against something, the Widow Kenworthy was for you.

Lydia knew the Knights of Labor wanted to improve the lot of the working man, but she wasn't sure how. Perhaps there was some literature lying about. As she looked around the foyer she was interrupted by the tall, slender presence of the widow herself.

"Lydia, my dear. I'm so glad to see you here. Maybe they'll print this one?"

"There's always hope, I suppose."

"Oh, come now, try to be optimistic." Mary Kenworthy liked Lydia, and wanted to see her do well in this new, modern world of feminine professional possibilities. "I loved that little piece you wrote on the heathen Chinese among us—stealing good jobs, making slaves of their children, smoking opium. It made my blood boil! I'm sure they'll print it if you submit it." Cleansing Seattle of its Chinese population was a cause near and dear to Mrs. Kenworthy's heart. She saw them as a constant threat to white workingmen. Unfortunately for her, the rest of Seattle was fickle in its prejudices. Like the rest of America, they loved the phenomenally hardworking Asian "John" when they needed him, but were likely to set upon him as a mob when hard times changed their mood.

"I submitted it," Lydia said. "I sent it to the *Weekly* instead of the *Times*. I thought they might be a bit more appreciative of an investigation of that sort."

"'Investigation' indeed," sniffed the older woman. "I confess I

15

was not completely comfortable with you marching around those little alleys, talking with those…those people.”

“I was a bit nervous about it myself.” She didn't say so, but she had a far more difficult time speaking with the white workers who felt no compunction at all about treating a woman with a note pad as if she were a dancehall girl. The Chinese, on the other hand, were respectful in the extreme, cautiously looking around all the while they spoke. They had evidently reckoned that speaking with a white lady was not in the best interest of their long-term health.

“It doesn't matter, anyway—I'm getting married tomorrow night.” She said it as if she had just announced that she was going shopping.

“Tomorrow night?”

“Yes, it's got to be right away. We're going to go work as missionaries in China.”

“You're…? Oh my.”

“I was speaking with Reverend Steele at a reception this afternoon—”

“Oh yes, I read his book. He's doing wonderful work with the Asiatic heathens. Perhaps with his help they will progress at home, and can stop coming here. But why on earth do you want to go there?”

“Reverend Steele suggested that I would enhance my prospects as a journalist considerably merely by being in China. I don't know if he is right, but I know I'm not doing anything for myself here.”

“I see,” the widow hesitated. “But are you going to save souls or make a career?”

“Good question. I'll let you know.” She smiled distractedly.

Henry Wasserman of the *Seattle Weekly* approached them, cigar clenched between his teeth.

“Ladies,” he mumbled through the stogie as he put his finger to the brim of his hat.

“Henry, this is my good friend Miss Lydia Burke.”

“We've met,” Lydia said.

This was news to Wasserman, and he didn't have the social grace to lie about it. He looked at the high cheekbones, the light brown hair, and the slender figure and thought surely such a creature would leave a lasting impression on his mind. "I don't remember you," he concluded abruptly, stating the obvious.

"We spoke at the *Weekly* last month. You were explaining that I might want to consider having babies as an alternative to reporting news, as I was probably more qualified for the former."

"Burke, Burke," he mumbled as he tried to place the name. "Lydia...'L. C. Burke?'"

"Yes." Lydia was surprised that he was able to put it together. "After our last chat I thought I should have a better chance at publication as 'L. C.' than as 'Lydia.'"

"True enough!" He took the cigar from his mouth and looked closely at her face. Eventually he smiled and shook her hand vigorously—so much so that she was a bit startled. "I have 'L. C. Burke's' article on the 'Heathen Chinese' on my desk. If that's you, you can have a job." Lydia withdrew her hand and dropped her jaw. "We don't pay much, but you won't starve either. If you can keep up you can have twenty-four column inches a month. Be at my office tomorrow. In fact, why don't you cover this damn Knights of Labor nonsense for me so I can go home?" He didn't wait for an answer before he tipped his hat and started for the door.

Mrs. Kenworthy was the first of the two women to realize her mouth was agape. Lydia might have stood that way a good long while had the older woman remained silent, but the older woman spoke up to point out the obvious: "No doubt this complicates your plans."

"Plans?" Lydia repeated the word as if she couldn't quite place its meaning.

"Your wedding."

"Wedding?" It was a more significant word, and seemed to help her find her way out of Wasserman's smoke. "Oh my God, I'm supposed to be getting married."

17

"And going to China."

"Oh my God, I'm going to China."

The events she had set in motion had developed a momentum of their own, and suddenly she needed to put a halt to them, with as little embarrassment as possible. A few hours earlier Seattle had seemed a dead end, a soggy and rowdy outpost of civilization that offered her only useless anonymity. When her agile mind recognized the Reverend's predicament as a chance to change all that, she thought she was quite clever to seize it. Certainly Christopher needed to be maneuvered a bit to make it all work, but ultimately she was confident she knew what was best for him. Now, with the sudden opportunity at Wasserman's *Seattle Weekly*—the chance to be a real journalist without relocating to the other side of the planet—she realized she had been too clever by half. At that moment her family, her church, and her friends were feverishly preparing a modest wedding ceremony that would take place in less than twenty-four hours whether she wanted it or not. Not knowing how to straighten out the mess, she took a deep breath, straightened her back, and marched forward into the Widow Kenworthy's parlor to listen to a lecture on the Knights of Labor.

Christopher never imagined a wedding like this. Actually, he had never imagined his wedding at all, but if he had it would have been much less modest. This allegedly blessed event seemed more like a sewing bee. Lydia, whom Christopher had imagined would be terribly disappointed at having a perfunctory ceremony, instead seemed intent on simply moving things along. While he was away at college, she had bided her time writing little newspaper pieces on weddings as lavish as Seattle society could conjure, so Christopher was mystified that she seemed satisfied with such a spare ceremony. She did appear a little preoccupied and distracted, perhaps even distressed, but Christopher supposed there was no accounting for a girl's emotions in affairs of this sort.

A very few friends and family gathered around them in the home of Reverend Bemis, and listened as Reverend Steele spoke a few words, finally granting Christopher permission to kiss his bride. He briefly felt her lips touch his, then opened his eyes to discover she had already turned back toward the Reverend. He looked like a fool, and all in all, it seemed a fitting end to such a cursory event.

None of this mattered, of course. There was a far more important issue at the forefront of his mind—the wedding night. Now they were legally together, and connubial bliss was scarcely hours away. He was unaware of it, but there was a faraway smile across his face as he stood among the joyful little group of guests and well-wishers. Even Lydia, otherwise occupied with little conversations at the makeshift reception, noticed the placid grin that would not go away.

"What are you smiling about, Christopher?" she asked as she was carrying a platter of something somewhere.

He responded by looking up and down her pleasant if modestly curved frame, now free to imagine without guilt what was beneath the petticoats. Still beaming, he simply shrugged his shoulders.

"For goodness' sake, Christopher!" And she and her platter were off. The reprimand did not matter; tonight she would be his.

A knock on Rev. Bemis's front door—pounding, really—broke through his vaguely carnal reverie. He opened the door to see a boy, evidently a sailor. "Yes?"

"This the home of Revern' Bemis, sir?"

"Yes, it is. He's around here somewhere."

"Not him, sir. I need to talk to somebody that's stayin' here. Revern' Steele?"

Steele heard his name and made his way to the vestibule. "I'm Reverend Steele, young man."

"Cap'n sent me to tell you, Revern', he's debarking tonight 'stead of tomorrow. Storm's comin' in and he wants to beat it."

"Can't we wait until after the storm passes?" Christopher shot in. By this time the small crowd had gathered around them in the vestibule.

"We're not a passenger boat, mister; we carry freight. We're loaded down and the Cap'n don't want to lose it in the harbor." The sailor didn't seem to care either way. "Revern' if you want a ride to San Francisco you'd best grab your bag and be aboard afore the hour's up." The boy tipped his little hat, and started back into the weather.

Steele closed the door and turned around to face the guests wearing the resigned smile of a man who had faced far worse difficulties than this. "Well, that's it then. Christopher, Lydia—or should I say 'Mr. and Mrs. Jones,'—it's time to go."

Christopher, mentally accommodating this new wrinkle to his primary objective, the consummation of his marriage, turned to his wife and tried to put the best face on it. "Things will be fine, dear. We'll just have to say goodbye to our friends and launch our marriage along with the ship."

"No," Lydia replied without hesitation. Heads turned.

"No?" asked Christopher. He looked around nervously at their guests.

"No," she said, again. "I can't possibly take care of my arrangements and go in an hour, nor twenty-four hours." Her mind was racing, but she tried to soften her tone. "It simply won't work. You'll have to go without me, Christopher. I'll catch up with you in San Francisco."

Christopher's smile was now completely gone. The ramifications of this decision were brutally clear. "But Lydia, my dear, we should, well, be *together* on our first night as *husband* and *wife*, don't you think?" Even the dullest present was now entirely aware of his foremost concern.

"Impossible," she stated flatly. "I'll meet you in San Francisco, and that's that."

"But Lydia," he implored as he began to stammer, helplessly groping for words that might change her mind without simply blurting out that he might die if he did not make love to her this very night. His agonizing search for words conveyed his meaning to everyone present, embarrassing and infuriating Lydia. Reverend Steele, sympathetically amused at Christopher's frustration, put his arm firmly around the groom's shoulders and gave him a good shake.

"Come, my boy," he said with a broad smile. "A love so strong and healthy will certainly survive a week's separation."

Christopher made one last effort. "Why can't we just let this ship go? We could book passage on a passenger steamer in a few days' time, couldn't we?" He was almost begging.

"Sorry, my boy. The church can't afford to pay for our passage twice."

Despite his best efforts, Christopher Jones was leaving Seattle a pure and chaste man.

As the ship made its way North through Puget Sound toward the Pacific, the skies cleared and the swells calmed. The voyage had begun smoothly and Christopher couldn't have been more furious about it. *Storm*, indeed! Steele decided to let Christopher stew in silence for an hour rather than attempt to talk him out of his justifiable rage. Just as the Reverend was about to cheer him up with a prayer Christopher declared, "I'm seasick."

As it happened, it turned out to be an infuriatingly splendid evening to go above deck and get some air. The seasoned traveler stood at the railing and breathed deeply of the cold sea breeze beneath a newly cleared sky filled with ten billion stars, as Christopher parted company with his dinner.

"Feeling better?" inquired Steele, who had seen much worse.

"Much, thank you. At least my stomach feels better." Still turning the events of the day over in his mind, Christopher thought that it would have been nice to see Lydia at the pier, but he knew that she was probably busy doing, well, 'things.' He was never sure what they were, but she always seemed to be occupied doing them. Steele read this in Christopher's face, which was still a bit ashen, and patted his traveling companion on the back.

"Your wife and mine will join us in San Francisco within a few days, and all will be well. Don't worry, my boy."

Christopher took a deep pull of the salt air, then changed the subject. "Will we be on a freighter to Hawaii as well?"

"No, we'll be a good bit more comfortable. There is a regular passenger line running between San Francisco and Honolulu every week. It's practically like a train running across the Pacific, only with better food."

"How's the food in China?"

"Horrible, but we make do. Perhaps as they become more civilized their palates will improve as well, eh?"

Christopher did not want to offend the great missionary, but he was starting to wonder how he ended up in his current situation. A day ago he lived in Seattle, a single man casually considering his post-graduate options, and all of a sudden he found himself a married—yet somehow chaste—missionary on his way to faraway China; he wasn't at all sure how or why this transformation had occurred. He thought back to the pre-sermon reception at which Lydia chatted with the Steeles. He remembered her pointing at him as they had their heads together.

"Uh, Reverend Steele?" he began haltingly.

"Yes, brother Christopher?"

"Who was that 'other couple' Lydia mentioned?"

"Oh my, tragic story, that. Jonathan and Cynthia Braden—a brand new missionary couple. They seem to have disappeared."

"Disappeared? How?"

"Well, I don't know precisely. I have a small collection of telegrams, three or four from different people, each offering various details but no real explanations. One of them mentions something about Jonathan and a dance hall girl, but I'm sure if anyone like that were involved it was just a matter of, uh, well—"

"He must have been trying to save her. Her soul, I mean." Christopher saw that the Reverend needed some help.

"Yes, obviously. At least it stands to reason."

"What about the other telegrams?"

"They were more confusing. Something about Mrs. Braden and some firearms. I didn't know what to make of it." The minister scratched his head. "Why do you ask?"

"At the reception, the one before your sermon, Lydia was discussing something with you at your table, and you all seemed quite serious."

"Oh yes, we had just pieced together the news and concluded that with the Bradens well and truly gone, we would be quite short-handed. You see, we now have treaty arrangements that allow us to go further into the interior of China than ever before, and I need a younger man's help." He paused a moment and patted his younger companion on the back. "Your dear Lydia came to us like an angel, an answer to an unspoken prayer." Christopher had to smile when he heard that description. She was certainly angelic in appearance, but he wouldn't imagine an angel to be quite so high-strung.

"It's true," Steel responded to Christopher's tacit skepticism. "She discussed our dilemma with us and immediately volunteered that you are a skilled linguist, which is exactly the sort of person we need in China."

"There must be something about China I don't know. I speak French and Spanish, a little German."

"A man who has studied scripture and language for four years is the perfect man for the job. The important thing is you have the aptitude and the faith. And your Lydia will be an ideal helpmeet." The Reverend smiled benignly. "Not incidentally, she will make an excellent correspondent for the *American Missionary*, and any other missionary magazine. There are many of them."

"Correspondent?" The question had not yet cleared his lips when the answer emerged from his brain. Lydia, he now understood, had stumbled on a path into serious journalism: the missionary press. The *American Missionary*, and a dozen other monthly magazines just like it, was the public link between the vast missionary enterprise and Protestant America. These journals were generally well-written and widely read, and they were the essential to the task of maintaining interest and funding in the effort to evangelize the world. "So," Christopher continued, a little more enlightened than before, "you discussed journalism with Lydia?"

"She seems to be quite a good reporter, and she'll only get better as she puts her pen to the service of the Lord."

"Yes, of course," Christopher agreed passively, but he had no illusions about whom Lydia's pen would serve. So there it was: he was going to China to preach the gospel so Lydia could establish her credentials as a serious journalist. He suddenly recognized, a little late, that her writing was no mere prenuptial pastime. She had other aspirations, larger ones, and it dawned on Christopher how little he knew her. Still, he was not angry, necessarily. This could be a good thing, he reasoned. She would get what she wanted, he would learn all about a new culture, and before any of that transpired he could legally take her clothes off her. There was much to look forward to, not least of which was a trip to Hawaii, which made him wonder for the first time why they had not simply taken a boat directly from San Francisco to China. He put the question to Reverend Steele.

The old missionary stared out into the cold darkness for a while, the calm smile that usually graced his face utterly gone, he watched the stars on the horizon as the ship rose and fell on the swells of the Pacific. Christopher couldn't imagine how such a simple question could alter his mood so quickly, so gravely. Finally the old man's sardonic grin returned.

"Your life has changed more than you know, Christopher," he said, using his first name for the first time. "The most successful missionaries in the world reside in Hawaii, and we need to attend their church for a few weeks before going to China, or so I've told our parent board. We're going to toil and perhaps die among heathens in a desolate kingdom on the other side of the world. We can forgive ourselves a month in paradise before we commit ourselves to that."

And on that happy thought the two men turned their backs on the stars, descended belowdecks, and crawled into their hammocks for a mostly sleepless night.

CHAPTER TWO

Their stay in San Francisco, brief as it was, had provided new depths of disappointment. When Reverend Steele and Christopher had gone down to the wharf two days after their arrival to meet their wives, they discovered that one of them was still in Seattle. As he watched Mrs. Steele carefully descend the gangway, quite alone, Christopher's heart sank. He strained to look beyond the older woman to see if, perhaps, Lydia was simply lagging behind, although that would have been radically out of character. In any case, the look on Mrs. Steele's face—something between anger and pity—told him all he needed to know: his wife was not on this boat.

"Mrs. Steele," Christopher said, once the Reverend had embraced his wife and properly welcomed her to dry land, or at least the dock that was attached to dry land. "Where is Lydia?"

"Mrs. Jones seems to have," she searched for the right word, "disappeared."

"What? Oh my God! What do you mean?"

"I have not seen her since the wedding, but I'm sure she is fine." The woman's voice was dripping with disdain. "An older woman, a Mrs. Kenworthy, delivered this note to me the night before I left."

Christopher quickly opened the note Mrs. Steele handed him.

Christopher,
I cannot leave just now. I will catch up with you in
Honolulu.
Lydia

"That's it? It says almost nothing." He implored Mrs. Steele as the reverend took the note from his hand.

"As I said, young man, your wife successfully avoided me from the wedding night until now."

"Relax, Christopher," the Reverend sought to relieve the young man's obvious anxiety. "The note, brief as it is, makes clear her intention to catch up with us in Honolulu.

"Yes, I'm sure," said Mrs. Steele in a tone that didn't quite conceal her hostility.

Christopher was too focused on the central point, namely that Lydia was not there, to notice the woman's tone of voice. Reverend Steele heard more clearly, and once he had dispatched Christopher to fetch his wife's bags he asked for clarification.

"You do not think young Mrs. Jones is as good as her word?"

"I know that there are a good many things occupying that child's mind, and being Christopher's wife is not among them," Mrs. Steele sniffed.

"Hannah," Steele almost never addressed her by her first name, but he was quite taken aback. "Whatever do you mean? She seems a perfectly Christian girl to me."

"A perfectly ambitious girl, if you ask me—and you did. I can't tell you any one thing she said or did, it's just a feeling I get. I don't believe that woman will ever set foot on a boat."

"I'm sure you're wrong, but time will tell."

Upon their return to the parsonage a local church had provided for their use, Christopher immediately sat down to write his new bride a plaintive letter imploring her to hasten her departure. Then he, like the Steeles, arranged their bags and prepared for the next leg of their journey: Hawaii.

* * *

Honolulu, as it turned out, was anything but the sleepy little Polynesian village of grass huts Christopher had expected. Quite the contrary, the city left Christopher feeling as though he had traded one San Francisco for another. Far from the primitive tropical paradise he thought he would find, Honolulu presented a bustling city with electric wires strung over the busy streets for trolleys and telephones, and people of every imaginable color and hue clogging every passageway. As the party of missionaries navigated their way through the busy traffic of stevedores, donkey carts, pushcarts, and pedestrians at the wharf it was clear that, all expectations aside, this was an entirely different sort of jungle.

The Reverend Archibald Tubbs, rotund and mutton-chopped, was there to greet them with a number of young native men to carry the party's luggage. Christopher was immediately relieved to see the strong young men, because to this point carrying luggage had been his primary function as a missionary.

"Kalani!" barked Tubbs in the general direction of the young men. The newcomers wondered what sort of exotic command this might be, but it turned out to be the name of one of the boys. He was a smiling, muscular young man who looked like he may have been a teenager, maybe older, but Christopher found all of their exotic faces to be ageless somehow. Kalani, who seemed to be in charge, started directing the other three boys in a variety of unintelligible phrases, concluding with the Hawaiian command to get going, *"Hele on!"* His companions immediately started hoisting bags, trunks, and boxes into the donkey cart, chatting away in the melodious linguistic mish-mash that is Hawaiian pidgin. The sonorous mix went by his ears so quickly Christopher could not quite separate the English from the Hawaiian, let alone the Portuguese, French, and Scandinavian elements of the tongue, but the sound of it held his attention as if it were music. He wished Lydia were there to hear it.

"Christopher," Reverend Steele interrupted him. "This way," he said, guiding him by the arm over to where Rev. Tubbs and Mrs.

Steele were waiting for a trolley. A few moments later they boarded the open-air car and ascended the hill, rising above the city to the accompaniment of the clanking steel wheels beneath them. Christopher could see the four young Hawaiian men walking in the distance behind them, disappearing into the rest of the human traffic as the missionaries effortlessly rose above the city toward the more sedate neighborhood above it. Reverend Tubbs spoke as tour guide and historian in his clipped Boston accent, pointing out the churches and other improvements outsiders had brought to the Island over the last seventy years, leaving out the saloons, slums, and brothels that form the social bedrock of any great city.

As their trolley rose high above Honolulu, the vista caught the missionaries unawares. The vast panorama that lay before them was a lush patchwork of dense tropical forest and agricultural fields, all of it surrounded by the meandering frame of black volcanic sand that gently yielded to the turquoise waters of the Pacific. None of the newcomers had ever witnessed such a vision, and certainly no magic lantern slide or daguerreotype they had ever seen could possibly do it justice. Their sense of wonder at this first glimpse of Eden was disturbed only by the unlovely sound of Tubbs's droning narration.

"And over there," Tubbs gestured at one of the larger patches of yellow, "is a cane field that has done very well for us. Very well, indeed."

"You own it?" asked Steele.

"Some of it," Tubbs answered, evidently surprised that an American like Steele could be so ignorant about real estate finance. "I remain a minister, Reverend, like my father before me, but I also invest in several operations here in the islands." Terms like "invest" were alien to Steele's life experience, which had been spent almost entirely studying the Bible or traveling the world cajoling others to do so. Recognizing Steele's confusion, Tubbs explained the rather uniquely developmental role American missionaries had played in Hawaii. "You see, Reverend, we missionaries, especially my father,

29

were instrumental in reforming the landholding system here in the islands. Where once there were endless acres of untamed nature that produced nothing but subsistence for native families, we have created productive estates and great surpluses. My father actually wrote the land reform bill for King Kamehameha III."

"Where did the native landholders go?" asked Christopher.

"Who?"

"The families that owned the small plots before they were combined into large estates."

"Oh, well, it's hard to say." Tubbs shrugged his shoulders dismissively. "Many were hired as plantation workers at first, but the natives are not a hardy strain—dying off, you know—and they tend toward laziness. We've found that Chinese and Japanese coolies are better workers, almost like ants, and stay on the job longer. And efficient labor keeps the plantations profitable. The return was much better before the McKinley Tariff, but we still turn a profit."

"*Which* tariff?" Christopher asked, but Tubbs seemed not to hear him as he pointed to another yellow stretch of agricultural productivity, in which he also owned a stake. Saving souls, it seemed, could be quite a profitable enterprise.

A quarter of an hour later they had arrived at the Tubbs "parsonage," which was not the humble missionary's house that Christopher expected, but a three-story affair with an expansive veranda and long, well-manicured green lawns. Commanding views of the harbor below could be had from anywhere on the property, but from the deck above the veranda and the widow's walk above that, the view was absolutely spectacular. As Steele and Christopher continued gazing at the paradise around them Christopher wondered aloud how anyone could get any work done amid so much distracting beauty. At precisely that moment a pretty young native girl passed by on the lawn, carrying a load of laundry at her waist and Christopher's gaze at her backside, and the Reverend responded, "Good question,

Christopher." Hopefully the boy's wife would arrive soon, Rev. Steele thought to himself.

Such a vast household required some help to maintain it, and the visitors noticed various native staff here and there, some inside the house, others on the grounds. Christopher once again noticed the melodious pidgin he'd heard down at the wharf. The native patois gave the place an exotic ambience, in contrast to the interior of the Tubbs house, transplanted directly from Boston. Bookshelves and family photographs lined the walls, and electric lamps illuminated the dark overstuffed chairs, which were arranged just so. The blend of musical language and traditional New England appointments added a touch of the surreal.

Once in the house Reverend Tubbs passed off the guests to Mrs. Verna Tubbs who, aided by the lovely native girl Christopher had just seen carrying the laundry, escorted the missionaries to their rooms. Christopher closed his door, dropped his bag to the floor and his body on the bed, gratified to be in a place that did not continually roll from port to starboard. The sounds of a busy house at mid-afternoon, however, were not conducive to napping. To the mixture of chatty voices in the house was added the sound of the Tubbs's daughters practicing the piano. Scales—endless scales, going up four octaves, then back down, then up a semitone for another four-octave ascent, before descending to begin yet again. And *again*. Sleep, however desirable, was elusive amid the diatonic din, so he rose from his bed and approached the little writing table, where he began a letter to his wife.

"*My Dear Lydia*," he began, but crossed it out in favor of *Dearest Lydia*, which seemed more intimate, less formal. What to say? He wanted to ask *why the hell am I here and you are not?* But that would accomplish nothing, or worse. "*I am truly sorry you could not join us in San Francisco. Like you, it is beautiful.*" The thought of her pretty face gave him a pang of loneliness. "*I miss you terribly. I can't wait for you to get here so that we might enjoy a few days of this paradise together. Of course, there is no cable between Hawaii*

31

and the mainland, so I will send this note by packet, which should find its way to you within two weeks. It is my fondest hope that you will be here before then, and that you will never see this note until we return to Seattle, together, years from now." 'Years from now,' the words echoed in his head. What the deuce have I gotten himself into? he wondered. With that forlorn thought, he sealed the note in an envelope, returned to his bed, and eventually found sleep amid the piano noise that could not possibly be called music.

The next morning Christopher followed the smell of frying ham down to the kitchen where he found the Reverends Steele and Tubbs at the table, the former quietly eating his breakfast while listening patiently to the latter talk of his investments. Tubbs's three daughters were busy helping their mother snap beans at the opposite end of the long table.

"Ah, Christopher!" Steele looked like a drowning man who had just been thrown a life preserver. "Sit down. Join us."

"Yes, do," agreed Tubbs. "You'll be ready for some breakfast, no doubt."

"I won't argue with you there. I believe it was the smell of this food that woke me, or I'd sleep another day."

"Our young assistant does not sleep or eat well aboard ship," Steele noted in an aside to Tubbs. "But I think I've probably brought him to the perfect place for food and rest."

"Indeed you have," agreed Tubbs. "Penelope," he said to his oldest daughter, who did not respond, but rather stared at Christopher, transfixed. This elicited unkind giggles from her two younger sisters. "Penelope," her father repeated, a little more insistently.

Startled and embarrassed, the sixteen-year-old blurted, "Yes, father?"

"Could you get a plate of breakfast together for our guest?"

With all eyes upon her she was quite unable to speak, but managed to quickly nod her head up and down as she wordlessly rose from the table, tripped on the hem of her dress and fell to the floor. As she scrambled to her feet she fervently wished she could somehow disappear. She turned briefly to give her two giggling sisters a look of absolute fury before assembling what dignity she could and continuing to the sideboard to prepare a plate for Christopher. The young missionary seemed to have a tragically debilitating effect on her.

"Jane, Martha, you may go begin your lessons," Tubbs said to his two younger daughters.

"But, father, it is Saturday," argued one of them, to which their father responded with a raised eyebrow that told them, *leave now*. And so they did, unsuccessfully attempting to hide mischievous grins as they left the room.

The suddenly mute Penelope set the plate in front of Christopher, tried to say something but could not, and turned plaintively to her father as if to beg permission to leave. Her father, clearly puzzled at his otherwise normal daughter's sudden ineptitude, nodded his assent and watched her disappear. "I can't imagine what's come over her," said Tubbs quite honestly, although he was the only one in the room who enjoyed such ignorance.

"Probably just a little indigestion," offered Mrs. Steele. "Don't you agree, Christopher?" she offered, eyeing his discomfiture suspiciously.

"Delicious ham," Christopher responded.

Reverend Steele sought to reassure his wife. "I'm sure Christopher's wife will be joining us soon."

"Surely," Mrs. Steele responded, not believing a word of it.

Tubbs, slowly catching up with his company, began to sense that Rev. Steele's young missionary might be a threat to his daughter's chastity. His gaze came to rest on Christopher's face and stayed there.

Steele broke the awkward silence when he saw two natives approaching the open kitchen door, recognizing both of them from the day before. The boy had carried their luggage, and the laundry

girl who helped them to their rooms. "Tell me about these two
Hawaiians, Reverend. Do they live here with you?"

"Kalani and Muanu? Goodness no! They both have the morals
endemic in their race, which is to say none." He looked directly at
Christopher and continued, "So you wouldn't want them living in
the house with your daughters."

"No, of course not," Christopher agreed a little too quickly.

"They work here and there, doing this and that, but you have to
stay after them. Lazy as the rest of their race."

"Are they husband and wife?" asked Mrs. Steele.

"Cousins. But that doesn't mean much. They all seem to be
cousins. Faithless as cats."

"But surely you've converted them," said Reverend Steele.

"Certainly, but that doesn't mean they could be considered true
Christians." This statement, met as it was with puzzled silence,
seemed to require further explanation. "For them Christianity is
too often amalgamated with their own pantheon of gods and idol
worship. They'll come and sit through a sermon on Sunday morning
and still leave an offering to the volcano goddess, Pele, on Sunday
night."

"That's common enough," said Steele, who had spent a lifetime
weaving Christianity into the fabric of native cultures. "It begins
that way, otherwise the native has no foundation, no associations
by which he can make his new faith comprehensible. But we've
found that through continued teaching, preaching, and prayer
the Christian Gospel gradually supersedes the superstitions of the
native's youth. His faith grows through practice."

"Yes, that's all very well," said Tubbs, evidently uninterested in
being educated in the ways of saving heathens. "But we preach
to them on Sundays. If they need constant encouragement and
instruction perhaps that would be good training for your young
missionary here, Mr. Jones."

Christopher, seeing the cautiously curious Penelope hovering in
the hallway out of one eye and an opportunity for escape out of the

other, agreed emphatically. "I'll get to it this very minute." As he rose from his chair and headed for the door to the backyard where Kalani was loading some crates onto a cart, Steele called to him.

"Christopher, you'll need this!"

"What?"

"Your Bible, of course."

"Uh, say there... Kalani, is it?" Christopher asked as he escaped through the kitchen door to the backyard where Kalani was loading some empty crates.

"Yeah, brah. Dat me."

"I was hoping to accompany you on your rounds. I'd like to see Honolulu, get the lay of the land, so to speak."

"Why dey watchin'you like dat?" Kalani gestured at the crowd of Anglo-Saxons staring out the kitchen window who were, variously, supportive, suspicious, curious, and lovelorn.

"I can't imagine, but I'd be grateful if you would allow me to come with you today."

"You look like maybe you gotta get away, little bit?"

"Uh," Christopher hesitated as he looked back over his shoulder. "Quite so."

"Sorry, brah. Kalani gotta work today."

"I'll work with you," Christopher offered, hopefully. That got the young Hawaiian's attention.

"You help Kalani work, brah?"

"Love to."

Kalani let out a little laugh at the thought of it. "You got da Jesus book."

"Excuse me?"

"Da Jesus book—der in you hand, brah." Kalani indicated the bible Steele had given him. "How come?"

"I like to read it sometimes."

"You gonna be talkin' Jesus book all day?"

"Well, no, unless you want me to."

"I don't want."

"Fine."

"Fine."

Christopher helped load the rest of the empty crates into the donkey cart, joined him while he fetched the donkey and happily began his odyssey with his new object of conversion. Mostly he was just happy to be free of the prying eyes and oppressive atmosphere in the Tubbs household. Kalani led them down first to the central store where he left the cart and crates with a list of provisions for the Tubbs family. Then back up the hill they walked with the donkey to another household where they spent the rest of the morning splitting and stacking wood. Kalani produced a burlap bag and shared his poi and breadfruit, which Christopher found utterly unappetizing, but after the morning's labor he was thankful for it.

"Back to the store, then?" Christopher asked.

"No, brah. Down da road there's another farm. We gonna shovel out dey stables, little bit."

"Well, we should be about it then. Wouldn't want the horses to slip in their own shit!"

"You don' mind shovel da dung, brah?" Kalani looked incredulous.

"No. I've done this before."

Kalani shook his head. "You a different kind o' missionary."

Christopher thought Kalani's comment a curious statement. He remembered the Northwest missionaries who tried to outdo each other working with the Indian tribes around Seattle. Living and breathing the Protestant faith in hard labor and subduing nature, they would work themselves to exhaustion in an effort to instill a proper Protestant sense of industry in the "heathens." These Christians had a hell of a time convincing the Northwest natives that toiling in the soil was superior to hunting, fishing and enjoying life, but it wasn't for lack of trying.

36

Christopher and Kalani arrived at the next farm and spent an hour or so shoveling out the stables. Christopher, now a filthy, sweaty mess in his once-white shirt and wool slacks, put another shovelful in Kalani's wheelbarrow and asked a question before the native carried away the steaming pile of nitrates. "What did you mean when you said I was a different kind of missionary?"

"You work a little bit. You make jokes. Missionaries don't work. Dey just talk about da Jesus book, and dey *very* serious. Dey make da money and take da land and watch the Hawaiian work. Or da China man. Or da Filipino man."

Christopher reflected ruefully on Tubbs's absurd comments on the 'lazy' natives.

"I think things are different in Hawaii," he said as he resumed shoveling.

"Where you from?"

"Seattle," he plopped another load in the wheelbarrow.

"Where dat, Californy?" Kalani grunted as he hauled the loaded vessel over to the dung pile.

"Washington."

"You know da president?"

"No. Seattle is in the other Washington, on the west side of the country. North of California and Oregon. Missionaries work with the Indians there. I think missionaries work hard everywhere. Except Hawaii, evidently. Anyway, I'm not really a missionary. I just work for one. I'm a writer, sort of."

"What you doing here?"

"We're going to China."

"Seem like everybody in China coming here."

"The coolies, you mean?"

"Yeah, dey cut da cane, most. I do dat sometimes, too, but most I do a job here, a job there, and stay away from da big cane fields. Dey got bosses there in da fields, make you work like a slave. I like it out here where it's free." Plantation labor, like the Old South, Christopher thought.

"When you go to China, boss?" Kalani resumed the conversation.

"After my wife gets here."

"How come she not come wit you?"

"She was supposed to, actually." He explained the series of delays, starting with her missing the boat in Seattle, then failing to show up in San Francisco, and the excuses he made for her sounded unbelievable even to himself. Kalani stated the obvious.

"Maybe she not comin'?"

"Yes," Christopher conceded, dropping his gaze to his filthy shoes, "maybe she's not."

For the rest of the day it seemed there was always one more thing to do, another little place to stop, do a little work, collect a little money, and move on. They would talk a bit, eat a bit, and Kalani would answer Christopher's endless questions about Hawaii, its people and history, the missionaries, and on and on. Kalani's portrait of the early missionaries was generous enough, but of their descendents he had nothing good to say. According to Kalani, the sons of the missionaries used their parents' influence to change everything—from the laws of the land to the morals of the people— to favor themselves, those Kalani referred to as "the Americans."

"But they're not 'Americans,' Kalani. If they were born here, doesn't that make them Hawaiian?"

"Dey don' look like no Hawaiian I know. Don' dress like Hawaiian, don' speak Hawaiian, don' share like Hawaiian. No *aloha*."

"'*Aloha*'?"

"Yeah, *aloha*," Kalani repeated, as if it was the most self-evident thing in the world, but Christopher tilted his head and squinted in eyes in the universal pose of confusion, so Kalani explained further. "*Aloha*, it's da spirit, da big spirit dat's everywhere—da sharing, da love. I got food, so you got food. I got a roof, so you got a place to stay. You get it?"

"I think so."

"Good, 'cause dem American Hawaiians don'."

* * *

Reverend Steele had treated himself to a long walk along the punchbowl—the great volcanic crater above Honolulu—taking in the view of the ocean at sunset. He was sure he would never tire of the sight of it. As evening fell, and his legs grew weary, he returned to the New England comforts of the Tubbs house where he expected to hear Christopher report on his first foray into conversion. Christopher, to his surprise, was not there, nor would he be until much later that evening. He had been gone all day, and as the hours passed, no one was terribly concerned about his extended absence, except of course Penelope, who saved him a plate of dinner in the kitchen and waited impatiently for his return.

The Reverend sat across the table from the young girl. He watched her remove Christopher's plate from the table to keep it warm on the stove. It was a hearty helping of roast beef, yams, boiled carrots and kidney beans—*always beans with these people*, the Reverend thought to himself. He looked at her kindly as she covered the dish with a linen napkin. She was easy to read, and this chapter of her life could not possibly end well.

"It was kind of you to keep a plate warm for our young friend."

"He'll be hungry, I'm sure," she responded a little self-consciously.

"I imagine his wife will be here soon." He waited for Penelope to respond to the observation, but she was silent.

"I said—"

"Yes, Reverend, I heard you." She just wanted the man to stop talking about this absent "wife," but it seemed to Steele that they understood each other, so he spoke plainly.

"It's all right, Penelope. These feelings you are experiencing will pass. They are a natural part of life."

The girl blushed slightly, mortified to have her crush held up to her face, but she didn't think herself a child and had no wish to be spoken to as if she were. "I'm sure I don't know what you mean, Reverend," she said as she stared primly at the table. Penelope lifted her head to look directly into the Reverend's eyes as she continued. "'Wife?' Mrs. Steele says Mrs. Jones will not be coming at all. She said they're not really even married."

Steele hardly knew how to respond. He was incredulous at this sudden burst of assertiveness from this little church mouse. Dumbstruck, he wanted to say something about having performed the wedding ceremony himself, although he knew perfectly well her implication was not so much the absence of a wedding, but rather the absence of a *wedding night*—hardly the sort of thing he could properly discuss with a sixteen-year-old girl. His intention had been to gently urge the girl to forget about the young man, but she responded, at least momentarily, like a bulldog clinging tenaciously to a bone. As he searched for the words to respond the bone in question knocked on the door.

Penelope lunged toward the door and pulled it open, standing behind it as Christopher entered the kitchen without noticing her. She assumed her usual posture of staring at the floor. Steele, on the other hand, caught an eyeful of him and tried to squint his way to some sort of an answer as to why the freshly pressed white shirt and slacks he wore that morning were now a damp, dingy gray, wrinkled in unimaginable ways.

"What happened to you?" asked the Reverend.

"Beg pardon?" Christopher responded innocently enough, but cognition lagged only slightly. "Oh, my clothes. I worked with the Hawaiian boy all day. Shoveling shi…uh, shoveling out horse stables, chopping and stacking wood, and so on. Dirty work, but pleasant company."

"But you're not dirty, as such, just unkempt, in an extreme sort of way."

"So I am!" he responded enthusiastically, then settled into a placid grin, evidently feeling no need to share further.

"Christopher?"

"Hmm?" Christopher was reflecting on how much he had enjoyed the day and had already lost the thread of the conversation.

"Your appearance?"

"Oh, sorry. Yes, I was actually a filthy, stinking mess a while ago. But after a good day of work we met Kalani's friends at the beach—a congenial group of young men, by the way—and the lot of them cast me into the sea. Some sort of initiation to the Islands, I suppose. Anyway, it was great fun, and the cleansing waters of the Pacific washed away all evidence of stable work and, I hope, its unflattering aroma. I think the smell of the sea is preferable."

"Indeed," said Steele. "And your efforts at converting Ka... Klahan... the young man? Perhaps his friends as well?"

"Kalani? Hmmm, that's difficult. It's complicated by their experience with the descendants of the missionaries here in Hawaii."

"How is that?" demanded Reverend Tubbs, who had been standing in the corridor for the last few moments, eyebrow arched.

"Oh, hello, Reverend," Christopher said. "Sorry for my appearance. I've had quite a day with the natives, you might say."

"Obviously," he observed dryly. "You were saying that we descendants have complicated the conversion of the natives? Enlighten me."

"Well, sir," Christopher stumbled, searching for the right words. "I suppose it's all a matter of perception, but they seem to think that, while the original missionaries were sincere disciples of Christ, their descendants are more concerned with controlling Hawaii and its wealth. They enjoy the Bible—'Da Jesus Book,' they call it—but they seem to sense a certain hypocrisy because the children of the people who came to save their souls now seem to have dispossessed them of their lands, leaving them more or less dependents and laborers on islands that used to be theirs."

"The children of the people who saved their souls *created* all the wealth of their country," Tubbs corrected him.

"I'm sure you're right, Reverend, but I don't think they see it that way. As I understand from talking with these native boys, Hawaiians simply didn't think in the same terms we do regarding wealth and property, who owns what, and so on. And concepts like *aloha*,

41

which imply a shared responsibility for each other—"

"One day with a group of native boys and you've become an expert." Tubbs interrupted icily. Christopher looked around the room, embarrassed at being brought up short by his host.

"I'm sorry, I only meant… I was just trying to relate what I learned of them, from them. I meant no disrespect."

"I've talked to the natives, young man. I have many of them in my congregation."

"But Father," interjected Penelope, "Perhaps Christopher actually listens!"

As her father glowered at the girl Christopher noticed her for the first time. "Oh, hello, uh…"

"Penelope," she helped him.

"Yes, that's right—Penelope! When did you get here?" he asked, quite unaware that she'd been in the room the entire time.

"Penelope saved you a plate of food." Reverend Steele grasped the opportunity to change the subject.

"That was kind of you. Thanks so much, but I ate a king's feast with the boys down at the beach. We caught fish, and ate poi—ghastly stuff, but very filling—and I really couldn't eat another bite." Having inadvertently insulted both Rev. Tubbs and his daughter, he sought an excuse to leave the kitchen. "Well then, I'd better change out of these clothes." And with that he was off, leaving Penelope sitting quietly under her father's glare next to the meal she had saved for Christopher.

Christopher wondered how he had walked into that embarrassing trap. Tubbs was obviously offended at Christopher's effort to interpret the native point of view, but attacking him like that hardly seemed charitable. Just then he was interrupted by the sound of a foot tapping at the bottom of his door.

"Open the door, Christopher." It was Reverend Tubbs.

Christopher opened the door only to be pushed out of the way by Tubbs, who entered carrying a stack of books up to his chin with both hands. The older man dropped the pile—twelve volumes or more—next to the writing table.

"There!" Tubbs looked sternly at Christopher. "After you've read these, come talk to me about what we've done to the natives." Without giving Christopher a chance to stammer another apology, he turned on his heel and left the room, slamming the door behind him.

Awkward, Christopher thought to himself, but perhaps it was a situation he could study his way out of. And so he picked a book off the top of the staff and read himself to sleep.

Cantonese writing had no letters. The Chinese seemed to prefer many thousands of indecipherable, nearly indistinguishable pictures to anything Western eyes might call a letter. Christopher agonized over the little linguistic diagrams that were obviously designed for the express purpose of driving white men crazy. This was how his hours in paradise were slipping away from him—staring at these miserable symbols until his eyes rolled back in his head. Reverend Steele started him with an hour of instruction immediately after breakfast each day. Christopher devoted the ensuing daylight hours to making some sense of the morning's instruction, while Steele went out and enjoyed his celebrity status on the island. The midday meal gave Christopher a break from the demonic diagrams, eating a New England meal while avoiding Reverend Tubbs's disdainful glare, Penelope's desperate glances, and her sisters' furtive mocking. A few post-meal minutes of contrived conversation in which Tubbs and Christopher pretended not to loath each other, and the latter would escape back to his room for more Cantonese study accompanied by the sound of one or another of the Tubbs girls knuckling out some offense to music on the piano in the parlor. Christopher suspected he would never speak Chinese.

Each afternoon he stole back to his room to write a quick note to Lydia. This gave him an excuse to descend the hill to the post office by one o'clock, when the letters from the morning packet would have arrived. Each day he delivered his letter and inquired with a nonchalance he did not feel, if there were, perhaps, a letter for him. And each day there was not. Crestfallen, he would stand on the deck outside the post office, look at the ships coming and going at the wharf, and think seriously about flinging himself upon one of their decks—as a paid passenger if he could come up with the money, as a stowaway if he could not. He wanted both of his feet back on the mainland where he could stand before Lydia and ask her why—*why, oh why?*—she had sent him away. But of course there was always the forlorn, unreasonable, and pathetic hope that she might be on her way to him at that very moment, which carried the dreadful possibility that they would pass each other at sea. The fantasy was just enough to hold him on the island.

After the daily late-afternoon disappointment, he still managed to get some time with Kalani each day, ostensibly to convert him, but in reality to stay out of the Tubbs house for a while. They mostly just talked, each sharing with the other anecdotes about his homeland. At length, Christopher did go so far as to invite him to church on Sunday, and very nearly kept a straight face when he suggested that Kalani would enjoy Reverend Tubbs's sermon.

"Yeah, brah, Kalani love to listen to dat man blow wind. Anyway, I go to that church near ever' day. I do mo' work der dan anybody."

"I mean come there to worship, not work."

"I do dat befo' too. I don' tink dey like me there so much on Sunday."

"Okay, very well, just think about it. I'm supposed to be converting you, after all."

"Good luck, brah."

"Thanks."

"Ah, don' be like dat. I like da Jesus book, you know dat."

"Yes, I appreciate that, but you mix up the Christian teachings with all the rest of the Hawaiian pantheism."

"'Panty...?'"

"Pantheism. Your multiplicity of deities?" Kalani tilted his head and squinted, as if that might bring Christopher's words into focus.

Christopher tried again. "Your many gods. You know, Kane the creator, Ku the war god, Lono the peace god, Kanaloa the god of the ocean, and so on."

"Hey, you pay attention good, brah," he gave his white friend a pat on the back. "But you don' see dat it's mo' betta dat way, da Hawaiian way? We don' gatta choose between dis one o' dat one."

"Yes, that's very generous of you, but Christian missionaries prefer that you take their religion whole, without combining it with all these other gods."

"Dat's a problem. You really believe all dat stuff?"

Christopher sighed. "I hope so."

On Sunday morning Christopher and the Steeles joined the Tubbs girls on their ritual walk to church. The Reverend Tubbs and his wife were, of course, already at the church preparing for the morning service. The younger girls, Jane and Martha, each took one of Christopher's arms as if to prevent his escape, and peppered him with an endless series of questions about the impossibly exotic land known as Seattle. Did they really have Indians? (Yes, they were actually there first.) And logging camps? (Yes, but not downtown, as they had imagined.) Did he wear a six-shooter on his hip around town? (No.) Wolves? (Yes, but again, not downtown much.) And on and on the girls monopolized Christopher's time and attention as Penelope, ever uncomfortable speaking in front of him, silently wished lightning would strike both of the female chatterboxes and reduce them to quiet little piles of ashes.

Once at the church the group dallied in the narthex, which served as something of a social center where various congregants exchanged gossip and other Christian essentials before the service began. Forgetting herself for a moment, Penelope nudged Christopher and pointed into the sanctuary.

"Look, it's your new convert" she whispered.

"So it is. His name, by the way, is Kalani. He's worked at your house for years."

"I know his name," she said, a bit defensively.

"Who's that girl next to him? Isn't that your laundry girl?"

"*Was* our laundry girl," she corrected him. "Father fired her for 'questionable moral behavior.'"

"What on earth does that mean?"

"It means," Martha chimed in, "that Father heard that sailors were coming to her little hut on the beach road late at night."

"How would he know such a thing?"

"Who knows?" It was Jane's turn. "The only thing that matters is that Father suspects. That's enough. I can't believe she'd show her face around here."

"Besides," Penelope rejoined the condemnation. "Church is hardly the place for a prostitute."

"On the contrary," Reverend Steele joined the group. "I can scarcely think of a better place for a prostitute. Shall we take our seats?"

The service began, and after what seemed like a very long time, it ended. In the interim there were hymns, prayers, an exceedingly lengthy sermon, and of course the collection. Reverend Tubbs's sermon was devoted, in all of its cruel duration, to making the point that Christians, although they praised The Father, The Son, and The Holy Ghost, really just had one God. This bit of biblical theory left the *haoles* bored, if they were actually listening, and the natives confused, or at least unconvinced—native Hawaiians usually found Christianity a few Gods short of a full deck. Eventually, as if to prove God's mercy, the sermon came to a close, giving way to the most important part of any church service—the collection. This particular ritual turned out to be surprisingly entertaining, if a bit awkward.

Protestants had become bounteously adept at collecting money in recent years, especially the evangelical-missionary variety. No offering was too small, and certainly none was too large. But on this particular Sunday, when the fallen Muanu extended her hand to drop her coins in the basket, native dignity and Christian contempt collided. The Reverend Tubbs, offended at the girl's temerity at showing her face in his church after he had dismissed her from his service, had been watching and waiting to see if she would further her offense by dropping her tainted silver into the basket. And when the moment came he placed his girth between Muanu and the usher holding the plate as he hissed, "We will not accept the wages of sin in this church!"

Muanu, the simple laundry girl, looking angelic in her pale blue dress with its lace collar and cuffs, assumed a decidedly defiant posture. If Tubbs had expected her to bow to his condemnation he would be disappointed, as she spoke directly to the Reverend amid the hushed congregation. "You have reduced us to slaves and whores. If you won't accept the wages of sin, you shall have no wages at all." And with that she dropped her coins in the basket and curtsied before the red-faced Tubbs, who trembled like a volcano on the verge of eruption. Mrs. Tubbs, at the organ, began pumping out the closing hymn, either to rescue her husband from this hideous moment or to prevent him from making it worse. Either way, the organ music delivered the congregation from their humiliation at the hands of this native girl.

After the service the little group of missionaries watched as Kalani and his cousin exited the sanctuary—she, stoic and defiant, and he typically benign.

Steele nudged Christopher. "You should go after them."

"Me? Why?" asked Christopher.

"Balance the condemnation they received here with some true Christian charity—perhaps even forgiveness." The old man was clearly disgusted with his colleague's performance with that poor laundry girl, prostitute or not.

"Surely not," interrupted Penelope. "You're not going to be seen talking with that harlot, are you Christopher?"

"Of course I am." Christopher was surprised at Penelope's sudden ability to speak in his presence, and found he preferred her mute. He excused himself and caught up with Kalani and Muanu as they walked off the church grounds.

"I'm so sorry," he said, a little breathless as he caught up with them. "I'm new at this church myself—"

"I know who you are," Muanu interrupted him, still spoiling for a fight.

"You do?"

"You are the new *haole* with the Tubbs family," she spat out the name. "I was there the day you arrived with the others. You stared at my backside until I thought I would have to pull your eyeballs out of my skirt and return them to you."

"I didn't... I mean, I don't remember—"

"Yes, you do," she corrected him.

"See here, I'm a married man!" he exclaimed in a feeble attempt to exert some control over this conversation. Kalani came to Christopher's rescue.

"He da one I tell you about," he said to Muanu, "You know, da one who tinks he gotta wife."

"Oh," said Muanu, nodding her recognition. "That's sad."

"Look," Christopher said, trying to elbow his way back into the conversation. "I just wanted to apologize for the way Reverend Tubbs spoke to you. It was unfair and, well, unchristian, if you ask me. I feel terrible about it."

"You do?" Muanu seemed genuinely surprised by the apology. She squinted at Christopher for a moment, examining his eyes. "Hmmm!" she concluded the examination. "You are not like the others."

"Oh, no!" Kalani laughed. "I could tell you dat much! I see Christopher almos' every day. He *hoa pili*," he said, using the Hawaiian term for close friend.

"This *haole* is *hoa pili*?" Muanu was skeptical. She peered at him again. Satisfied with what she saw, she shrugged her shoulders and concluded, "Okay. Good day, Mr. Jones."

She laughed as if she had found some ironic amusement in his name. She put her arm in Kalani's and walked away. A few paces hence she turned to look at Christopher, whose eyes were exactly where she knew they would be. He cringed, but she just smiled and continued on her way.

Christopher's 'wife,' Lydia, who had no intention of ever going to Hawaii, let alone China, arrived at the offices of Bliss Shipping in Seattle precisely at 9:45 for a ten o'clock appointment with the owner, Warren Bliss, who was yet to arrive. His secretary, an Asian man, whom she figured to be Chinese, wore a long, braided pigtail. He offered her a slight bow and the slightest of smiles as he told her "The Captain" rarely arrived before eleven o'clock.

"I'll wait, thank you."

The secretary acknowledged her with another bow and returned to a raised desk, at which he evidently worked in a standing position all day. After watching the man methodically roll several documents into cylinders and shove them into pigeon holes, she ventured a question.

"Why does 'The Captain' always arrive so late to work?"

"Perhaps it is better you ask the Captain," returned the soft, slightly accented voice. Further questioning would probably be useless but she tried anyway, only to find her initial impression was correct.

She sat in silence until slightly after eleven o'clock when the Captain, a.k.a. Warren Bliss, briskly strode into the office directly past Lydia without noticing her. He gave Mr. Li a pat on the back and announced that he would like coffee brought to his desk, his voice disappearing as his office door closed behind him.

"'The Captain,' I presume?" asked Lydia, which Mr. Li answered with a nod. He had obviously forgotten their appointment, so she rose to approach the door. Mr. Li interceded, placing himself her path. With another bow he said, "Please to sit. I will tell The Captain you are here." Mr. Li poured the requested coffee, placed it on a silver tray and entered the office.

Moments later Lydia was seated across the desk from Warren Bliss, furious, but trying not to appear so. "Good morning, Captain," she greeted him. "I'm Mrs. Jones, from the *Seattle Weekly*. We had an appointment an hour ago."

"Oh please, call me Warren," evidently more concerned with what they would call each other than the fact that he had left her stewing in the anteroom for an hour.

"Mr. Bliss—"

"Coffee?"

"No, thank you."

"As you like," he said as he lifted his coffee cup to his mouth.

Lydia waited until he had a mouthful of coffee before asking, "Are you smuggling illegal Chinese workers into Seattle?"

The coffee sprayed from his mouth, followed by coughing and sputtering as his face turned a dark shade of red. Eventually he found oxygen, then a handkerchief to wipe his face, and finally words. "You do get right to the point, don't you, Mrs. Jones."

"Saves time—I've already lost an hour waiting for you." She observed him for a moment as he continued to mop his face with the handkerchief. "You are familiar with the steamer *North Star*, I believe."

He rolled his eyes. "I've heard of it. It belongs to the Canadians these days."

"The Canadian government seized it when it was discovered to be smuggling Chinese into America."

"In truth, dear lady," a condescending smile crept across his lips, "the Canadians are remarkably unconcerned about human cargo, so long as they receive their share of the profits."

"Their share? The Canadians have a stake in this?"

"To say the least. They've actually legislated it. Unlike the American version, the Canadian Chinese exclusion law is such that it doesn't actually exclude anyone, it just makes them pay fifty dollars a head on their way to America."

"The Canadian government profits from violating the Chinese Exclusion Act?"

"What does the 'L' in 'L. C. Jones' stand for?"

"Lydia. Can you please explain how Canada profits from U.S. law?"

"Certainly, Lydia—may I call you Lydia?"

"No."

"I didn't mean to presume—"

"Canadian profiteering?" she prodded him.

"As you like, *Mrs. Jones*." This woman was no fun at all. "The vast majority of Chinese who come to Canada have no intention of staying there."

"They're all on their way to the States, is that it?"

"Yes. Canada welcomes each and every Chinaman with a fifty-dollar head tax on his way in, knowing full well the little yellow fellow is already on his way out. No one really wants to stay in Canada. Too cold." He noticed Lydia had turned thoughtful, obviously reflecting on something. "Yes?" It was his turn to prompt her.

"What you say fits with something a Canadian customs agent told me."

"You went to Canada?" Bliss raised an eyebrow at the idea of this woman traveling, perhaps unaccompanied, between Seattle and Vancouver.

"I had to go there—I wanted to see your boat. I thought the customs agent I spoke with was just offering the customary rudeness to Americans they all seem to practice up there, but he was quite specific. Now let's see," she said as she turned back a few pages in her notes. "Ah, here it is. 'The yellow bastards come here to enter your damn country, and you can't stop it, and we don't care.'"

"Such language."

"I'm quoting." She flipped forward in her notes and resumed. "So why did they take your boat if you were simply playing your part in this international fraud?"

"*I* wasn't doing *anything*. The ship's master was supposed to be making supply runs to Vancouver, not smuggling Chinese. Then the silly man got caught smuggling taxable items *into* Canada, so they seized my boat. I have a lot of people working for me, and I can't help it if one of them develops a taste for smuggling."

"So they don't mind smuggling into America, but smuggling into Canada is prohibited?"

"They like to collect their customs duties, evidently." He paused for a moment, and was about to resume when Mr. Li interrupted them in his ever-so-serene voice, "Captain, you have other appoint-a-ments."

"Thank you, Li." He returned his attention to Lydia. "If you don't have any other questions—"

"Actually, I'd like to see your ships' manifests for the last six months."

"*Appoint-a-ments*," insisted a decidedly less serene Mr. Li.

"I generally don't invite reporters to go through our records, and I don't think I'll change that policy for you." Such cheek! But he couldn't help but be impressed by it.

"You claim not to have any human cargo. It's a matter of simple bookkeeping to verify that. This can actually help you, Mr. Bliss."

"I'll see if we can scare up some records for you."

"When? I would like to see them now if I could."

"*Appoint-a-ments!*"

"I'll send someone to your newspaper with them."

Lydia did not believe him for a minute, but she knew she could find him again. So, just as the Chinaman opened his mouth Lydia raised her hand to silence him. "'Appoint-a-ments.' I know, I know." She crammed her notes back into her bag and left the room. Bliss watched her go, then turned to his secretary.

"Li, collect some shipping data for me, will you?"

"Captain, surely it is not wise to give manifests to this woman?"

"No, of course not. Just collect a bunch of innocent manifests and change the ship names, or create whole new ones. I don't care, just give me a stack of useless paper to deliver to this woman."

"Yes, Captain."

"And get me every article she's ever published."

"Yes, Captain."

"Li," he called to his secretary as he was leaving the office. "We don't often get an opportunity like Mrs. Jones."

Mr. Li shook his head slowly. "Captain too smart for his own good."

Among the books that Tubbs instructed Christopher to read were several histories of the missionary endeavor in Hawaii. Christopher left the stack of books where Tubbs had unceremoniously dropped them, but rather than hole up in his room he usually did his reading in the family's parlor. It was a nice way to relax after a day of studying, and the atmosphere in the parlor felt very much like the little reading rooms he nearly lived in at college. After several hours isolated in his room studying Cantonese he wanted to feel like there were people around him, and he could always count at least two: Penelope and one of her parents. Within moments of sitting down in a chair and opening a text Penelope would magically appear. Soundlessly taking up a position in the chair opposite Christopher, she would pull out her cross-stitching and proceed to inadvertently poke holes in her fingers while she surreptitiously stared at the object of her crush. Within moments of her arrival one of her parents would take up a third position to keep an eye on them both. Christopher would have been happy to assure them that he was no threat to Penelope's adolescent chastity, but such a conversation was beyond imagining.

This particular evening the Tubbs parents were less diligent than usual at protecting their daughters from the young missionary from the Northwest. Luxuriating in the privacy, Penelope forgot herself and gave up any pretense of needlework in favor of dumbly gazing at Christopher while he read. After several minutes of this Christopher, without looking up from his book, said, "Penelope, is my hair on fire?"

Startled, she responded, "Brother Christopher, why would you ask such a thing?"

"I was just wondering why you were staring so."

"I was doing no such thing!" Embarrassed and flustered, she returned to her stitching with a vengeance. Christopher grinned, offered that he must have been mistaken, and returned to his book.

"What are you reading, brother Christopher?"

"I'm working my way through that stack of books your father offered for my edification. This dusty old volume here was published about thirty years ago. It's called..." he paused as he flipped to the front cover and read, "'The Hawaiian Islands: Their Progress and Condition under Missionary Labors, by Rufus Anderson.' Old Rufus mentions your grandfather, repeatedly."

"That's probably why Father condemned you to read it. What does Old Rufus say?" She smiled shyly at their shared joke.

"Just that you've all done a fabulous job bringing Christianity to this benighted race of Polynesian savages, which unfortunately decreases every year."

"Father says it's their immoral living that reduces their numbers."

"No doubt," Christopher dismissed the topic. "Anderson concluded the volume, way back in '65, with some concern about your father's generation, the sons of the original missionaries. He wrote that..." he paused again as he found the last chapter, "Ah, here it is. 'They will be exposed to the temptations of wealth, of ambition, and possibly to the paralyzing influence of a declining population.'"

"What does that mean?"

"It means that the generation of whites born and raised here, rather than look after the race their parents came here to save, is likely to feed on its dying corpse and take the islands for themselves."

"Oh, my!" the girl's eyes were wide with shock at the words she just heard.

"That's a rough interpretation, naturally. Your father might read it differently."

"Indeed he might!" boomed the voice of Reverend Tubbs, who obviously had a gift for showing up at the most inopportune moments. Christopher, having waded through a couple of Tubbs's books already, was now less inclined to back down than propriety required. He was a guest, after all. Problem was, he could not help himself.

"There really doesn't seem to be a lot of room for interpretation, Reverend. In fact, I read in another one of these books you so generously loaned me—thanks, by the way, I'm really enjoying them—it said that the Congregational church threatened to excommunicate any missionaries who acquired real estate privately. That would hardly square with your father's work on land reform, creating private land holdings under King Kamehameha III."

The reverend looked for a moment as if his temper would get the better of him, but suddenly he became ostentatiously calm.

"Christopher, perhaps it would behoove you to see one of the great plantations in action. Why, the productivity and wealth the whites have created for the natives here can hardly be expressed in words. You really need to see it for yourself."

"Love to," Christopher agreed, always eager to see more of the island and less of Reverend Tubbs. "I'll go tomorrow."

Christopher got a later start than he wanted because Reverend Steele insisted that they do their lessons before he headed out to the plantation. Tubbs assured him that he would get there in plenty of time to observe operations as long as he left right after lunch. There was always a passing wagon on which he could catch a ride.

So it was afternoon before Christopher walked along the beach for a couple miles, breathing deeply of the moist Pacific air before turning up the coast trail where he hoped to catch a ride up to the vast cane farm. Kalani had mentioned that he was working out at one of the sugar plantations, so he hoped that he would meet up with his friend for the ride home.

The walk along the beach reminded him yet again that he had truly found paradise. So beautiful to the eye, the images melded with the smell of the sea and the shifting sand beneath his feet. Yet it remained something of an empty experience without Lydia there to enjoy it with him. Where was she?

The day grew blisteringly hot, but all the passing wagons Tubbs promised failed to appear. And the more the sun baked his brain, the more he felt like a real missionary. So he walked and thought, and thought and walked, and as he did so it occurred to him how little progress he had made on his ostensible mission to convert Kalani and his friends to Christianity. Given the Hawaiians' experience at the hands of the missionaries' descendants, the idea that he would be able to induce young Kalani to accept Jesus Christ as his Lord and Savior was starting to seem a bit absurd. The richness of the native spiritual traditions would be hard enough to compete with if it were not for its amazing adaptability to new belief systems. Clinging to basic truths—*aloha*—Hawaiians could find similar faiths and add them as they liked.

As the sun beat on Christopher's brain a theological plan started to take shape in his head. He imagined that he might truly convert Kalani, and his lovely cousin, too. He would give them a few choice parables from the New Testament, leavened with sympathetic examples of the ways the teachings relate to his own sordid life, and that, he imagined, should just about do it. Christopher would then bring his newly Christian manservant to Tubbs and display him as his first trophy in a long, prosperous career of saving heathen souls.

As these fantasies and others came and went, the sun continued to sap the strength of the sweating missionary. Christopher began to wish he had provisioned himself for the trek, but he had expected to catch a ride by now. Where was all the traffic, for God's sake? *Watch it, Christopher—don't want to use the Lord's name in vain just because you're a little hot and thirsty, and maybe just a trifle delirious.*

Relief finally came in the form of darkness. The sun began to set, and a tired, thirsty, hungry, missionary allowed himself to collapse at a spot where the trail opened onto the beach. He watched the orange sun fall slowly into the sea. He wanted to sleep, but the sting of hunger and thirst would not permit it, so he waited for sunset to restore his stamina somewhat.

He rose in the humid night air to resume his trek toward the plantation. He forced his legs to plod forward, and immediately slipped on a pile of donkey dung, but he didn't care enough at this point to bother wiping it off. He just lay there.

He thought he heard a noise. The sound of a burro's hooves struck his ears a few moments before he could make out its shape in the twilight ahead of him. He wasn't sure of its reality, but hearing a mirage seemed unlikely. A moment later, as it came toward him, he could see that the burro was pulling a wagon, empty save for two riders. It was going in the wrong direction, but the exhausted missionary, having lost his enthusiasm for saving souls, resolved that he would happily accept a ride if it would only take him back to his own little bed. And as he raised his arms to stop the wagon's advance he noticed its occupants for the first time: Kalani and Muanu.

"Brah," barked the smiling Kalani to the bewildered missionary. "What you doin' all way out he'?"

"I... uh," stammered Christopher. "I was looking for you."

"You find me, brah," said the smiling Kalani. "You wanna ride?"

Christopher was overwhelmed with a sense of deliverance. If his mind were not struggling under the weight of overexertion and the legacy of sunstroke, he might have found irony in who was saving whom. And Muanu appeared to him like some Polynesian angel of mercy smiling benignly down on him from her perch. She seemed

57

to read his mind, at least inasmuch as he clearly wanted something. "You want food, drink?" she asked, holding up a canvas bag. Kalani had already locked the brake in place, hopped down, and assisted Christopher into the rear of the wagon, where Mauna joined him. She reached in her bag, from which she produced some bread and a skin filled with wine.

"Water," Christopher protested when he tasted the wine. "I need some water. I'm afraid I didn't plan well for my walk today and I'm terribly thirsty."

"S'okay, brah," Kalani said over his shoulder. "Have a little bread with the wine, s'good as water."

Christopher knew better, but his hunger and thirst got the better of his judgment, and he permitted himself a generous helping of wine with his slice of bread. Then another. It felt good on his empty stomach. At some point the wagon started moving again, but Christopher wasn't entirely aware of it. Kalani—ostensibly the object of the day's journey—was driving the wagon but had ceased to exist in Christopher's head, which was lying heavily upon Muanu's thigh. She held him to keep his head from rocking back and forth as the little cart bumped about on the undulating path. Christopher wasn't sure how he came to be in this position, but both parties seemed comfortable with it, so he lay there contemplating the softness and warmth of his 'pillow.'

Christopher's perception of time, like the rest of his senses, save his sense of touch, were lost in the mists of wine and woman. After some undeterminable period of time Kalani brought the wagon to a halt and the missionary reluctantly lifted his head along with the rest of his body and followed Muanu toward a little hut. Christopher might have recognized his surroundings in the daylight, but in the night's darkness he had no idea where he was. "Where are we?"

"My house," Muanu replied.

"Have you a lamp?" he asked as he stumbled over something. "I can't see a thing." He heard Kalani's voice in the distance saying something about a candle. Christopher, dangerously lightheaded, slipped to his knees. He was startled by Muanu's touch as she knelt beside him to offer assistance. He felt her body against his, and her breath on his ear as she whispered, "It is alright, Christopher. You'll be okay here." The flash of a match and then the gentle glow of a little candle illuminated Muanu's face only inches from his own. He stared at her unabashedly, only because he wasn't aware he was doing so. He thought he heard Kalani speak, saying something like "Go ahead. It's okay. It's good." But it was the kiss that made him aware of his body. In the back of his mind were echoes of many stern voices, none of them his own, telling him to turn his back on temptation, to be strong, to deny himself this feeling that had suddenly enlivened every inch of his skin. Eventually the kiss ended, and when he opened his eyes to see Muanu's exposed breasts before him the scolding voices fell silent, powerlessly mute. In all his life this particular image had never been his to behold, and he found it awe-inspiring. Muanu could not stifle a small giggle when she noticed how the sight of her breasts had lulled him into fish-eyed stupidity. She smiled with a certain sympathy as she placed his hands upon them, then occupied her own hands unbuttoning his shirt.

His thoughts were not really thoughts at all, but rather a series of impressions based on total immersion in his physical senses. Flesh against flesh, it seemed she must have had more than two hands. There was kissing, then there was not, and then it resumed. His faint efforts to exert some control were met by gentle yet firm instructions to lie back, relax, and enjoy. Christopher was content to follow instructions. He could feel himself just barely inside her, and yet he also felt her moist pelvis pressing against his hip. He couldn't make sense of this, and this cluster of sensations was the only hint of dissonance in an otherwise harmonious flow of pleasure. He ignored it, but his mind circled back to the curiosity, mingled in a tangential way with another question, *where is Kalani?* But this lasted only a moment, and again he drifted back into the little world where only he and Muanu existed. He reached to his side to caress her buttocks as she ground her pelvis against his thigh, and he realized with a start that the wet orifice he felt around his member could not possibly be what he assumed it was. And as the possibilities fought their way through the fatigue and inebriation protecting his brain from reality, Christopher pulled his mouth from Muanu's neck, his face from the nest it had made in her hair, and looked down to see the top of Kalani's head. The significance of this sight was thundering into his consciousness just as he heard voices outside the door. Suddenly he was blinded by a bright flash of lamplight, which protected him from the horrified expressions of the Reverend Tubbs, his wife, Reverend Steele, his wife, and assorted others, standing at the opening to the little hut and aghast at the tangled mass of carnality they had stumbled upon.

Thus ended the missionary career of Christopher Jones.

CHAPTER THREE

Reverend Steele sat alone on the veranda of the Tubbs' mansion, staring at the ocean, unable to escape the sordid scene he had witnessed a few nights before in that heathen hut out by the beach. Now the tropical sunset held no beauty for him, as if paradise had been lost yet again. He watched the sun, surrender to gravity and drop into the sea. It is too hard to fight against natural forces like gravity—or a young man's animal instincts. The weight he felt left the old man disconsolate. He chastised himself for being so severe, but he was even angrier with Christopher for putting him in a position in which he seemed to have no other choice. My God, he thought, what would happen to them if they made their way to China and Christopher started buggering little boys? His continuation with the mission was simply out of the question, and Rev. Steele had made no effort to speak with Christopher since—he could barely bring himself to think of it—since he discovered him as part of that bestial trio. Christopher, for his part, seemed to have disappeared. And what choice did the boy have? He could hardly be expected to show his face among civilized society again. And that is what hurt; he liked Christopher. Several times since they met he had occasion—usually when Christopher's skeptical approach led him to some hilarious, unorthodox observation or another—to consider Christopher a blessing.

"Forget about all of this, husband." Mrs. Steele interrupted him and offered this advice along with a cup of tea, but her husband made no effort to respond. She set the cup down next to him and tried again. "We shall be fine. We will find another replacement."

"Yes," the reverend agreed, albeit reluctantly. "But I was excited about having this boy around. He was so... so different."

To say the least, Mrs. Steele thought to herself, but in consideration of her husband's despondent mood, she said nothing. True, Christopher had engaged in a monstrous act, but it was clear to her that he had been made a tool of the savages—no less than he had been a tool of that woman, his so-called wife. Why, he would not be there at all were it not for Lydia's designs on a writing career—a career, for pity's sake! Anyone with eyes could see that Christopher pined for the girl, and Lydia used his weakness for her like a puppet master. Now the poor boy was lost in the woods and Lydia had quite disappeared. It made her sick to her stomach, still more so that they had unfinished business with the little minx.

"Husband, we must notify the boy's wife in some way, mustn't we?"

"But she answers no letters. We don't even know if she is in Seattle at all." The thought of that innocent young girl brought Rev. Steele a new sense of grief. "Oh my," he realized for the first time, "I married that poor girl to a... a sodomite! I must do something." He paused then resolutely concluded, "She must be told."

"But you must be discreet, my dear."

"Yes, but I must say *something*. I feel responsible."

She brought him his writing box. "You'll find the right words, husband. You always do." And with that she patted him on the hand, kissed his forehead and left him to his duty.

He felt strongly that the message should be sent with utmost urgency, but there was no cable linking Hawaii with the United States. He would simply have to send a letter by packet to San Francisco, where it could be cabled to Seattle. But thinking through such details was simply an unconscious method of procrastination. He had to find precisely the right words to convey the seriousness of her husband's weakness, without explicitly identifying his crime in writing for the telegraph operators to read. After all, people went to jail for such things, and he would not wish that upon Christopher, however heinous his transgression. He would find something scriptural.

Lydia Jones sat alone at her desk amid the clatter of the Seattle Weekly press room. She was trying to tease some meaning out of a decidedly mysterious telegram. The Western Union boy had delivered it the night before and she had immediately read it with great curiosity, but very little comprehension. She moved to an unoccupied corner of the newsroom, and studied it anew. It was clear that Steele was trying to say something without actually saying it, let alone leaving a written record of it. The two terms he relied upon were "faithlessness" and "Leviticus 18:22." She peered at the words as if focusing on the individual letters might bring clarity out of the fog, and did not even notice that yesterday's news, the shipping magnate Warren Bliss, had sidled up beside her. Bliss, ever the gentleman, interrupted her meditation with a subtle, then more insistent, clearing of the throat. Having failed to get her attention by esophageal means, he simply asked permission to sit down across from her. "I thought I might find you here. I was hoping we could continue our conversation of the other day."

She raised her head from the paper on the desk. At first she was irritated at the interruption, but as she was about to say something unkind she noticed, again, how handsome he was. Ten years earlier he was probably almost pretty. Suddenly, she had nothing to say.

"It's me... Warren. Warren Bliss? You must remember me." Although he wasn't at all sure she did.

"Oh, yes, of course. I'm just working on a... problem, of sorts."

"Perhaps I can help."

You want a part of this mess? She had precipitously married her long-time beau to jump at a writing job, and just as quickly disposed of him to secure a better one, but always vaguely imagined she would find a way to fix things—put everything right. The telegram, however, seemed to indicate that events had gotten completely out of hand. Having dispatched the amorous Christopher to China via

Polynesia, she was now in receipt of a cryptic communiqué from the tropics suggesting her husband had disappeared, and this local businessman wanted to help?

"No," she dismissed the offer. "It's just family stuff—impossible for an outsider to understand."

"I come from a family myself, you know, but I understand, I think. Well, you wanted to look at our manifests from Bliss Shipping? I have several here," he said, putting the valise on his lap. "The documents are not readily comprehensible to the layman, or lay*woman*. Perhaps we could discuss them together over lunch or tea?"

They met that afternoon, and the next. Then they began meeting in the evening after work, sometimes over dinner. So began the brief courtship between the shipping magnate and somebody else's wife. Handsome and wealthy, he was not terribly interesting, but it sufficed that he was interested in her, or appeared to be. If she had admitted the situation to be what it was, she would have been scandalized, so it served her purposes to fool herself for the time being.

Lydia's ambition, her marital status, and casual disregard for anyone else's opinion, gave her freedom of movement society usually reserved for matrons and prostitutes. With Christopher thousands of miles away, she had the advantages of marriage without actually having to tolerate a husband. As a female writer, people grudgingly accepted her tendency to be out and about asking people questions, and generally snooping around. Her parents did not like it, but after Mary Kenworthy intervened on her behalf their objections ceased, or at least subsided to a dull grumble. Going off to meet Warren for dinner could, with only a little duplicity, be passed off as a meeting with a source as long as he brought along his ridiculous valise stuffed with papers of some sort. And so, sitting across from her in a secluded booth in the magnificent dining room of the Madison Hotel, Warren passed another useless and utterly fraudulent ship's manifest to her in the candlelight.

The waiter offered wine, but Warren, understanding his prey, feigned indignation. "There will be no alcohol at *this* table." Then turning to Lydia he spoke much more gently. "I'm sorry the subject came up. Perhaps your good writing on the temperance movement will spare us such embarrassment in the future." The waiter, who had served him alcoholic beverages on countless occasions, shrugged his shoulders and moved on. Lydia, however, was deeply moved.

"Thank you, Warren. Your sentiments are rare in such a town as ours."

"I know," he said, shaking his head. "If it's not the Chinese and their opium, it's the Norwegians and their beer—truly tragic." As he spoke he filled her glass with drinking water from the carafe the puzzled waiter had brought them.

"But you were a sailor for so many years. Isn't it a bit unusual for you to advocate temperance? I mean, as one hears it the first thing a sailor does in port is seek out a bottle of rum."

"I'm an unusual man." *To put it mildly*, he thought to himself before quickly changing the subject. "You seemed troubled as you read that telegram last week, or was it two weeks ago?" He nodded toward the well-fingered envelope protruding from her bag.

She thought a moment before answering, but she wanted to talk. She missed the way she used to chat with her young women friends, now busy with their husbands and babies. This man was somehow different—he could talk with her and listen almost as her girlfriends had. She decided she could confide in him.

"It's from my husband's superior, Reverend Steele." She waited for a reaction, but clearly none was forthcoming so she pushed on. "He explains that Christopher, my husband, is no longer a missionary, but he doesn't explain why. Well, not really, anyway."

"'Not *really*'?"

"Well, you read it." She thrust the note at him.

MY DEAR MRS JONES STOP I HAVE DISMISSED YOUR HUSBAND STOP A MISSIONARY MUST LIVE A CHRISTIAN LIFE STOP THIS INCLUDES THE OLD TESTAMENT AND LEVITICUS 18 22 STOP YOUR

HUSBAND HAS CHOSEN FAITHLESSNESS STOP I
SUGGEST YOU HAVE YOUR UNION ANNULLED STOP

Warren looked up slowly, still holding the telegram between his
thumb and forefinger. "This is very troubling."

"I agree, but I don't know why. What does it mean?"

"You are not familiar with Leviticus?"

"Well, no," she admitted. She had always been a church-going
Methodist girl; she just hadn't paid much attention. "I am a good
Christian, but I always left the Bible study to Christopher. Are you,
perhaps, more conversant with the Old Testament?"

"Generally, no, but I think I recall this one."

"What does it mean?"

Bliss drew close to her and lowered his voice. "It means, dear
lady, that your husband is a sodomite."

"What?" she demanded. Heads turned toward their booth.
Lowering her voice, she insisted, "That can't be—not Christopher.
He has always been decidedly, almost improperly, interested in
women." She paused to consider the notion for a moment, but then
shook her head, rejecting it again. "It just couldn't be."

Warren peered at her over the cable, just barely managing to
suppress a grin. "The Reverend recommends that you have your
marriage annulled." He waited for a reaction, but her mind was
elsewhere. Showing no sign she heard him at all, she reached over
and retrieved the telegram from his grasp. She peered intently at
each line, searching for some meaning she may have missed in
the first hundred readings of it. Warren stretched his hand across
the table and gently enfolded the hand that held the offending
document in his own. "It will be all right," he whispered.

"Are you sure?" she asked, a little defeated.

"Yes, it will all be all—"

"Not that—Leviticus eighteen-twenty-two! Are you sure of what
it says? You're unfamiliar with the rest of the Bible, so maybe you're
not certain of this one verse?"

He looked at her closely and was relieved to see that she implied nothing by the remark. This woman was unexpectedly naïve. "You're right. I'm sure I've mixed it up with some other verse."

"I want to know for sure," she insisted as she cast her glance about the great dining room.

"Well, I don't carry a Bible with me, Mrs. Jones."

"Hotels have Bibles in them, don't they?" She didn't wait for an answer. "Ask that waiter to fetch us one."

"I really don't think—"

She started to rise from her chair, waving across the room to the waiter.

"All right, all right," he relented. "Just sit down... please!" She did so, completely unconcerned with his embarrassment. He made eye contact with the young waiter and with a slight nod of the head had him scurrying to the table.

"Yes, sir, have you changed your mind about the wine?"

"Never," he snapped. "I assume your rooms have Bibles in them?"

Well, this is a new one, thought the waiter, unable to keep the corner of his mouth from turning up ever so slightly as he responded. "Sir?"

"I'd like you to bring one—here, to our table. Thank you."

As the highly amused but utterly perplexed waiter hurried off, Warren returned to the subject of Rev. Steele's advice. "Reverend Steele recommends annulment rather than divorce, did you notice?" He didn't wait for an answer. "That would indicate, or at least imply, that your marriage was never actually... well, never actually occurred. At least it wasn't made complete."

"What do you mean, 'never—" she caught his meaning as the words passed her lips, and she blushed deeply. The question seemed fair enough given the evening's revelations about Christopher. "If I understand your question, the answer is no, the marriage was never consummated."

"I would never ask such a thing," he lied. "No gentleman ever would," he lied again. "I just wanted to point out that if you are

67

eligible for an annulment, and evidently you are, it is a far less complicated thing than a divorce—and much better for your future prospects, as well."

"And what, I wonder, are the consequences for one's prospects for marrying a deviant?"

Warren hesitated an awkward moment. "I'm sure I don't know."

"What's the difference between an annulment and a divorce?"

"In legal or practical terms?"

"Either—no, both."

"All right. In legal terms, divorce means you had a true marriage and it failed for whatever reason, and you are legally dissolving it. Annulment means the marriage never really existed, that it was somehow fraudulent from the start. For instance, if one or both parties were below the age of consent, or the groom misrepresented himself, or—"

"Or if the marriage were never consummated?"

"Exactly."

"And the practical terms?"

"Hmmm. To put it most bluntly, I'd say that in the case of annulment you're regarded as a woman who's been wronged, but in the case of divorce you're more likely to be taken as a fallen woman." He watched as her face fell. "I am sorry."

"I prefer annulment."

At that point the waiter, who was enjoying himself immensely, arrived, Bible in hand, smiling sweetly. "Here you are, sir."

Warren dismissed him with a decidedly unfriendly glance, and began thumbing through the pages to the twenty-second line of the chapter in question, eighteenth Leviticus. He stopped and stared benignly at his dinner companion.

"Read it to me," Lydia ordered.

"As you wish." He indulged himself in the slightest smile before continuing. "'Thou shalt not lie with mankind, as with womankind: it is abomination.'"

They sat in awkward silence for a long moment, she obviously sorting through a dozen conflicting thoughts, he enjoying wondering what they might be. Finally she stood up, collected her things and announced, "There's someone I must speak to."

"But we haven't finished our meal," Bliss protested.

"I'm sorry," Lydia said as she got up. "I have to go."

As she scurried out of the Madison Hotel the waiter came back to the table and asked simply, "Sir?"

"Kindly wipe that smirk off your face and bring me a brandy."

"Of course, sir."

Lydia sat in the parlor of the Kenworthy home, rattling on at a relentless pace until the widow insisted that she take a moment to breathe. Sheer momentum seemed to propel the words out of Lydia's mouth, as if she were talking downhill. The older woman urged her to slow down, gently at first, but to no avail; then more persistently, and finally by leaving the room on the pretense of fetching some tea. She made the tea, but did not bring it into the parlor until she heard the younger woman's pacing slow, then stop. At length the sound of petticoats collapsing into a chair, followed by the slow, rhythmic clicking of fingernails on oak, told her that the younger woman had regained her composure and she re-entered the room.

"So, you believe Christopher has hidden peculiarities?" the widow asked gently, setting the tea service down on the table.

"Not so hidden, I'm afraid."

"But do you believe it?" the older woman persisted. Lydia was not so glib now, thinking before she responded.

"I don't know what to think. It certainly doesn't seem like him."

The widow sat down beside her young friend and neither of them spoke for a moment. She took Lydia's hands in hers. She thought about the boy, then began to speak of him as if he were dead. "Remember how brave he was during the fire?" In Seattle *the fire* referred to just one event, the great fire of 1889. Lydia shook her head ruefully. For two terrifying days the wooden city burned—twenty-five city blocks from the waterfront, to skid road, through the business district, and up the hill to within feet of the Kenworthy house. Flames spread from rooftop to rooftop, consuming everything in its path while men fought the fire every way they knew. Christopher was just home from his first year at college when he found himself with the Seattleites battling the flames, tearing down buildings in mostly vain attempts to create firebreaks, working himself to exhaustion in a losing battle against the voracious beast that consumed his city. As the flames approached the Kenworthy home, Lydia had found him and led him by the hand up University Avenue, pleading with him to save this place that was sacred to her.

"Yes, I remember," said Lydia. "He must have trudged up and down your roof with those wet blankets and water buckets two hundred times," she said, referring to one of the only methods that seemed to save the homes on the periphery of the fire. Soaking quilts and blankets and spreading them over the roofs retarded the flames from the falling embers just long enough to give people a fighting chance to extinguish them before they consumed the structure below. The ambient heat dried the blankets quickly enough, so Christopher climbed repeatedly out onto the roof with buckets of water, drenching and re-drenching the protective covers. Finally, after two days of fire, as the dawn rose over the smoldering city it seemed safe to rest. Christopher lay his aching body down on the Kenworthy floor and slept there until evening.

"He saved my house just because you asked him to, like a lovesick puppy," said the widow. "He didn't even know who I was."

"And now I've ruined him," Lydia blurted out, suddenly overcome with guilt. "I married him and abandoned him at the same time, and now I've turned him into a... a sodomite!" She wished she knew another word for it, something less biblical.

"There, there, dear," Mrs. Kenworthy tried to console her, but Lydia would have none of it. It was all her fault, she insisted. "Well, perhaps you can rehabilitate him through love and charity. Over time, of course."

"What? Rehabilitate him, how?"

"Love and charity, as I said."

"But I don't want him back." Lydia's voice began to rise. "Everything is going so well just now. I have my job, and… everything."

"And what might 'everything' be? You have another suitor?" She began to suspect that the young woman didn't know her own mind.

"No, of course not." But, of course, she did. She had come for comfort and absolution, but here was Mary Kenworthy telling her to be responsible. This was not working at all.

"I have to go, I think." Preferring not to face any more dilemmas, she bade goodnight and returned to the night air, leaving her friend wondering what could possibly be going through Lydia's head.

Walking down to the trolley stop, Lydia puzzled over why the discovery of Reverend Steele's veiled meaning disturbed her so. After all, the minister's revelation merely made permanent the recent changes in her life she loved so well. She was well rid of Christopher and all of his plaintive longing for her; she had the job she always wanted, and a wealthy, worldly gentleman showed interest in her. Yet when she stepped on the back of the trolley and looked out at the city lights reflected in Puget Sound as the car started its slow ascent toward Capitol Hill, she felt a vague emptiness.

A pragmatic gal, she simply pretended to feel fine and stepped off the trolley at the top of the hill and walked back to the Madison Hotel. From the street she could see Warren still seated at their table, now joined by another gentleman. She was relieved that he had found another companion after she had abandoned him. That problem solved, she simply went home.

Once back in her parents' house, she slipped up to her room to seek the solace of sleep—always her favorite escape from her family and whatever else threatened to bother her. But as she lay in the darkness she could not help but be troubled with concern for Christopher. What had become of him? Was he hiding among the natives—libidinous heathen girls and boys nearly naked in the tropical heat? Day after day his pathetic letters had continued to arrive postmarked "Honolulu," but she hadn't received one in nearly two weeks. She wondered if he had finally interpreted her silence as his dismissal. She would never have left Seattle, but before she met Warren she would have welcomed Christopher back. Now everything was different—more different than she knew.

As these concerns wandered through her sleepy head and threatened to cohere into something like guilt, she simply reassured herself that Christopher would be fine. She pushed all troubling thoughts safely away and went to sleep. Yes, Christopher would be fine.

"What you name?" asked the Chinese overseer, who looked Christopher up and down as if he were some strange curiosity.

"Christ-o-... Christ-i-an?"

"No, Christopher," he corrected him, but the overseer had already moved on.

"What you other name?"

"Jones." *That one should be difficult to mangle*, Christopher thought.

Still scribbling in Chinese on a ragged piece of paper, the Chinaman repeated "Jo-n-ah. Jon-ah Christ-i-an." Christopher, now Jonah, at least on this ranch, didn't care. He was too busy looking at all the backbreaking labor happening around him, wondering if he had the strength to do it. He saw Chinese laborers sweating in the hot sun, carrying enormous bundles of cut sugar cane on their backs that still other Coolies had cut under the blistering sun. Their bodies seemed to be endlessly in motion, defying the heat, working through the cane.

"I'm not sure I can do this."

"Do wha, Jonah?" the overseer asked.

"That," 'Jonah' said, pointing to the cane cutters.

"No, you no do dat," the overseer laughed in his thick pidgin. "White people work inside." Christopher wanted to look up at the sky and thank God for the sweet, if heavily accented, words he just heard. Twenty minutes later, when he found himself in a muggy stable, wearing a pair of rubber boots, standing on a mucky floor full of horse shit, he was less inclined to prayers of thanks. Thus he started his new life as Jonah Christian amid the sickening sucking sound his rubber boots made as he carefully adjusted his stance in the ankle-deep horse dung combined in irritating dissonance with the buzzing of the flies feasting on his bare back. It was too hot in this enormous barn so he took his shirt off and let his suspenders hang from his waist as he tromped around the stable, his oversized boots sloshing in the muck as he shoveled it from here to there. If he kept his back covered his shirt would afford him a modicum of protection from the hungry flies, but it was just too damned hot.

Jonah Christian, formerly Christopher Jones, was grateful to have the work, if not exactly happy about it. Kalani had talked to someone who had talked to someone else, and within a day Jonah had found himself doing odd jobs, some of them extremely odd, on a sugarcane plantation. Cutting cane was out of the question, as the overseer had told him—they had Chinese contract labor for that job—but there was plenty of work closer to the domestic side of the plantation that a poor *haole* could do. The family, wealthy descendents of humble missionaries, seemed happy to have a good, trustworthy white fellow there in any case, certain as they were that the Chinese would steal from them. And trust was important, hence Jonah's new name. He thought he would make his new start complete with a new identity, lest the family fire him upon discovering they harbored the race-mixing, sexually indiscriminate fallen missionary named Christopher Jones. Their man would be a secular working sort of fellow, inadvertently renamed Jonah Christian by a distracted overseer with minimal English.

He tossed the last shovelful of a load onto his wheelbarrow, which he then hoisted to haul over to the great mountain of dung he was creating outside, behind the stable, where it would be left to dry and bake itself into a nitrate-rich mountain of fertilizer. But as he hove the barrow upward he forgot to curl his toes inside the too-large rubber boots. The deep, moist mixture of mud and dung worked its powerful suction on his right boot, holding it in its putrid grasp as his stocking foot came free to land in the fetid muck, immediately seeping between his toes. He pulled his foot out as quickly as he could, which made no difference, and tried to hop on one foot while still pushing his carts full of dung. It was better than starving, probably.

The afternoon social was, as Reverend Steele found almost everything else on this island, enchanting. The plantation house was like a great open lodge through which the ocean breezes constantly flowed. Like a river of purifying air, the salty wind rejuvenated the soul. His wife had already been escorted away from him by a group of daughters and granddaughters of the missionaries who were now the landed aristocracy in the islands. The Steeles would be leaving for faraway China in a couple of days and the locals wanted to have one last shot at the famous missionaries. Feeling a bit forlorn at the thought of leaving, Steele wandered about the house and grounds chatting momentarily when it was required of him, but mostly just soaking up the Hawaiian atmosphere, which he still found magical. The islands were everything he had heard and more, but he was also taken by the native opulence of this particular ranch, owned by the descendants of missionaries, that he mused a little whimsically on the life choices he had made.

The grounds beyond the house contained cultivated gardens where the owners fought against nature to create a little bit of New England in Hawaii. Then there were stables, an enclosed riding arena, and beyond these the vast expanse of cane fields teeming with Chinese contract labor, coolies. The contrast between their lot and the extravagance through which he toured brought him back a little closer to the earth. It reminded him of his mission—of who he was—which was decidedly not landed gentry. On the spur of the moment he decided to go speak with the laborers, if he could possibly do so without causing them difficulty, and he turned toward the cane fields that lay in the valley beyond the stables.

As he walked by the open western end of the cavernous stables he heard a familiar voice barking out an unfamiliar stream of profanity. As the old man stood in the entrance, the afternoon sun at his back, he was but a silhouette to the sweating laborer within, whose boot had stuck in the muck, but whose foot had not. He watched as the man he knew as Christopher hopped on one booted foot over to a tub of water, cleaned the dung off his bare foot as he angrily flung a soiled sock to the ground, hopped back to his boot, and stepped into it. Jonah squinted at the unrecognizable silhouette in the entryway, some two hundred feet distant, and then went back to shoveling.

Steele was dumbfounded. He couldn't help but ask himself, *had God brought him here?* The reverend's final departure imminent, he wondered if he should offer the young man forgiving words, perhaps even his hand in friendship. It was not an opportunity he had expected to have, and he wondered if the coincidence had a larger significance, but his reverie was interrupted just as he was about to walk into the stables.

"Had enough of the party, Reverend?" It was Lorrin Thurston, one of the most powerful *haoles* on the island, who came up beside Steele, cigar in hand. It was a casual question, but Thurston seemed to command answers when he asked questions, however casual.

"Mr. Thurston, you startled me."

"Sorry about that," he said, utterly unconcerned. "I see we had the same idea. I come to these things because I have to, but after an hour of small talk I have to escape them—the Brahmins."

And so they chatted there in the stable doorway. The two men had not crossed paths before, but Steele had heard of Thurston more than once since he had been on the island. Thurston, a lawyer by training, seemed to have his hand into everything, yet he clearly displayed an appetite for more. Former Minister of the Interior, current legislator, and not incidentally publisher of the daily *Honolulu Advertiser*. Naturally, he was the son of missionaries. Steele was not sure what to make of him. Dressed like a Boston lawyer, his clear gray eyes bore into whomever he spoke with, giving the impression that he not only knew more than they, but he could make a good guess at what they were thinking. Unlike most of the powerful men on the Island, who favored longish hair and flowing beards, Thurston kept his brown hair cut short, like his beard, and meticulously groomed. At a couple inches short of six feet, he projected the image of a much taller man.

Steele turned his attention back to Jonah. "See that young man over there mucking out the stables?"

"Unfortunate fellow, yes. You'd think they'd have a coolie doing that sort of work."

"His name is Christopher Jones. You wouldn't know it to look at him just now, but he's an educated man—Wesleyan University—and really quite intelligent."

"No, you wouldn't," responded a skeptical Thurston.

"He used to work with me. He is a good man, I think, but for all his talent, he was not right for our sort of work. Not quite, anyway. But more to the point," continued Steele, suddenly anxious to take advantage of this opportunity to clear his conscience, "he writes exceedingly well—and quickly—and has splendid organizational habits."

Thurston, by this time quite aware he was being petitioned, considered the man standing next to him. "Tell me, Reverend, if he is so gifted, why is he shoveling shit?"

"He needs work, obviously."

"But he was working for you. A missionary, right? Why did you let him go?"

Steele paused before answering, but the clergyman lied to no one and he wasn't going to start now. "I found him morally unfit for missionary work."

"But you think he is morally fit to work for me?"

"You are a lawyer," Steele spoke without thinking. Thurston paused a moment, then the slightest hint of a smile crossed his lips.

"Point taken."

The two men stood silently for a moment, watching the hapless young man in the distance push on through his distasteful chore. At length, Thurston said he was sure he could find some work more suited to the boy's academic talents, despite his obvious skill at stable cleaning. Steele thanked him, but asked Thurston not to mention their conversation to him, explaining that he would just as soon his part in the job offer remained unknown. He was certain that a brief interview with Jonah would convince Thurston he was a man of who could be of use in some higher purpose.

The old man was enormously relieved to have tied up this loose end before he cast himself out of this Eden. His deed done, his conscience clear, Steele decided to return to the social and his wife, rather than continue on to the cane fields to visit the coolies. Chinamen would constitute the entirety of his society soon enough, and all of a sudden Steele felt tired. As he turned to take his leave, Thurston asked him a final question.

"Reverend, one more thing, if you don't mind. Can he play baseball?"

"Well, I don't know," Steele answered, more than a little puzzled by the question. "I suppose so. He *is* an American."

As Jonah approached the baseball field he saw the group of men tossing balls back and forth. Some of them looked as if they were dressed for a cricket match, while others looked as if they had just left the office. One of the latter was the strange man who invited him here, Lorrin Thurston. Still mystified as to why he was there, but glad this Mr. Thurston had interrupted his dung hauling at the plantation to ask him if he could play baseball, Jonah reviewed the conversation in his mind.

"What? Yes, of course." He was a little confused by the question.

"Any particular position?" asked the stranger, an unlit cigar clenched between his teeth.

"Usually in the outfield, but I can play anywhere I supp—say, what's this all about? Who are you?" Jonah asked, wiping his hands on his pants.

Preferring to ask questions, Thurston had ignored Jonah's.

"What's your name, son?"

"It's, uh, Jonah, Sir," he answered a little hesitantly, still unused to saying it. "Jonah Christian."

"It is, is it?" Thurston replied in some amusement. Whatever this boy had done was evidently serious enough to warrant a name change. Thurston made a mental note to look into it. "I hear you're something of a scholar, appearances to the contrary. We've got plenty of those, but if you can play baseball, maybe I can use you. Be at the park by the palace grounds tomorrow for a friendly game. Four o'clock."

Use me for what? he wondered, but if it was anything besides moving horse manure, he knew he was in no position to be choosey. So he tacitly accepted the mysterious invitation, which sounded much more like an order, and showed up at the designated place at the appointed time in newly washed but sadly tattered shirt and trousers. "Jonah!" Thurston called out as he briskly walked toward him, hand extended in welcome. "Take this," he said handing him a mitt. "It seemed a safe assumption you wouldn't have one. Now take your place at shortstop." Thurston himself trotted over to first base while Jonah happily thumped his fist into his glove, enjoying the smack of the leather, the smell of fresh air, the fact that there was neither shovel nor horse excrement anywhere in the immediate vicinity.

Jonah knew he had been put at shortstop as a test; if you do not know how to play the game, he realized, it will be revealed at shortstop sooner than any other position. The idea that he was being challenged on baseball electrified him as much as it confused him. Finally, something he actually could do! The other players seemed to be a combination of businessmen, lawyers, and their assistants, and these teams were likely to have fewer power hitters among them than the lumberjacks and longshoremen with whom he had grown up playing ball. It turned out to be a game of infield hits—a busy day for the shortstop—and Jonah spent the afternoon happily scooping grounders out of the dirt and slinging them to waiting Thurston at first base. Better still were three double plays, one of which required Jonah to go horizontal to snag a line drive, scramble to his feet and make the throw to first before the runner could make it safely back. He also enjoyed swinging the bat—infinitely preferable to a shovel—and drove in a couple of runs, including one by Thurston. All in all, he felt sure he had passed the interview. There was one play, however, that was a lot closer than it should have been. A young Hawaiian, about Jonah's age, hit a routine grounder to Jonah at shortstop, but ran so fast that he was barely able to throw him out at first base. Jonah looked to Thurston at first base and whistled admiringly. Thurston nodded his acknowledgement ruefully and shouted over to Jonah, "Willie is a bit faster than most."

A native named Willie? Jonah wondered to himself. Willie was the third out of the inning, so Jonah asked Thurston about the fleet-footed native while they trotted back to the dugout, which was really just a sideline with a bench.

"Willie is a fast one, that much is certain," Thurston observed. "Doesn't hit or field particularly well, but if he can lay down a bunt or get any kind of hit he's as likely as not to reach first base safely."

"I've never seen anyone go from the plate to first that fast," Jonah shook his head. "Doesn't look like someone you'd expect to be named 'Willie,' though."

"It's common enough for the natives to take English names. His surname is Kaae, if that makes you feel better. He's one of the Queen's secretaries—more like a gopher, actually. I imagine she's got him running all over Honolulu."

"Can't outrun his debts though!" one of the other players chimed in. Thurston looked at the man sharply; he immediately fell silent and walked to the opposite end of the bench.

An hour later Thurston's team had the game won and he was obviously pleased with his new shortstop. As the players walked off the field, each team congratulating the other, Thurston, sweaty and smiling, put his hand on Jones's shoulder and said, "Nicely done, Jonah. Walk with me." And they proceeded to walk in the twilight of a perfect Hawaiian sunset toward Thurston's office, where the lawyer got directly down to cases.

"I do not need another secretary, but I need a highly skilled amanuensis from time to time—someone who is able to do research but not so full of himself that he disdains to do mundane tasks and run errands. I am guessing from your last job that, although you have a college education, you do not hold yourself above such labor."

"Well, no." Jonah tried not to sound overly desperate.

"Then I shall try you out, if the work seems amenable to you."

"Would I have to work in your barn?"

"Don't have one."

"In that case, Mr. Thurston, I gratefully accept."

Thurston filled in the details of his work and expectations, and Jones did his best to pay attention, but he was nearly giddy sitting as he was in a fine leather chair, surrounded by morocco-bound legal volumes in numbers he had not seen since he was in college. Deliverance was his; he was home—figuratively home, that is. Literally, he didn't have one. His little bunk among the coolies was a dubious perquisite of his employment at the plantation, and now no longer his. Thurston seemed to read his mind.

"Obviously you won't be able to stay at the plantation any longer. There's a boarding house down the street from here. You can stay there."

"Could you write out a reference for me?" the young man asked tentatively. "I'm sure they wouldn't accept a stranger off the street, especially one dressed as I am."

"I'll just call them." And with that, Thurston walked over to the hitherto unnoticed telephone on the wall and secured Jonah a residence in moments. Jonah, unsure his emotions could withstand another miracle, took his leave to see his new home, afraid he might weep tears of joy in front of his new boss. He wanted to ask how it was Thurston knew so much about him, but he simply had to leave before he said or did something to nix his deliverance.

"And another thing," Thurston's voice halted Jones as he headed out the door. "There is a haberdasher around the corner. Go there in the morning and buy a decent suit. Put it on my account—I'll deduct it from your wages. If you show up for work dressed as you are, somebody is likely to hand you a shovel."

CHAPTER FOUR

Working for Thurston was not the warm, collegial affair that working for Reverend Steele had been, to say the least, but the expectations were much clearer. Both the capitalist and the holy man were men of clear purpose, but while the latter sought to nurture, love, and uplift all of God's children (regardless of the actual results), the former sought to use God's children to accomplish *things*. People were either on Thurston's side or in his way, and it was definitely safer to be one than the other. Jonah understood his place in Thurston's machine and found the clarity liberating. Missionary work, by contrast, had just confused him. The whole idea of converting people to a set of ideas he himself was still unsure of had been unsettling, and it left him feeling adrift. He never knew quite what he should be doing at any given moment. Put him in an office with research and writing to do, on the other hand, and he was like the proverbial fish in water. Still, however muddled he felt about his old job as a missionary, he missed actually liking his boss. In contrast to the easy rapport Jonah had with Steele, trying to converse with Thurston on anything besides business or baseball was like cuddling up with a pineapple.

His new identity as the amanuensis to power, emboldened Jonah. He was smart enough, but in Thurston's employ he found it useful to be strategically obtuse. The lawyer-magnate-legislator seemed to subtly intimidate nearly everyone, except when he dispensed with the subtlety. Jonah's recent experience taught him that he could survive nearly anything, even Lorrin Thurston, so he saw no advantage in suffering intimidation. He simply didn't bother with it, freely asking questions or questioning directives, which alternately impressed and exasperated Thurston. But the newspaper baron-lawyer-legislator was a master of self-control. His anger was generally channeled into cold, calculated responses, which sometimes resulted in curiously unidirectional dialogues that consisted of a series of questions from Jonah and a series of cold stares and raised eyebrows from Thurston. So it was when he discussed the mysterious McKinley Tariff with Jonah.

"Mr. Thurston?" The older man looked up from the papers on his desk to see Jonah standing in the doorway. He made no response beyond the stare that communicated his displeasure with the interruption. Accordingly, Jonah continued.

"I'm typing this editorial for you, and you mention, as everyone does, the 'McKinley Tariff' as the source of all Hawaiian economic troubles. I'm afraid I don't know anything about it. Could you explain a bit?"

Thurston lowered his chin and cocked his eyebrow, offended at the temerity of this boy—expecting that he should take time from the business of running a law firm, daily newspaper, and untold investments and business arrangements to educate him.

Jonah began a retreat. "I can see you're busy. We can talk later."

Tilts head, both eyes widen with incredulity.

"Right. Okay then, sorry to bother you."

Jonah returned to his desk and set his typing chores aside. He began assembling a disorganized collection of Thurston's notes into an outline for an editorial, but the new Jonah couldn't resist the temptation to write some introductory and concluding phrases, and maybe just one complete paragraph. *This stuff practically writes itself, anyway*, he rationalized. He looked up and saw Thurston emerge from his office and walk toward the teakwood shelves that lined the opposite wall. He began pulling rolled piles of documents from several different pigeonholes. Each of the rolls was neatly tied up with a single strand of red cloth tape. Thurston unceremoniously dropped them on Jonah's desk and turned toward his office.

Stopping at the door, he turned back to Jonah. "You'll notice at the end of the shelves a letter file cabinet—the one you have had your hands in and out of several hours a day for the last few weeks. You will find more documentation about the McKinley Tariff under either 'M' or 'T,' depending on your organizational fancy at the moment *you* filed them there."

"Right. Thank you, sir," Jonah said to the shutting door. Strategically obtuse, indeed. He went to the Amberg Peerless letter file cabinet—"letter" referring to the revolutionary alphabetical organizational system, rather than what was actually filed there. The file drawers were designed to hold documents lying horizontally between leaves of cardboard, all of which was pressed down by a thin metal bar on a spring. All in all, Jonah found it a vastly superior method to pigeonholing documents, but the Thurston office was at that moment in transition from the old method to the new. Still, he wished there were a way to make the files stand vertically because his neck got sore after a few hours of tilting it to look inside the horizontal leaves.

Jonah was startled at what he found. First, in the last fifty years, Hawaii, under the guidance of the missionary landowners, had become a sugarcane satellite of the United States. And, second, the recently passed McKinley tariff suddenly kept all the cane out of America with a huge tariff wall.

What to do? To some men, Thurston among them, the obvious solution was to make Hawaii part of the United States. And this was the recommendation of the editorial Jonah typed up for his boss. He paused to ponder some of the obvious complications to this scheme. First off, what would they do about the Queen? Americans, after all, were committed democrats, not monarchists, and having a queen on the public payroll would hardly do. Thurston was obviously suggesting annexation but implying abdication. The young man's contemplation was interrupted by a familiar voice.

"Christopher?"

He recognized the young woman's voice even before he looked

up and saw the Reverend Tubbs's oldest daughter standing before his desk.

"Penelope? How'd you know I was here?" He nervously glanced toward Thurston's office door.

"It's a small Island."

"Yeah? Try walking around it sometime."

"News travels quickly, and it isn't easy to disappear." She looked around the cluttered anteroom where Jonah had his desk. "Is that what you were trying to do, Christopher, disappear?"

"Are those for me?" he asked, indicating the large envelopes she held in her hands, and not incidentally changing the subject.

"Yes, they are. Father said I should just send them back. Actually, he did send the first letter back with a note explaining that you could not be found."

"What? Was it from my wife?"

"No, I'm afraid it was from someone's law offices, same as this one," she said as she slid the large envelope across his desk. He stared at it, reluctant to open it while Penelope was standing there, but she showed no indication that she had any intention of leaving.

"Thanks so much for bringing this by, Penelope, but I'm afraid my boss is a bit of a tyrant, and I really should be getting back to work—"

"'Tyrant?'" Thurston calmly repeated as he walked out of his office. "I've been called worse, I suppose."

"Good afternoon, Mr. Thurston," Penelope said, as if she were addressing her favorite uncle.

"Penelope! Good to see you, my dear," he said as he disappeared back into his office.

Jonah slumped in his chair, looked up at the smirking Penelope without actually raising his head, and asked in a low voice, "You know each other?"

"Our families have been friends for a couple of generations," she replied matter-of-factly.

It dawned on him, rather uncomfortably, that Thurston must

know everything about him, his real name and his escapades on the island. Of course he did; Thurston knew everything about everyone. And he must have made the same scandalous conclusion that everyone else did. He slumped further into his chair at the thought of it.

"Aren't you going to open it?" Penelope indicated the envelope.

"No."

"But aren't you curious? I am."

"The mails are a private affair, last I heard."

"Oh, I'm sorry, really I am." She looked genuinely distressed. "I don't mean to be nosy, but I did save it from the trash, and I carried it all this way for you..." Her voice trailed off.

"You live barely a mile from here."

"But still, I'm just so curious."

Thurston reemerged from his office with a note in his hand. "Penelope, my dear," he said, smiling at the girl. Jonah wondered if he had ever seen the man smile before. No, he decided, he had not. "Would you kindly deliver this note to your father for me?" He didn't wait for an answer before he commented on the envelope on Jonah's desk. "'Law Offices of Hanford & Hanford,' eh? What is that, your annulment?"

"Annulment? Why would I get an annulment?" Jonah stammered.

"Given the tenuous state of your marriage, combined with your recent embarrassing history, what else could it be?"

"I don't know, but I'm sure it's nothing of the sort."

"Yet you still haven't opened it."

Jonah looked at Thurston, then Penelope; they gazed back expectantly. "Very well, I'll open it." *Walked into that one*, he chastised himself as he ripped open the envelope and read the signed, countersigned, witnessed, and notarized document, with enclosure, from the Law Offices of Hanford & Hanford notifying him that his marriage was, in fact, null and void. Not only was it over, according to the document in his hands, it had never occurred in the first place. Jesus!

"Well?" Penelope prodded him.

"You'll be all right." Thurston patted him on the shoulder—another first, but he was too stunned to notice it. "It's better for you this way. You won't have to carry the weight of a divorce. Legally, your marriage never existed."

"You mean," Penelope asked breathlessly, "He's a bachelor?"

"It means he has never been anything else," Thurston confirmed. The girl beamed.

Thurston instructed Jonah to give Penelope a ride home. He deeply desired to be alone to contemplate the non-existence of his marriage. Ordering him to alone with this lovelorn girl was like directing him to dip his fresh wounds in saltwater. He could hardly decline such an order from his boss, but that did not stop him from trying.

"Perhaps I could just walk her to the trolley. I've really got a lot of work to do here. Thurston responded with the by-now familiar look of mild incredulity that one of his directives was not being immediately acted upon. "Right, sir. I'll go get your carriage."

And so he escorted Penelope around back, where she stood looking on, still grinning, as Jonah harnessed the horse to the little carriage, which had just enough room for two. He helped her up, and once he joined her there she locked her arm in his and boldly placed her head on his shoulder.

"Oh, Christopher, isn't it wonderful? You're not married to that horrible woman anymore. Mrs. Steele told me all about her. I don't know what you saw in her in the first place, but that's all over now. You're a bachelor!"

"So it would seem," he said glumly. "A bachelor named Jonah—Jonah Christian, by the way. Christopher Jones is the name of a notoriously debased missionary who dare not show his face in polite society. Thurston obviously knows my old identity—he has secrets on everyone—but I still need you to call me Jonah."

"I'm happy to call you anything you like, *Jonah*."

As they pulled out onto the street they passed Willie Kaae, who was slipping into the back door of Thurston's office.

"Hello, Willie," Penelope waved enthusiastically with her right hand, keeping her left securely fastened to Jonah's arm.

"Is there anyone on this island you *don't* know?" Jonah asked quite seriously.

Willie disappeared into the building without acknowledging them. His left eye was purple and swollen.

"Oh my goodness, I wonder what happened to his eye?"

"He had an unfortunate encounter with a baseball."

"A baseball?"

"He runs like a gazelle, but certain advanced fielding techniques elude him, like placing his mitt between his face and an approaching baseball," Jonah explained. "Now I'll repeat my question: is there anyone on this island you don't know?" Penelope was already devising a future for the two of them, and didn't bother to respond. A better question, it occurred to Jonah, was what the hell was Willie Kaae, one of the Queen's secretaries doing skulking about the law offices of Lorrin Thurston, Her Majesty's greatest antagonist.

Jonah reined the horse around and pulled to a stop on the other side of the street, down about one hundred feet, where he could see anyone coming and going from the office.

"Let's sit here for a moment and talk, shall we?" he asked Penelope. "Tell me, do you hear anything of the Steeles?"

"Yes, we received a letter yesterday. They've arrived in Shanghai."

Jonah regretted that the clergyman had already gone on without him, and he'd missed his chance to make amends. "I miss the old man, but I don't suppose he misses me," he said softly.

"It's hard to say. We're more or less forbidden to speak your name in the house. Since the 'incident,' you ceased to exist."

"Ceased to exist, did I?"

"Well, yes. We are forbidden to speak the name 'Christopher,' which unfortunately is a fairly common name, and we know—"

"Just like my marriage! Is banishing me not enough? Why is it that people need to declare that I never even existed?"

"Don't worry, Jonah. I know those natives must have tricked you somehow. I know you would never behave so without their evil influence." She went on to make more excuses for him, but Jonah was no longer listening. He was watching Willie Kaae emerge from Thurston's building. Thurston lingered in the doorway, out of sight, but Jonah thought he gave Willie a little pat on the back as he left—a familiar gesture from a man who seldom made them. Curious.

"Jonah, are you listening to me?" Penelope peered intently at him.

"I'm sorry—my mind wandered."

"Oh, you're terrible, but I don't mind. Now take me home, but be sure to let me off before we're within view of my house. My father would happily have you arrested if he saw us together." Penelope obviously relished the intrigue.

"I'm sure Reverend Tubbs would love that, but I don't think Mr. Thurston would have ordered me to drive you home if he thought that were a possibility. I may be disgraced, but strangely I'm much better connected than I used to be."

"So you are, Jonah. So you are. Soon it won't matter. I'll ask Mr. Thurston to talk to Father, and I'm sure he'll straighten everything out. They've been friends ever so long and—"

"You used to be so quiet."

"You used to be so married." Again, she beamed.

In a very large, and very empty, house in the Pacific Northwest, Lydia Bliss, formerly Lydia Jones, formerly Lydia Burke, sat alone wondering what it was she should do. She found married life with Warren Bliss every bit as unconventional as her engaged life to him had been. They were never alone together, yet she was often alone. Warren kept the oddest hours, and by the time he did finally conclude an evening of meetings with various and sundry business partners and return home, she was asleep. On weekends he would stop by the office, just to "check on things," and return hours later with Mr. Li in tow, who would busy "The Cap-y-tahn" and himself with shipping logistics in Warren's study for most of the rest of the day. Li would emerge from the study from time to time to bully the Chinese kitchen staff in words Lydia could not begin to understand, but whatever he said seemed to work because the food was always better when he was there. In short, her life was as empty as most of the splendid rooms of their Capitol Hill mansion. She missed having a purpose. She missed having a job.

Warren turned out to be more of a curiosity than a companion to her. In her years as Christopher's intended she was accustomed to turning the persistent young man's advances away more or less constantly. She never realized that she would miss the attention. Naturally, she rejected his advances effortlessly, almost automatically, as a Christian girl must. What puzzled her now, as a married woman, was the complete absence of carnal advances from the man who was actually entitled to them—her husband. After going through some considerable anxiety about their wedding night, it was surprising to her that the consummation failed to occur. Being as she was, inexperienced and unsure of herself, if he wasn't going to bring it up, neither was she.

They had, of course, made something of an attempt. It seemed to start well, and the complementary body parts seemed to find one another, but the exercise did not proceed much farther than that. In fact, the inconclusive nature of the event left her confused as to whether she was still a virgin. The closest they came to discussing it was the next morning when Warren explained in the gentlest terms that, given the "horror" of her first marriage, she could have all the time she needed to heal her mind and spirit. "*I can wait, my love,*" he assured her. Each time she hinted that he could have her if he wanted her, he offered some variation on the same patient, loving reply: I can wait, my love. Had she done something wrong, she wondered? Again, she was not sure.

Another event that failed to occur was the transfer of responsibility for their social life—or more aptly, the social side of Warren's business life—from the staff of Bliss Shipping to Mrs. Bliss herself. She had looked forward to it, arranging dinner parties and such, but she was unable to pry the position away from Mr. Li & company, as she referred to her husband's secretary and his little army of coolies. So, with nothing to do and no one to do it with, she began to ponder the possibility of resuming her career as a journalist.

When she sat down with Mrs. Kenworthy and explained her thinking she found her mentor's reaction disappointing.

"Have you discussed this with your husband?" Mrs. Kenworthy asked the question that Lydia would find more exasperating each time she heard it.

"Really, I don't think he would even notice if I went back to work. Would he approve? I can't think why not. I have nothing else to do."

"Nothing to do? My dear girl, wives are generally expected to occupy themselves with their children."

"I haven't any."

"Yes, obviously, but Lydia, don't you suppose that will change?" Mary looked at her young friend pityingly.

"No, I don't." She began to fidget; this conversation was taking an entirely unexpected turn.

"Oh, of course it will. You could be pregnant already. How far were you from your last cycle on your wedding night?" In Mrs. Kenworthy's progressive circle, female friends could be candidly clinical.

Missing the point entirely, Lydia said, "I'm not sure. Why do you ask?"

"It is a euphemism, my dear."

"What is?"

"Your 'wedding night'?"

"Euphemism for what?"

"For the sexual act of love."

"'Wedding night' is a euphemism for...that?" Lydia visibly squirmed on the widow's brocade settee.

91

"No, not generally, but in this case, yes. My point is, depending on where you were in your menstrual cycle when you've been having *marital relations*, you could well be with child already." Mrs. Kenworthy wondered about the young bride's naiveté. This was her second marriage, after all.

"Oh, that isn't a problem. We haven't had '*marital relations*.'"

"You haven't had... why not?"

"He told me he understood that I had been through a traumatic experience and that I should give my emotional wounds time to heal."

"Time to heal?" Mary's eyebrows, and her voice, lowered skeptically.

"Yes, he assured me—several times, actually—that he would not make any, um, demands before I was entirely healed."

"Healed?"

"Stop doing that! Why does this puzzle you so?

The widow Kenworthy had enjoyed a long and loving marriage to a man she missed very much; she knew something about traumatic loss, and Lydia had suffered no such thing. Lydia's annulment was something less than traumatic—practically a non-event for her. Mary gently reminded her that she had married Christopher not to get a husband, but to get a job.

"Yes," Lydia protested, "but to discover one's husband is a... a *sodomite*!"

"Warren?"

"No, *Christopher*! How could you think such a thing about Warren?"

"About a husband who doesn't want to have sex with his wife?"

"Of course he *wants* to. He just respects that I don't want to, or haven't wanted to—not entirely, anyway."

"Ah, I see." And indeed she did see, but could not understand how Lydia did not. This could not possibly end well.

* * *

"Come." Lorrin Thurston employed an impressive economy of language when giving orders. He uttered the single syllable as he strode quickly past Jonah's desk, dropping a sealed envelope there as he did so. Jonah caught the envelope and scrambled to catch up with his boss, who by now was in the street, climbing into a carriage. Once they were underway Jonah asked the obvious.

"Where to?"

"Look at the envelope."

Jonah noticed it was addressed to the Prime Minister. "Oh, the Aliiolani Hale. Outstanding! I love the palace."

"Hmm." Thurston grunted a spare acknowledgement of the younger man's enthusiasm. For Jonah, of course, the government palaces and the monarchy were exotic curiosities, whereas Thurston found them embarrassing legacies of an inferior race with pretensions.

"I want you to deliver this envelope to the PM's office, and get a receipt," Thurston instructed.

"What will you do while I'm doing that?"

"I will be present at your side, a civilized yet somehow threateningly authoritative presence. That is the only statement I wish to make."

"How pleasant," Jonah shrugged. "May I ask what the envelope contains?"

"You may, but you will receive no response." Thurston had a gift for putting a chilling end to any line of inquiry he preferred not to pursue. The two men rode on in silence beneath the late morning sun. But as the palace came into view, apropos of nothing Thurston surprised Jonah with the information he sought. "The envelope contains a memorandum of understanding on our constitutional principle."

"'Constitutional principle?' You mean the 'We the People' sort of thing?"

"Something along those lines. Our constitutional principle, as

Hawaiians, is that the monarch shall reign, but not rule."

"Like the English? The queen sits as a figurehead while Parliament runs the government?"

"Yes, only more so."

Jonah mulled this over for a moment before speaking. "It seems so strange, though. When I think of the Hawaiian monarchy I think of the warrior King Kamehameha. I couldn't imagine him accepting anything less than rule."

"Kamehameha is dead, and so is monarchy. Or at least monarchical rule," he corrected himself. "We saw to that with the new constitution of 1887."

"Ah, yes, 'The Bayonet Constitution.' I've heard of it."

"An unfortunate and inappropriate appellation," Thurston responded dismissively. "The King did not sign it at gunpoint; there were no weapons involved. The new constitution saved Hawaii and its treasure from being squandered by a king who happened also to be a profligate drunk with the unfortunate habit of killing the people around him when it suited his whim."

"That was the Queen's brother?"

"Yes, may he rest in whatever peace he deserves, which is to say none."

"I suppose it's safer to have that sort of fellow reigning without ruling."

"Quite so."

"But the Queen seems a different sort, so regal. I hear she's very learned and disdains alcohol."

"Her reign is young yet, and it is not possible to know if she is susceptible to the indulgent qualities of her race." Thurston sought to tutor the young man. "But we cannot tailor a new constitution for the peculiarities of each individual monarch. Democracy works. The monarch, king or queen, must respect the constitution. She must reign—"

"—not rule?"

"Precisely."

Once at the Aliiolani Hale palace the ritual went as Thurston planned. The two men walked unmolested to the Prime Minister's offices, where Jonah, Thurston standing benignly at his side, delivered the envelope to a young secretary—a native dressed in a gray suit that looked as though it had been purchased at Brooks Brothers. He then collected the requested receipt and turned to go.

"Just a moment, Mr. Thurston," the young man was about to make the offer Thurston knew he would make. "I'm sure the Prime Minister would like to see you. Could you wait a moment?"

"Jonah," Thurston turned formally to address his aide. "You may walk back to the office. I'll be here for a little while."

Jonah took his leave and started walking through the great halls of the Aliiolani Hale building. Descending the grand marble staircase on his way to the exit he realized that he had stumbled into a damn good job. Thurston was always up to something, meeting with one high government official or another, and Jonah had an insider's view of all of it. He felt as though he were in the midst of something exciting—he just wasn't quite sure what it was.

Coming out of the cool marble building into the sunshine, he decided to treat himself to a walk up the block past the Iolani Palace, the Queen's residence, though it was slightly out of his way. The great palace, barely ten years old, was actually the second royal palace. The first royal residence was the government building he had just left, the Aliiolani Hale, but the King who built it found it somehow unsatisfactory, so he built the much larger Iolani Palace across the street and left the original for his Parliament. The King's pet project went through three different architects before it was done, and the final product was as impressive as it was unique. The gray brick façade was elegantly ornate, with grand pillared porticos on the first two sprawling floors, which supported a collection of penthouses above. At something of a loss to describe it, Thurston's paper coined a new term, *American Florentine*, to describe the building's curious blend of Old and New World design.

To say the Iolani Palace was 'just across King Street' from the Parliament building was a bit misleading. Once Jonah did cross King Street there was still a two-acre stretch of meticulously manicured grounds between him and the palace, which included an entryway that rivaled most avenues in northwestern America. As he leaned casually against a coconut palm and took in the view, he was treated to another spectacle he would never have witnessed back home: the Queen and her retinue returning to the palace. As he watched the small parade of carriages—three of them, actually—led to the entryway by two mounted guards, he saw that the first was filled with men in suits, all of whom he recognized as legislators or cabinet members. The Queen and consort du jour were in the middle carriage, and the hindmost was filled with what he imagined must be the Hawaiian version of ladies-in-waiting. And one of them recognized him as soon as he recognized her—Muanu.

What on earth was the erstwhile laundry girl and alleged prostitute doing in the Queen's retinue, he wondered? The shock of seeing her would have been severe under any circumstances, given the way they parted, but seeing her materialize as part of the Queen's escort was otherworldly. Muanu had seen him, he was sure of it, and her deliberate gaze told him that she wanted him to know it. He stayed there hoping she might approach. He pretended to be a tourist, appreciating the architecture as long as he reasonably could, hoping the palace guards would not come and escort him away. Mercifully, she appeared at last in one of the great porticos on the second floor. Forgetting himself, he raised his hand to wave, but she immediately signaled him to stop. She gestured north, toward Richards Street, then moved her hand eastward. Accordingly, Jonah casually walked to the north end of the Palace and turned to the right and continued on to the corner of Richards and Hotel Streets. Moments later she met him there.

"You are surprised to see me, Mr. Christopher?"

"To say the least! But I'm glad of it. What are you doing with the

Queen?"

"I am *hanai* cousin to the Queen. I work here at that Iolani Palace now."

"I still don't understand how *hanai* works, but you're obviously not working here doing laundry. I mean, I saw you riding in a royal carriage, for goodness' sake."

"We cannot discuss this now, not here." She changed the subject when she noticed the cut of his new clothes. "Kalani told me you changed your name. 'Jonah'?

"Yes, I am now known as 'Jonah Christian.'"

"And Kalani said you were working in the stables. This cannot be true," she said as she gently brushed the back of her fingers across the lapel of his suit. "At least you are not dressed for such work."

"I'm a different man now. I work for Mr. Thurston, at the newspaper."

"'*Elelu kea!*" she muttered under her breath.

"What does *that* mean?"

"It means 'white cockroach.'"

"I take it you don't like my new boss?"

"I do not." Her voice softened. "But I'm sure you are no more like him than you are like Reverend Tubbs. But it is not good that you are so close to bad people all the time. No *aloha*. We must speak of this further."

"Does that mean I may see you again?" he asked hopefully.

"Yes, you may see me."

"Here, at the palace?"

"No, you must never come to see me here."

"Well, where then?"

"I have a house—not the one out on the beach road. It's one of the Queen's properties here in town. She chooses to keep me close, but not too close."

"Why? What do you do there?"

"Come to my house, late tonight. It is on the end of Kinau Street, over there," she pointed to the east.

97

"Good. Fine, I'll see you tonight," Jonah stammered, struggling to comprehend his good fortune.

She gave him that hint of a grin he recognized from the first time they spoke at the Tubbs's church. It seemed to say that she was amused by him, which was fine with Jonah, as long as it got him through her door.

Jonah was profoundly thankful that his boss never returned to the office that afternoon, because he found it nearly impossible to focus on his work after his encounter with Muanu. She was, after all, the only woman he had ever known intimately, not that he remembered the uncompleted, confusing, humiliating event with any sort of clarity. Still, the memory, and all its hazy images of female scent, exposed flesh, and tactile moistness, had tremendous power over him. At least the recollection had the power to completely obliterate his ability to concentrate on his work as he anticipated seeing her that night. He spent the rest of the afternoon as if in an extremely agitated dream.

Jonah locked the building up and walked toward his boarding house. Knowing that the evening meal would have already been served and put away by now, he stopped at a Japanese noodle shop for dinner, toyed with his soup until he acknowledged that he couldn't make himself eat, and continued on his way to his boarding house. The old Chinese woman who ran the place gave him the same smile and "arro-hah" he received each night, then paid him no more mind. He walked past a couple of short-time tenants playing cards in the parlor, nodded and wished them a good evening, proceeded to his room, and lay down upon his bed. He looked over at his writing table where the terrible papers from the Law Offices of Hanford & Hanford still lay there menacingly, but for the first time the sight of them gave him no sting. Nor did they have the power to distract him from his coming visit with Muanu, which completely occupied his mind and made time pass very slowly. She said to come "late," but what did that mean? *These natives are so casual about time*, he thought. Finally, when he could wait no longer, he rose, let himself out the back door to the little deck that ran the length of the back wall, and descended the staircase to the street.

Jonah spent the next hour aimlessly walking the streets of Honolulu before finally arriving at the end of Kinau Street where he stood in front of what he knew must be Muanu's little white clapboard bungalow.

She greeted him at the door with a different smile than the one she left him with earlier. This one was warmer—more friendly, less superior. She drew him in, closed the door behind him, and whispered "*Aloha*," as she pulled his head down to kiss him. The gesture sent his mind racing, but it need not have; it was just a kiss, not a promise. She led him to a little sitting room that contained two wicker chairs and a couch. With high hopes, he sat on the couch and waited for her to join him. To his disappointment, she sat in one of the chairs opposite.

"Tell me about your work for Mr. Thurston," she asked politely.

He would much rather have kissed her again than discuss his job, but he clearly was not the one making those decisions. "It's hard to describe, really. I work mostly at his law offices, but I end up running down the street to the *Advertiser* building—that's his newspaper."

"Everybody knows that!" Muanu laughed.

"Oh, sorry, I suppose they do. Anyway, it's much like being back at college, except that the work actually matters to somebody. I'm always researching or writing something for him, or typing up notes from meetings. He belongs to a 'secret organization' that doesn't seem to be a secret to anyone, so I handle the logistics for that as well."

"The Annexation Club? Yes, everyone knows of this." She laughed again as she said it, but then grew more somber. "They are dangerous, but of course these are dangerous times."

"Dangerous times? How so?"

"No, we will not talk of such things right now. What else do you do?"

"Baseball seems to be part of my job, happily, the best part of all. We play baseball a couple of nights a week. It's almost like being back home."

"You smile when you talk about baseball, Jonah. This is good to see. You carried so much pain before."

What an odd thing to say, Jonah thought. Before he could ask Muanu what she meant, she asked another question.

"Have you let go of your wife, the one you never had?"

Her directness startled him, and he regretted that Lydia's memory had intruded on their evening. "I'm trying to. And it is exactly as you say—legally, as it happens, she was never my wife." The concept of annulment still puzzled him. "I was fooled."

She looked at him for a moment, seeing a trace of the old agony in his eyes. "Let it go. *O ka mea ua hala, ua hala ia.* What is gone is gone. There is no use in crying over the wounds others have inflicted upon you."

He said nothing, but found comfort in the lyrical Hawaiian words, and the softness of the voice that carried them. He was, it occurred to him, more comfortable in Muanu's little home than he had been since he came to this island. Perhaps it was just the satisfaction of finally being in the same room with this woman after anticipating it all day, but he suspected it was more than that.

For the first time, he looked around and noticed that the house was actually just two large rooms, a large one in front divided by bookcases and a small room in the rear, presumably the bedroom. The bookcase contained no books; instead, its shelves were filled with small potted plants, boxes, and jars filled with what looked like herbs and dried plant leaves. He recalled Reverend Tubbs's accusation that she was a prostitute. The accusation seemed plausible after his one evening with her, but that no longer made sense at all.

"What is it you do for the Queen, Muanu?"

That insouciant grin crept across her mouth again, as she curled her legs beneath her in the chair and rested her chin on her fist. "What do you think I do, Jonah?"

"I haven't the foggiest. It's clear that Tubbs was wrong about you."

She ignored his pointed comment about that night. "I am *kupua.*"

"'*Koo-poo-ah*'?" Jonah repeated, inviting her to explain what it could possibly mean.

"There is no simple way to explain it to you completely" She searched for an analogy. "You have in America, the Indians or natives. Sometimes they have healers—"

"You are a medicine woman?" Now they both groped for a common understanding. "Or a shaman, a spiritual healer?"

"Ah, you know of such things." She found this encouraging.

"Well, a little. I studied religion in college—we all did—but mostly just our own, though. I guess they slipped in a word or two about other faiths once in a while." He wondered how he had ever run into the concept. "Oh, yes, the missionaries." It was starting to come back to him. "The home missionaries would drive our instructors crazy telling us all about Indian faiths."

"What is a '*home* missionary'?"

"Well, we have foreign missionaries, what I was supposed to be, who go to foreign places like China, Africa, and the Arab lands—but it's hard to preach there without getting killed. So we also had what we called 'home missionaries' to convert our Indians to Christianity."

"'*Your* Indians'?" She shook her head and laughed. "Really, Jonah."

But Jonah had no idea what she was getting at, so he continued. "Yes, some of the missionaries came back with a completely different point of view than our professors. They saw all kinds of parallels between Indian faiths and Christianity, especially things like the story of creation, and Jesus' admonitions against greed and so on. A visiting missionary would speak one day and our professors *corrected* him the next. I guess they didn't like having the theoretical theology of the classroom distorted with worldly experience." They laughed about that for a moment, then Jonah turned his attention back to Muanu. "So, kupua. Shaman to the Queen?"

She began to look uncomfortable with the topic. "It is an uncertain time. *Huna kupua*, or 'secret wisdom,' is a violation of the Queen's Christian faith. She does not combine faiths as easily as someone like Kalani," she explained. "Kalani told me that frustrated you, the way he simply added Christian Gods to Hawaiian ones."

"'Christian *God*, singular, thank you. That seems like a lifetime ago."

"Yes, I can see that." Kalani, the source of so much embarrassment for Jonah, remained the connection he and Muanu shared. He could not imagine that she would talk to him or grant him the warmth of her smile so readily were it not for their mutual friendship with the gentle giant.

"So, if the Queen is uncomfortable with you as a *kupua* why does she keep you so close?"

"The Queen carries conflict inside her heart. She is not simply Hawaiian."

"She certainly looks Hawaiian," Jonah said, a bit confused.

"I do not refer to the color of her skin, but the very old contest for her mind and her heart. She is caught between two worlds—yours and mine."

"Western and Polynesian?"

"Yes. She was educated in the Royal School, a boarding school run by New Englanders who teach Hawaiians that Western ways are the only correct path, and that Hawaiian ways are savage or superstitious. She absorbed white wisdom, *haole* faith. She was told that the way of *aloha*, the way of love, was wrong—was unclean. She knows in her bones that this is not true, but in her mind she is not so sure." Muanu sighed. "Whichever way she chooses, part of her will believe she is wrong. She speaks the precise English of the Protestant, but in her spirit she is Hawaiian."

Her description of the Queen's 'precise English' brought to mind another question. "Muanu," he began. "Your English is very precise.

Why don't you sound more like Kalani?"

Her quiet, mischievous grin was unsettling. Was she amused, or just toying with him? he wondered.

"I attended the Punahou School, *ka Punahou*, a missionary school. Congregationalist. I was taught by missionaries."

"How do you learn *huna kupua*?" he pronounced the words carefully and looked to her for acknowledgement that he got it right, which she gave with a nod, "Studying with American Congregationalists?"

"You do not!" She laughed at the thought of it. "I stayed for eight years instead of twelve. The Queen's brother, King Kalakaua, paid my tuition—he was very generous—but I learned the ways of *huna kupua* from my grandmother, and I knew in my heart that it was the true way. What I heard at school every day was someone else's truth—*haole* truth—and after eight years I wanted no more of it. I was a disappointment to many people, but unlike the Queen, there is no conflict in my heart. I know what is right for me."

"I wish I could say that."

She smiled sympathetically and shook her head. She joined him on the couch. "You are no missionary, Jonah. A missionary would never make such an admission—admit that he was unsure of anything. But you are honest, and you have been through much."

"How do you know so much about me?"

"You tell your story on your face, in your eyes, the way you move. And the *kupua* sees not just with the eyes, but with the heart."

"You have to tell me more about this *huna kupua*."

"First, you tell me what you know of shamans."

"It isn't much, really. I think they seek healing through earthly deities, like animal gods, and they use chants and dances, plants and herbs—magical types of things, I guess." He felt suddenly childish, trying to explain spiritual things to her.

"*Huna* is similar, but not completely. Yes, there is dancing—you've heard of the *hula*—and chanting. You see my shelves behind you. Plants and herbs are part of this. But this is only about the practice in this world. *This is not the only world.* The *kupua* understands *Po*, the inner world. In *Po* there is no separation of people, time does not move in a straight line, and love is more powerful than gravity."

"Like some sort of heaven?"

"Perhaps, but you think of heaven as some faraway place, where good is separated from bad, and the only people who are there are dead. *Po* is part of everyone's existence, though they may not be aware of it."

"So, is the *kupua* some sort of priest or *Kahuna*?"

"*Kahuna*? No, but it is similar. '*Ka*' means light, '*huna*' means secret. The *Kahuna* is more like a priest. The *kupua* is many things and one thing," Again, she struggled to find words he would comprehend. "*Kupua* is the trickster, playing harmless games with other people's senses. Sometimes the traveler of distant places, or maker of magic, or," she drew her face close to Jonah's and whispered playfully, "the reader of minds."

"Oh, my," said Jonah. "I'm afraid I might be in trouble, in that case."

"It is all right," she reassured him. "You only *think* your heart is in your pants. That is because it is easier to know how to relieve the ache between your legs than the pain in your heart."

"Um... uh, what is the 'one thing'?" Jonah blurted out, eager to change the subject.

"I don't understand," she said benignly, clearly enjoying Jonah's discomfiture.

"You said the *kupua* is many things and one thing. What is the 'one thing'?"

"Ah, yes. Healer—the *kupua* is always a healer."

"That explains the plants and herbs, I guess."

"It does, but those are secondary methods. Love is the most powerful medicine."

"It is?"

"Yes," she said as she rose to her knees on the couch and bent down over him. "It is." She pulled his head close and kissed him deeply. After several moments she moved her lips from his and whispered words in his ears he did not expect to hear. "Go home."

"Why? Things are going so well."

"So they were, and so they shall."

"I may see you again?" he said, a trifle too anxiously, eliciting that little laugh from Muanu again.

"Yes. Perhaps we can help to heal each other."

"You need healing?"

"Yes, Jonah, we all do. As I told you, these are difficult times." And with that she ushered Jonah out the door, with the most beautiful parting words he had ever heard. "Come tomorrow night."

CHAPTER FIVE

Henry Wasserman, Lydia's former employer at the *Seattle Weekly*, trudged through the rain up the steps to the Bliss house, valise in one hand, umbrella in the other, cigar in mouth. He was a little irritated when the Chinese servant opened the door and ushered him in—*My God, they're everywhere*—but he was relieved to get out of the drizzle. The young man bowed after accepting first his umbrella, then his hat, and finally coat, which Wasserman found a bit comical. And with a "Please to follow me," and yet another bow, he led him to the drawing room and went to fetch the mistress of the house.

Lydia entered through the room's large double doors a few moments later.

"Mr. Wasserman, how nice of you to stop by."

"Call me Henry, please." *Henry?* Before she became Mrs. Bliss such familiarity would have been deemed contemptible indeed. What a difference a fortune makes.

"All right, 'Henry,' what brings you to Capitol Hill?"

"Well, I know your life has been very busy the last few months, what with your engagement and all, but you were in the middle of a story when you left—a very important story—and I'd like to know if you'd be willing to give your notes and research to another reporter who could finish it."

"Well, I—" Lydia struggled to find the words to make her request.

"It really doesn't make any sense to have someone start over from scratch when so much of the work has already been done."

"I agree, really I do. I only hesitate because I'd really like to finish the piece myself."

"You would? What would your husband think?"

She suppressed the desire to scream, though she was tempted to tell him she did not give a fig what her absentee husband thought about her writing. She could not help but notice a nearby flower vase that would have gone nicely up along the side of Wasserman's fat head, but she resisted this as well.

"Actually, I would like to finish this article and then remain at the paper," she stated with assurance she did not feel.

Wasserman thought about this for a moment. The idea of having a well-connected society woman penning features for his paper was enticing, however unconventional.

"All right," he agreed. "It should raise an eyebrow or two having 'Mrs. Bliss' appear as a byline in the *Weekly*."

"Actually, I'd like to keep my original byline, 'L. C. Burke.'" Now it was Wasserman's eyebrows that were raised.

"Somehow I think it's best that I don't ask what your husband will think about *that*." He was a wise man, in most cases, but there was more going on here than anyone had anticipated.

To everyone's astonishment, Warren appeared completely unconcerned about Lydia's return to journalism. At breakfast the next morning, when she rather awkwardly suggested that she might like to "write an article or two" for her old paper, he was all smiles.

"Lovely idea, my dear. It will give you something to do."

"Well, maybe more than an article or two. I thought maybe it could be my job again."

"Really? Good for you, my love. Just try to get home early enough to remind the servants that this is our house, not theirs," he said with that winsome smile that was closing so many deals lately. His unconcern about Lydia rejoining the business world seemed to be completely genuine, as he added one small question. "Lydia?" Now the other shoe will drop, she thought.

"Yes?"

"You'll still be available as the hostess for our dinner parties, won't you?" That was the one part of the job Mr. Li could not handle himself.

"Certainly," she said, relieved, although she had harbored some hope that there would be a slackening of social requirements. The dizzying array of dinner parties, large and small, had only increased since their wedding. The guests included not only clients and potential clients, but often their lawyers as well—wool suits and sideburns everywhere. Warren explained that it was useless to grease the wheels on the engine only to discover the wheels on the caboose had locked up. She took that to mean he did not want anyone speaking common sense in the clear light of morning, questioning deals that had been inked in the fog of cigars and brandy the night before the Bliss mansion. In any case, there were many such engagements—smaller, to be sure, than the gala engagement parties, but too many of them to ever feel as though life were normal. In fact, there was nothing normal about their life.

The night after Jonah's first lovely evening with Muanu he came back to her, as instructed, as he did the next night, and the next, and the next. At first, it was much like the first night, full of conversation and questions, confusing concepts and more baffling explanations. She continued to take the measure of this funny young haole, and as the string of evenings grew longer, she allowed him simply to be there. She wasn't sure why, but she liked having him there in the house when people came for her services. Usually they came to purchase herbs, but sometimes they required the shamanistic rituals of chanting or rhythmic movement, which she could not allow Jonah to watch, but he could not help overhearing from the next room. More than once an American sailor would come seeking some exotic potion to cure whatever he had caught, and Jonah realized that this sort of activity must have convinced Reverend Tubbs that Muanu was a prostitute. Of course the old puritan would think the worst if he heard sailors were seen leaving Muanu's little grass shack out by the ocean, he thought to himself. Perhaps he had gone to her hut that night expecting to find immoral activity.

All thoughts of his past life would evaporate when Muanu, having finished with a visitor, would come back behind the bookcase and join him on her little couch, usually saying nothing as she curled into the warmth of his arm, laying her head on his shoulder. They would sit quietly for a long time, sometimes ending the silence with aimless conversation; other times she would simply rise from the couch and lead him by the hand to her bed. But what Jonah found he loved most of all about being with this woman was the time they spent lying together in the quite darkness after making love. Just being there was the easiest thing he had ever done.

One such night, as Jonah lay on his back with Muanu's naked body curled around him, she asked, "How is the Tubbs girl, Penelope?" He had told her about the girl's unfortunate crush and her tendency to find excuses to stop at Mr. Thurston's office, but he was surprised that Muanu would ask about Penelope. "Why, are you jealous?" he teased, but Muanu could not be teased. Their relationship was such a strange synthesis of platonic affection and sexual comforting that her fondness for Jonah left no room for possessiveness. She did not take the bait.

"Do you treat her gently when she intrudes on your time?" Muanu pressed him.

"I think so. It's not my habit to be cruel to anyone."

"But she has experienced cruelty," Muanu observed. "Her father is not a kind man. Girls who grow up in the household of such men need healing."

"Healing? How?"

"Love."

"Her father loves her, I'm sure. He just doesn't show it much."

"That damage is done. She simply needs to get away from there, though she probably will not do that. That is why she seeks you out—you are an escape for her, without leaving her father."

"Interesting theory, but I'm not the mate for her." Jonah could not imagine another woman intruding on his time with Muanu.

"That is wise, Jonah. A girl so wounded, so fragile, should be first guided by the touch of women."

Jonah blinked and swallowed, puzzled by the turn the conversation had taken. "Excuse me? I don't think I heard you right."

"Men are consumed by their own desires. If she were to find comfort and release through love it would have to be with a woman, or women, who can guide her slowly, allow her to play. Men, especially young men, approach girls so desperately." She smiled a little, at the thought of his desire.

Jonah laughed at the thought of this traditional girl having sex with a woman—or women. "I really can't see Penelope allowing such a thing."

"It is not what you can imagine, Jonah; it is what Penelope can imagine that matters. You find women beautiful, do you not?"

"Indescribably so."

"Then what makes you think she would not? And if she could speak her desires to one who could speak them back, she would begin to become whole."

Jonah did not believe a word of it, but it brought to mind a question that had been on his mind since that night in her little shack with Kalani. "Muanu?" His tentative tone signaled that he was venturing into uncomfortable territory.

"You wish to speak of the night in my house with Kalani? What would you like to know?" she asked matter-of-factly.

Only Muanu's openness permitted him to speak so freely. "Well, it's Kalani, or rather, what he did to me. That sort of thing is actually against the law where I come from." He struggled to find words to make sense of what had happened. "I guess that doesn't matter. What I mean is, well, I just don't understand why he did, uh, what he did."

She shook her head gently. "He did not do anything to you. He shared something with you—something beautiful."

"I really don't understand."

"You were in such pain, Jonah."

"I was dying of thirst and hunger!"

"No, your soul was in agony. Your heart. Think of the relationship you had with your wife, how she continually pushed you away. You were too long denied human touch. You were not just a hungry man denied food, but a starving boy who had been led to a great feast, but not allowed more than a small taste of delicacies before you. You needed release—I gave it to you. Kalani helped."

"But men don't do that with other men," Jonah insisted plaintively.

"Of course they do. It is *Aikane*, or *ho'okamaka*, the relationship of a man with a man. He is your friend, and he helped you generously."

This, like so much else Muanu said, just confused Jonah. "Does Kalani like women?"

"Yes."

"Then I obviously don't understand."

"*Aikane* is a tradition of affection of men for men, and women for women, that exists everywhere, but it is not embraced everywhere. In Hawaii it was. A great chief would always have his *aikane*, boys he liked. Kamehameha had many. When your Captain Cook came—"

"He's not 'my' Captain Cook. I'm American. He was English."

"As you wish. When the *English* Captain Cook came here one hundred years ago, many of his sailors took Hawaiian boys as *aikane*, though not the Captain. He would not accept the women, either."

"The crew 'went tropical,' as they say?"

"Yes, *as they say*. But it continues, often, between Hawaiian boys

111

and *haole* visitors. *Haoles* believe they seek pleasure; they do not understand is that they seek healing from the wounds your world has inflicted on them."

Every so often one of these summary judgments Muanu issued on western society left Jonah a little defensive, and he reacted defensively.

"Muanu, I'm not sure our society wounds our people. We seem to have come out of it well enough."

"Because you are powerful?"

She was mocking him and he knew he was being led, but he saw no alternative but to follow. "Well, the *haole* nations are undeniably powerful, don't you think? The British rule most of the world, for heaven's sake."

"You conceive of power in a small way, Jonah. Yes, big ships with big guns and mountains of money are powerful things—in one way. But if you do not know how to live in harmony with all that surrounds you, if you cannot love and accept your *kakane*, your fellow humans, what power can you really have?"

Jonah actually understood the point she was making, a rare moment. "I think I see. We have another way of saying it, if I remember correctly, 'What does it benefit a man to have the whole earth and not the knowledge of God?'"

"Yes, this is what I meant to say. It is from the Bible. The book of Mark, I think."

"Please," Jonah feigned indignation. "*Da Jesus book!*"

It was late, and despite a moment of clarity Jonah was now more confused than ever about what had happened that seminal night on the beach road. He hoped the walk back to his boarding house would help clear his head; as it happened, it did not. He lay down in his bed, and eventually came sleep and dreams, of little huts and sinuous dancing. For the first time in a very long time, he did not dream of Lydia.

* * *

When Lydia returned to the offices of the *Seattle Weekly* to reclaim her desk, she wondered why the men there—and they were all men—couldn't be as casual about her return to work as her husband had been. As she breezed through the room as casually as she could, someone shouted, "All hands on deck—*it's the Captain's wife!*" So much for a casual entrance. The staff crowded around her desk, welcoming her back and asking how she found married life, being rich, and so on. Never had she received this sort of attention anywhere, let alone at the paper, and she liked it. She was a curiosity. She dressed, it occurred to her, much more expensively than she had the last time she was here. She wore a smart shirtwaist from New York, unlike the ordinary dresses she used to wear to the office. Adjusting her attire might be wise, however painful, but ultimately she decided against it and affirmed to herself, *I can afford to dress well, and by God, I shall.* Besides, she reasoned, the dowdy old office could use some brightening up.

After a few more minutes of pleasantries and 'welcome backs' the gawkers around her desk dissipated when they noticed Wasserman standing outside his office, arms akimbo, cigar clenched in a most unhappily jutting jaw. It was very clearly time for everyone to get back to work, and she was glad of it.

She had organized all of her notes into files, and the files into a hatbox, which she now hauled up onto her desk. Joyfully she removed the papers from the box and started organizing them into logical piles on her desktop. She began to reimmerse herself in the arcana of smuggling Chinese labor into the United States. She was out of her gilded cage and was happy to be busy documenting real human misery.

As she pored over her sources she started outlining the material and tagging the papers with straight pins accordingly, although she hated poking holes in her papers. It would be much more convenient if there were some way to bend the pin into some sort of clamp to keep the papers together. Pinned or clamped, the organized papers made it clear that she had ample documentation from official sources like the customs service, law enforcement, businessmen (like her husband), and posturing politicians. These documents did not, however, add up to a complete story. Government officials liked to pretend that they had everything under control, whereas the business community, which hired so many of the illegal immigrants, claimed that they had nothing to do with getting them there, as if they had simply fallen from the sky. Her husband, with his houseful of Chinese, fit unfortunately well into this category. Did the smugglers work for someone else, or did they control their own operation? The smugglers remained unknown or unavailable, so she decided to talk to the people who were most likely to have the intelligence she required: the human cargo.

When it came to Chinese labor, she could hardly find a better repository of it than her own house, which included four Chinese servants, all male—*boys, really*, she thought—with little work to do, and lives that bore no resemblance at all to the average immigrant's existence. Still, they had migrated from China, and that was the experience about which she wished to learn. The problem with talking with her own servants, however, was that she had a terrible time keeping their names straight. This is not an effective way to ingratiate oneself with the help. They all had one-syllable names that had unfortunate homonymic relationships to certain English words. Pi (pronounced "Pee"), Fuk, Ah, and Qwok were names she simply found it difficult to utter with a straight face. Remembering which name belonged to whom defeated her completely. Not that they were any better with their less-than-careful pronunciation of her name. Responding to her husband, it was always, "Yes, Cap-y-tahn?" To Lydia they responded with a half-hearted attempt at "Mrs. Bliss," which sounded more like "Missy Biss." She did not like it.

Still, she began with the sources closest to home. Her first attempt to engage in casual conversation with them was illuminating, but not in the way she had hoped. Two of them were in the kitchen when she approached. It was a small victory that she was able to speak their names.

"Ah, Fuk," she paused, pursing her lips to prevent the corners from turning up. "How are you boys this afternoon?"

Blank stares.

"I thought we might chat a bit—get to know each other better."

Ah and Fuk glanced at each other, then turned their opaque looks to Lydia.

"Well, uh, you have known the Captain so much longer than you've known me," she continued amiably. "I thought you might like a chance to get to know me better."

There followed awkward silence—awkward for Lydia, that is; the servants seemed happy to spend the rest of the afternoon in that impenetrable silence. Finally Ah turned to Fuk, then back to Lydia, and said, "No thank you, Missy Biss."

Well then, she thought as she stood there feeling like an intruder in her own kitchen. Clearly, approaching them in groups would not do. She would have to catch them in isolation—one at a time, when they could not reinforce each other with those deadly glances.

The Queen, seated at her great desk, looked up from her work at Muanu's interruption. Ever gracious, she smiled once she had refocused her eyes. "Yes, Muanu?"

"Your Majesty, Fraulein Wolf is here to see you."

"Very good, my child. I hope she can bring some clarity to this muddle," she indicated the legislative correspondence on her desk. "It seems every single legislator has at least one bill, and every other legislator has one that opposes it."

"Yes, Ma'am," Muanu agreed. "I was unaware that Fraulein Wolf had experience in such things." In fact, Muanu knew the Fraulein possessed no such experience at all, but to suggest such a thing to the Queen would have been insubordinate. The bounteously buxom

Fraulein Wolf—no one ever uttered her first name, Gertrude; she was always "Fraulein Wolf—had come into the Queen's service a year earlier to teach Her Majesty German. The Queen, it seemed, had developed an inordinate fondness for the handsome young German who directed the Royal Hawaiian Band, who in turn recommended the Fraulein as an instructor. Fraulein Wolf, once in the Queen's employ, immediately began insinuating herself into Her Majesty's inner circle as the personal spiritual medium to the Queen. Gettogethers with the dead had become fashionable in recent years. President Lincoln's wife had been known to have the occasional séance in the White House to chat with her dead son and various deceased friends and relatives. Tarot card readings, séances, trances, had become more commonplace recreational pursuits since Mary Lincoln's day. Evidently there was something about the approach of the twentieth century had everyone seeking reassurance from the other side.

Muanu, herself a practitioner of occult arts of a sort, was always inclined to give a would-be spiritualist the benefit of the doubt, but she had quickly seen through Fraulein Wolf as a scheming fraud with a disagreeable accent. The first time the Fraulein revealed her pretended spiritual gifts to the Queen was in the middle of a language lesson when, during the rhythmic repetition of German verb forms, she slipped into a "trance" in which she saw and conversed with King Kamehameha I. As proof of the authenticity of the conversation she revealed a detailed description of the King, which impressed The Queen tremendously, but Muanu knew that Fraulein could have acquired all such information at the library—or in ten minutes of conversation with a native Hawaiian. Nonetheless, the isolated Queen saw in her German teacher a direct line of communication to her royal forebears, and when the Fraulein came out of her trance in dramatic disorientation—swooning had also become quite popular for sophisticated women—she opened her eyes to find the Queen enraptured. Muanu, whom the Fraulein had scarcely noticed before, balanced the Queen's enthusiastic reaction with a cold, piercing stare that left no doubt as to what Her Majesty's attendant thought of the language teacher's spiritual prowess. Thus was born an icy mutual hatred, as Muanu watched the Fraulein become one of the Queen's closest confidants.

"Bring her in, please, Muanu," the Queen directed. "And stay with us, if you will. She'll be reading her tarot cards and I think you'll enjoy it." She began to clear her writing table of distractions.

"Yes, ma'am," Muanu cringed.

Muanu fetched the woman she loathed so sincerely. She assumed that the spiritualist must make her own dresses, because she had adapted the European style of the low-cut evening gown, one that revealed nearly all of her generous cleavage, with the light and airy flow of the traditional Hawaiian wraps. Muanu led the immodest charlatan to the Queen, who greeted her warmly, and guided her to the round teak table in front of the grand fireplace.

"Would you like something, dear Fraulein?"

"Thank you, Your Majesty, but no. I think we should get right to work," the Fraulein replied importantly.

'Work', indeed, scoffed Muanu silently.

"May we lower the lights, Your Majesty?" The Queen responded with a nod to Muanu, who managed not to grimace as she rose to do the German's bidding. She drew the drapes and dimmed the lamps, creating a dusky atmosphere in the room. The ambient light rose and fell as the wind occasionally blew through the open windows. The Fraulein produced a single candle from her bag, and placed it in the center of the table before lighting it.

"I thought we were reading tarot cards today," Muanu asked as innocently as she could manage.

"The spirits have directed me otherwise," responded the Fraulein. "They will speak through me directly."

The Queen wanted to make the exercise as efficient as possible. "I would like specifically to address the issue—"

"Please, Your Majesty," said the medium, imperiously holding up a hand to silence the Queen. "The spirits will know what you wish to discuss. I am but the messenger—telling me will accomplish nothing." Muanu was appalled, knowing full well that if she attempted such a gesture she would likely lose the hand she held up. Liliuokalani, however, merely nodded her understanding of the medium's instructions.

"Please place your hands on the table," she said, as she did the same. Her accent, usually barely detectable, became thick as she began the séance. Muanu had to admit to herself that the Fraulein's accented English—*Pleeze plaze you hahnds on zee tahble*—gave the bogus exercise a dramatic flair. "Quiet... your mind," she said, drawing the final word of each sentence into a long, accented whisper. "Quiet... your heart. Gaze... into the flame. Let the flame be your only thought." And so they sat in the expressly quiet room, the only sound the rustling of the curtains as the wind blew. Together they slipped into something like a collective meditation, relaxed by the movement of the flickering candle and the accented moans of the Fraulein. The peace settling over them was shortly interrupted by a sharp knock on the table. "It is all right," reassured the Fraulein. "It is merely the spirits announcing their presence." Muanu wondered what sort of device the Fraulein had under her petticoats that accomplished this little trick, but she knew an investigation under the table would meet the Queen's disapproval.

"The spirits are concerned for the Queen. She bears the burden of many decisions."

Such insight! Muanu could hardly stop herself from rolling her eyes.

"You wish to know what is best for your people."

"Yes, yes I do," responded the Queen, her voice rising.

"The crown will become strong. The people want a strong queen... a queen who will also make them strong" the medium intoned.

"Yes, but how?" the Queen asked anxiously.

"The state must grow richer. The spirits say the Queen knows how to do this."

The Queen did not break the silence, but she did indeed know the answer—a lottery. It was the idea that one royalist advisor after another had suggested, the same 'gambling bill' that had led to the revolution of 1887 and the miserably confining constitution she hated so passionately. Yet there it was, a means to refilling the state coffers that could just as easily bring down that very state.

"A man will cross the sea bringing great wealth. He will help the Queen. I see a name... no, I see two letters. There is a 'C' and there is an 'S'." Fraulein Wolf dramatically rolled her head, her eyes tightly closed.

"C. S." whispered the Queen. "It must be Clause Spreckles," she said to Muanu. Spreckles was the richest of the Hawaiian sugar plantation owners, a German immigrant who had made a vast fortune there. Unlike most of the other large landholders, he was a fierce royalist who had advised the Queen's brother, King Kalakaua, to use a lottery to raise funds. He was currently living in San Francisco, but would soon be crossing the sea to return to Hawaii.

The medium continued. "There is another man. He does not bring money. No, something more powerful—an idea. The Queen can trust this man. I see more letters. He is a Mister T... E... E. Yes, Mister T. E. E."

Muanu could see the Queen thinking deeply about this. She turned to her young attendant and repeated the initials, *Mister T. E. E.* Muanu nodded her understanding; she would write them down as soon as the séance concluded. At that moment Fraulein Wolf went through a brief trembling fit that perfectly communicated the impression that she was returning to her body, after which she slumped down in her chair and breathed heavily for a few moments. Finally she lifted her head and looked calmly at the Queen, ignoring Muanu entirely, and asked, "Your Majesty, did anything happen at all?"

"Yes, my child, you were very helpful. Thank you, once again." She patted the Fraulein's hand and rose to leave, giving one last look to Muanu to remind her to write down the mystery man's initials.

Muanu grabbed a piece of paper and spoke the initials as she wrote them down, then leveled her eyes at those of the medium.

"I wonder why it is that 'the spirits' prefer to identify our saviors with initials rather than names."

"I'm sure I don't know," snapped the Fraulein as she began packing up her candle.

"Yes," Muanu smiled sweetly. "I'm sure you don't."

Lydia had been looking for an opportunity to question one of her husband's Chinese servants alone, having failed abysmally in her effort to question two of them together. It occurred to her that it was strange to think of them as *her husband's* servants, and not her own, but therein lay the tale of their wedded life—she was a guest in her own house. Accordingly, easy opportunities for chatting with the staff simply did not exist, so she resolved to create one. One morning she waited in the sitting room outside her bedroom for one of the servants whom she knew would come. She knew that Pi, a slender young adolescent of around eighteen (it was impossible to be sure), would be coming up to change her sheets and make her bed. When he walked by in his silk shirt and pants that looked to her very much like pajamas, she waited a moment, then slipped into the room after him.

The boy heard the door click shut and saw the mistress of the house leaning against it. His eyes grew wide as he tried to comprehend, or miscomprehend, the situation.

"Pi," Lydia began, "I'd like a moment alone with you, if you don't mind."

Now the boy's confusion turned to fear as his eyes darted about the room searching almost frantically for another exit. Seeing this, but not understanding, Lydia approached him in an effort to reassure him that he was safe, but her proximity made things worse. "Please, Pi," she tried to comfort him, "I won't need you for long," she said, putting her hands on his slim shoulders.

"No, Missy Biss! *Preeze!*" he squealed in desperation as he slipped past her and ran out of the room, down the stairs, and directly into the den where Warren and Mr. Li were working. A few minutes later she heard the two older men laughing uproariously. "Oh, God," she moaned aloud, as she realized what had just happened. The pretty boy thought she was trying to seduce him and the rest of the men were apoplectic in their laughter about it. *God help me*, she lamented to herself. *This should add an interesting wrinkle into my relationship with the boys in my house.*

Clearly, if she were going to get some first-hand accounts of Chinese labor being smuggled into the United States, she would not be able to do it in the comfort of her own home. *It might be nice to stay out of the house for a while, anyway*, she thought. Off to Chinatown.

Muanu came through the door to her little bungalow that night to find Jonah on her couch reading yet another history of Hawaii.

"What do you know about mediums?" she asked, frowning.

"They're neither small nor large."

"*Haole.*" Her voice was quiet and firm, telling him in a single word that she didn't want to hear any jokes.

"Sorry. Well, I'm sure you know more about them than I do. I mean, that whole otherworldly, spiritual sort of thing seems much more your area of expertise than mine."

"I'm not talking about spirituality. I'm talking about Germans who claim to be able to speak with spirits."

"Ah, *frauds*. Yes, that *would* be more my area of expertise. They're remarkably popular these days in America, and here too, I suppose. Otherwise intelligent people trust—and pay—these charlatans who claim they can put them in touch with the dead, which is the strangest part to me. I mean, once you're truly done with someone on earth, why would you want to bring them back?"

121

"How do they convince people, these frauds?"

"They perform tricks of one sort or another. I visited one once with some friends from college. It was like seeing the fortune teller at the fair. She made the room quiet and dark, lit a candle, and when the spirits arrived they announced themselves with a rap on the table."

"A rap on the table?"

"Yes. But one of my more forward friends reached up the wretched woman's dress and found a lever with a knob on the end of it pressed against her knee. It smacked the tabletop when she put her knees together. Took all the fun out of it. Until the medium felt my friend's hand on her knee."

Muanu muttered something about "a lever... a lever between her knees" as she sank into the couch next to Jonah.

"What's this all about, anyway? Have you met one of these industrious charlatans?"

"The Queen keeps one," Muanu admitted. "Fraulein Wolf. She came over today to convince the Queen to introduce a lottery."

"'Fraulein Wolf'? I know her, I think. Attractive gal, big... uh, yes, I know her. German accent, right?"

"How do you know this woman?"

"I met her at a party one night with Mr. Thurston. It's part of my job to know who is selling what, so no matter how much I drink I have to make notes on every conversation I hear as soon as I get back to the office."

"And your notes on Fraulein Wolf?"

"None on her, but she was on the arm of an oily man. He runs a company that he thinks could handle a lottery—print the tickets, handle sales, rewards and such—and he was trying to convince Thurston to support the idea. He obviously had no idea who he was talking to."

"The man's name?"

"Evans, I think. Yes, Evans. He didn't give his first name, just T. E. Evans."

* * *

The next day Muanu felt truly apprehensive when she led a caller to the Queen. He was tall and thin, with wet black hair, and he carried a leather valise full of papers.

"Your Majesty," Muanu said as the bile rose in her throat. "I would like to present Mr. T. E. Evans."

The Queen looked at Muanu with hope in her eyes. Just as the Fraulein had prophesied, here was 'Mr. T. E. E.' in the flesh!

CHAPTER SIX

Lydia Bliss was getting nowhere, no matter how much walking she did through the streets of Chinatown. She still had a list of Chinese contacts from the work she did on the "Heathen Chinee,"—her first feature printed in the *Weekly*. The list was less than a year old, but already it was hopelessly obsolete. Her contacts were no longer there. Chinatown, like any other immigrant neighborhood, looked to outsiders like a static slum rather than the dynamic way station it actually was. New immigrants came, found temporary comfort and respite in the company of familiar faces; once they had made their cash and connections, they moved on to make their way in the economic maelstrom of the American West. Sometimes they found hard labor and a better life, and sometimes hard labor and death, but they always found it somewhere else.

Tired of walking, and quite hungry, her logical next stop was a restaurant that had been run by the Chang family. The hand-painted sign above the door read simply enough, "Restaurant." Single women entering public eateries always caused something of a stir, so she steeled herself, but when hers was the only white face in the room she received rather more attention than she liked. A young Chinese man came to wait on her, but he was quickly shooed away by a much older man in a torrent of Mandarin that seemed to say, "go work in back, I'll take this one."

"Missy Burk-ah," said the venerable Mr. Chang, making a valiant attempt at pronouncing Lydia's maiden name, Burke.

"Mr. Chang, you remembered me! I was beginning to think everyone I knew in Chinatown had abandoned the place." She smiled with genuine relief.

"We ah still he-yah, Missy Burk-ah. It very nice to see you," he said sincerely. He had not actually read the piece she had written about Chinese immigrants, the one he had contributed to, in which she concluded that as a group, the Chinese were a generally filthy, stinking, opium-smoking, and debased infestation of whores, pimps, and sundry human vermin. Lydia had serious second thoughts about these conclusions by the time she finished writing the piece, but it seemed to be what people wanted to read—it was definitely what her editor wanted to read—so it went to press as the bigoted piece of slander it was. In her personal interaction with her sources, however, she had always treated them with the same warmth and respect she was surprised to receive from them. Consequently, Mr. Chang, a kind and trusting soul, remembered her fondly.

"We bring you very good meal, Missy Burk-ah. You ah special guest he-yah."

"Lovely. I must admit, I could use a good meal. But I wonder if you wouldn't mind sitting down with me. I'd like to ask you some questions about your experience coming to America—as a Chinese immigrant."

"Yes, I am Chinese," he responded, not quite getting her request. "But I am citizen of America for many month now."

"I know. What I mean is, I wanted to talk to you about how you came here—how most of the Chinese came here." By this time the other patrons, Chinese all, made no attempt to conceal their eavesdropping. Mr. Chang looked at them sternly, then turned kindly to Lydia and beckoned her to follow him. He led her into the kitchen, to the table at which his family ate their meals. He turned to the young man again, apparently his son, and let loose another river of Mandarin, the gist of which seemed to be, "go back out front," or at least that is what the young man did. Then he started barking at the family generally, and they stopped their labors, and joined

125

them at the table. A young girl, perhaps fourteen years old, spoke to Lydia in perfect English. Mr. Chang and his wife would continue to be Chinese even if they stayed in American for a thousand years. The son, who was nearly a man when he immigrated, would be forever caught between two cultures. But their young daughters, despite their traditional Chinese raiment, were quickly becoming American girls.

"Excuse me. My father says that you are a nice lady, that we should trust you and answer your questions," the daughter said demurely. Lydia suddenly felt terrible about her 'Heathen Chinee' article. The young girl continued, "Father's English is not good. We, his children, will translate for him, but first you will eat."

It was clearly their tradition to eat in silence, which Lydia acknowledged, but she could not quite bring herself to conform to the convention, so they tolerated her questions. There were five children, four of whom were girls. The firstborn son, the boy who was running the restaurant out front while they ate and talked in the back, was clearly second-in-command.

Through his daughters, Mr. Chang revealed all the immigration stories and methods he had heard. He knew of many subterfuges for getting into the United States from China, like the "paper sons" scheme, which was something of a cottage industry in Chinese port cities. Legal Chinese Americans would dummy up bogus document packages—*papers*—full of family information, letters and testimony, photographs, "proving" a familial relationship to would-be Chinese "sons" who would buy the package. Documents in hand, the "paper son" would use them to bypass U.S. Customs agents, who had no idea how to question the veracity of the papers. It was a good deal for both the Chinese American who could make money from Chinese exclusion, and for the immigrant, who otherwise would have to find another, possibly more dangerous route into the country.

"How much can one make selling such 'paper sons'?"

Mr. Chang scratched his chin a moment and looked off into the corner. He seemed to be not so much contemplating the answer, but rather whether he should divulge it to Lydia. Finally he spoke with the slightest grin, and his daughters chuckled before one of them finally translated the answer. "My father says he would not know exactly how much these papers would cost," then she leaned toward Lydia conspiratorially, "but two 'paper sons' could possibly bring enough money for a poor Chinese immigrant to open a restaurant like this one." And with that the girls giggled behind their hands.

"But that is not how you came to America, Mr. Chang."

"No," the daughter continued, without waiting for translation. "My father and brother took a boat from China to Canada, then took another boat from there to here. This is the way most come. They sent for my mother, me, and my sisters a year later."

"Yes, but he didn't just hop on a boat in Vancouver and sail into Seattle. The American Customs agents would have arrested him on the spot."

The father smiled at this translation. As he spoke he shook his head, remembering an adventure that he was very glad was behind him. His daughter nodded as she listened. They were all familiar with the story, but listened reverentially as their father imparted to them their family lore.

"It was not so long ago, really. A little more than two years ago. The boat to Canada was no problem. They gave fifty dollars to the Canadian Customs man, who pointed to the American smuggling boat."

"Showed them the way to a smuggling vessel?"

"Yes. Very helpful. Then they boarded the American boat. A Chinaman took all the money they had left, and then they made their brief voyage in the dark of night. They arrived in Port Angeles, and the ship left them there."

"And how did they get to Seattle, with no money, and presumably no English?"

"They walked."

"Walked? That's nearly a hundred miles!"

"Yes, it was hard, but now they are here, and we are happy."

"Do you remember the name of the smuggler, the man who seemed to be in charge on the boat?"

"Yes, everyone who comes that way knows him. Mr. Li, but it is not his boat, even though he acts like it. He works for a white man."

Li was a common name, Lydia reminded herself. There must be a thousand of them in the State of Washington, but she did not have a good feeling about this.

"Do you remember the name of the boat?" she continued.

Mr. Chang thought for a moment, and answered in English. "It was *Stah, the Stah of Noth-ah.*"

"The 'Stah'...*The North Star*?" Lydia asked as her heart sank.

"Yes," responded Mr. Chang, pleased that she understood his English. "That is the one."

"Muanu," Jonah whispered in the darkness of her bedroom. She was uncharacteristically restless in the bed as he tried to sleep, just as she had been uncharacteristically aggressive in their lovemaking a little while earlier. "Are you all right?"

"No one is all right in Honolulu just now. We hear the thunder roll before the storm arrives."

"Yes, I suppose it would be hard to sleep with all that rolling thunder in your head. Perhaps you'd like to tell me what you're talking about."

"It doesn't matter. It was all set in motion so long ago. We were divided, then conquered, but it happened so gently no one seemed to notice." She was uncharacteristically solemn. "It was Penelope's grandfather who did it, you see?" Muanu was trying to tell him something, and Jonah began to realize that they wouldn't be sleeping anytime soon.

"Ah, I should have known the Tubbs family was behind it!" he declared, hoping to tease her out of this mood. "What is it that Penelope's grandfather did?"

"He wrote the 'Great Mahele' law for King Kamehameha. It divided the islands up into little private bits of land. It separated Hawaiian from Hawaiian. It turned Hawaiian land into private property."

"But private property clarifies things. Otherwise you don't know who owns what. Once you know whose is which you can get busy and do something with it. It spurs industry and self reliance. We draw strength from it."

"And, in your way, you are very strong. But do you love land you do not own? Do you love the people on land you do not own?"

"I suppose I'd have to get to know them." He was still determined to make her laugh.

"*Haole!*" she scolded, as she leveled her gaze at him.

"But Hawaiians *did* have private landholdings——I've been reading up on this stuff—it's just that the chiefs held all of it."

"——As your father held your land for you when you were a child. And on that land he held you close, loved you, looked after you. In that protected place you thrived and grew strong."

He understood her lesson. "Well, that doesn't really describe my childhood, but we'll accept it for argument's sake. Still, at some point, to continue your metaphor, the child grows up and gets his own land. How does that happen if the chiefs own all of it?"

"A grown man can abide on his father's land. That is togetherness, connectedness—*Po*. Harmony in this world is the path to the inner world." She saw Jonah do that skeptical head tilt he always did when she spoke of spiritual things, so she reverted to logic, the only language he seemed to understand. "Jonah, if every son of every father is always looking for his own land, you will one day run out of it."

"On the islands, perhaps, but Americans always seem to satisfy their restlessness by moving West."

"Was no one there?" she asked sincerely.

"In the West? Mexicans, Indians, but lots of empty space."

"Empty space? There is no such thing, especially if part of the emptiness was Mexicans and Indians."

129

"Well, Indians lived in the Dakotas, for example, but they didn't live in settlements. This was true as recently as fifty or sixty years ago. The Indians were nomadic; they followed the vast herds of buffalo rather than establish towns. So—like Polynesians, I suppose—no one owned any of that property."

"But now it is owned?"

"Oh yes, of course. It's full of farms and towns. It's civilized."

"Did you civilize the buffalo as well?"

"Nearly extinct, as it happens."

"The Indians?"

"Not much better than the buffalo." He was beginning to see her point.

"And so it is with what is left of the Hawaiians."

They fell quiet for a few moments. The lightheartedness with which Jonah began the discussion could not survive the demise of an entire race. In the silence Jonah thought about the way everything seemed to simply move out of the way when western civilization appeared. The buffalo shot, Indians fought and negotiated onto ever shrinking reservations, and the Hawaiians simply disappearing. Before Muanu he had never really wondered how that happened.

"You are about a tenth of your original numbers?" he asked.

"Yes, something like that."

"Everyone who writes about Hawaii comments on the disappearance of the Hawaiians."

"And why, according to all of these scribbling 'everyones,' do we disappear?" Of course she knew the answer from her years at the missionary school, but she decided to make Jonah say it.

He swallowed and debated whether to make up a palatable lie. "It seems to be the general consensus that it is due to Hawaiians' lack of morality."

"Some would call that 'lack of morality' love," she said, as she ran her fingers gently across the back of his hand. Her spirits were lifting at the shift to a subject where she felt an advantage. "I believe, Jonah, that you are a convert to this way of thinking."

"Praise the Lord!" he said, also relieved at the new turn the conversation was taking.

"Of course," she signaled that they were still discussing this, "I have heard this silliness many times. First at Punahou, then many times at church. Then, when boys and girls get older, after six or seven years of school, the girls grow breasts, their hips become round; the boys have erections they feel they cannot control. That is when the teachers and preachers grow feverish, telling us over and over how sin and lust destroyed a race."

"I take it you didn't buy their argument."

"I did not. After my eighth year I could listen to it no more. Every night I would talk with my family, especially my grandmother, about this and so many other crazy *haole* things. 'How can love kill us?' I would ask. My grandmother was wise. She knows the ways of *huna kupua*, but she remained silent until I started asking questions. She liked your Jesus book, like me, but she was sure the *haole* preachers had never read it."

"That's the same thing Kalani said!"

"Yes," she smiled at the mention of her cousin. "Kalani knows a little of the *huna*."

"Whatever became of him, by the way? I mean, he couldn't have continued to work for Reverend Tubbs after we were caught in your hut."

"You won't believe it."

"Try me."

"He has joined the Royal Hawaiian Police!"

"You can't be serious!"

"I know, it sounds so silly, but he is so strong, yet so gentle— exactly the kind of man we can trust to do what is right. If we had more such men the decisions of Hawaiians might actually matter today."

At last they both became quiet at the thought of Kalani in uniform, and they held each other in the darkness and drifted off into a troubled sleep.

* * *

Within the hour Lydia was back at her desk, sitting alone in the halo of lamplight in the otherwise darkened newsroom. It was late in the evening and everyone had long since gone home. The lamp on her desk illuminated several overlapping piles of notes and documents that Lydia was poring over with new, more skeptical eyes. In particular, she was examining the manifests that Warren had brought to their first few meetings. She had requested them at their initial interview, but by the time they arrived she was far more interested in the man than his paperwork. Now, that ratio was inverted, she started going over the documents with a magnifying glass, and she could see that they were frauds—absolutely phony in every case. The manifests for the *North Star* indicated it was carrying cargo it couldn't possibly hold—lumber, for instance, which would be difficult to load onto a sixty-foot sloop, unless your purpose was to watch it sink to the bottom of Puget Sound. The fancy embossment for the ship's title, on closer inspection, turned out to be a second sheet of paper seamlessly glued over the original ship's title. She scraped it off with a hairpin and found the authentic ship's name beneath it, *The Tempest*, which was one of Warren's larger vessels.

She was angry with herself. If she had paid more attention to these bogus documents than she had to his winning face and parade of social engagements she could have... what? Would she have exposed him publicly as a smuggler? She honestly did not know what she would have done, but certainly she never would have married the man. And with that lonely thought, she went to his home.

Once back at the house she was relieved to discover that Warren and Mr. Li were, as usual, not there. She went directly to her room and changed into a filmy French nightgown, which she knew would give her a measure of privacy from the servants as she walked about the house. Since her ill-fated attempt to question Pi, the slightest hint of her femininity was enough to send the boys scurrying from the supposedly libidinous mistress of the house. With her modest décolletage immodestly exposed to just above indecency—the outlines of her breasts were clearly visible through the pale satin—she knew she would scare her androgynous Coolies into hiding for the evening. Sure enough, on seeing her descending the stairs, Ah and Fuk immediately turned around and walked the other way, presumably to alert Pi and Qwok that "Missy Biss" was on the prowl again. The floor safely vacant, she slipped into Warren's study unobserved and immediately began looking for verification of Mr. Li's smuggling activities.

She found nothing related to Mr. Li's activities in any of the drawers, which was logical enough. This was Warren's den, after all, and if Mr. Li really were running the Chinese transport operation, it made sense that any damning records that existed would be down at the shipping offices under Li's lock and key. What she did find raised a new sort of questions. In a valise on the floor next to his desk she found several signed shipping contracts, which was not unusual in of itself, but on closer inspection she could see that several of them were for the same boats, on the same dates. She was no expert in shipping, but simple arithmetic indicated that these ships were severely overbooked. *What*, she wondered, *was Warren up to?*

She became more methodical, going through every single drawer, box, and cabinet in the room looking for anything she could find to make sense of these papers, but she didn't find much to illuminate the material in the valise. She did, however, find a spare set of keys to Warren's offices down at the pier. As she sat on the floor among the piles of papers, barely dressed in her satin gown, the servants eventually emerged from their hiding place and peeked around the door, alarmed that this interloper was going through their master's papers. Ah was the first to speak.

"Missy Biss, perhaps it is not wise to touch Cap-y-tahn's papers." His voice carried a warning.

Lydia did not appreciate the interruption or his tone. She raised her eyes from the information she was examining and looked at the two servants for a long moment before she spoke. "You forget that I am not a guest here. This is my house."

"But Missy Biss, the Cap—"

"The 'Captain,' *my husband*, isn't here, so my opinion is all that matters at the moment. You may go."

The two servants stared at her impassively, refusing to move an inch. It was clear to Lydia that these two did in fact consider her no more than a guest in their master's house—an unwanted guest at that. Equal parts frightened and furious, she rose from her spot on the floor to face them, which was difficult because she stood a half head above the taller of the two; Ah's and Fuk's eye's were uncomfortably level with her breasts. Unreadable as ever, yet somehow smug in their victory, they stood aside to let her pass from "the Captain's" inner sanctum. But rather than retiring to her rooms, the unvanquished *Missy Biss* walked directly to the telephone on the wall, and asked the operator to connect her with the police.

"Hello, Police?" She looked directly at the surly servants as she spoke and saw their demeanor change dramatically as their eyes grew wide at the word 'police.' "This is Mrs. Bliss on Capitol Hill. There are two Coolies in my house who refuse to leave." She paused as they desperately waved their hands at her, mouthing something like '*No, preeze!*' She continued, "Yes, I feel quite unsafe. Would you send an officer around right away? Thank you." As she hung up the phone Ah and Fuk, who had no interest in seeing what the police would do to a couple of Chinese who were accused of threatening a white society woman, raced out the front door into the rainy night, never to return, she was quite certain. Unfortunately for them, in their quite reasonable terror of the authorities, they had not noticed that once Lydia had rung up the operator she then depressed the receiver cradle, disconnecting the call. Her conversation with 'the police' had in fact been a conversation with dead air, but at least the arrogant little men were out of her hair, probably forever. It was after midnight, she was exhausted, and Warren still wasn't home.

She needed to get some sleep and see if any of this made any more sense in the light of morning.

Warren Bliss knew he should be nervous, but once he and his assistant, Mr. Li, had passed the point of no return in the execution of their scheme, he felt a certain contentment. He sat grinning serenely and accepted a cup of strong green tea from his companion, who seemed to be apprehensive enough for both of them. Li was more than a little anxious about this whole notion of 'wiring' money. Why not just put the money in a big box and carry it with you on the boat? Or divide it in parts and send a satchel of money with each of their servants? He had been sending and receiving money from China that way for years, and it always worked.

"Li, relax, this is the safest way to send the money," Warren reassured him.

"But, 'wire'? How send money on a wire? It make no sense." Warren noticed, not for the first time, that when Li became excited his otherwise crisp English slipped slightly into pidgin.

"It's not the money itself that is sent on a wire," Warren explained. "It's simply a message that is sent from one bank to another, securely transferring funds from this bank to that one. It's a little more difficult than that when we transfer the cash to European banks, but only a little."

Li did not understand this process at all, but protested the part he did understand. "But we have money in many, many different banks!"

"Li, please, come and sit." Warren removed his feet from the ottoman in front of him and patted his hand where he wanted Li to sit, which his assistant dutifully did, although he would much rather have run through the rain down to the bank and started loading their cash into a lockbox. Warren gently rubbed his companion's knee as he spoke. He had long since learned that gentle physical contact soothed Li when he was upset, and it seemed to work now. "Do you

135

know why I sent you with deposits to all those different banks?"

"If one bank close, all money not gone?" Li guessed.

"Partly, yes, but mostly it was so I could keep each account small enough that I would be able to wire, that is, transfer the entire account without attracting attention. When you have a lot of money in one spot everyone finds out one way or another. When you move that much money, it becomes the subject of gossip and speculation, and God knows we've had enough of that." Li smiled at that, and Warren gave his knee a little squeeze. "So we've had all these other accounts set up through which we can *transfer* the sums before they can be traced or otherwise obstructed."

"Very well," Li surrendered. "It is enough that you understand. I do not believe I ever will. I have work to do." And with that, he rose, kissed the top of his Captain's head, and went back to his little desk, leaving Warren with his tea and banking receipts.

Warren stared out of the great window that lined the back wall of his office, overlooking the busy pier. The steady drizzle against the glass reminded him why he would not miss this place. The difficult part, though, would be leaving so much money on the table, but he reminded himself not to get too greedy; every step of the plan had already increased their take dramatically. The evolution of the scam actually developed out of a clerical error some years earlier. Two of his agents had sold the same cargo space to two different buyers at the same time, accepting the standard ten-percent deposit from each of them. It occurred to Warren as he was helping his agents sort out the mess, that if he increased the standard deposit from ten to, say, twenty-five percent, and sold the same cargo space many times over, rather than just twice, one could simply collect money for nothing—lots of it. Multiply that double deal through the entire fleet and you would have a fortune. All one would need is a willingness to leave the United States before the purchasers of the cargo space discovered they had been robbed. But of course, he knew he could never come back either, which struck Warren as a splendid idea every time it rained.

Greed, however, was not to be denied. He could double the take—and triple the risk. Rather than just walking away, he could sell the entire shipping line as well, leaving the new owners with an overpriced business, tied up in contracts they could not possibly honor. Adding the purchase price of the shipping line to the kitty would more than double what he could get from the cargo swindle. He would be rich beyond his dreams. It would be difficult to pull off, of course. Timing would be critical. The trick would be to arrange the sale of the business just before the shipping contracts were scheduled, which meant the former had to be arranged before the latter were executed.

At forty-three, Warren Bliss had been in the shipping business long enough to know something about supply and demand. The railroads were insanely overbuilding—too many companies were building competing lines for the same freight, all on borrowed money. That, Warren understood, was a house of cards just waiting to come crashing down. As he read about these financial shenanigans in the daily press he thanked Providence (he was something of a Deist) that ships on the sea required not one single foot of track. Happily, however, those industrial pioneers who were overbuilding the railroads were also facilitating a dramatic expansion in the amount of freight shipped from the interior to the coast, which would then be shipped across the sea on one of Warren's boats. And who laid all the track for these robber barons of the rails? Chinese Coolies who came over on ships like Warren's, under not-so-loving guidance of men like Mr. Li. Warren had arranged to make money coming and going. And after the big payoff, working for money would be an obsolete concept.

As a merchant and a seaman Warren had seen the world, and he knew that there were places he would fit much better than Victorian America. To this end, he had already purchased a small palace in the Greek Isles, under an assumed name, of course. By the time he and his small group of Chinese companions were there, the financial knot into which he had tied so many businesses would be just starting to unravel. And by the time these business-owners and their lawyers had traced the financial and legal morass in which they found themselves back to Warren Bliss, the man using that name would have vanished. By the time they located the banks where all the funds were deposited, the money would also be gone.

Among those who would be left in Seattle holding worthless contracts would the lovely Lydia Burke-Jones-Bliss, whose wedding contract would also be null and void. Warren could rationalize almost every aspect of this colossal con—the railroad barons, for instance, would probably be broke in a year, anyway—but the pain he would cause Lydia, well, that was harder to swallow. *Surely she understood by now, or was beginning to understand my lack of desire for her*, he told himself. *She couldn't possibly be that oblivious.* In any case, it had worked out well enough for her, had it not? She had the career she wanted, and unlike most journalists, she was rich, at least for the time being. Still, to be so publicly unmarried twice in so short a time would be, well, awkward.

Lydia woke to the sound of the doorbell. She waited for one of the servants to answer it before she realized that the door-keeper had fled the night before. The cook would still be there, but he would certainly consider it beneath his station to answer the door. She donned her robe and descended the stairs to see who had come calling.

It was a bicycle messenger from Bliss Shipping; she recognized the boy's face. He handed her a letter and with a tip of the cap was on his way into the crisp, clear December day. It was one of those days in the Northwest when the rain took a rest, and the clouds broke to reveal a clear view of the Olympic Mountains beyond Puget Sound. Breathtaking.

"Quok," she raised her voice toward the kitchen. "Coffee, please." The cook sent the houseboy, Pi, out with green tea, as usual, rather than the coffee she requested. They went through this ritual daily, but as she was starting to like the tea, she didn't mind the little rebellion so much. She sat down and opened the letter, which was brief, and to the point.

> *Dearest Lydia,*
> *I'm afraid I've been called away on business. Some of the deals we were setting up a few months ago in Chicago are suddenly on shaky ground. I hope to be back within two weeks.*
>
> *As Ever,*
> *Warren*

Lydia saw her chance. She abandoned her tea, dressed, and sent for a cab to take her down to the pier and the offices of Bliss Shipping. Once there she breezed past the office staff on the lower floor and took the lift up to the third and top floor where Warren kept his offices. Mr. Li was not at his customary post in the anteroom where he usually jealously guarded access to 'The Captain.' Perhaps he joined Warren on this mysterious business trip. In any case, his absence would make things much simpler. She produced the keys she had found the night before, hoping one of them would unlock his office door. The second one did the trick. Once inside, she turned the lock behind her and immediately began rifling every cache of papers she could find. Alas, what she found were empty drawers, which told a tale of their own—most of the files had obviously been removed, presumably destroyed. But enough remained to verify the picture that had already been forming in her head. She could see by the additional shipping contracts and schedules she found that Warren was playing a highly sophisticated version of the old "runaway dog" con. She remembered Christopher telling her about the proverbial drifter who made enough money to get along by selling his dog, which would return to him in the night and move on with the drifter to the next town, where he would sell the same dog to someone else.

Warren was selling—and reselling—cargo space instead of dogs, and it suddenly occurred to Lydia that he would need to be a lot further away than the next town to escape the men he was cheating. She knew at that moment that she would never see him again.

On the carriage ride back up to the house she went over in her mind their history together, all of the dinner conversations, parties, and the evening meetings. Warren had always conducted business in informal situations that included oceans of alcohol. Among the invited were not just the business chieftains, but often their lawyers, so that he could, as he explained, eliminate as many layers of skepticism as possible. In retrospect, even the series of engagement parties had been but a chain of business meetings disguised as celebrations in which he used champagne and caviar—or beer and smoked salmon, depending on the company—to grease the skids for reluctant business partners cum dupes. Then their honeymoon, in which she hardly saw her new husband; instead she was entertained by the wives of Chicago railroad magnates while Warren negotiated God knows what sort of deals with them. Railroad men don't need to negotiate shipping contracts—there must be another wrinkle to this scheme.

This last notion continued to play on her mind after she arrived back at her house, which now sat empty. The last two servants were gone; evidently they too knew The Captain was not coming back, or they knew where he was and had gone to join him. Looking back, she could see that they had always been closer to her husband than she had been. She was the latecomer, the window-dressing for their con game, and she obviously didn't fit in this peculiar little Oriental boys' club. *Enough of that*, she told herself, and sat down to her writing table in her empty house. She started organizing the notes for what she sensed would become a much larger story than the Bliss Shipping's interest in smuggling Chinese labor. As she worked she was irritated from time to time by a teardrop that would smear the ink on her notes.

* * *

"Jonah," Thurston stood in the doorway of his office and gestured with a faint wave that his assistant's presence was required. It was after dark, and Jonah was anxious to escape the office and see Muanu, but disobeying Thurston was never an option. He followed the publisher into the inner office and sat in one of two overstuffed wingback chairs he kept for clients. Thurston, rather than sit behind his desk and deliver instructions from that Olympian position of authority, produced a bottle of Scotch and poured two drinks before sitting in the chair next to Jonah's. *This is new*, Jonah thought.

"You've learned a lot since you started working here, Jonah."

"Yes, sir. I suppose I owe much of that to you."

"Of course you do." Thurston was not given to false modesty. "But, as they say of the proverbial horse, you can take him to the library but you can't force him to read the books. You've done well."

Jonah wondered what the man was getting at. And when he gestured for Jonah to drink his Scotch, yet took none for himself, Jonah wondered what he was up to.

"Are you waiting for me, Jonah?" he said, indicating the man's tumbler. "Very well," and with that Thurston tossed back his drink and placed the empty glass on the desk. "Ah, it refreshes one's attention at the end of the day, does it not?"

"Yes, sir." Jonah dutifully followed suit and felt the sting of the alcohol warm his throat.

"The committee meets here tomorrow, you know, in the conference room."

"Yes, sir. It's on my schedule."

"I want you in the meeting this time." A night of firsts. Jonah had always arranged the meetings, made sure members knew when and where to go, delivered messages and so on, but he had never been allowed in the actual conference room. It was, after all, at least *supposed* to be a secret organization, and Jonah was barely more than an assistant. Thurston saw the incredulity in Jonah's face. "I

141

want more complete minutes and stringent organization from here on out. I need you in the room for that." He paused and looked at Jonah. "I also want a record of who is committed and who is not. You will take notes. This, of course, will make you an accessory to anything that at some later point is determined to have been treasonous." He said it as if he had made an observation on the weather.

"Treason, sir?" So this was what the drink and friendly conversation were leading up to. It was time for Jonah to make his choice: stay or go. Thurston looked at Jonah impassively, choosing to let the boy work it out for himself. Jonah thought back over Muanu's observation that Hawaii's fate had been determined decades ago. She believed that all they were doing now—whites and natives— was playing out the details; he wished he knew what she had meant by that. Now Thurston was offering him a front row seat to the next big events, as long as he could keep his mouth shut. All that was required of him was a little treason.

"I'll be there, sir," Jonah said, feeling vaguely as if he were stepping off a cliff.

They were interrupted by a knock on the outer door. Jonah answered it and found the fleet-footed Willie Kaae standing in the doorway clutching a leather valise to his chest, looking nervously over his shoulder. He slipped through the partially open door before Jonah had a chance to greet him.

"Why was the door locked?" Willie demanded.

"It's after hours," Jonah answered matter-of-factly. He could see that Willie was nervous about being seen there. "Perhaps you have brought us something from the Queen?" Jonah asked a little playfully.

Willie regarded Jonah suspiciously.

"It's all right, Willie," Thurston said as he emerged from his office. "There isn't much Jonah doesn't know. Although I'm not always sure how he knows it. From now on I want you to make your deliveries to Jonah at his boarding house. The less you are seen around here the better."

Willie relaxed a little. "Good. Coming here puts my stomach in knots. What if someone from the Palace saw me?"

"All the more reason for you to meet at the boarding house," Thurston said. "We wouldn't want you to become dyspeptic, now would we?"

"Thank you, Mr. Thurston."

"Your eye is looking better," Jonah offered.

"Thanks. I think I'm going to stick to foot races from now on. I'll leave baseball to the *haoles*."

"Good night, Willie," Thurston dismissed him. Willie, who knew an order when he heard one, emptied the valise of its papers, set them on Jonah's desk, and scurried out the back door.

"He does move quickly, doesn't he?" Jonah observed.

"If only he could catch a baseball," Thurston responded ruefully.

"He catches papers rather well," Jonah said, fingering through the stack of them Willie had just left on his desk. "This looks like memoranda from the Queen's staff. And this one here," he held a group of handwritten pages up to the light, "this seems to be a rough outline for a speech, or something like that."

"Written very carefully, you'll notice," Thurston said, pointing to several blank spaces, where the subject of the sentence was indicated by a line, or a single capital letter followed by a long blank. "She knows better than to put treasonous ideas in print."

"This is the Queen's writing? These are her personal papers?"

"Yes, I'm quite familiar with her hand."

"So, Willie is a spy." Jonah confirmed the obvious.

"You already knew that or you wouldn't have toyed with him while he was standing there like a trapped animal. Not very nice of you, by the way."

"What did you mean about the Queen knowing better than to 'put treasonous ideas in print?'"

Thurston held up a document. "It's difficult to tell from this incomplete scribble, but it's been clear to me for some time that she is contemplating abrogating the Constitution."

"You mean the Bayonet Const—sorry, the Constitution of 1887? I know she hates it."

"Of course she hates it; it's the only thing between her and absolute power." He saw that Jonah's face had gone ashen. "What's the matter, boy? Beginning to understand what you've signed up for?"

"It looks as if two sides are forming, each accusing the other of treason. It can't end well," Jonah stated simply. "So, yes, now that I see what's at stake, I'm a little nervous."

"Well, I suppose you ought to be," Thurston allowed. Turning his attention to the trove of stolen papers, Thurston rubbed his hands together. "Well, let's see if we can't piece together what sort of constitutional changes she's contemplating, here," said Thurston as he started reading through the pile. "Hmm, what do you make of this?" he said, handing a page to Jonah.

"It says 'double from twenty-four to forty-eight.'"

"Of course, that fits with this here," he said pointing to another page. "It's about voting requirements. She's eliminating, or perhaps just drastically reducing the property requirement for voting."

"Oh, like the United States?" asked Jonah. Thurston ignored him.

"And here she wants to extend the suffrage to all males who can read and write."

"I see," Jonah too began to piece the queen's plans together. "She proposes to double the size of the legislature, from twenty-four to forty-eight delegates, but at the same time she wants to eliminate the property requirements that effectively disenfranchise most Hawaiian men, meaning that *haoles* like you would probably lose your advantage in Parliament."

"Yes, and it gets worse. Look at this," he indicated a page on the court system from his Bayonet Constitution. "She's crossed out Article Sixty-Five of the Constitution. She wants to reduce the life term of Supreme Court judges to six years, and here she's crossed out the line that says that the justices' pay 'shall not be diminished during their continuance in office.'"

"Which could compromise the independence of the court."

"'Compromise'? She wants to cripple it."

"I think you'll like this section even less," Jonah said, indicating another line from the Constitution of 1887 that had been violently struck through. "It's your beloved Article Seventy-Eight, with which you so effectively bludgeoned the Queen's predecessor."

"What? Let me see that." He took the offending page from Jonah's hand and looked at the strike-through, so deep that it actually ripped the page at one point. The Queen had obliterated the line that read, *any act of the reigning monarch shall be done and performed by the Sovereign by and with the advice and consent of the Cabinet.* "She wants to be free to act unencumbered by the Cabinet or courts," Thurston thundered.

"Just like a real Queen," Jonah said, but Thurston did not see the humor in it.

In the still darkness of her bed, Muanu sensed that Jonah was uneasy as he lay on his back, hands behind his head. She rolled on top of him and eased up his body in a serpentine motion until her mouth was on his neck. As she administered this loving attention she felt his muscles relax, and his right hand moved from behind his head to clasp her buttocks. She lifted her lips from his neck and in a barely audible whisper said, "Let it go."

"Oh, sorry," he said, releasing his hand.

"No, Jonah, not that." She replaced his hand to the spot that always made him so happy. "Let go of what is troubling you. It is late, and there is nothing you can do about it now. The knot will untangle while you sleep."

CHAPTER SEVEN

The knot did not untangle. Nonetheless, Jonah put his conscience in his pocket and dove into his new role as coordinator for the Annexation Commission.

He needed to educate himself. He gathered sources and laid out a timeline of political events, going back to the Bayonet Constitution. The trick here was to balance Thurston's interpretation with other sources, which told a startlingly different tale. He took over the conference room, where he would have more table space to spread out his documentation, and started reading. By lunchtime he had reached some conclusions. First, 'committees,' 'leagues,' and various organizations had come and gone for years, but they were all essentially the same thing: a vehicle for Lorrin Thurston to displace native Hawaiian leadership and ultimately annex Hawaii to the United States.

As a legislator, cabinet secretary, lawyer, and publisher, Thurston seemed to have but one purpose: the Americanization of Hawaii. His methods were both consistent and effective. First, he would form some sort of political or social organization with one clear purpose, and associate with other organizations that might oppose him on nine issues in ten, but Thurston would promise to make common cause on that tenth issue and thereby win support for his confederacy on a crucial point. Then he would make life a misery for those who resisted him, painting them into a corner and force them to make a dangerous political move. Thurston then would marshal public opinion and turn their blunder against them. Political jujitsu.

By this pitiless and methodical approach, Jonah's boss was, as it turned out, already an experienced, stealthy revolutionary. The documents made clear that he had orchestrated the events that led to the Bayonet Constitution in precisely the same way he seemed to be doing now. In the 1880's King Kalakalua, the Queen's brother and predecessor, had been doing the unthinkable: he was trying to govern Hawaii with Hawaiians instead of *haoles*. As a profligate spender, womanizer, and drunkard, however, he was hardly the best man to sell such a plan to the island's whites, who were not likely to be fond of slogans like "Hawaii for the Hawaiians" in any case. To make matters worse, some of the king's schemes to fill Hawaiian coffers, like licensing opium dealers and running a lottery, struck even Hawaiians as profiting from social misery, which of course they were.

By 1886 Thurston had had quite enough. He formed a secret organization, "The Hawaiian League," devoted, as Thurston wrote in their secret charter, "to secure efficient, decent and honest government in Hawaii." And just in case any of the members thought they were joining a social organization, Thurston added, "To the securing and maintenance of government of this character, we do hereby pledge our lives, our property, and our sacred honor." Oh my. What at first glance seemed very high-minded and patriotic, actually became explicitly racial in the following paragraph. Members pledged not to "oppose or oppress the white citizens of this Kingdom," and to obey "military superiors in their necessary efforts to protect the white community against arbitrary or oppressive action of the Government, which may threaten the lives, liberty or property of the people." *Military superiors?* Jonah was surprised at the terminology. Did this mean that the whites had their own army? A little more digging and Jonah found that they did. Thurston's group could call on the assistance of "The Honolulu Rifles," an armed group of three companies of whites of various nationalities, many with military experience abroad. Although there was considerable overlap in the memberships of the Rifles and Thurston's four hundred-member Hawaiian League, the two organizations were ostensibly separate. When the government became concerned about the numbers of guns and ammunition coming into the country for them—some one thousand cartridges per member—the lawyers of the League filed papers to have the cargo released. Thurston's political league, in other words, had a military arm.

The mass meeting, however, was Thurston's most effective weapon. As a politician and newspaper publisher, Thurston was a keen student of public opinion and the manipulation of same. Skillful propaganda, always with some kernel of irrefutable truth at its core, was essential to whip some strategic segment of the public into a frenzy of indignation. By the summer of 1887 Thurston had his secret political organization and private army in place. All they needed was a pretext for action, and the King's announcement of his opium and lottery bills provided one.

Thurston used his newspaper and other publicity channels to call a mass meeting to intimidate the King. Lest the King miss the point, Thurston selected the Rifles' armory as the most expressive venue for the meeting. There a massive crowd heard speaker after speaker stand before a phalanx of uniformed and armed private soldiers, and denounced the King and his cabinet. Finally, Thurston himself read out a set of resolutions for the crowd to support through vociferous acclamation. The mob, under Thurston's expert guidance, resolved on the spot that the King must fire his cabinet and accept a new constitution. Thurston, as coincidence would have it, had already drafted a new one for the occasion.

The King was frantic. The Rifles arrested and exiled the King's prime minister, and the miserable monarch could only assume that he would be next. In a fit of desperation he sent for as many diplomatic representatives as he could find. The American, British, French, Portuguese, and Japanese representatives listened politely as the King offered to place his kingdom in their hands, hoping that they would give it back once the crisis had passed. The delegates listened in embarrassed silence until finally the British consul explained as politely as he could that this sort of thing "just isn't done."

So the King miserably awaited the arrival of the Committee of Thirteen representing the Hawaiian League—Thurston and his twelve disciples—while the whites' army stood at attention outside the palace. The Committee handed the King Thurston's new constitution. The King dolefully looked out his window at the precise rows of armed men, removed his pen from its stand, and set his signature to Thurston's constitution, effectively disempowering himself.

Jonah stopped annotating his timeline long enough to reflect ironically on Thurston's insistence that "Bayonet" was an inappropriate appellation for the Constitution of 1887—that no one held a knife to the King's throat. *Only a lawyer*, he mused. Yes, the bayonets were actually across the palace grounds from the King's throat, but they must have been the most memorable feature of the day, outside of the new constitution itself.

"All right, all right, let's call this meeting to order," Thurston barked over the din. The collection of aging white men milling about the conference room reduced the cacophony from a roar to a murmur as they took their seats. Tobacco smoke filled the air, and flowing facial hair decorated woolen vests. Thurston kept his beard closely cropped, but all the other men in the room looked like elders from the Bible, with great white auras around their faces, except for those who chose to sculpt their beards into more creative renderings. There were mustaches that looked like expropriated horse tails, and muttonchops that fairly billowed from the sides of faces. Jonah found a chair against the wall and scratched his clean-shaven chin as he contemplated the danger these men faced every time they lighted a cigar.

Thurston strode to the front of the room and, by way of bringing the meeting to order, asked the committee, "News or questions?"

149

"I would like a report on your trip to Washington last fall," responded a long white beard at the table. "Will annexation meet a receptive audience in the American Congress?" "Here, here!" barked another. The committee was anxious to know that Washington would welcome their efforts, and that had been the purpose of Thurston's mission. The Hawaiian legislature had sent him to Chicago to oversee arrangements for Hawaii's presentation at the upcoming world exposition there, but he took advantage of the opportunity to make an additional trip to Washington on behalf of the Annexation Committee. He had rather enjoyed the idea of the Hawaiian government financing his investigation into the possibility of eliminating it.

Thurston paused while the assenting murmurs died down, and then he said simply, "They are anxious to have us." Another round of happy mumbling, and Thurston began to fill in the details. "While I was there I spoke with the Secretary of State, James Blaine, who as you know has recently died, and he was then most enthusiastic about acquiring Hawaii."

"A lot of good that does us—the support of a dead secretary!" interrupted one of the muttonchops.

"Secretary Blaine appointed our present U.S. minister, Mr. John L. Stevens. I assure you, Mr. Stevens shares the late Mr. Blaine's support for us."

"And what of the living members of the American administration?" demanded one wag.

"The new Secretary of State, Mr. John Foster, assures me that Hawaii would be a welcome addition to the United States." Thurston was in his element, parrying their jabs.

"And Congress?"

"They are supportive, to a man," Thurston lied expansively. In fact, he had received no guarantees from anyone in the American government. With the exception of the now deceased secretary of state, American officialdom had played its cards exceedingly close to the vest, refusing to tip their hands as to what they might do if he, say, offered to give them the Hawaiian Islands. The incomprehensibly noncommittal phrase that fell from every congressman, senator, and secretary's lips was "a fair hearing," which was as much as they would promise him should he produce a treaty proposal for annexation. Thurston expected a warmer reception to the prospect of controlling a paradise that just happened to occupy a key position in the Pacific shipping lanes. Although he did not doubt his ability to turn a "fair hearing" into a successful treaty, he knew anything less than a firm American commitment would result in an epidemic of cold feet among his co-conspirators, so he led them to believe the U. S. government was solidly behind them. This convenient untruth was a mirror image of the con he offered American officials who asked about Hawaiian sentiments toward annexation. They were understandably reluctant to acquire a population that did not want to be annexed, but Thurston assured each and every one of them that the vast majority of island residents were deeply desirous of becoming American citizens. He happily showed them the bogus data his staff dummied up to prove his point.

Jonah watched as another of the long white beards rose to speak. "All that's fine, Thurston. But at this point you seem to have prepared the United States for an offer that is not forthcoming. The Queen will not consent to annexation, let alone offer it, and if we simply stage a coup—assuming we don't get killed in the process— the Americans will see us as no more legitimate than freebooters."

"I have discussed how a revolution here might be perceived in America with the current Secretary of State, Mr. Foster," Thurston spoke truthfully this time. "He understood—and seemed to think the rest of America would understand—that if the Queen violated the constitution, that is, if she sought despotic power, defenders of the Constitution would have no choice but to revolt. Americans despise despotism and do not confuse self-defense with treason— and neither should you." He paused while his words took effect, then lightened his tone. "Mr. Christian?"

"Uh, yes?" Jonah was a little startled to be called upon.

"Summarize our efforts to this point, if you please."

"All right," Jonah continued a little uncertainly. "Where shall I start?"

Thurston looked at Jonah impatiently. "The last legislative session, perhaps."

"Certainly, sir." He hoped he could remember the notes he had written out that afternoon. Hawaiian politics was a kaleidoscopic cluster of factional discord, constantly combining and recombining in unsteady alliances as one group vied for advantage over another in a game that would ultimately determine the sovereignty of the archipelago. The most important of these factions, for immediate purposes, was the Reform Party. It was led by the men in this room; white businessmen whose ultimate goal was union with the United States. Their name was, unfortunately, infuriatingly similar to the *National* Reform Party, also known as the Palace Party, or at other times the King's Party, never mind that there was no longer a king, given that he was dead. These were mostly Hawaiians, anti-American in every case, who favored the king's scheme to fill the state coffers with proceeds from opium sales and a lottery. They held the sons of the missionaries in passionate odium.

Jonah tried to stop all these factions from tripping over one another in his mind as he began to speak. Looking out at the room full of hairy-faced men staring back at him, he wished he had a beard to hide behind. "Gentlemen," he cleared his throat before continuing, "the last legislative session could hardly have begun more badly for the committee. The Reform party," *you fellows*, he noted mentally, "failed to achieve a majority in the legislative assembly."

"We were a little busy trying to save our businesses from the damned McKinley tariff, young man!" interjected one of them rather defensively.

"Yes, of course," Jonah continued. "Nevertheless, the result was that no one party gained a majority. Turning disaster to advantage, however, this committee orchestrated a strategy of legislative paralysis, effectively bringing Her Majesty's government to a standstill. Each time a cabinet and prime minister was selected, the Reform Party either found enough votes among the other parties to oppose it, or would bring down the government shortly thereafter with a vote of no confidence. One cabinet, in fact, lasted no more than twenty minutes."

"Here, here!" one of them shouted among a chorus of happy mumbles.

"The Queen," Jonah continued, "has at long last ended up with a cabinet she neither wants nor trusts. We understand from the Queen's staff that she finds this untenable and that she may be preparing to promulgate a new Constitution." The assemblage lapsed into silence.

"And that presents us our pretext, gentlemen," Thurston concluded for Jonah. "Thank you, Jonah. That was very succinct, despite the flourish." Jonah smiled, nodded silently, and returned to his seat.

"Suppose she doesn't do it?" asked one of the gray beards. "The Cabinet we've given her would never approve abrogating the constitution."

"Better yet," said yet another, "what if she *does* do it. If she successfully promulgates a new constitution, she can simply give herself the power to have us arrested."

"We fight," answered Thurston. "We are not defenseless. Our Honolulu Rifles are a match for the palace guard and the police, should it come to that." He looked around the room at his co-conspirators. "Come now, gentlemen, this is exactly what we worked so tirelessly to achieve. Let's not shy away from the result when the Queen hands it to us. Everything is in place. We have but to await the Queen's next move."

"Let's hope it isn't to put a noose around our necks," offered one of the mutton chops to murmurs of agreement.

* * *

"Muanu, are you awake?" Jonah whispered in the warm darkness of her bedroom.

"I am now."

"There was something you said a few nights ago—it's been bothering me. Something about how none of the political infighting between the Assembly and the Queen matters. You said it was all decided long ago." Having found himself at the center of a conspiracy against her queen, he was more than a little interested in any theory that suggested it did not matter.

Muanu rolled over to face him. "You would not understand. It is not about politics."

"Okay, then what *is* it about?"

"Stubborn *haole*," she yawned. "If I try to explain this to you, will you go to sleep even if you do not understand?"

"I promise."

"Good. Listen carefully: It is about wholeness and separateness. Good night."

"That's it? C'mon!"

"I'm just teasing you," she laughed. "I'll explain," she said as she settled her head into the soft cradle between his neck and shoulder. "You were telling me about how wonderfully productive you Americans are, each of you on your little piece of the earth, because you *own* it. Each of you, separate from the other, work, work, work. The Hawaiian is different. For a hundred generations he found strength in togetherness, wholeness, sharing—*aloha*. Together, beneath a chief, we lived on land that belonged only to the kings and the chiefs, worked as much as we needed to, and lived abundantly. By owning nothing, we had everything. Then about sixty years ago the missionaries convinced King Kamehameha III that we should each own little pieces of earth, like you."

"Fee simple."

"What?"

"That's what we call it. You have one piece of land, with one owner—land in 'fee simple.'"

"Simple for who? *Haoles*, that's who. It was not so simple for the Hawaiians. It would not be hard to guess who would get all the land. As I told you before, the law was called 'The Great Mahele.' An American missionary wrote it—Penelope's grandfather. He thought it would be better if Polynesians were more like Americans." She chastised him, "I told you all about this the other night, but you didn't read it in one of your books, so you don't try to remember."

"The land reform law? Yes, I've read about it."

"Yes, you read what it meant in property, but not what it meant in spirit. We were together before, whole and strong. After the Mahele, we were divided—separate and weak. The royal family tried to give favor to one Western power after another—French, British, or American—but nothing mattered after the Mahele; Hawaii had ceased to be the land of Hawaiians."

"But the Queen is still Hawaiian," Jonah protested weakly.

"But she cannot rule. Mr. Thurston and the American party are our rulers more and more each day. The Mahele made that possible, and the Bayonet Constitution ensures it will remain so. Her Hawaiian subjects beg her to replace the constitution with one that would make her truly Queen—a strong Hawaiian leader like the Kamehamehas— but it is useless. The Kamehamehas ruled over half a million loyal subjects. Now there are only... I don't know how many."

"Forty thousand, give or take," Jonah said.

"Forty thousand—a tenth of what our number was a hundred years ago! So you see, the deed is already done."

"I see... You obviously don't speak about this with the Queen."

"It is not my place to speak of such things. You forget, I am there as a shadow of her own spirit, a reminder to her Western head that she still has a Polynesian heart. I am a token of another time, another way. She has many advisors, and they compete for her attention and argue for their policies and projects," Muanu said bitterly. "And the fraudulent Fraulein Wolf and her Mr. T. E. Evans have persuaded the

155

Queen to sanction a lottery to raise money, to give the Hawaiians the new constitution they want."

"She has already decided this?"

"Yes, she will announce it in a few days, when she closes the legislative session."

"I see." Jonah was already calculating the effects of a lottery bill on the Commission's efforts.

"At last, the *haole*'s questions have been answered!" she yawned. "Now this little member of the remaining forty thousand is going back to sleep."

Muanu slept, but Jonah didn't. He had no idea Thurston's pretext was coming so fast, and gift-wrapped with the offensive gambling bill, no less. As he closed his eyes and tried to sleep, he thought he could hear the approach of rolling thunder.

Henry Wasserman, Editor-in-Chief of the *Seattle Weekly*, turned over the last piece of paper in the stack, leaned back in his chair and let out a low whistle. Lydia had been slumped in a chair across the desk from him, waiting for him to finish reading the article. She looked at him impassively. In the preceding two weeks she had cried all the tears she had, and now was merely numb. She knew she had given him a blockbuster, but she found no joy in it.

"Can you prove all this?" he said at last. He pointed at the article on his desk, as if it might burn his fingers if he touched it again.

"Yes, sadly, I can prove all of it."

"When did you find out he sold Bliss Shipping to the railroad?" Wasserman grilled her.

"Their executives showed up at the pier about a week after Warren left town. They were kind enough to show me the records of the deal after I provided them evidence that they were the new owners of a hundred or so bad shipping contracts. Did you know you can actually see someone's blood pressure go up?"

The editor shook his head peevishly. "But you have no statement from Warren, not even a denial. If he shows up the day after we run this and claims that it was all just a case of bad bookkeeping, well, then we'd have a major libel case on our hands—even if he is your husband."

"I do have a statement from Warren. It's an admission of sorts. It arrived two weeks after he disappeared. It contains some personal details I'd prefer to keep out of the paper. Read it—you'll see." She dug a letter out of her bag and handed it to her editor.

> *Dearest Lydia,*
> *By now I'm sure you've ascertained that my business trip needs to be prolonged more or less indefinitely. I have conducted a series of business transactions that some will no doubt see in the darkest possible way, but I assure you everything is quite justifiable, if not entirely legitimate.*

"'Justifiable, if not entirely legitimate?'" Wasserman read aloud. "What the hell does that mean?"

Lydia laughed darkly. "If I know Warren, and I'm not at all sure I do, it means that what he is doing is profitable and our laws are rather an inconvenience."

Wasserman made a disapproving snort and read on.

> *I have taken the liberty of contacting our lawyer on your behalf. The firm of Hanford & Hanford, which handled your annulment from your first husband, would be happy to do so again. I have left them a signed statement affirming that our marriage was never consummated and therefore qualifies for annulment.*

Wasserman stopped again, looked up at Lydia, but said nothing. Lydia, uncharacteristically subdued, especially under the circumstances, broke the silence. "As I said, there are certain details

I would like to keep out of the paper."

Wasserman continued reading.

> *I am sorry that it will not be possible to leave you a lump sum of money, as that would undoubtedly be confiscated by the authorities in short order and I see no reason to send any contributions their way. The house, however, is yours. I have had the title transferred into your name—your maiden name— and the requisite paperwork awaits your signature at offices of Hanford & Hanford.*
>
> *Despite appearances, despite what you might think, and despite the despicable things you will surely hear about me, I have grown quite fond of you. You might even say that I love you, in a way. But this is an opportunity that we could not pursue together, and so I bid you, alas permanently, adieu.*
>
> *As ever,*
> *Warren*

Wasserman wordlessly handed the letter back to Lydia. After a long moment, he said, "I'm sorry."

"Thank you."

"Well, at least he left you the house."

"A grand gesture, but a false one. By the time I signed for the title, not to mention my latest annulment, any number of creditors had already filed suit to seize any of Warren's assets they could find. Who ends up owning that house is anyone's guess, but there's no shortage of claimants" Lydia observed bitterly.

"But it *could* be you, once all of the legal wrangling is done."

"In which case, I'll sell it. I'll have to leave. I'm a twice-married maiden. My humiliation is just too large for a small town like Seattle."

Wasserman understood, and he was unusually sympathetic. "Look," he said. "You're a helluva journalist, for a woman, and an expose like this should get you a job in any major city you care to work in. We're running this, which means that in addition to all the short pieces you've published, you'll have two major investigative pieces under your belt, er, so to speak."

"But I'm part of the story myself. Doesn't that make me look like something of an accident?"

"Look, I know you're good, and I'm willing to say so in writing," he offered. "Besides, you're 'L.C. Burke again.' No one outside of Seattle need ever know you were 'Mrs. Warren Bliss.'" She blinked back tears. The thought of denying her identity, like a common criminal, hurt. Wasserman leaned back in his chair and thought for a moment before speaking. "There's a new national syndicate, just put together last year. UPI—United Press International. They're headquartered in Chicago, but if you get sick of that town—it's lousy with immigrants—they'd probably send you somewhere else. I've got friends there. I'm sure I can get them to hire you," he insisted. "Besides, they've got the World's Fair in Chicago this year. 'The Columbian Exposition!' The whole world's going to Chicago. They'll need all the extra hands they can get." She was touched at his unexpected attempts to encourage her, and it dawned on her that perhaps her work really was good.

"Chicago. I'll go home and pack."

CHAPTER EIGHT

January 14th

"Why doesn't he speak?" Jonah asked the other men in the room, mostly members of the Annexation Committee. He watched the distraught man pacing back and forth in the anteroom to Thurston's office. At times he would stop pacing and turn to the others, his face would drop into the most plaintive expression, his mouth would open as if to either speak or cry out (it was hard to tell which), but no words would come. He mopped his brow and resumed pacing. In between short, shallow breaths, he made sounds that were somewhere between a moan and a whimper, but no words.

"I'm sure I don't know," said Thurston, who almost certainly did know why the man would not speak, but seemed content to let this drama play out without his guidance. "Why are you so late to work?"

"It's Saturday," Jonah answered.

"Oh, so it is." Thurston nodded absentmindedly.

Jonah turned back to consider the distressed walker. "Who is this man? He looks familiar."

"He's the Prime Minister."

"That's not the Prime Minister. Whatsisname is the—"

"Whatsisname was the PM day before yesterday. This fellow got the appointment yesterday. It seems the job disagrees with him."

"Clearly. But why is he here?"

"Evidently he wants to tell us something, but he looks as though he may need to weep a bit first."

Jonah looked around the room. "Isn't one of you a doctor?" he asked in a low voice.

"I know a thing or two," answered Serrano Bishop, although he had no real medical training. Bishop was one of the long gray beards on the Committee.

"Well?"

"Let me think a minute, will you." The man scratched his head. "Ah yes, I know just the thing. Fetch him a brandy, Jonah. If that doesn't work, slap his face once or twice."

Jonah dismissed the notion of slapping the prime minister, but rushed to get the brandy from the cabinet in Thurston's office, which elicited a stern look from a few of the men.

"I keep it for medicinal purposes," Thurston explained. Meanwhile Bishop administered the brandy, which the distraught PM at first declined, for he was devoted to the cause of temperance. Then, with a 'what the hell' shrug of his shoulders, he took the tumbler and tossed the entire contents down his throat."

"Another," gasped the diminutive, half-caste Prime Minister—a political veteran who enjoyed the perquisites of life in the Royal Party, but never imagined he would have to endure a position of actual authority. He offered his empty glass to the doctor.

"He *can* speak," said Jonah with feigned surprise, which met stern looks from the other men. If these men were good at anything, it was looking stern.

"I've seen the speech," the Prime Minister spluttered. "She's… she's… Oh, it's just terrible!"

"She's what?" Bishop prodded the poor man as he handed him another brandy, which disappeared as quickly as the last.

"When she pro… pwoh… pro*rogue*—," he searched for the right word. He was no longer mute, but his words were beginning to slur.

"When she prorogues the legislature," Thurston helped, offering the formal term for the ceremony at which the Queen concludes the legislative session for the term.

"Yes," the Prime Minister continued. "Today, after she pro… after

161

she sends them home, she's going to give the speech!"

"What speech is that?" Thurston asked gently, knowing the answer as well as Jonah, thanks to the intelligence supplied by Willie Kaae.

"My God, man. She's going to prom... promote, no..."

Not this again! thought Thurston. "*Promulgate?*"

"Yes, she's going to *pro...mul...gate* a new constitution."

Silence. It was as if all the air were suddenly sucked out of the room. All at once the men of the Annexation Committee seemed to cease breathing and looked at one another. They knew they were face to face with the pretext for revolution that Thurston had promised them, and a part of each man had wished it would never come. Many had been with Thurston five years before when they forced the Bayonet Constitution on the King, and the experience had tested their nerves rather more severely than they would have liked. They also knew that had it ended in failure they would have faced execution as traitors. Now, here they were, once more into the breach, and somehow the shock was all the worse for knowing it was coming. The whole island had been abuzz with rumors that the Queen was considering a new constitution. Petitions from her native subjects had been pouring in from every corner of the archipelago, begging her for a new charter—or rather a return to the old, pre-Bayonet version. Somehow few of the Annexation Committee members—the very face of white power in the islands—believed she would actually take that fateful step, despite their calculated efforts to provoke it.

"Prime Minister," Thurston broke the silence. "Why have you come here to tell us this news?"

"Because, well, I... I didn't know what to do! I can't just hand the government over to the Queen, can I?" The question was not rhetorical; he hoped for a plausible way out.

"Of course not," Thurston assured him. "That would make you as treasonous as she. So, you are here for our advice?"

"Yes, yes—and your support."

"When is the Queen to put forward this new constitution?"

"Today, or tonight, after the ceremony. There is to be a speech, at the palace, where she will announce the new constitution and all its particulars."

"Good. You've made a wise choice in coming here. This is what you must do." Thurston had the attention of everyone in the room. "When the Queen asks the cabinet to sign her constitution, as she certainly will, you must refuse."

"How do I refuse the Queen?" The PM aghast.

Thurston calmly laid out a plan. "Insist that you need time to read the document. Assert your leadership of the Cabinet, get them on your side—especially the Attorney General—and persuade them to declare the throne vacant. The Queen is committing treason against our constitution and government." He ended with an intentional flourish.

"Say there," interrupted Bishop, "what are you doing as prime minister, anyway? We all thought Ol' Whatsisname was doing a splendid job."

"He was one of yours." The PM had begun to regain his wits. "The Queen wanted one of hers—me, evidently. With one of her own in place at the end of the session, she thought she it would be easier to offer her new constitution."

"Clever," admitted Bishop.

"It was easy enough for them to do," admonished the PM in a fit of defensiveness. "Your side always seems to be happy to vote a government out just for the sport of watching it fall. On the last day of the session you put up no fight at all as the Liberals pushed through a vote of no-confidence to vote out the cabinet you yourselves put there just a couple of weeks ago—and you just let it happen! The next thing I know I get to be prime minister just in time to throw out the constitution I swore to uphold—yesterday! Oh, this is just terrible—and it's all your fault!" He dropped into a chair, wringing his hands.

"But no matter what the queen wants, only the legislature can propose changes or amendments to the constitution," protested one of the graybeards.

"Yes, I suppose that's why I'm so upset. This isn't a legal maneuver. Oh, this can't end well."

"You must return to your offices at the Aliiolani Hale," Thurston instructed.

The PM's eyes grew big. "I won't! They'll have me killed."

"No one is going to have you killed, good fellow," Thurston chuckled. "You're the prime minister, after all."

"I'm not going anywhere," he said, clutching the arms of his chair. It was clear to everyone that the man was not going back to the palace without dragging that chair with him.

Jonah turned his attention to the Prime Minister, who had taken to hiding his face in his handkerchief again. "Come along, Prime Minister. I'll hide you at my boarding house. I don't stay there much these days, in any case."

"Thank you, Jonah," Thurston said, dismissing one problem and turning to another. "Gentlemen, under the circumstances I don't suppose our attendance at the prorogation ceremonies would be advisable. Her Majesty can offer her congratulations to the native legislators without our help. I will meet with the Cabinet beforehand, or as many of them as I can gather. Let us meet back here immediately after the Queen's speech. Jonah!" he called as his assistant was guiding the ever more feeble Prime Minister out the door.

"Yes, sir?"

"Once you get our friend comfortably situated I want you at the Queen's speech."

And with that the meeting adjourned into a bright Honolulu Saturday morning unlike any other.

The prorogation ceremony—an almost entirely native affair—was brief and dignified, but it ended with a cliffhanger. The Queen invited the assembled to return to the Palace grounds that evening to hear her address "the request of some 8,000 Hawaiians," which left little doubt as to what the speech would be about. Eyes grew wide through the gallery and a murmur rose as the queen and her retinue filed out.

After the ceremony the press and diplomatic corps attempted to buttonhole anyone who could tell them definitively whether the Queen had decided to issue a new constitution—the press so they could file their stories in time to get them on the next packet to San Francisco, the diplomats so they could see to the safety of their nationals in the event of revolutionary violence.

"Hey, Christian!" shouted one of Thurston's reporters from the *Honolulu Advertiser*. "Is she doing what it sounds like she's doing?"

"Beats the hell out of me," Jonah lied. "Just write what you want. The boss will tell me how to fix it before it goes to print."

Meanwhile, Thurston met with several cabinet members at the office of Attorney General Arthur Peterson. These men, a combination of half-castes and noble natives of the Liberal Party and various independents, all nursed a loathing of Lorrin Thurston as a man who stood for everything they hated—most especially his anti-monarchical fanaticism and his thinly veiled schemes for *haole* rule of the Island. They also hated that they shared his desire to avoid the chaos they all knew would ensue in the event of an illegally promulgated constitution.

"Well, Thurston," began Peterson, "you've pushed her into a corner with all of your legislative shenanigans. You've made the kingdom damn near ungovernable. What the hell did you expect her to do?"

"I should think the better question is what do you expect to do? You have something of a disaster on your hands," Thurston replied coolly.

"Where is the prime minister, anyway?" asked the foreign minister. "Does he know something we don't?"

"Gentlemen, you must act," Thurston redirected the conversation. "You can't just throw out a constitution by executive fiat. Responsibility for constitutional amendments lies exclusively with the legislature—*you know that*. Violate that law and you put yourselves in a state of revolution against the government. If you support the Queen you'll be guilty of treason."

John Colburn, the Minister of the Interior, seethed. "What would you have us do, *Thurston?*" he practically spit the man's name. He hated Thurston, and hated even more finding himself in a position where he had to listen to Thurston's guidance. One of the most infuriating things about Thurston was that he always had an answer, and this afternoon was no exception. He was always ten steps ahead.

"What you must do is obvious: You must declare the Queen in violation of the constitution and the throne vacant," Thurston forged ahead, oblivious to the Cabinet's incredulous looks. "Send a request to the American Minister, Mr. Stevens, asking that he land troops from the *U.S.S. Boston*, to maintain the peace."

"Why, I wouldn't even know how to begin such a request!" protested Peterson.

Thurston had thoughtfully already drafted the request himself. "Here," and he handed it to the attorney general. "Sign the request under your authority as the chief constitutional defender in the kingdom, and the American minister could hardly refuse. I'll deliver it to Minister Stevens for you."

"I'll deliver it myself, thanks," the attorney general said, tucking it into his breast pocket, but Thurston suspected the man would not have the courage to actually go through with it. At length, Peterson looked up and said, "Thurston, your conduct is unfathomable."

The editor shrugged off Peterson's insult. "Momentous events are at hand, and it is up to us to shape them. Contact the American minister; I really don't see what choice you have."

The attorney general leveled his gaze at Thurston, and measured his words carefully. "I won't sign her new constitution, but don't expect me to overthrow the monarchy for you."

"As you wish, gentlemen, but I would assume you will be careful to keep yourselves always on the right side of the constitution." The threat was less than subtle and Peterson looked as if he were about to spring at Thurston, when there was a bang on the door. The cabinet members froze in place, looking at Thurston as if he might know who was coming; he had anticipated everything else.

"I believe you have a visitor," said Thurston, breaking the silence, if not the tension.

"Who's there?" shouted Peterson.

"Queen's Messenger," returned a voice from the other side of the door. Thurston recognized the voice as that of Willie Kaae, and he went to open the door.

"Mr. Kaae, what a pleasant surprise," said Thurston. "You've news from the Queen?" Willie was shocked to see Thurston there, but continued with his mission.

"The Queen requires the presence of her Cabinet in the Blue Room at once" Willie announced.

"I'll let myself out," Thurston said to Peterson. And with that Thurston took his leave of a group of men who found themselves in the very disconcerting position of needing Thurston's support while very much wanting to kill him.

The Queen entered the palace's Blue Room, where the Cabinet members who could be found rose to acknowledge her entrance. They were enormously relieved to see the Queen enter alone, without the guards or marshals whom they feared might be coming to force their collective hand. Their nerves had gotten the better of their imaginations as they had walked through the growing throngs of natives in front of the palace, and they were beginning to fear for their lives.

"Where is the prime minister?" asked the Queen.

"We've not been able to find him, your majesty," answered

Colburn. "But I believe we have a quorum, in any case."

"So we do," acknowledged the Queen. "Sit down, gentlemen." She rang a bell and Willie Kaae entered the room carrying a blue satin pillow in both hands, upon which was a thick document on official parchment. The Queen dismissed Willie with a nod of her head as she took the document and placed it on the table. Turning to the last page, she looked at her ministers and declared, "Gentlemen, I have here Hawaii's new constitution. You may sign it now in order that we may grant the desires of our countrymen."

A most awkward silence fell upon the chamber.

"Gentlemen?" the Queen prodded. Peterson, by default, was the first to speak.

"Your majesty, well, it is my duty to convey the sense of the Cabinet that it would be premature to sign the constitution at this time."

"'Premature,' Attorney General?"

"Yes, Your Majesty."

"Perhaps the Attorney General would tell us why?"

"Well, Your Majesty, we have not had the honor of reading the document."

"The Attorney General, albeit in his former capacity as legislator, has had a draft of the document in his possession for nearly a month. Indeed, it is to this fact that he owes his position as Attorney General today."

"I'm sorry, Your Majesty. It was my impression that it was simply a draft document, that is, a document to be discussed with the cabinet, amended, and eventually submitted to the legislature—as per constitutional law." Peterson looked at his shoes.

The Queen stared at the Attorney General, tacitly offering her displeasure at being schooled on matters of state. Another minister began to speak, but she held up her hand to silence him that she might allow the Attorney General the opportunity to squirm in discomfort a moment longer. Finally, she spoke.

"We do not believe that an institution that is run by bribery and corruption, an institution that is paralyzed by factional fighting and petty disagreements, should be allowed to deny the Hawaiian people their rights."

"I beg Your Majesty's pardon," rejoined Peterson. "But the legislature *represents* the Hawaiian people."

"The Queen represents the Hawaiian people," she responded with quiet authority. Her contempt for Peterson's position was clear, and he knew better than to argue further. "Gentlemen," she began, her voice calm and dignified, but clearly conveying her opinion of this uncooperative cabinet—a cabinet assembled expressly for their cooperative nature. "I do not seek your counsel. The plain fact is that my people have demanded this constitution, and they shall have it. Look out at the palace grounds; they are gathering now to receive this gift, and I shall give it to them."

"Your Majesty," Peterson spoke. "I beg you to reconsider. There are powerful interests arrayed against us."

"I do not serve 'interests,' I serve Hawaii."

"There could be violence," Peterson persisted. "Let us wait, perhaps only a few weeks—a small delay that will enable us to prepare for contingencies. The safety of your subjects hangs in the balance. Your Cabinet cannot support you at this moment."

There it was: The Queen could not force her Cabinet to sign the document, but neither could they prevent her from taking her case directly to the people in a few hours time. They could do no more than beg her to delay.

"Very well," the Queen relented, and the Cabinet members exhaled in relief. "You are not required to sign the constitution. It is your privilege to accompany your queen on the palace balcony this evening when I address the Hawaiian people."

"Yes, Your Majesty," said the demoralized attorney general, whose stomach twisted as he wondered what the Queen would actually say on that balcony.

* * *

As evening fell torchlight illuminated the palace grounds. Thousands
of native Hawaiians and the occasional *haole* crowded in front of
the palace awaiting the appearance of their queen. They anticipated
big news.

As Jonah weaved his way through the crowd, moving as close to
the front as he could, he hoped he would see Muanu. He wanted to
warn her. The possibility of physical danger was still several hours
away, but the certainty of its coming increased his anxiety about
her safety and he needed to convey the urgency of the situation to
her. A murmur rose through the crowd as they saw the Queen pass
by a window. Jonah looked up and glimpsed Muanu among those
in the royal retinue. His heart fell as he realized they would not be
speaking to each other that evening.

A cheer erupted from the crowd as their Queen appeared on
the balcony above them. She smiled benignly at the gathering as
her subjects continued to cheer. Surrounded as he usually was
by the enemies of this queen—the landholders, the sons of white
missionaries, the annexationists—Jonah had never witnessed the
outpouring of love that these native Hawaiians clearly felt for their
sovereign. So many in this crowd had been petitioners, asking their
queen to give their country back to them, to take power away from
the white, propertied island elites and restore it to the crown, which
they believed was their true representative. At last, facing the crowd
below her, her Cabinet (less the prime minister) standing behind
her, she slowly raised a hand to settle the crowd, and after the roar
quieted to a murmur, she began to speak.

"My dear subjects, I have listened to the thousands of voices
of my people that have come to me," she paused for effect, "and
I am prepared to grant your request!" The crowd exploded into
rapturous applause and cheering at the words. Jonah, seeing for
himself the native passion that the Annexation Committee would
have to confront, felt a rising sense of panic. And he was not the

only one. He could see the Cabinet members, eyes wide in disbelief, nervously glancing at each other as if to ask, *did she really say that?*

"The present constitution," the Queen resumed, "is full of defects. It is so faulty, in fact, that I believe a new one should be granted. I have prepared one consistent with the wishes of the dear people." Again, the crowd erupted. They were proud at this assertion of power, and they made this volubly clear. The Queen's expression, however, hardened as she held up both hands to quiet the crowd. "I expected to proclaim a new constitution today as a suitable occasion for my dear people. But with regret I must say I have met with obstacles that prevented it." Disappointment turned to disbelief as the mood of the crowd, so euphoric only moments earlier, absolutely deflated. Scattered protests erupted here and there, but most awaited further words from their queen, whose own face masked her feelings. "Continue to look toward me and I will look toward you. Keep me ever in your love," she concluded firmly. "I am obliged to postpone the granting of a constitution for a few days. I must confer with my Cabinet and after you return home you may see it received graciously. Return to your homes peaceably and quietly—you have my love, and with sorrow I dismiss you."

For a moment Jonah was as confused as the rest of the crowd, but one thing was clear—she did not go through with it. She had stood at the precipice of revolution, but stepped back, much to the disappointment of her subjects and the relief of her Cabinet, who, Jonah noticed, had begun to breathe again. He saw the Attorney General wiping his brow with a handkerchief as he filed back into the palace behind the Queen. The crowd, meanwhile, dispersed slowly, as if unsure of what they had witnessed. So many had petitioned for a new constitution, and were so sure that they would have it, only to see it held just out of reach, and several tear-stained faces communicated their collective misery. For his part, Jonah was enormously relieved. Standing amid the crowd, the potential for confrontation became real to him, and the human dimension of the conflict was sobering. Perhaps, he speculated, that is why the Queen pulled back from the edge.

"Mr. Thurston," Jonah blurted out as he burst into his boss's law offices, ignoring the other twenty or so people in the room. "She didn't do it. She spoke to an enormous crowd about the new constitution, but she didn't promulgate it. I think she's looking for a way out of this."

"Thank you, Jonah," Thurston said, and then returned his attention to the meeting Jonah had just interrupted. "As I was saying, gentlemen, the Cabinet needs some spine. They are timid men, but they want to do the right thing and we must support them in that. We should, as far as possible, make this appear to be a contest between the Queen and her Cabinet, leaving a clear field for the Annexation Committee to act. And act we must—boldly. I believe a committee of safety, consisting of thirteen members, should be appointed immediately. This committee can steer other organizations and establish control once the throne is officially declared vacant."

Bishop seconded the motion, and the graybeards began discussing a chairman, which position Thurston refused at once. The chair was then proffered to his legal associate, William Castle, who immediately accepted. The wheels of the Committee ground forward as if Thurston and all the other men in the room had not heard a single word Jonah had said. He had just stormed into the room and announced that everything they were doing was unnecessary, yet there they were, continuing on as if he had said nothing at all.

Jonah noticed a stack of petitions on the table next to Thurston, and everything became clear. The petition read, in professionally printed type, *We the undersigned declare Queen Liliuokalani to be in attempted revolution against the Constitution and Government and pledge to support the Cabinet in resisting her*. They had their pretext, whether the Queen actually promulgated the constitution or not, and they were not about to give it up simply because she had failed to play her part. Already at least one hundred signatures graced the several petitions. Jonah recognized several of them—a veritable Who's Who of the financial power and Protestant leadership in Honolulu.

Having set things in motion Thurston seemed content to let the other committee members move things along. Jonah slipped to the front of the room and leaned forward to quietly ask his employer how they had acquired so many signatures so quickly. "I sent some messengers down to the business district and the market, made some calls letting people know where the petitions would be. It wasn't difficult, Jonah," he replied in a low voice. He turned back to another committee member and started discussing strategy.

The group of thirteen had already broken into small groups dealing with various issues. Two others manned the phones in the office. Another spread a map of the city next to another map of the island, pointing to weapons caches and plotting the disposition of the Honolulu Rifles. *This must be what a war room looks like*, Jonah thought. Something about the no-nonsense efficiency, the single-minded focus on their task, was slightly unnerving. This collection of men represented the doers of society—men of rock solid achievement who never encountered an obstacle they could not overcome through intelligence, hard work, and diligence. Among these thirteen men were several lawyers, a few bankers, railroad presidents, plantation–owners, and industrialists, all of whom had spent their careers changing the face of Hawaii and growing very wealthy. Nearly all of them were current or former members of the legislature, and possessed an intimate knowledge of the dynamics of power both inside and out of Hawaiian government. As the single-mindedly successful top percentage of the population, they were hardly representative of Hawaiian society, or any society for that matter. Jonah would have felt more comfortable if there had been a poet or scholar among them.

"Jonah," Thurston had an idea. "Go fetch as many of the Cabinet members as you can. They'll be with the Attorney General, probably at his office."

Jonah jumped at the chance to escape the war room and the Committee's antiseptic preparations for violence. He was eager to bring the cabinet to witness this scene—hopeful that it might bring the deadly reality of their situation into focus.

A little more than an hour later Jonah came back with three Cabinet members sullenly in tow: the attorney general and the ministers of interior and foreign affairs. The men in the room, as busy as when Jonah left, barely acknowledged the cabinet ministers while continuing their work. Thurston gave a nod to the chairman, who then called the meeting back to order. "Mr. Thurston, you have the floor."

"Mr. Peterson," Thurston put the Attorney General on the spot, "did you enjoy the Queen's speech?"

"I'm sure your man here, Mr. Christian, told you all about it. The Queen has decided not to promulgate her new constitution."

"*For the moment*," Thurston corrected him. "The document exists, and she has not withdrawn it, but rather postponed promulgation until certain details can be worked out—presumably the arrest and execution of this committee. I assure you, however, that we are not details to be disposed of so easily."

"No one wants a confrontation with you or your Rifles," said Peterson, making it clear to Thurston and the rest that he did not recognize the fig leaf of separation between the Annexation Committee and the Honolulu Rifles.

"Gentlemen, allow me to outline the sense of this Committee for you," Thurston redirected the conversation to the three Cabinet members present. "First, we are, to a man, prepared to support you, the Cabinet, against the Queen. Second, we recognize, as should you, that the Queen is in fact already in revolt, the throne vacant, and the monarchy abrogated." The cabinet ministers turned ashen, mouths agape, as Thurston continued. "And finally, we are united in the opinion that the solution to the current crisis, for the safety of the Hawaiian people, is annexation to the United States." Thurston paused again, carefully reading the ministers' reactions before summarizing their new reality for them. "Gentlemen, the Queen has set events in motion that cannot be stopped. If you will lead, we will back you—otherwise, the Committee will act alone."

Peterson understood for the first time that events were entirely out of his hands; he had been no more than a pawn on Thurston's chessboard. He could not speak. This was preferable to the reaction of the ministers of interior and foreign relations who, evidently, could not breathe.

"Go home, gentlemen. I will contact each of you in the morning," Thurston dismissed them. "In the meantime, we'll be doing the Cabinet's work for you."

January 15th

Thurston's voice was far less pleasant to wake up to than Muanu's, Jonah thought as he rubbed the sleep out of his eyes. He sat up on the edge of the couch he'd slept on in the office and rubbed his back in an attempt to push his spine back into its natural position. He looked at the clock and wished he had not; it was 5:30 in the morning. He had been asleep not quite three hours before waking to Thurston's directive to, "Get up and fetch my horse." Once his eyes were able to focus he saw Thurston crisply dressed in a suit as if it were any other business day, rather than a revolutionary Sunday morning.

"Well?" Thurston demanded.

"Right. I'm on my way," protested Jonah, who would have been more convincing if he were not stretching his way through a tenacious yawn. "Where are you going at this hour, anyway?"

"I'm on my way to Colburn's house to see if the Cabinet has found its spine, or rather see if I can put some steel in their collective backbone for them. It is time for them to choose a side," Thurston said unequivocally. "And *you* are going out to Bill Castle's house," referring to his law partner and chairman of the Committee of Thirteen. Castle was perfectly representative of the Annexation Committee: the son of missionaries, American educated (Harvard, naturally), and now a wealthy lawyer with investments scattered around the islands. "The Committee will meet at Castle's place at 10:00 AM and determine our next steps. I'll report on what I hear from the Cabinet."

"So, theoretically, I could sleep a little more?"

"If you must, but after we meet at Castle's you'll be accompanying me to the American minister's office. He needs to be apprised of events. And I need to be apprised of how far he is willing to extend American assistance to the Committee."

"You mean you don't know? You've been in more or less constant contact with this man for the last year. He and Captain Wiltse," Jonah referred to the commander of the *U.S.S. Boston*, which was anchored in Pearl Harbor. "They're practically members of the Annexation Committee. Surely, it's no secret where they stand."

"Where they *stand* and what they'll *do* are different propositions, and our necks may have to stretch between the two interpretations."

"Suddenly I'm not very sleepy."

"It focuses the mind, does it not?"

"The prospect of hanging? Damn right. This has got to be the strangest revolution in the history of government."

"Strange?" Thurston thundered. "How is the Queen different than any other monarch, ever searching for a way to extend her power at the expense of her subjects?"

"But who's really in revolution here? Sure, the Queen is seeking to overturn the five-year-old constitution. But in defense of that constitution the Committee wants to end the monarchy entirely, which would also seem to be rather a revolutionary act." Jonah began to warm to the topic. "And then there's the Cabinet—what a mess *that* is. I mean, if they follow your advice they'll be abandoning the Queen's revolutionary course, but they'll still be in power as the executive authority of the kingdom, which will cease to *be* a kingdom through their support for you, and therefore make them revolutionaries as a result of their refusal to revolt." He had run out of breath.

"Jonah," Thurston studied his assistant thoughtfully for a moment. "I think I'm turning you into a lawyer."

"Huh?"

"Now go get my damn horse."

Once Thurston was gone Jonah briefly considered the possibility of sneaking in an extra hour of sleep, but knew it would be hopeless, and so he went to his boarding house to find a change of clothes and wash up. He decided then that he had to alert Muanu to events so that she could absent herself from Honolulu and any possible bloodshed. But first he would have to get cleaned up a bit.

He opened the door to his room and immediately heard a scream of panic. *Oh shit! I forgot all about the prime minister*, thought Jonah as he recovered from his initial shock at the man's scream. He reassured the shivering minister, huddled a corner in his drawers, that everything was okay.

"Oh, Mr. Christian, it's you. I thought the Queen's Guard had come to kill me." His teeth still chattered.

"You know, I really don't think they're going to kill you," Jonah comforted him. "The rest of the Cabinet has been in regular communication with the Queen and she hasn't threatened any of them, not even Peterson, and you know what a bastard he can be."

"Do you think it would be safe to go home?"

"Indeed, I'm sure of it."

The Prime Minister looked doubtful. "Perhaps I could stay here for just one more day?"

"Certainly, Prime Minister—you are welcome to stay as long as you like. But you'll have to excuse me, I need to wash up a bit and go see someone."

"Of course," said the Prime Minister, as he crawled back into Jonah's bed and pulled the covers over his head.

Jonah quietly slipped into Muanu's bungalow without waking her. He watched her sleeping and thought how nice it would be to join her. He sat on the bed beside her, and she opened her eyes and pulled his hand up to her face. She slid it under her head like a pillow and closed her eyes again.

"Muanu," he whispered, "we need to talk."

"We need to sleep," she moaned softly, her eyes still closed. "We'll talk later."

"I can't stay long. I have meetings to attend to," He said gently.

Muanu propped herself up on her elbow, no longer interested in sleeping. "Mr. Thurston has you in meetings on a Sunday? What is happening, Jonah?"

"It's the confrontation you knew would come. The Annexation Committee has rejected the Queen's new constitution, and the Queen as well. I'm afraid it could get violent, depending on events."

"What 'events'?"

"I don't know, exactly. But there are two armed camps, each claiming the other is in revolt and illegitimate. I think the situation has become quite dangerous. I would feel better if you would get out of Honolulu, maybe even off the Island. You have family on Kauai, don't you?" He stroked her hair.

Muanu sat up suddenly and slid her feet to the floor. "I'm not going anywhere, except to go inform the Queen and stand by her. It is not her habit to listen to me, but I think she will today."

"Believe me, Muanu, the Queen is already well aware of the situation—Thurston has been rather bold about the entire process. Look, you said yourself that this was inevitable, indeed, that the substance of it happened sixty years ago with the Great Mahele."

"Yes, Jonah, that is what I said. But my place is with the Queen."

"There are safer places."

"And more dishonorable ones, as well. I will be at the palace." She rose and, as she dressed, Jonah regretted that he might be seeing her naked body for the last time. As she had so many times, she seemed to read his thoughts. "I do not know how this will turn out, but we will not see each other again, Jonah."

"Muanu, no. This isn't fair."

"I can think of nothing that has happened here in the last several generations that is fair, Jonah. I wish you would take the advice you offered me," she said, softening her tone. She looked up at him, and put her hands around his face. "Go. Go far away and be safe," although she knew that he was no more likely to accept such advice than she had been. The young man who seemed to spend every night reading the history of this kingdom was unlikely to pass up a front row seat for its demise.

She caressed his face a final time, and she was gone. He stood alone in her room, thinking that all the kindness and comfort he had experienced here had vanished, too. Muanu was not a woman with whom one could argue, and Jonah knew that hers was not a mind to be changed. It was clear that their time together was well and truly at an end.

By the time Thurston came riding up to Castle's house at a quarter to ten Jonah was already there, propped against the hitching post with an oh-so-vital cup of coffee in his hands.

"You look like hell," offered Thurston, as he dismounted.

"Thanks. It's been a rough morning."

"Why, did you go to see that native spiritualist who works for the Queen?"

"She's not a spirit—hey, how did you know about her?" Jonah asked, nonplussed as usual with Thurston's ability to know all things. Quickly deciding he'd rather not know, he shrugged his shoulders and let it go. "How was your meeting with the Cabinet?"

"Fruitless, much as I expected. They can't commit to any specific course of action, the timid bastards. Still, they're useful in that posture. They can triangulate coordinates for us, even with their heads in the sand. That's as good as having them on our side."

"What do you mean?"

"If the cabinet were united with their Queen she would be emboldened to push things through. With the cabinet on the fence, however, she'll be afraid to move, while we will suffer no such reticence. That's as good as having the Cabinet with us." He paused for a moment and looked at Jonah. "I suppose you lost this one, too?"

"Lost what?"

"The girl. You didn't expect her to stay with you once you'd joined a revolution against her queen, did you?"

Jonah affected a casualness he didn't actually feel. "Never really thought about it one way or the other. I don't think she did either."

"Oh well, you'll find another one. God knows Penelope never seems to be very far away from you." This drew a beleaguered look from Jonah, to which Thurston responded with a cold laugh. The man was grateful for a little levity, however dark, before jumping back into the revolution. "Is everyone there?" he indicated the Castle house.

"Yes, and they've been busy. They've settled on military leadership, and now they're planning a mass meeting. It's as if you were here directing things, even when you're gone."

"That is among the reasons we will succeed, Jonah. Come, let's join them."

Once inside Jonah took notes when asked to, but mostly he just watched as the wheels of the Committee's revolution continue their inexorable forward motion. The Committee decided there would be a mass meeting the following night to publicly denounce the Queen and her constitution, and one of the members took to the phone to activate a calling tree, whereby everyone in each of their intertwined organizations would be informed and instructed. The news spread quickly and intentionally—thousands notified within hours—not so much through a grapevine as through a family tree. Years of intermarriage and interlocking land and business interests had created a coherent and powerful network that encompassed the lion's share of the financial power on the island. The previous night Jonah had been impressed with the number and passion of the native subjects massed in front of the palace as they practically begged their Queen to wrest power from the white element—the missionary party, as the Queen would say. But after observing the Committee of Thirteen he could see that their ruthless efficiency might after all be a match for native numbers and intensity. He could not help but think of Cortez's small company ruthlessly bringing down Aztec Mexico almost four hundred years earlier.

"The outstanding issue," William Castle's voice interrupted Jonah's reverie and everyone else's activity, "is what the Americans are willing to do." All eyes turned to Thurston.

"I am aware of this, gentlemen, and I am going to speak with Minister Stevens in less than an hour. Can someone lend Jonah a horse?"

As the two men approached the American mission on horseback they could see the tall, thin frame of John Stevens, American minister plenipotentiary, waiting on the veranda.

"Mr. Thurston, good afternoon."

"Your Honor, thank you for seeing us."

"I did not expect you to bring an assistant."

"I assure you he is quite trustworthy," Thurston said, which Jonah thought was as close as he had ever come to giving him a compliment. "Minister Stevens, may I introduce Jonah Christian, lately of Seattle, Washington—U.S.A."

"Ah, an American. Good for you," Stevens said in his clenched Maine accent that somehow conveyed the impression when he spoke to you that he would rather not. "Well, come in then."

Once in Stevens' office Thurston came right to the point. "I'm sure you are aware of events at the palace."

"I've heard. Perhaps you'd like to give me your version of events, Mr. Thurston?"

"The Queen is plainly in revolt against the constitution," Thurston began. "A Committee of Safety has been created to help reestablish responsible government. As a representative of that committee I request that you direct Captain Wiltse of the *U.S.S. Boston* to deploy troops to maintain safety in Honolulu."

"Who, Mr. Thurston, is currently in control of the government buildings?"

"The Queen's government, of course."

"Then there is nothing I can do." Stevens had a hell of a poker face.

"But, Your Honor, you can end the monarchy right now. This is the opportune moment."

"I would like nothing better, believe me, but it is simply not possible for me to direct Captain Wiltse's men to counter revolution in Hawaii. Mr. Wiltse has civilian informants who can determine if American lives and property are in need of his protection, but I cannot accept a request from an extra-governmental entity." He paused in thought, then said cryptically, "If your committee controlled the government, then we might speak officially."

"But you would land troops to protect American lives and property?"

"I believe that is what I said." The minister was reluctant to be explicit, but Thurston pushed.

"And you would accept a request from a provisional government, so long as it could demonstrate that it was indeed in control of the government buildings?"

"Yes, Mr. Thurston. Now, I believe I have said enough." Stevens rose to escort his visitors to the door, peremptorily concluding the interview.

As they mounted their horses to take their leave Jonah saw that barely perceptible smile that occupied the corner of Thurston's mouth whenever the man had one more ace up his sleeve. In this case, given Stevens' discouraging reception, Jonah thought the smirk might be more show than substance.

"You look awfully optimistic for a man who was just abandoned by one of your most important supporters—the only one who controls a battleship, actually."

"Abandoned? Not at all," said Thurston, cocksure as ever.

"I'm not sure we were in the same meeting. The one I attended featured the American minister telling you that you were on your own, best of luck, write if you get work, best wishes."

"Jonah, you might as well be a deaf man. I could have sworn I heard the man promise to deploy troops."

"Yes, in the extremely unlikely event that the government turns itself over to the Committee of Annexation, and you accomplish A, B, and C, and the stars align just so."

"Anything else?"

"Yes, actually. Even if he were to call in troops, he wouldn't use them in support of the Committee. He said he'd only use American soldiers to safeguard American lives and property, presumably in that order."

"Jonah, you can read the notes but you can't hear the music," Thurston offered an uncharacteristic metaphor. "As long as American troops are on the streets of Honolulu it won't matter why they're there—everyone in the Queen's party will assume they are here in our support, even if they were explicitly told otherwise."

Jonah contemplated this, and the musical metaphor, as they rode their horses down the residential streets toward downtown Honolulu. He was beginning to suspect that Thurston, fully committed and past the point of no return, was simply choosing to see every event in its most positive light, until Thurston interrupted his musings.

"Have you noticed those fellows behind us?" Thurston asked.

Jonah turned and looked. About fifty feet back were two men in suits on horseback. They both halted when Jonah turned to look at them.

"They're Marshal Wilson's men."

"You mean Charlie Wilson?" Charlie Wilson was fanatically devoted to the Queen, and in charge of the police and constabulary on the islands. "Why haven't they arrested us?"

"They've been following us since we left Minister Stevens' house. If they assume we are in alliance with the Americans then they will believe they have much to fear by arresting us. Let us preserve the illusion as long as possible." *Perhaps Thurston's pipe dream may pan out after all*, Jonah thought.

Back at the Aliiolani Hale the rump cabinet, led by the attorney general, sat glumly around the prime minister's office. It was not just that they thought *someone* ought to use the space, but rather that they actually hoped the prime minister, whom they very much wanted to see, would make an appearance. He did not. The chief of police, whom they were hoping would not appear, did, naturally. Appearing in the doorway of the absent prime minister's office like a dark cloud, the chief found a way to make a bad day worse merely by showing up. Marshal Charles Wilson was a mixed blood Hawaiian who devoted his life to Hawaiian sovereignty and his queen, in that order. It wasn't that the cabinet officers did not love and respect the man—they did—but his devotion to the cause of Hawaii for the Hawaiians would be most inconvenient at this particular moment. They were searching for some way to avert a crisis, and this man would almost certainly make it all worse. In defense of Hawaiian sovereignty Wilson could be both daring and something of a hothead. He had, in fact, led a failed revolt against the queen's predecessor, King Kalakauah, in retaliation for signing the Bayonet constitution. As strange as it might seem to the unacculturated observer that a man who had led an armed, albeit unsuccessful, rebellion would be appointed marshal of the kingdom, it seemed perfectly logical to the queen. His object in taking up arms against the king had been to replace him with his sister, Liliuokalani, whom he correctly believed would seek to replace the hated Bayonet Constitution. The queen may also have taken some comfort that, despite his predilection for rebellion, he was a demonstrably ineffectual revolutionary.

"Gentlemen," a surprisingly subdued Marshal Wilson greeted the cabinet officers. "I have come from the Queen." The men in the room sat up in anticipation of what he might say. They feared more surprises from the palace. "Her majesty has decided to withdraw her constitution, permanently." The cabinet officers slumped back into their chairs, clearly unimpressed with the marshal's revelation. This was not the reaction Wilson had expected. "She is planning to declare this publicly, from the palace veranda," he elaborated. Still no reaction. "In front of everyone!" Nothing. The gloomy cabinet might have sat in depressed silence until the marshal took his leave, except that Peterson was afraid he might go off and do something particularly stupid.

"It doesn't matter, Marshal."

"Doesn't matter? Nonsense! Of course it matters," Wilson roared. "Did you not hear me? I said that the Queen, despite the overwhelming desire of her subjects, has decided to withdraw her constitution in order to maintain peace and safety in the kingdom, and she is planning to declare it—"

"—publicly!" Peterson finished the sentence for him. "I heard you, we all heard you. But she can say or do anything she likes and it won't change a damn thing," insisted an increasingly frustrated and impatient attorney general.

"Why not, may I ask?"

"Because, as one of those extremely well armed American marines in our harbor might say, we're fucked."

"Mr. Peterson!"

"Marshal, please. Thurston and the rest of them don't care what she *does*; they only care what she *did*. When she even hinted at that damn constitution, she handed them the excuse they've been waiting for—agitating for. At this point they're deaf to anything else she might say."

"Then have them arrested," protested the marshal. "Give me the order and I'll execute it immediately."

"No, don't!" the foreign minister cried, lurching forward in his chair.

"I won't do any such thing," the attorney general assured him. "I'm no more interested in a visit from the marines than you are."

"What on earth are you talking about?," interrupted Wilson. "As marshal of the kingdom I have every right to arrest someone who is in revolt against her majesty's government." He did not bother to add that he knew this from painful experience.

"As attorney general—the chief law enforcement officer in the kingdom—I will sanction no such arrest."

"And why not?" Wilson demanded.

"Because we, the cabinet," Peterson paused and looked at his colleagues around the room, "what's left of it, anyway, are fairly certain that arresting the Annexation Club or its leadership will result in the landing of armed troops from the *U.S.S. Boston*."

"So the American minister shall decide who governs Hawaii? I won't stand for it!"

"You don't have a choice. In fact, *you* don't matter. I, my dear Marshal, do not matter. Lorrin Thurston matters. Minister Stevens matters. Battleships with great big guns and hundreds of armed marines matter."

The marshal thought for a moment. The other men could tell he was calculating numbers in his head. "Commander Wiltse doesn't have more than 175 troops on board the *Boston*. I have 500 men at my disposal."

"Fool!" the foreign minister was on his feet now. "Fighting American troops is suicide!"

"And even if your superior numbers helped you against superior American arms, it is highly unlikely that Captain Wiltse would allow you to fire upon his troops without, in turn, turning the fire power of that damn battleship upon us. In which case it wouldn't matter how many men you had at your disposal, because they'd all be blasted to pieces." He shrugged disconsolately.

Wilson's shoulders slumped. He knew they were right, if indeed those were the intentions of the American minister, but no one could be truly certain of that.

"Ahem," Colburn, the Minister of the Interior, nudged his way into the discussion. "There is also the not insignificant matter of the Honolulu Rifles."

"Nonsense," countered Wilson. "The Rifles were disbanded nearly three years ago."

"Allegedly disbanded," said Peterson. "They simply moved their membership to the fraternal order of the Knights of Pythias."

"But that's just an American social organization, like a Masonic lodge."

"Except that this one is really a rebel army." Now Peterson was really worried. "They continue to import weapons and ammunition, drill, take target practice, just like any other army. I'm sure they'd be handy in a fight."

"Incredible!" thundered Wilson. "I know those men."

"Not as well as you thought you did, evidently."

Marshal Wilson sat down, one more officer of the government slouching helplessly in a chair, wondering what on earth he was going to do. He could not help but recognize that the cabinet, by refusing to assist the Queen, were in effect supporting the revolution against her without risking their necks. Suddenly he couldn't bear to be in the same room with them. "Damn cowards," he muttered as he rose from his chair and left the room.

Back at the Castle residence the members of the Committee of Thirteen were showing signs of fatigue, but they continued to push forward with their work. "Mr. Thurston," the chairman interrupted their discussion. "It is late, and I think we should wrap things up for the day, but I would like to hear a summary from you beforehand."

"Of course." Thurston paused a moment to arrange his thoughts. "As things stand, the cabinet will not interfere—they are entirely incapacitated by events. That being the case, we can proceed with a public meeting tomorrow night and declare the abrogation of the monarchy without fear of arrest. Most importantly, we can count on the support of American forces as we move forward."

"Minister Stevens has made this commitment to you?" the chairman sought reassurance.

"Yes, this afternoon when I met with him," Thurston exaggerated.

At the back of the room Jonah held his head in his hands and fervently wished his boss had not just told this enormous lie to the Committee. Sure, he was giving them the confidence to move forward, but who knew if they were marching confidently up the steps to the gallows? Not for the first time, Jonah wondered what he had gotten himself into. This depressing thought was interrupted by Bishop's voice.

"I move that a formal request for the landing of an American naval force be sent to Minister Stevens and Captain Wiltse."

"Seconded," said somebody.

"So moved," said the chairman with a bang of his gavel.

"I move that Lorrin Thurston be deputed to organize an agenda for the public meeting."

"Seconded."

"So moved." And with the bang of the gavel Jonah could hear the night's sleep he longed for disappearing into the night.

January 16th

On Monday morning the Marshal was once again in the Aliiolani Hale trying to convince the attorney general and other assorted government officers that they should damn the risks of U.S. intervention and just arrest the conspirators. His audience was unmoved.

"We've been over this," protested the attorney general. "The foreign minister called you a fool, you called us cowards… It was only yesterday, don't you remember?"

The Marshal persisted. "Do you know what they're doing right now? I'll tell you what they're doing—they're meeting at Thurston's office. Right down the street from the police station. I could arrest the lot of them and have them peacefully and quietly in jail before anyone in the American legation heard about it. No disturbance of the peace. No reason to deploy troops."

"A pleasant scenario, Marshal, but a fanciful one," said the singularly unimpressed attorney general. He imagined this was the same hot-headed impetuousness had led the Marshal to urge the Queen on to her ill-fated promulgation in the first place. "I'm sure these very careful and skillful men have prepared for such eventualities as your blundering into their inner sanctum and I'm certain they won't go down without a fight—a fight which, in turn, will flood the streets of Honolulu with American troops."

Willie Kaae was at the door again, but this time he was expected. He carried a box from the printer. Peterson opened it and produced a handbill from a stack of 500 of them. "Here, Marshal, have a look at this."

"What is it?"

"A last-ditch effort to preserve Hawaiian sovereignty. It is a proclamation by us, the cabinet, 'By Authority of Her Majesty the Queen,' as you'll read there on the top line. It makes official the promise you brought to us yesterday. You'll notice that it reads, 'the position taken by Her Majesty in regard to the promulgation of a new Constitution was under the stress of her native subjects.' Which means we are doing our best to take the blame from the Queen, and put it on people like you. No offense."

"None taken."

"At the suggestion of the foreign representatives, we also added a promise from the Queen that, quote, 'any changes desired in the fundamental law of the land will be sought only by methods provided in the Constitution itself,' unquote, which is really just a promise to obey the oath she swore when she became Queen." Peterson turned a glare on Wilson. "And if she *had* kept that promise instead of listening to people like *you* we wouldn't be distributing this silly damn humiliating document right now."

"You've met with the foreign ministers?" the marshal asked, unmoved by the attorney general's rising tone and pointed comments.

"Yes," the foreign minister answered, while the attorney general got his emotions back in check. "French, British, Portuguese, and Japanese. They're no more interested in seeing American troops in our streets than you are."

"You didn't invite the American minister—the only one who really matters?"

"Oh, we invited Mr. Stevens," the attorney general assured him. "He just didn't answer our summons. I imagine he would have found it awkward, seeing that no one, save perhaps Lorrin Thurston, would be happier to see the Queen deposed."

"But their advice was good," the foreign minister returned to the subject. "Even the American element of the population doesn't really want a change in government. They just want the Queen to play by the rules, so to speak. No more of this 'Hawaii for the Hawaiians' nonsense."

Wilson did not appreciate hearing the cause to which he had devoted his life casually labeled 'nonsense,' but as he saw the beloved kingdom slipping inexorably away he was not inclined to argue. "I hope you men are right," he acquiesced sadly. "I still think I should arrest the lot of them, but if you won't allow it, so be it. I will, however, confront Thurston."

"Please do," said Peterson. "May you have better luck with him than we have. But be back here by one o'clock this afternoon. The most important part of that document we're distributing is a call to a public meeting to ratify this. We're going to make this as legitimate as possible and show that damn Annexation Club that the popular will of this island is against them and for the Queen. You need to have your men in position to keep public order. The last thing we need is a public embarrassment."

"Too late," said Marshal Wilson, as he closed the door behind him.

CHAPTER NINE

As Marshal Wilson approached Thurston's office above the Bishop Bank on the corner of Kaahumanu and Merchant streets, the proximity of the center of the rebellion to his own police headquarters—barely half a block—irked him. The cheek! *These men really had no respect for the duly constituted authorities at all*, he thought. He climbed the stairs and let himself in the front door. They had not even posted guards, he noticed. Arresting these men would be as simple as a whorehouse raid. Before he closed the door behind him he looked up and down the street and noted the positions of the four detectives he had posted to keep an eye on the conspirators' comings and goings. It occurred to him, painfully, that he could simply defy the attorney general's order and use the men he had right there at his disposal to arrest the revolutionaries. But the prospect of going back to jail haunted him, along with the possibility that the whole thing could blow up in his face and then he, of all people, would bear the blame for the queen's ouster. *That*, he concluded, would be too ironic to bear.

Once in the building he followed the sound of voices down the hall to Thurston's conference room. From the casual banter he heard through the door he surmised that the meeting was just breaking up. He knocked on the door and Thurston's assistant, that damned American kid, answered it.

"Marshal?" Jonah said, with some surprise.

"I would like a word with Mr. Thurston," Wilson said evenly. Thurston was already weaving his way to the door when he caught sight of the blue of Wilson's uniform. All conversation in the room ceased as each man anxiously wondered if things were about to get complicated. They had taken the precaution of deputing replacement Committee members should they be arrested, but they all sincerely hoped that their next steps would not be toward the police station under armed escort. Thurston, outwardly cool, opened the door wide and invited Wilson in with a casual sweep of his arm. But as Wilson entered the room Thurston peered into the hallway and saw exactly what he hoped he would see—nothing and no one. Wilson had come alone. The attorney general had obviously not given him authority to make an arrest. Thurston was not holding all the cards, but he sensed that the Marshal was not allowed to play his own hand.

"May we speak privately, Lorrin?"

"Gentleman," Thurston addressed the room. "Would you leave us alone for a moment?" The Committee members breathed a sigh of relief as they filed out of the room. They could see as well as Thurston that Wilson had come to plead, not demand.

"Look at this," Wilson said plaintively as he handed Thurston the 'By Authority' proclamation from the Cabinet. "It includes everything you've demanded, including the Queen's promise to live by the letter of the constitution. I beg you, Lorrin, stop. Cease this rebellious plotting before innocent people are hurt. Allow our country to remain a kingdom."

Thurston regarded the man whom he had known for so many years. "Charlie, I am sorry for your countrymen, but what guarantee have we that the queen will abide by the constitution? It is like living on a volcano. There is no telling when it will explode."

"Suppose we replace the Queen with another royal? Princess Kaiulani will soon be of age. You yourself could sit on a board of regents who could reign during her minority."

"You would sacrifice your queen to save the monarchy?"

"I would sacrifice my life for it."

Thurston paused for a moment. Sensing that Wilson posed no

193

real danger to the revolution, Thurston had lost interest in the conversation. "I have great respect for the Princess, Charlie," he said gently, "but things have gone too far. We are going to abrogate the monarchy entirely, and nothing can be done to stop us."

Wilson could not believe the temerity of this man. He wanted to kill him that moment. His jaw clenched, and he began to shake. He turned silently to leave.

"Is everything alright?," said Jonah, sticking his head in the room at the sound of the slamming door.

"Have a look at this," said Thurston, handing him the Cabinet's proclamation.

"Hmm," Jonah quickly scanned the document. "It appears she's answered your every complaint. I guess we can all call it a day and go home," knowing full well the committee's actions would not be halted.

Thurston ignored the comment. "Be at this public meeting at the Palace Square." Jonah nodded his assent. "And collect any other documents they distribute. I want you there until the end. Then hurry over to the armory where we'll be meeting; I want to know what has happened at Palace Square. And you might get to see the end of our presentation. It would be a shame to miss it."

Actually, Jonah wanted very much to miss it. For a fleeting moment he thought that his mission to observe the public meeting at Palace Square would allow him to slink back to his room at the boarding house and get some sleep, of which he had had very little. It occurred to him that Thurston had slept even less, if at all, in the last forty-eight hours, but showed no sign of fatigue. *How does he do it?*, Jonah thought to himself.

Even before the meeting started Jonah could feel the shift in attitude and purpose among the Queen's supporters. Their high-spirited aggressiveness from two nights earlier was utterly gone. As the speakers took the podium, each offering more instruction than exultation, it was clear that the Hawaiian nationalist movement had lost all momentum. There were perhaps half as many people in attendance than two nights ago, when the raucous crowd heaped adoration upon their defiant queen as she challenged the island's power structure with a new constitution. Now, amid an atmosphere of palpable fear and tension, the cabinet members and some nationalist legislators cautioned the crowd to avoid any behavior that might provoke a response from the revolutionaries. Several speakers openly acknowledged that the revolutionaries were on the alert for a pretext to overthrow the queen and Hawaiians must be careful not to provide them with one. *Talk about closing the gate after the horse has already bolted*, thought Jonah. Finally, the Queen's proclamation was read in both English and Hawaiian, and voted on by acclamation of the crowd, in the forlorn hope that a unanimous vote might forestall the movement they had unintentionally unleashed.

The crowd was nearly still. Having witnessed both rallies, Jonah could not help but think of the irony. Hundreds of nationalists had petitioned the Queen for a new constitution, yet they were now grateful for her renunciation of that same document. What a difference forty-eight hours makes!

Looking at his watch, he calculated that the Annexation Committee's mass meeting was probably still going strong. He was hurrying through the thinning crowd to make his way to the armory, when he heard a voice call out behind him. "Christian!" It was a shamefaced Marshal Wilson. Jonah turned toward him, but said nothing. "Tell Thurston what you saw here. Tell him everything can be as it was."

Thurston doesn't want it as it was, he thought to say, but did not. "I'll tell him," was all he said, and rushed on.

The atmosphere at the armory could not have been more different than the dirge-like meeting at Palace Square; it was positively electric. The venue itself, which doubled as a skating rink, was surrounded by sloping hills that created a natural amphitheater. A happily animated crowd packed the place. Jonah tried to estimate the size of the gathering, and came up with not less than 1,500, and maybe as many as 3,000. Advertisements for the meeting had ordered all businesses closed, "Per Order of the Committee of Safety." The order conveyed the impression that the Committee had already become the de facto government of the islands. Whole families had come, and their collective number lent a carnival atmosphere to the evening's orgy of antimonarchical denunciations. One speaker after another made dramatically effective, if self-serving, comparisons between their cause and that of the revolutionary patriots who won American independence from the British tyrant, George III. The crowd loved it.

Jonah tried to squeeze through the crowd to catch a word with Thurston, who stood to one side of the dais keeping an eye on events while he waited for Jonah's return. Thurston had already addressed the crowd, outlining their legal case against the Queen in popular phrases. With the constitutional argument made, subsequent speakers were free to address the issues more flamboyantly as they played on the enthusiasms of the crowd. One speaker identified himself as a fourth-generation American patriot, which might have seemed odd for someone who was fighting for the Hawaiian constitution, but, again, the crowd loved it.

As Jonah inched forward through the sea of well-dressed whites, he glimpsed the entire Tubbs family in the crowd facing the center of the platform. *Oh God*, he thought. He really didn't have the energy to deal with any of them—especially their blowhard of a father. The Tubbs family, like the rest of the crowd, paid attention to the speaker at the lectern, but Penelope, who seemed to have a sixth sense for Jonah's presence, looked directly at him. She could not wave or permit herself any gesture that might alert her father to his presence, so she winked. The gesture caught Jonah like a slap on the face. *Did that girl just wink at me?* he asked himself. The sweet little sixteen-year-old who could barely speak in his presence a few months ago now tossed him decidedly lascivious gestures right under her father's nose. He reminded himself that he did not have time to think about such things and quickly turned his attention to swimming through the crowd.

"What do you have for me?" Thurston demanded, once Jonah had finally reached the platform.

"Nothing new," Jonah panted. "The meeting was a just a recapitulation of the cabinet's 'By the Authority' proclamation. They're running scared."

Thurston was visibly pleased. "Excellent. Stay close. All that's left is a few minutes of citizen testimony, then a voice vote on the resolutions."

"I know. I was the fellow typing this out for you last night while the rest of Hawaii was sleeping, remember?"

Thurston ignored the comment, as usual. "Then the committee will adjourn to the meeting room in the Armory and determine our next move. Meet us there."

Jonah stood back and enjoyed the political circus. He had never seen anything quite like it. The crowd was having great fun; they seemed not to truly comprehend that they were supporting these men in revolution. The speakers stated and restated their right to assemble and express their opinions, to the crowd's vociferous approval, but their resolutions were clearly, if not expressly, treasonous. After a cacophonous "vote" on the Committee's resolutions that the Queen had revolted against her own government—this despite the fact that she had rescinded her constitution—the crowd mirthfully roared their resolve. They wandered off in cheerful clumps, as if they were ending a picnic, not launching a rebellion.

At the post-rally meeting, however, the difference between the crowd and the Committee was stark. The Committee members, although pleased with the meeting, were all business. Recognizing the momentum of events, rather than revel in their success they calculated how they could use it. William Castle, the Committee chairman, and some of the others were concerned that events might actually be moving too fast.

"If the government falls today we are not prepared to assume

197

control, and troops would be premature. We need more time," Castle pointed out.

"Agreed," said Thurston. "Jonah, type a request, will you? Standard diplomatic language. Request a forty-eight hour delay on 'assistance.' Do not explicitly refer to troops."

Jonah sat behind a desk and got busy typing. He was glad for something to do while the Committee started mapping out adjustments in their strategy and planning for contingencies.

"My point is this," Castle felt the need to clarify. "We crossed the Rubicon out there tonight. However careful our language, our intent was plain, and I don't see any way to turn back."

"Nor should we!" Thurston reminded everyone.

"Agreed, but if events get ahead of us we shall lose control of them. We can't save these islands from despotism if we are all dangling from ropes. Let us slow things down enough to allow us to form a successor government."

"Excellent idea," Thurston agreed, satisfied that no one was getting cold feet. "Jonah, have you finished that note?"

"Yes, here it is," he said as he peeled the dispatch out of the typing machine. Thurston looked it over and signed it, then handed it to Castle, who did the same.

"Take it to Minister Stevens, Jonah." He was reluctant to leave the center of the revolution. "But I thought you were going to have one of Mr. Castle's messengers deliver it?" he asked.

"No. Stevens likes you, as much as he likes anyone. You're an American, which helps. Take my carriage—and be quick about it," Thurston dispatched him.

Jonah had no sooner exited the building into the cool air of early evening than he felt a feminine arm slipped through his. He started. "Penelope? This is not a good time."

"What a splendid show you all put on this afternoon," she observed, ignoring his comment. "It was like going to the fair!"

"I really can't talk right now, Penelope. I have a rather urgent task to perform."

"How exciting! I'll go with you."

"Why didn't you go home with your family? I saw the entire Tubbs clan here, front and center for the revolution."

"Revolution? You're being a little dramatic, I think," she teased. "Take me with you. I won't get in your way, I promise."

"All right," he gave up, knowing that resistance was futile, "but you must stay put when we get to the American legation." He helped her into the carriage and grabbed the reins.

"We're going to Minister Stevens' house? Oh, good. He was over for dinner just last week."

"You must know everyone on these islands." By way of answering she snuggled up next to him and rested her head on his shoulder. "Penelope, do we need to repeat that conversation about proper behavior between sixteen-year-old girls and grown men?"

"I'm *seventeen* now—I had a birthday. And you're only twenty-three. We're practically the same age."

"You seem to have it all figured out. Have you set a date for our marriage yet?"

"I thought I should wait until you asked me, just for the sake of propriety."

He sought to redirect the conversation to the topic on his mind. "What has your father had to say about all this political tension the last few days?"

"I like the other subject better."

"Come on, there's always plenty of political talk around the Tubbs table. Your father wouldn't miss a chance to tell you girls what to think."

"My sisters are girls. *I'm* a woman," she declared, sitting up straight. He had to admit to himself, if not to her, that she had a point.

"Okay, you're a woman. Now, what has your father said about recent events?"

"Oh, all right, boring man! Father thinks it's all great fun. He slaps the table and makes jolly noises about how Mr. Thurston and the rest of them are really going to teach the Queen and her party a lesson, and from now on she'll behave herself, and so on."

"'From now on'?" Jonah repeated.

"Yes. That's what this is all about, isn't it? Making the Queen respect the Constitution, or the missionary party, or whatever they all call themselves." Penelope began to be bored by the political complexities.

"The Reform Party."

"As you say. I can't keep them all straight."

So he had read the crowd correctly. Even well-connected, informed observers like Reverend Tubbs perceived events as more of a reprimand than a rebellion. Few if any outside the Annexation Committee seemed to understand the moment. Believing that this was just another political shenanigan in an archipelago where they had become commonplace—where the Reform Party had *made* them commonplace—Hawaiians, white and native, did not truly perceive that their kingdom was on the verge of passing into history. He shook his head at what he had gotten himself into by taking a job with the increasingly duplicitous Lorrin Thurston. He thought about Muanu and Kalani and their loyalty to a way of life, as much as to a queen, and Jonah wanted to press Thurston on this, challenge his assumptions, make him explain why this was necessary. Suddenly he felt more like a thief than a political player. He felt a new urgency in getting the request to delay troop deployment to Minister Stevens. This had to stop, at least long enough to allow people to learn what was really happening.

Arriving at the American legation Jonah jumped out of the carriage and tossed the reins to Penelope. "Here, hold steady. I'll be right back."

An assistant opened the door. "Hey, Mr. Christian! You people have been busy, haven't you?"

"I have an urgent message for Minister Stevens."

"I'm afraid he's not here."

"What? Where is he?" This was not good news.

"I'm not at liberty to say."

"The message is from Lorrin Thurston and the Committee of Safety. It's urgent that I deliver it immediately."

The young man was about to go into his standard bureaucratic stonewalling when Jonah said, "Look, don't do this to me. Things are about to blow up around here. Let's make sure that we don't get too many people killed because you couldn't help me get a message to your boss." The assistant stared at him and said nothing. "It's a big responsibility," Jonah continued. "I'm glad you're the one making this stupid mistake instead of me."

"Oh, all right. He's on the *Boston*, over at Pearl Har—"

"I know where it is. Thanks," he said, as he was already on his way back to the carriage.

Jumping in, he took the reins from Penelope and snapped the horse into a brisk canter. For a moment he thought of unhitching the carriage entirely and galloping bareback to the *Boston*, but decided better of it. He would have better luck getting aboard ship if he did not look like a mad man when he approached it.

Penelope sat quiet, too startled by Jonah's violent approach to say anything, but eventually she collected herself. "What on earth is going on? Slow down, this isn't a racing buggy. You'll kill us—or someone else," she cried as he raced through the lighted streets of Honolulu, scattering pedestrians.

"We've got to get to Pearl Harbor."

"All right, but let's try not to kill too many people along the way." She wrapped her arms around him and sat unnecessarily close, and enjoyed the ride immensely for a moment until Jonah pulled back on the reins, bringing them to an abrupt halt.

"Now what are you doing?" she asked, not bothering to loosen her grasp.

"I just saw Minister Stevens heading the other way."

"So?"

"So... I'm not sure, actually. If he's already been to the *Boston*..." he hesitated, his mind racing.

"Could you finish a thought, Jonah? It's very difficult to follow you."

Jonah decided to continue on toward the landing at Nuuanu Street to see if he could catch a skiff out to the *Boston*. He knew at this point it might be more effective to take the note directly to Captain Wiltse, who would make the final decision on any actual deployment of troops. But when they approached the pier he saw two things that should not have surprised him at all, but did. One was the approach of several companies of U.S. troops and their artillery. The other was Lorrin Thurston, watching the procession of troops from a salient above Nuuanu Street. *How did he get here so quickly?* Jonah wondered.

He pulled the horses to a stop about twenty feet from Thurston and told Penelope to wait; he wanted her well out of earshot.

The two men spent a few silent moments watching the American troops, blue-jacketed sailors and olive drab Marines in immaculate, pressed uniforms, carrying heavy backpacks and long rifles as they marched in tight, disciplined formation. It was an impressive sight, and not a welcome one for anyone who might consider opposing them.

"You must have come directly here after you sent me to the American legation," Jonah asked at last. Thurston's duplicity surprised him and he wondered how much his boss would admit to.

"Yes. I wanted to see Captain Wiltse. Minister Stevens just happened to be here with Wiltse when I arrived."

"And you asked the American minister *not* to deploy troops?"

"Of course," he said, looking askance at Jonah, who silently watched the troops marching by for a long moment, then turned back to Thurston rather skeptically. "Stevens heard my plea for more time patiently enough," Thurston continued, "then he told me he didn't give a damn who runs the Hawaiian government at present, his duty is to protect American—"

"'Lives and property,' I know." Jonah shook his head.

"And therefore he was deploying troops on his own authority, against my wishes."

"That's what he said?"

"Yes, Jonah, that's what he said."

The two men regarded each other for a long moment. He didn't know whether to believe Thurston, or whether it mattered, but he found his boss's version of events unconvincing. Stevens and Wiltse both knew Thurston well, they understood that he was at the apex of the movement against the Queen, and they were known to sympathize with his cause. Why would they not give him a day's delay if he requested it? *If* he requested it. There was no immediate disorder in Honolulu—just an unprecedented level of tension. Thurston, for his part, was steely-eyed and inscrutable, but typically unperturbed by his underling's nearly insubordinate lack of trust.

"If we can dispense with this issue," Thurston resumed, "there is much work to do and very little time to do it. Can we do that, Jonah?" He turned toward his assistant, eyeing him carefully.

Again, Jonah looked at the troops marching by. "It appears as if events have gotten away from you, just as Castle feared."

"Hmm? Oh, yes, I suppose so," Thurston responded, though it was clear his thoughts had already progressed to his next move. He came back to Jonah's point with some irritation. "Jonah, we never controlled events, regardless of what Castle and the others might think. The best we could ever hope for is an opportunity in which we could find some advantage. Events occur—perhaps by our hand, perhaps not—and human reactions to them cannot be perfectly anticipated. We plan for a variety of scenarios and improvise the most coherent response we can muster. Now we have just such an event before us: Troops have landed, and now we take advantage of the opportunity, if indeed it turns out to be one. We will proceed as if we are in de jure alliance with the Americans. If the Queen and cabinet believe this they will either accept our victory as a fait accompli or call our bluff and resist."

"In which case...?"

"In which case we will probably lose and the Americans will

broker a truce based on the status quo ante, and we might live to fight another day."

"And if the Americans support the Queen's authority?"

"Then ultimately we all hang." Thurston took the measure of his young assistant, half-expecting Jonah to walk away.

For Jonah, he knew this was the moment he must choose to stay or go. Feeling like Faust, he made his bargain. "Well then," Jonah took a moment to swallow. "You were saying something about work to do?" he said, with a renewed interest in finding a solution that would not stretch his neck. But before Thurston could respond he was interrupted by the furious words of a royalist legislator shouting at him from across the street. "Damn you, Thurston!" An old Hawaiian waved his arm toward the American troops, now well down the road from them, and shouted, "This is all your doing, you bastard," then stormed off toward the palace.

As Jonah climbed back into the carriage, Penelope pointed back at Thurston. He had instructed his assistant to gather the annexationists at Castle's home, where they would renew their efforts to form a provisional government by the morning, when Hawaiians would awake to find themselves surrounded by foreign troops. Now he was having trouble pulling himself up onto his horse. Jonah resisted the impulse to run over to help him, waiting to see how bad it was. A moment later, with obvious difficulty, Thurston swung his leg over the beast and settled into the saddle, demonstrably drained by the effort.

"Is he quite all right?" Penelope asked with genuine concern.

"I don't know, but he'd better be. He's the one driving this tiger. The rest of us are just hanging onto the tail, hoping it doesn't bite our heads off."

"Tiger? What are you talking about? Are you delirious, my love? You know, you don't look much better than he does."

"We seem to have sworn off sleep the last few days."

"Well, I'm putting you to bed. Drive straight to your boarding house this minute."

"Can't. Gotta make some calls from the office first."

"Thurston's office? Good, that's just a couple blocks from your boarding house."

Once back at Thurston's office, Jonah stood in front of his desk for a moment, not quite remembering why he had come there. Penelope gently guided him over to the settee, gave him a slight push with her index fingers, which felled him like a redwood.

"Where is your list?" she asked the now-prone assistant revolutionary. "I'll make the calls for you."

"It's over there," Jonah said, making no attempt to resist.

His fatigue distracted him from tasks at hand, and he found himself staring as she removed her waistcoat to get down to work, which revealed feminine contours hitherto unseen. The fitted blouse she wore reminded Jonah of her earlier assertion that she was a woman, not a girl. *How had I not noticed this before?* he asked himself, as he curled into a better position to stare at her.

Standing before him, list in hand, she asked, "What shall I tell these men?"

"Committee of Thirteen meeting. Eleven o'clock. Castle's house." Jonah paused. "They're making the skirts tighter these days, aren't they?"

"You noticed? Will wonders never cease." Turning to Thurston's list she exclaimed, "Oh, I know all these men. Some of Father's closest friends. Why isn't Father part of your committee?"

"Because he's better at talking than keeping his mouth shut. Besides, he doesn't actually know how to do anything."

She nodded her understanding without offense; there are some points that simply cannot be argued. She began making the calls for Jonah, briefly explaining to each of them "Yes, this is Penelope Tubbs, so nice to speak with you. I'm assisting Lorrin Thurston…" Jonah opened his eyes to observe the girl while she stood there, posture perfect, making his calls for him. After the last of the twelve calls he could not help but ask the question that had been running through his mind the last several minutes.

205

"Penelope," he stifled a yawn, "what accounts for this change in you?"

"Change?" she asked with feigned dismay. She squeezed onto the couch where he lay, and bent over him.

"Perhaps 'total transformation' would be a better term. You've changed from timid church mouse to, well, uh…"

"*Woman?*"

"Yes, that's the word I was looking for."

She paused a moment, looking directly into his eyes, then touched his lips with hers, tentatively at first, then deeply. After a few moments she sat up. Jonah was no longer interested in the answer to his question, but she wanted to tell him. "Tragedy can affect people in different ways."

"What tragedy?"

"You were my tragedy, Jonah—you and your native tryst. You can't imagine what it was like in the Tubbs household the night my father and the rest of them found you in that hut on the beach road. I sat in the hallway that night and listened to the Steeles and my parents talk about it until morning. Oh, how it shocked them— shocked us all!"

At the memory of the horrified faces of the minister's and their wives, Jonah was suddenly deeply ashamed. "But why did you ever speak to me again?"

"Oh, I was absolutely broken-hearted, but at the same time I found it all a little unbelievable," she said with a small laugh that said she could still remember the pain, even if she had learned to deal with it.

"I wasn't terribly happy about it, myself. I ended up living in some pretty uncomfortable circumstances after that," Jonah pointed out.

Penelope went on. "I couldn't stand it. What I heard that night as they discussed and argued, prayed and cried, on and on, just didn't make sense to me. But nothing about the world made sense to me, really. I was this protected little child, safe in my father's house, utterly ignorant of anything beyond my house or my church."

"And?"

"And so I went to see Muanu."

"You... you couldn't have. When?" He began to consider the chronology of his own relationship with Muanu.

"The day after the Steeles left for China. Reverend Steele told me that I should forgive you, that we shouldn't judge you harshly, and all the New Testament generosity that my father generally ignores. It was Reverend Steele who suggested that I should seek Muanu out and invite her back to our church. He told me that in helping her, I could heal my broken heart."

"I'm guessing that it didn't work out quite the way the Reverend envisioned."

She rolled her eyes at that. "No, not quite. Muanu is so... *different* from anyone I've known."

"To say the least."

"I went to her house. When she opened her door and saw me standing there, she looked at me as though I were a lost little girl." She smoothed Jonah's hair absently. "There I was—the daughter of the man who fired her and called her a whore in public—and she just took my hand and led me in with the most sympathetic expression on her face. I followed her in, sat down beside her, and cried for most of the afternoon. She said nothing. She just stroked my hair and somehow made me feel comfortable and, well, safe. Yes, that's the word, *safe*."

"And you went back?"

"Yes, she invited me—no, *instructed* me to come back, like a doctor. At the end of my first visit I apologized for my behavior and she just pressed her finger to my lips, like this," she said, gently applying her index finger to Jonah's mouth. "She told me to rest, to love myself, and to come back the next day and we would talk. I think that was the part that got me—she told me to love myself."

"Isn't that in the New Testament, too?"

"*Da Jesus book!*" she corrected him, and they both laughed. "I went back many times, as often as I could, in fact. But she is busy, working for the Queen, and seeing people in the evening. She made it very clear that I should not come at night." She paused to look at Jonah, and he wondered if she knew that he was the reason Muanu was not available to her after dark. "But still," she continued, "she often made it seem like nighttime when I was there in the afternoon. She would draw the shades and light a single candle and place it between us. She would ask me to talk about whatever was on my mind, then guide me with questions, like 'what do you feel when you say that?' or 'what color is your dream?' and a thousand other questions no one else in the world would ask."

"And this changed you?"

"This changed everything. She led me to believe that I was good, not bad. She helped me understand I am not a bad daughter, I am a separate person. I was not evil because of the...," she paused, choosing her words carefully, "well, the sensations I felt, and how I responded. In that safe place I had the courage to try... things."

"'Things'?"

"Yes, Jonah. New experiences." She brought her face close to his and whispered, "Didn't she help you discover good things? Isn't that what you were *really* doing that night out on the beach road?"

Suddenly uncomfortable, he sat up. "I believe we were going to go to my boarding house and put me to bed."

"Why, Mr. Christian," she smiled and drew closer, "a good girl like me can't be seen accompanying a man into a boarding house."

"There's a back door. Very discreet."

"I'll come in for just a minute—just to see the place," Penelope said tentatively.

Jonah bit his tongue and rose from the couch, which until a moment ago had seemed like the most comfortable spot in the entire world. They left the carriage behind the office and walked silently to the boarding house. Once there he prudently led her up the rear stairs, his hand on her elbow. Outside his door, Jonah spied lamplight coming into the dim hallway. "Oh, God," he moaned. "The Prime Minister!"

"What about him? Father says he's disappeared."

"He's in my room."

"Really?"

"I'm afraid so."

There was nothing for it, so he knocked on the door, and announced himself. He wanted to avoid the shock and drama of his last encounter with the timid man, when he nearly scared him into a heart attack. The Prime Minister cracked the door barely an inch and peered through the crack to verify that it was indeed Jonah. He had opened the door and was standing there in his drawers before he noticed Penelope. He gasped and reached for a blanket to cover himself. "You didn't tell me you had company!"

"Hello, Prime Minister," said Penelope.

"Hello, Penelope," mumbled the P.M. and retreated into the room, as Jonah and Penelope closed the door behind them.

"Friend of the family?" Jonah asked.

"More like an acquaintance."

Jonah called into the darkened room, where they could hear him rummaging for his clothing; Penelope looked discreetly at her boot tops. "Prime Minister, you've been here for three days. Don't you think it's time you went home?"

"Do you think it's safe?" the parliamentarian asked as he stumbled into his trousers.

"Yes, I do," Jonah said, trying to hide his exasperation with the man. "Your government has collapsed for all practical purposes. I assure you that you're quite irrelevant now."

"Are you sure?" the man sounded uncommonly hopeful for a politician who had just been told he no longer mattered.

"Yes, completely inconsequential. No one has any reason to even think about you, except, perhaps, for their curiosity about your whereabouts the last few days." A thought suddenly occurred to Jonah. "If you tell them you've been in my room, believe me, they'll think the worst" he warned.

"What do you mean?" he asked as he emerged from the back of the room, pulling on his shoes.

"I have an inconvenient reputation in some circles. Think of a good story."

"Oh, thank you, Jonah," he stammered. "I appreciate your help. Really, I do. I'll go now." He pulled on his suit coat and something occurred to him. "Say, what are you doing here, Penelope? A bachelor's room is no place for a young girl, especially not a preacher's daughter."

"Prime minister," she lowered her voice conspiratorially, "I won't mention that this was your hiding place the last three days if you try to forget that you saw me here."

"Oh, very well," he stuttered as he collected the last of his things and approached the door under Jonah's guidance.

"Good night, Prime Minister," Jonah said, closing the door on the man. "Well," he said, turning to Penelope. "Welcome to chez Christian."

"Why thank you. It's lovely, if a bit claustrophobic."

"I prefer to think of it as 'cozy'."

"Mind if I take off my coat and make myself a little more comfortable?"

"You can take off anything you like," he said as he dimmed the lamp. Penelope removed her coat, then pulled a pin from her hair and let it fall around her shoulders. Jonah put his arms around her, pulled her hair away from her neck and kissed it gently.

"I don't want to wrinkle my blouse," she whispered. Jonah accepted the prompt and began unbuttoning the garment, then the belt, then the skirt. Dressed in only a thin cotton petticoat and bodice, she sat on the bed and pulled him toward her. He made no resistance. She had never been in a man's bed before, though she had spent many nights fantasizing about being in this bed with this man, and she reveled in the feeling of his body against hers as they kissed. His mouth explored her as he made his way from her lips, to her neck, to her breasts, still barely contained within the bodice. And as he laid his head upon them, he felt a calm come over him. She felt him grow still, and then he began to snore.

Her disappointment was leavened with relief; these were not precisely the circumstances in which she wanted to give herself to him, after all. With Jonah asleep she could enjoy this intimate, if cacophonous, closeness without worrying that it would go any further—for the moment. So she lay there, with the exhausted young American asleep on her breast, lightly running her fingers through his hair so as not to wake him.

"Jonah," Penelope whispered in his ear. "It's after ten o'clock. I believe you have a meeting."

"Hmm?" Jonah grunted. He raised his head, squinted his eyes at Penelope, not quite understanding where he was. Then he looked up and down the woman next to him and placed his head back where it was, tugged the top of the bodice down to reveal her left breast, and gently placed his mouth upon it.

"None of that," Penelope said, pulling his face up to hers. She kissed him and said, "You have to go."

"Oh my God, you're right." He had been asleep for over an hour and was grateful for it. The sense of exhaustion was gone, and the sight of Penelope in a state of undress was nothing less than inspirational. He was not sure, however, what had actually occurred in his bed. "Penelope, did we, uh...?"

"Don't worry, I'm still pure and chaste—in body if not in mind."

"So I was the perfect gentleman."

"No, but you were pleasant company."

Jonah let Penelope off a safe distance from her house, lest her father see who was bringing her home. He had no idea how she would explain why she was returning home so late, but with the city in upheaval there was no shortage of plausible excuses. He had no time to think about it as he turned toward Thurston's house. He actually found himself worrying about whether the man was still alive. It was with a mixture of trepidation and curiosity that Jonah approached Thurston's door, hefting the bulky typing machine in one arm. A Chinese servant answered the door, and welcomed Jonah inside.

"Where is Mr. Thurston?"

The servant answered by way of leading Jonah upstairs to Thurston's bedroom, where he lay across his bed, gray and perspiring. He had a few pages of scribbled notes on the bed around him, but it was clear that the effort of forming them into a coherent document had gotten the better of him.

"Jonah," Thurston greeted his assistant, trying his best to sound hearty.

"You still look like hell," Jonah tried to joke, "Only more so."

So the exhausted man wouldn't have to move, Jonah set the typing machine up on a table in Thurston's right there and threaded a piece of paper into it.

"Ready?" Thurston asked.

"Yes, if you think you can get through some dictation without collapsing."

"Shut up and type the following." Thurston began dictating a three-page diatribe outlining monarchical misrule in the island realm and the heroic efforts of the business class to save the native tyrants from themselves. Somewhere along the way he declared the monarchy abrogated, then concluded, "*All officers under the existing Government are hereby requested to continue to exercise their functions and perform the duties of their respective offices, with the exceptions of the following named persons: Queen Lilioukalani; Charles B. Wilson, Marshal; Samuel Parker, Minister of Foreign Affairs; W. H. Cornwell, Minister of Finance; John F. Colburn, Minister of the Interior; and Arthur P. Peterson, Attorney General—who are hereby removed from office.*

"You think you can depose the Queen and her entire cabinet

with a proclamation?"

"Only if it is well written. If you were a better lawyer you'd understand that."

"I'm not a lawyer at all."

"Don't quibble. Besides, if we work quickly, the American Navy will appear to have done the job for us—and in a very real way, they have. Resume typing. *'All Hawaiian Laws and Constitutional principles not inconsistent herewith shall continue in force until further order of the Executive and Advisory Councils. Signed...'* and so on."

Jonah typed the last few words, then handed the document to Thurston, who grabbed a pen and signed it.

"Now take this to Castle's house," Thurston directed. "By now the Committee should have finished an outline for the provisional government and staffed it with our members. We have but to choose a president."

"Well, that shouldn't be too difficult."

Thurston read his mind. "Not me," Thurston said with finality. Jonah was stunned. He had imagined that was Thurston's ultimate goal from the start.

"Why not you?"

"Because I would be unacceptable. I am the object of the undying hatred of half the population of Hawaii, and the fear of the other half. We need someone who is loved and respected. Tell them to give the presidency to Sanford Dole."

"Dole of the Supreme Court?" Jonah asked, thinking of the gray-bearded eminence of Hawaiian jurisprudence. Jonah had often seen the man in the company of the Queen and other Royalists; although a member in good standing of the business class, Dole had never been a member of the Annexation Committee, and in fact did not favor annexation to the United States.

"Yes, Dole is perfect. If all goes well he'll be the first governor of the state of Hawaii. The Americans will love him. Hell, even though he was born and raised here he went to Harvard and fought for the

213

Union in the American Civil War. Now go to Castle's house. Get things moving. This proclamation needs to be read and posted in public—soon!"

Jonah did as he was told. Arriving at Castle's house twenty minutes later, he found the Committee members—now "Executive and Advisory Council" of the not-yet proclaimed provisional government—busy as usual.

"Where's Thurston?" demanded Castle.

"Sick. He sent this. He's already signed it, and he'd like you gentlemen to do the same."

They gathered around Jonah to get a look at the proclamation. Each of them had the same raised eyebrows upon reading the words "are hereby removed from office" after the Queen and cabinet's names were listed. Still, one by one, each man signed the document slowly and carefully.

"All right," Castle called them back to work. "Everything is set except for the naming of a president."

"Thurston, obviously," said one of them, followed by general sounds of assent from the others.

"Good. A vote of the Advisory Council will make it official."

"He won't do it," interrupted Jonah.

"What?" said an incredulous Castle.

"He won't accept the presidency. He wants the Committee to offer it to Sanford Dole." Jonah could see the reticence of the men in the room. Thurston had been running this operation since before any of them were really aware what they had gotten into, and they were reluctant to hand the reins over to anyone else. Jonah, on the other hand, had been steadily losing faith in the man and thought putting an honest man into the leadership might not be a bad change of pace. Accordingly, he sought to preempt their arguments. "Look, Thurston's sick," said Jonah. "Very sick. I don't know if he's going to make it, and it won't do you any good to appoint a dead man president. That probably wouldn't impress the Americans."

214

The men in the room continued to regard Jonah skeptically. "He's a regular Nathaniel Bacon, for crying out loud." Now they were truly puzzled.

"Nathaniel Bacon?" Castle asked as their collective skepticism turned to confusion.

"Yes, you know—*Bacon's Rebellion?*" He could see from their expressions that this was not helping. "Virginia, 1676," he continued. "Nathaniel Bacon leads a rebellion against the colonial authorities in Virginia. On the threshold of victory Bacon gets dysentery—shits himself to death. The cause was lost. Hard to bounce back from that sort of thing."

Stunned silence.

"Dole would be a workable choice," conceded Castle, nodding and scratching his chin.

January 17th

Thurston sat up in his bed and pursed his lips as he considered the tale Jonah had just told him from the chair opposite the bed.

"Nathaniel Bacon?" he asked. "Really?"

"Hey, it worked," responded Jonah, a little defensively. "Those men were hell-bent on making you president, and they were understandably disinclined to accept advice from your lowly assistant on the matter."

"You might have just sent one or two of them over here to consult with me themselves."

"You have a point," Jonah conceded. "In fact, I figured you might have been dead by then, and that would truly have carried my argument."

"Sorry I couldn't accommodate you."

"That's all right. Anyway, you should be flattered. I didn't think those men were that fond of you."

"They're not, but people are accustomed to me being in charge."

He paused a moment. "And Dole?"

"He accepted the presidency, but it took some doing. Castle prevailed upon him to accept the job as a means to securing public safety, but Dole looked as if we had given him a fatal disease by the time we left."

Thurston leafed through the papers spread around him on the bed. His fever had passed in the night and he awoke feeling like a new man. Fourteen hours sleep had worked wonders on his health, and he was anxious to catch up on what he had missed while sleeping. Jonah, for his part, found being with his boss less uncomfortable now that he was certain he would not be the first president of Hawaii. Given what Jonah had learned of Thurston's methods and reflexive duplicity, that thought was simply more than he could stomach.

Upon waking and seeing Jonah sitting in his chair reading one of several newspapers, the first thing Thurston did was ask him for a status report. Jonah gave him the full story, starting with Dole's reluctant acceptance and concluded with the successful proclamation of the new government at two o'clock that afternoon at the Alliiolani Hale government building.

"The Queen's army is still in the barracks?" Thurston asked.

"We haven't seen a single uniformed Hawaiian on the streets. Not even a policeman."

"And we have occupied the government offices at the Alliiolani Hale?"

"At three o'clock this afternoon. The Honolulu Rifles are in place around the building."

"There was no resistance?"

"The Americans encamped on King Street, about sixty yards from the Alliiolani Hale. If the Committee were assaulted on their way to the government building the Americans were in perfect position to do something about it. Whether they would have or not is anyone's guess, but their position sure as hell suggested they might."

"So," Thurston concluded, hardly believing his own words, "the thing is done."

"So it seems," Jonah shrugged. "Now what?"

"Why, we go to Washington, of course."

The following day the remaining government buildings not already under the control of the provisional government were occupied, one by one, as native forces, sensing the futility of holding on, simply slipped away. First the police station, then the army barracks, and ultimately even the Queen's palace were occupied by the troops of the provisional government, formerly the Honolulu Rifles. The Queen retired to her house at Washington Place and raised her standard there, but the provisional government quickly made her take it down.

Two days later, on the nineteenth of January, provisional president Dole sent a deputation consisting of Castle and Thurston, accompanied by Jonah, to Washington DC to seek a formal treaty of union with the United States. Jonah was excited to make the trip, but the timing was difficult. The provisional government was barely two days old, and Jonah had spent the entire time working at a pace nearly as frantic as the three sleepless days of the revolution itself. There was simply no time to sort things out with Penelope. Ah, Penelope. His thoughts on that topic were utterly confused. She was too young, for one thing, but on the other hand she had somehow managed to become maddeningly alluring while he was not paying attention. This girl who had always managed to inconveniently pop up when he had no interest in seeing her seemed to have completely disappeared now that he could think of little else *but* her. Once again he was boarding a ship without the woman he loved, or thought he loved—it was hard to be sure.

Early that morning he followed Thurston and Castle up the gangway and took a last look at this enchanting paradise from the deck of the steamer *Claudine*. "Another beautiful January morning in Honolulu," he said aloud.

"Hmph," grunted Thurston in passive agreement. "What's the weather like in Washington this time of year?"

Jonah tried unsuccessfully to suppress a laugh.

CHAPTER TEN

"Holy Christ, it's *freezing* out there!" Castle said, clutching his collar to his throat as he stumbled toward the fireplace. Thurston and Jonah ignored the outburst, barely looking up from their work, as this was typical of the commissioner's entrances of late. William Castle was born and raised in Honolulu and had lived there his entire life, with the exception of four years at Harvard College, where he must have spent his winters huddled under the covers. In any case, the Washington winter, enduring into this unhappy February, did not agree with the man, but then neither did most of the other recent developments. They had a mess on their hands and the capital frigidity only seemed to make it worse.

Their foray into world history had begun so well. In a matter of three days they had led a small group of powerful and determined men in a successful revolution in which they depended on nothing but their wits, a bit of luck, and the U.S. Navy. That done, they set off immediately to offer up their newly non-monarchical archipelago to the United States, with which they had always been so close. The moment they arrived in San Francisco—three o'clock in the morning—Thurston woke the Port Authority and violated U.S. Customs law by going immediately ashore to break the story of the Hawaiian Revolution to every newspaper he could find. He wanted to make sure America heard his version of events before the royalists could share theirs. Thurston and Castle then held a news conference that afternoon—the first of many—and by the time the evening editions came out all the leading newspapers were in favor of annexing the Hawaiian Islands to the United States. (A notable exception was the San Francisco *Newsletter*, which denounced the whole business as "a fraud and a humbug.") Among those attending the press conference was a U.S. State Department representative who immediately telegraphed the contents of Thurston's January 18th proclamation of provisional government to Secretary of State John Foster in Washington. After a good day's work on the Barbary Coast the annexationists boarded the Northern Railway's Overland Express for Washington, DC, holding press conferences at every stop to tell the American reading public their story of Hawaiian redemption and deliverance from savage barbarism.

On their arrival in the capital the Hawaiian Commissioners— now universally known as the "P.G.'s," after Thurston's declaration of provisional government—were met by representatives of the Administration of President Benjamin Harrison. Harrison, alas, was already a lame duck, having been defeated by Grover Cleveland the previous November. The election had been a chance for the American electorate to reverse their decision to fire Cleveland four years earlier, which they had evidently decided was a mistake. The rejected Harrison administration would be in power only until March 4th, and the P.G.s hoped to use that power to expand the United States by approximately the square footage of the Hawaiian Islands, on their terms. They were about to learn a lesson in Washington politics.

Secretary of State John Foster took one look at the treaty Thurston and Castle had so lovingly crafted during their Pacific passage, and immediately set about eviscerating it. Where Thurston wrote persuasively on the advantages of admitting Hawaii as a state rather than a territory, Foster unceremoniously crossed out the entire passage. Thurston's inevitable protest was met with simple Washington hardball. Foster was blunt: "Would you prefer passage of your treaty, or would you rather watch it die in committee while senators argue whether Hawaii should be a state or a territory? Let us pass a simple treaty and Congress will work out the details later."

"But suppose they get it wrong?" protested Castle.

"Welcome to Washington, gentlemen. Getting it wrong is part of the process around here."

And so it went. Point by point, Foster hacked this bit and that from the draft treaty. Proposed improvements to the Pear River? Jettisoned. The laying of a Pacific telegraph cable? Excised. Preservation of Hawaiian labor contracts? Out. Sugar subsidy? Gone. Foster showed superior judgment and absolutely no mercy as he applied the meat cleaver to the Commissioners' beloved document. The commissioners received an object lesson in the difference between a wish list and a treaty. A week later Foster presented the commission with a draft treaty elegantly reduced to its essence. It recommended that the United States annex the Hawaiian Islands, in no particular form, as quickly as possible; the details, his slim document seemed to promise, would take care of themselves. Not seeing any alternative, the Commissioners shrugged their shoulders and accepted it. For once, they had a taste of how successive Hawaiian monarchs must have felt having their plans refashioned by American diplomats.

"I had hoped we might meet with President Harrison at some point in this process," Thurston said to Foster, as he handed Castle the pen he had just used to sign the draft.

"I'm afraid that isn't possible," Foster offered briskly without elaborating. Thurston, Castle, and Jonah all looked at the Secretary of State, awaiting an explanation, which was not forthcoming. As they walked out into the corridor, however, they spied the harried President walking toward them as he looked over some papers. Thurston was not about to let the opportunity pass.

"If you gentlemen don't mind, I'll take a moment to introduce myself to the President," Thurston said, not waiting for an answer. Foster shrugged and followed; an informal exchange of greetings in the corridor would be harmless as long as it went unnoticed by the press.

Before the Commissioners reached President Harrison an impeccably tailored, gray-suited burst of energy appeared seemingly from nowhere, leaning slightly forward, chin thrust upward, as he addressed the President in a high-pitched voice that was audible from anywhere in the White House.

"Mr. President! Mr. President! The spoilsmen are at it again! These Cleveland people are descending on federal jobs like bees to honey—*bees to honey*! The Civil Service Commission *must* be able to assert its authority with the President-elect's staff, not to mention the army of hangers-on who have descended upon us from Buffalo looking for a piece of the federal spoils!" By the time the man had made it through his first "bees to honey" declaration he had redirected the President down another corridor and the two men disappeared before Thurston had a chance to get a word with him.

"Who was that?" Castle asked.

"We used to call him Teddy," Thurston said, to everyone's surprise.

"You know him?"

"We were classmates at Columbia Law. Last I heard he was Police Commissioner of New York. Energetic fellow."

"Theodore Roosevelt," said Foster wearily. The mention of the man's name tired him. "He's one of the more ardent reformers around here—works on the Civil Service Commission. He wants to cure all the ills of mankind before he goes to bed each evening. His energy can be rather taxing, as you have seen."

"Indeed," agreed Thurston. "Why does the President tolerate him?"

"Theodore does his job—to say the least. Any number of people have pressed the President to fire him, but he stands by Roosevelt. He must find his earnestness refreshing, or at least unique. It doesn't matter, I suppose. In a few weeks he'll be out like the rest of us. Theodore will go back to New York and we'll never hear about him again." Foster turned back to the treaty. "Gentlemen, we have a good document here. The President will send it on to the Senate tomorrow for their advice and consent, and I think we should be able to wrap this thing up shortly. Hawaii will join the United States of America."

Castle and Thurston thanked Foster and pumped his hand effusively while Jonah assumed the suitable invisibility of a Washington aide. He had been observing how the young political assistants behaved themselves—no acerbic comments or questioning their masters' instructions—and thought about taking on their protective coloring. Jonah was certain Thurston must be a little envious of the Washington power brokers who employed properly servile minions; these protégés would never dream of questioning their mentors the way Jonah did. So he shouldn't have been entirely surprised that when they returned to their rooms at the Wormly Hotel, Thurston fired him.

"Excuse me?" the young man stammered.

"You heard me. You no longer work for the Law Offices of Thurston and Castle."

Jonah decided he would like to lick his wounds in private, perhaps in the hotel bar. "Well, I suppose that's that. I'd love to stay and chat, but I think I'll go look for a job."

"No need. You are now officially the Secretary of the Annexation Commission."

A little confused at this turn of events, Jonah asked, "What do you mean?"

"Well, for my purposes it means that the Hawaiian Provisional Government will pay your salary, which just doubled, rather than my modest little corporation."

"And who do I work for, exactly?

"You work for me, the leader of the Annexation Commission, of course."

"So, essentially nothing has changed."

"Essentially, no."

"All right, then. I guess I'll get right to work; I want to make a good first-impression in my new job."

So with a new title, which Thurston directed him to put on calling cards, and a new salary, which he would never have time to spend, Jonah shifted his focus from negotiation to lobbying. Now that they had their treaty, Thurston and Castle needed to propagandize the American public within an inch of its life. Facilitating that effort fell to the Commission's new secretary, who quickly came to feel like a combination of a scribbling monk and P.T. Barnum, writing and talking, booking his performers anywhere he could. He typed and submitted endless variations on Thurston's articles promoting Hawaiian annexation, and scheduled appointments for the Commissioners with the editorial boards of every newspaper and magazine within a three-day train ride.

Jonah's was writing back and forth with every editorial board in American, but his favorite correspondent was the unexpectedly lovely Penelope. No matter how busy, hectic, and generally impossible his schedule, Jonah found fifteen or twenty minutes to write to her every day. He started writing to her on the boat to San Francisco as an outlet for his anxiety at being so suddenly separated from her just as he had discovered his affection for her—profound affection. The image of her, nearly undressed, lying next to him in his little room in Honolulu both haunted and sustained him as boats and trains carried him further away from her. He sent his first dispatches to her as soon as they made port in San Francisco, and he was careful to include the address of the Wormly Hotel in Washington, should she be inclined, as he desperately hoped, to write back to him. This she must have done the moment his first letter arrived from San Francisco, because barely one week after the Commission encamped at the Wormly, the first of a steady stream of letters arrived, penned in Penelope's feminine hand. Each day the long-distance lovers would write a response to a letter written three weeks earlier—an epistolary echo of passion twenty-one days old. The cumulative subtext of these exchanges made it perfectly clear to both of them that if they ever again found themselves alone in a boarding house bedroom, things would end differently than the last time.

There was so much more to this young girl than Jonah had ever imagined, revealed to him now through the written word in which she conveyed thoughts and images that had rarely passed her lips, at least not in conversation with him. He imagined he could see Muanu's hand in this, and he was certain that she had coaxed Penelope into this self-discovery. She wrote of her faith, her feelings, her future, and how all three had changed. A very large part of this transformation was the diminution of her father in her worldview, from religious eminence to something life-size, human, and given to the same frailties as other men. What Jonah's banishment had begun, Muanu's tutelage had continued.

It was her talk of the future that Jonah found enticing. There lay in it the tantalizing notion of freedom—freedom from age-old expectations, from strictures and prohibitions, and from the land of her birth. She made him believe that they could go anywhere, and they shared their dreams of doing so in each other's company. As they idly scribbled these fantasies of seeing the world together, each assumed that they would see these exotic places as man and wife. Distracted by his own role in world affairs, this realization dawned on Jonah slowly, gently, and he admitted to himself that he liked the idea. He was, perhaps for the first time, finally falling in love. But he also wondered if the reason it was so easy to do so was because the object of his affection was so far away.

Now more than a month into their campaign for annexation, Jonah walked down to the lobby of the Wormly Hotel to drop off his latest epistle to Penelope and pick up the day's papers, the most pleasurable part of his job. Always an inveterate newspaper reader, Jonah never dreamed he would have a job that required him to read the papers—all of them. And this particular day the *New York Post* carried an article he could not afford to miss. It announced that Princess Ka'iulani, whom Lorrin Thurston had sent off to finishing school in England four years earlier, was coming to America to plead for her kingdom. "Hmph," he said to himself as he folded the paper and put it under his arm. "*This* should be fun."

225

* * *

Theo Davies slammed the *Manchester Guardian* on the table before him, paced back and forth in his den and just generally fumed. The former British consul to Hawaii, and currently guardian of the kingdom's Princess Ka'iulani, was incensed at the American reports reprinted in the paper he had come to regard as "that damn rag." These articles depicted native Hawaiians as savages, practically cannibals, who should welcome their rescue from barbarity by the white leaders of the Hawaiian sugar interest. And the press did not even get that right—Davies himself was a member of the "sugar interest" that was being blamed for the revolution. He had made a fortune in the stuff as owner of one of Hawaii's "Big Five" sugar companies, Theo H. Davies & Co. Davies knew Thurston and the rest of them, and saw them as part of the political class— meddlesome know-it-all lawyers who would do the world a favor if they would just concentrate on making money instead of making laws. Thurston's businesses were not about sugar, they were all about politics: journalism and law. *Sugar interests indeed!*

Thurston, however, had also given the man his greatest treasure. Four years earlier Hawaii's then-Secretary of the Interior, Thurston, had insisted that the thirteen-year-old Princess Ka'iulani finish her education abroad. Thurston had liked the girl and detested the King—her uncle Kalakaua—so he believed the best chance for her to be educated sensibly would be if the job were done far away from the royal family. Her father, a Scottish businessman named Archie Cleghorn, agreed completely. Cleghorn was a member of the Hawaiian House of Nobles, and a royalist to the core, but he had no respect for the profligate King. It was the last issue upon which Thurston and Cleghorn would agree.

Contemplating this history, Davies walked up the colossal staircase in his Southport mansion to the Princess's rooms. When he knocked on her door the lady-in-waiting, Mrs. Whatoff, answered. She welcomed him into the sitting room where he found the Princess studying French verbs; it seemed she was always studying something. When she had arrived as a girl of thirteen she was free-spirited, mischievous, and full of fun—given to pillow fights with the Davies children and playing whirlwind games of tag through the Victorian house, leaving a swath of destruction in her path attesting to all the pleasure the children were having. In the intervening four years her King and most of the relatives between her and the throne had died, leaving her a heartbeat away from ruling Hawaii, and she was determined not to make a hash of it. She became grimly studious, mastering the academic canon and learning four languages, so it was no surprise to her guardian that he found her bent over her books. The image of this poised and accomplished girl reinforced in his mind that the decision he had made was the correct one.

"Princess, you must go to America," he announced abruptly.

Princess Ka'iulani looked at her guardian as if he had just ordered her to jump out the window. Only a couple weeks earlier he had come to her rooms with a cable in his hands that read: QUEEN DEPOSED STOP MONARCHY ABROGATED STOP BREAK NEWS TO PRINCESS STOP. And now this? She was starting to wish the man would just stay downstairs.

"It is the only way," Davies continued. "The average American has a completely absurd understanding of Hawaii and the average Hawaiian. They have been led to believe that you're an entirely backward race of heathen savages, beating on drums and boiling missionaries in cauldrons." It was a common image in American newspapers. "I'm sure," Davies went on, "that Thurston and his Commission are doing nothing to disabuse the public of this barbarian claptrap. But you," he paused a moment, looking at the elegant girl, stylishly dressed, surrounded by books, "your appearance would put the lie to all such nonsense."

Ka'iulani closed her book slowly. "Please don't ask me to do this," she said in a voice barely above a whisper. She was horrified at the idea of jumping into this political fray.

"Your kingdom is slipping away as we speak, Princess. Thurston has dethroned your Queen, and now he is in Washington trying to give the country to the United States. Let us not look back on a lost kingdom and wonder if you could have done something to stop it."

She looked down on the table of French verbs that had just become painfully irrelevant, then around the room in which she felt so safe, and finally nodded her head in silent assent.

"Good girl! Now, look at this. I've written a statement for you to release to the papers. It should get you some advance attention in America. If all goes well the new President—I can't remember his name—"

"Grover Cleveland," the Princess offered.

"Yes, Cleveland, thank you. If we create enough of a public stir, he won't be able to ignore you. You may have a chance to plead Hawaii's case directly to the one person who can do something about it."

The Princess nodded again. Then, curious as to what her first public utterance to the world would be, asked, "What does the statement say?"

Jonah looked up at Thurston and Castle, who stood before him, their arms crossed.

"Well, read it," Thurston directed. "Let's hear what the former heir to the throne has to say."

Jonah read Princess Ka'iulani's words, reprinted in the *New York Post*. "'Four years ago, at the request of Mr. Thurston, then a Hawaiian Cabinet Minister, I,' the Princess, that is, 'was sent away to England to be educated privately and fitted to the position which by the constitution of Hawaii I was to inherit. For all these years, I have patiently and in exile striven to fit myself for my return this year to my native country. I am now told that Mr. Thurston will be in Washington asking you to take away my flag and my throne. No one tells me even this officially. Have I done anything wrong that this wrong should be done to me and my people? I am coming to

Washington to plead for my throne, my nation and my flag. Will not the great American people hear me?'"

"Oh my, she sounds angry," said Castle. "Did she write that, do you think?"

"Probably Davies wrote it for her. She's smart—very smart—but I think Davies will be guiding her through this," answered Thurston. "Like most Brits, he loves monarchy, and like everyone, he loves the Princess."

"So," said Castle "Davies and Ka'iulani have jumped into the fray."

"Yes, I think it's trouble for everyone," said Thurston. "And there's always a way to work trouble to our advantage. It's just a matter of waiting to see how it plays out." He shifted gears. "Jonah, have there been any statements about this from the royals?" Thurston was referring to the Queen's representatives, who had arrived in Washington three days behind the annexationists. The Queen's representatives, including Prince David, second in line to the throne behind the Princess, had all been in Washington trying to get an appointment with someone, anyone, in the outgoing Harrison Administration. So far they had been unable to get through the door.

"No, I haven't heard anything about the Princess from the royals."

"Then they'll be as surprised by this as we are. If they knew she was coming they would be doing as much advance publicity for her as they could. No," Thurston concluded, "this is Davies' operation, and it's not an authorized one."

"You don't think the Princess wants to displace the Queen?" asked Jonah.

"No. No, I don't. But it wouldn't hurt us a bit if it appeared that way."

"An apparent palace fight?" Castle picked up on Thurston's line of reasoning. "I'm sure a subtle comment or two, dropped here and there, should help create the image of a royal dissension—a scramble for power between the deposed Queen and her heirs. I don't suppose the Americans would be eager to hand power back to a bunch of grasping royals."

"Yes," agreed Thurston, "but we must be careful not to say anything that can be attributed to us in print. In fact, volunteer nothing. We're sure to be asked about the Princess anywhere we go, especially those damned parties." Thurston, never a social soul, had quickly learned to detest Washington's favored work environment—the cocktail party.

"When is our next one?" Thurston inquired.

"Tonight," Jonah answered. "And seeing as how the Princess was kind enough to mention you twice, Mr. Thurston, I think it would be nearly impossible for you to avoid the topic."

"When will she arrive in New York?"

"Tomorrow afternoon." Jonah had already checked the schedule with the shipping line. "She is going to make a statement to the press from the pier."

The Commissioners stared at Jonah.

"I know," he responded to the unspoken command. "I'll be there." And with that he grabbed his bag and headed out of the Wormly Hotel into the Washington snow. He trudged to Union Station, where he bought himself a train ticket to New York City.

Gotham was every bit as cold as Washington, but the food was better. The best part about being a P.G., Jonah decided as he finished his steak, baked potato, and perfectly spiced vegetable preserves, was the Provisional Government expense account. One more hot cup of coffee and he bundled up in coat, gloves, scarf, and hat, and descended to the pier to join the lesser mortals—journalists—who awaited the Princess in the frigid New York air. They huddled together on the dock next to the massive, ship, the *Teutonic*.

At last Princess Ka'iulani appeared with an entourage of five—rather modest by royal standards—and Jonah was stunned by what he saw. The young woman was beautiful—stunning, in fact. This tall, slender mix of Scottish and Hawaiian blood was familiar, yet exotic, with gentle features, a sensuous mouth, and piercing black eyes that gave away precisely nothing. What Jonah did not know was that the Princess was severely nearsighted—the crowd was nothing but a blur to her. The Port Authority had placed a lectern for her on the pier, but she chose to walk directly past it, standing with nothing between her and the blurry throng. The crush of reporters pushed forward, and the Princess seemed momentarily nervous, but she recovered quickly. She bowed her head, looking almost demure, then raised her chin and spoke in a loud, clear voice.

"Seventy years ago Christian America sent over Christian men and women to give religion and civilization to Hawaii. Today, three of the sons of those missionaries are at your capital asking you to undo their fathers' work. Who sent them? Who gave them the authority to break the Constitution which they swore they would uphold?" she paused dramatically. "Today, I, a poor weak girl with not one of my people with me and all these 'Hawaiian' statesmen against me, have strength to stand up for the rights of my people. Even now I can hear their wail in my heart, and it gives me strength and courage and I am strong—strong in the faith of God, strong in the knowledge that I am right, strong in the strength of seventy million people who in this free land will hear my cry and will refuse to let their flag cover dishonor to mine!"

The moment she finished reporters began barking questions, which she ignored as she and her lady-in-waiting left under the protective escort of the Port Authority. The reporters could only watch as the Princess disappeared into a nearby, presumably heated, building. Her guardian, Theo Davies, however, stayed behind to answer questions on the Princess's behalf. Regardless of the question, the answer was always some variation of the same theme: *Lorrin Thurston is a pirate and America must not allow his piracy to succeed*.

Jonah stood among the reporters, scribbling away as if he were one of them. As they dashed away to their warm offices to get their stories into print, Jonah looked over the Princess's words on his notepad. The young woman was arresting in both appearance and speech. If the royalists turned her loose to fight for the crown, who then, he wondered, would be restored to power: the Queen who had made so many miscalculations and enemies, or the fresh new Princess? Castle may have been more prescient than he knew when he speculated about an intra-palace competition for power.

He walked to the nearest telegraph office and had the Princess's words cabled to the Wormly Hotel. He could not resist sending a little tag of his own. He grabbed a piece of Western Union stationery and wrote out a brief postscript and handed it to the operator. "Here, add this, please." It read, "'Hawaiian-as-savage' argument was kicked off the pier this evening, where it presumably drowned."

"So, she was really that impressive?" asked Castle. Thurston, less surprised, took his nose out of the press clippings Jonah had collected for him and slid the sheaf across the table to his fellow commissioner.

"Read these and see for yourself. The press seems to love her—or love the fact that she's poised, beautiful, and speaks like a refined Brit." Thurston was still waiting for some opportune event to pop up and allow him to turn all this to his advantage. "So what is she doing now, Jonah?"

"Enjoying herself tremendously," Jonah said as he reached for his notepad and started flipping through the pages. "She is attending a series of receptions in her honor in New York and Boston, after which she will arrive in Washington, probably right after Cleveland's inauguration. The royals believe that she will have a much better chance of a presidential meeting than any of the rest of them."

"Is she talking to the press or is Davies doing it all?" Thurston asked.

"She's talking to the press almost daily, and turning them to the royal position, one by one. You're quite the buccaneer in her interpretation, by the way. She's really something," Jonah said, taking the opportunity to rib his boss a little.

"I'm aware of the Princess's charms, Jonah. I'm the one who sent her to school abroad for all this finishing that now seems to impress everyone so damn much."

"But you haven't seen her since she was a girl of thirteen. She's a woman now. Seventeen-year-olds can be far more mature than I once thought."

"Indeed?" Thurston responded with a sidelong glance. "That is Penelope Tubbs's age, is it not? And how is young Penelope, or have we kept you too busy to check your mail?"

"Never *that* busy, I assure you. Actually, I haven't received anything for a couple of days. The Honolulu mail must have hit a bottleneck somewhere en route."

"Or her father put a stop to her correspondence when he found out on whom she was spilling all the ink."

Jonah fidgeted anxiously with his notepad. "I'll sort all of that out when I get back to Hawaii."

"My dear Castle," Thurston said to his partner, while still observing Jonah. "I believe the Commission Secretary is in love."

"Fine thing, that is! Now he won't get any work done," grumbled Castle.

"Not so!" insisted Jonah, eager for a chance to change the subject. "I give you," he declared with mock solemnity as he handed some papers to Castle, "the galleys of an article that will appear in the March issue of *Forum* magazine. It is by a certain Captain Alfred Thayer Mahan—a naval theorist who teaches at Annapolis. It's all about Hawaii being 'key' to the Pacific and how absolutely essential it is for the United States to have her. It looks like something Mr. Thurston would have written, only with more nautical terminology, fewer legalisms, and generally tighter prose."

Thurston gave Jonah a droll stare.

Castle glanced over the pages. "Do I actually need to read this, or do you have a précis for me?"

"Here you, go sir," said Jonah as he handed another type-written sheet to him. "As is my habit, I've prepared a one-page, point-by-point breakdown of the piece for you, lest either of you actually have to read anything."

"Jonah, please," admonished Thurston, knowing that the humorless Castle too often took Jonah seriously.

"How did you get this, anyway?" asked Castle, looking at the article galleys as if they were perhaps stolen.

"Alcohol, mostly. While you gentlemen spend your evenings among the most upstanding and respectable elements of American society, I spend mine drinking with the lowest of the low—writers— and making new friends among them with every round I buy. I can only imagine what percentage of our expense account goes to keeping the reporters in this town inebriated."

"I've calculated it," said Thurston. "You don't want to know."

"But it's a system that works," Jonah happily continued. "For instance, I can also tell you that the Princess—although she doesn't know it yet—will be on the cover of the April 1st issue of *Housekeeper's Weekly*."

"And you learned this—," Castle wondered.

"By drinking with a friend of their Washington correspondent, who was good enough to introduce me before he slipped under the table."

"*Housekeeper's Weekly* has a Washington correspondent?" asked Castle.

"Yes, and he can hold his liquor much better than the fellow from the *Post* who introduced us. Evidently they like to stay abreast of legislation involving the American home and family, like temperance, ironically enough."

"The cover of *Housekeeper's Weekly*," Thurston repeated to himself, still looking for that elusive opportune event.

"All of which brings up an issue," Jonah tried to bring Thurston's attention back.

"Issue? What issue?" mumbled Castle, who had turned back to

the Mahan article.

"The issue of who goes where," Jonah answered.

"Yes?"

"Every night, well, not every night, but a couple of nights a week you two gentlemen are out at the nicest mansions and establishments in Washington, eating rich food with diplomats and senators, while I, wretched scribe, drink my liver into submission in the subterranean taverns of Washington with the dregs of the fourth estate."

"I thought you liked journalists," objected Thurston.

"That's beside the point."

"Well, what *is* the point?"

"I want to go a Washington cocktail party—just once—and I think I've earned the reward."

Castle and Thurston looked at each other. Neither responded right away, as they tried to think of a reason to reject the request, which gave Jonah an opportunity to press his case.

"I've got an official title now. Shouldn't I have a chance to embarrass you in public?"

"Well, when you put it that way…" Thurston began to relent.

"And keeping me out of the taverns for a night will probably save Hawaii fifty dollars in investigative expenses."

"What do you think, Bill?" Thurston asked Castle. "Do you think we can trust our lovesick young secretary among Washington's social elite?"

"Not for a minute, but we've faced greater peril. Let the boy come along."

"All right, then. When?" Thurston asked Jonah.

Jonah had already selected the occasion. "Tomorrow night. You're going to a dinner at the Townshend Mansion in Dupont Circle—very posh. Just a block away from the British embassy on Massachusetts Avenue. But the most important thing about this party is who will be there."

"Okay, I'll bite," said Thurston. "Who?"

"Some of the luminaries of New York journalism. E. L. Godkin—"

"'E. L.'?" Thurston wasn't pleased.

"*Edward Lawrence* Godkin. Sorry. Editor of both *The Nation*—probably the most influential of the national news weeklies—and the daily *New York Evening Post*. His opinion, as you might imagine, carries a lot of weight."

"Who else?"

"Another one of the *Post* editors, Rollo Ogden, who also contributes the lead editorial for *The Nation* from time to time. Ordained minister who chose journalism over the pulpit, but as we all know, for editorialists anyway, that's really just trading one pulpit for another. He's something of a protégé of Mr. Godkin, and very smart."

"Is that all?" asked Thurston, suspecting it was not.

"No. Carl Schurz should be there as well. He and Godkin see things much the same way, but don't like each other—at all. They were part of the group that bought *The Post*, but couldn't work together. Schurz writes mostly for *Harper's Weekly* these days, which competes rather successfully with *The Nation*."

"Godkin and Schurz agree on issues but don't like each other?" asked Castle quizzically.

"Yes," Jonah said, trying to remember some of the boozy conversations that brought this intelligence. "Something about Godkin's pugnacious Irish blood and Schurz's German arrogance. I don't remember exactly."

"Given the way you acquire so much of your information," grumbled Castle, "it's a wonder to me that you remember any of it."

Jonah wanted to point out that drinking with journalists was just the most social method, among many others, he used to keep his superiors informed, but decided it would be a waste of breath. "Anyway, be careful with these men. They're very smart, very influential, and they are predisposed against annexation" he warned.

"Why is that?" Thurston asked, unable to imagine why any American would be reluctant to acquire so lovely a place as Hawaii.

"They fear that the United States is abandoning its traditions, that acquiring Hawaii would be like embarking on a career of imperialism." Jonah thought he was stating the obvious.

"Nonsense," responded Thurston. "We're not asking to be a colony—we want to actually join the United States as one of them!"

"Well, tomorrow night you should have a chance to make that argument. I'm just pointing out that you ought to be prepared."

"Indeed," agreed Castle. "I'll memorize that Mahan article right now."

"Godkin and Schurz, Irish and German," mused Thurston, shaking his head. "A couple of immigrants telling Americans what to think."

"New Americans tend to be the most American of the lot, I think," Castle observed.

"I hope we get the chance to find out."

The Townshend Mansion was large, ornate, stylish, and brand spanking new. The house itself was part of a renewal of Dupont Circle begun some twenty years earlier when respectable houses started replacing the workers' shanties. Once the new British embassy was constructed there the neighborhood's recently elevated identity was secured, and General Townshend and his money could comfortably risk construction of his residence in the newly fashionable environs. It was truly something to behold. He felt as if he was at a diplomats' pleasure garden. Having spent the bulk of his time in hotels, libraries, and of course taverns, it had painfully occurred to him several times that he might as well have stayed in Seattle. But this mansion was something he was sure he would never have seen in the Pacific Northwest. The gargantuan electric chandeliers brightly illuminated a foyer which was larger by far than the whole house Jonah grew up in. It contained a number of staircases that went God knows where, but created the impression that you could get lost in this place. The adjacent rooms were open to the central salon, creating alcoves of sedately chatting partygoers that were somehow also connected to the larger social jungle—that word seeming particularly apt due to the plethora of large potted plants around the room.

"If you're going to gawk like that, at least do it with your mouth closed," Thurston admonished Jonah. "I'm afraid you're going to drool. One would think you had never seen a mansion before." The two older men looked as if they were having second thoughts about including Jonah.

"Sorry," Jonah said without meaning it, as he took a drink from an anonymous man in a tuxedo who held a tray of them. "Look, over there, it's Godkin and Ogden," he said nodding toward a corner where the two men were talking.

"Excellent," said Thurston, turning to Castle. "Shall we see if we can turn their publications to our advantage?"

"Indeed!" And with that the two commissioners adorned themselves with their most political smiles and proceeded across the room, Jonah lagging a respectable subordinate's distance behind.

"Which is whom?" Thurston asked as they walked.

"Godkin is the one with the big brush of a mustache and close-cropped beard," the secretary whispered.

"And Ogden?" Castle asked.

"The other one," Jonah said, wishing there were some way to do so without making the man feel stupid. "Next to Godkin, there. Tall, thin, glasses, no hair."

"Gentlemen," Thurston grandly offered his hand to Godkin. "I'm Lorrin Thurston and this is my associate, William Castle. We're with the Hawaiian Commission, here to—"

"We know who you are," interrupted Godkin, accepting Thurston's hand absently as the four men went through the rituals of introduction.

"So," Godkin began, "You're the missionary scions who conspired with Minister Stevens to dethrone the Hawaiian Queen, she of unpronounceable Polynesian syllables?"

"Lilioukalani," Thurston pronounced helpfully. "And I assure you there was no conspiracy with Minister Stevens. Much to my frustration, he made it abundantly and repeatedly clear that American troops would be used only to protect—"

"'American lives and property,'" Godkin interjected. "I've heard. What amazes me is that you actually expect us to believe that. Stevens was no more than a tool of Secretary of State Blaine, and Blaine has wanted to acquire anything he could get his hands on his entire political career."

"I can't speak for the deceased Secretary of State, but—," Thurston began.

"Have you ever spoken with him?" demanded Godkin.

"Well, yes, once, but only briefly," admitted Thurston a little uneasily. He had not expected a cross examination.

"And when was that, exactly?" Godkin persisted.

"Last year. September, I believe. I found the Secretary to be a congenial host, but we spoke only of the McKinley tariff and the violence it had wrought on the Hawaiian economy," he lied.

"And you didn't speak to him about annexing Hawaii?"

"No. I did not." Thurston's curt response signaled his abandonment of diplomacy with Godkin, whom he could see was immoveable. Thurston quickly determined that he was not interested in trotting out his rhetoric for the man's disapproval. Castle, less nimble, proceeded according to plan.

"Gentlemen," Castle interrupted expansively, "Let us not talk of the past, but the future. Hawaii can provide America with untold advantages if we are joined. For instance—"

"I do not see what 'advantage' we could possibly have by taking possession of the Islands that we do not now have without possessing them, except perhaps being saddled with the public debt of Hawaii—some four million dollars that you annexationists wrote into your treaty with Mr. Foster," emphasized Godkin.

"But this is not really a gain to us," Rollo Ogden chimed in, "for we have a debt already."

"Indeed not!" It was Carl Schurz, who had sidled up to the conversation uninvited.

"My dear Carl," Godkin welcomed his old adversary. "Allow me to introduce you to Messieurs Thurston and Castle, of the Hawaiian Commission."

"Ah, yes," said Schurz in a German accent that was entirely too thick for a man who had been living in America for decades. "I have heard much about them," he snarled, which actually sounded more like '*Ah haff hurt mooch about zem.*' A smirk crept across his face as he talked. "In fact, I was in New York to hear the Princess speak about them, especially Mr. Thurston."

"Oh, I was there too," said Jonah without thinking, which gave the whole group of dignitaries an opportunity to pointedly ignore him to his face.

"May I introduce the Commission Secretary, an American from Seattle, Mr. Jonah Christian," said Thurston, giving Jonah a sidelong look to remind him to mind his place.

"Perhaps you would tell us a little more about your mission here, gentlemen?" Schurz asked, assuming control of the conversation he had just joined.

"It would be my pleasure," Castle said quite sincerely, eager to put forward the Captain Mahan's arguments after studying them all afternoon. "As you know, the Americans first came to Hawaii as a missionary enterprise, spreading the Gospel of Christ to the benighted heathens, which they have done with much success."

"And how are you measuring this 'success,' Mr. Castle?" Godkin interrupted. "By the number of heathens you convert or the general reduction of their numbers?"

"I assure you the missionaries had nothing to do with the declining native population, which I agree is alarmingly sharp," Castle launched into an explanation that seemed entirely out of place in the grand foyer. "It is the natives' defective social morality that is to blame. Really, the chief contributor and most lethal influence on the native is their heathen superstition. The kahunas—sorcerers

and medicine men—are very influential among the natives, dealing
in deadly witchcraft and its antidotes of propitiation of demons
by incantations and sacrifices—*sacrifices!*" he cried. "Of course,
Hawaiians are also prone to drunkenness and the wanton behavior
that generally follows."

"Perhaps, then," Ogden pointed out, "you should re-evaluate
your estimation of the missionaries' success." The others chortled.

"But you must consider what the missionaries have to work
with!" Castle continued earnestly. "The natives suffer the defects of
any tropical race. They are, you see, a somewhat child-like people."

"We've heard all this before," Ogden responded dismissively.
"And frankly, it doesn't improve by repetition."

"But, sir—" Castle started to protest before Ogden cut him off.

"No, please, allow me to give the synopsis as I understand it, and
you may correct my misimpressions. You see, I had the pleasure the
other night of listening to Secretary of State Foster hawking this treaty
of yours at the National Geographic Society. I understand that you,
Mr. Thurston, were there doing the same thing the previous week?"
Thurston, having all but washed his hands of this conversation,
acknowledged Ogden's question with the barest hint of a nod. "In
Foster's recitation of Hawaiian history," Ogden continued, "the
American missionaries imparted a knowledge of Christianity to the
natives, gave them a written language, founded schools for their
education, and prevailed upon them to adopt the dress and comforts
of civilization. Just inspirational stuff! These selfless missionaries
gradually created out of a barbarous race a civilized nation, that
also happens to be utterly unfit for self-government, and oh by the
way, destined to speedy extinction by its own vices. Moreover," he
held up a hand to forestall the objection Castle was opening his
mouth to make. "Under these conditions, Mr. Foster tells us that
for more than half a century Americans were the real administrators
of public affairs—the power behind the throne. But if the natives
were mere figureheads, and the American missionaries and their
descendants were the true administrators, we might be forgiven

if we question whether you have accurately located the source of governmental deterioration." Ogden closed with a flourish, to the great appreciation of his fellow journalists.

"But that is exactly it, gentlemen," Castle rejoined. "Mr. Foster is a brilliant man, surely, but he put it too plainly. The natives have been constantly engaged in governance, or at least spending the government's money, willy-nilly, while the Americans struggled to put things right once they've made a mess of them."

"Or perhaps you just don't want to let them run the government of islands you've come to own almost entirely," Ogden suggested.

"We don't actually—"

"What is the total population of the Hawaiian Islands?"

"About ninety thousand, I should think."

"And what is the total number of the white population?" Ogden pressed. Castle, unsure of the answer, turned to Jonah.

"Just under two thousand white souls," Jonah said, recognizing better than Castle where this was going, but feeling helpless to do anything about it.

"Ah, thank you, young man," Ogden smiled benignly at Jonah. "And yet those two thousand whites own more than seventy-four percent of the entire property of the Islands, and the natives, excluding the royal families, hold less than one percent? And amid this almost incredible discrepancy in property-holding, you actually have property qualifications for voting, do you not?"

Not one of the Hawaiian commissioners bothered to answer.

"So," Ogden continued, "you effectively control what little there is that you don't already own through your domination of representation by restriction of the franchise that would never, ever be legal in the United States."

"Well, I think that's putting too fine a point on it, really," observed Castle—a good lawyer—as he searched for a way to deflect this criticism. "Americans can hardly be criticized for owning wealth that they themselves created out of formerly fallow fields. But, be that as it may, we should consider the strategic and commercial advantages to the United States of a union with Hawaii. Dr. Mahan—"

"*Captain* Mahan," Godkin corrected him.

"Oh, yes, thank you—you know him?" Castle asked a little uneasily.

"Yes, but please go on," Godkin smiled as if he were handing Castle just enough rope to hang himself.

Castle turned nervously to Jonah again, as if to ask *what have you got me into?* "Well, gentlemen," he began, projecting confidence he did not feel, "you certainly understand Hawaii's *key* position as the crossroads of the Pacific."

"Ah, yes, I've read Mahan's stuff," Godkin said. "Makes much of this whole 'key' thing.

"Indeed," Ogden agreed. "He's infected Senator Morgan with it. Chairman of the Senate Foreign Relations Committee. I'm sure you gentlemen know him—he wants Hawaii and every other speck of land in the Pacific, Atlantic, or any dirty little rock in any other body of water you can find. I saw him trot out all this prattle with charts and graphs and all sorts of silliness. His main argument, like Mahan, is for a big navy, the Nicaraguan canal, and coaling stations thick as blackberries. The Senator has this naval chart of the Pacific and western Atlantic, and it was covered with converging lines of bright green that intersect with each other—in a way that is little short of miraculous—at the Hawaiian Islands! Thus making it plain to the comprehension of a child, and by truly childish methods, that the Hawaiian Islands are the true 'crossroads of the Pacific,' and that we must have them or forever lose our self-respect."

"I can't speak to your self-respect," said an increasingly exasperated Castle, "but you might want to consider whether you'd be more comfortable with Hawaii under the control of the British navy."

"Nothin' but a dog-and-sausage argument," grumbled Godkin.

"I assure you it's more than a dog and... what?"

"Dog and sausage," Godkin repeated to his perplexed listeners. This curious label brought even the disgusted Thurston's attention back to the conversation as Godkin resumed.

"A certain man bet that his dog would eat five dollars' worth of sausage in an hour. Finding the animal's appetite failing before his task was accomplished, he stimulated it by keeping another dog on a leash nearby, allowing the animal to make occasional dashes at the sausages. This never failed," Godkin explained. "It seems to me that whenever we're about to swallow any little island or dependency for which the American public seems to have no appetite, the likes of Senator Morgan or Captain Mahan, or you, my dear Commissioners, always try to rouse it by pretending that England or some other power is after it."

"I don't imagine you'll take much comfort in your dog-and-sausage story when the British Navy, in possession of the key to the Pacific, makes your Nicaraguan canal all but worthless to you." The color had begun to rise in Castle's face.

"The comfort I take," responded Godkin, with just the hint of an Irish lilt mingled with his Irish ire, "is in traditional American policy—the policy of Washington and Jefferson—free trade with all, entangling alliances with none. As things are, we have no foreign possessions to lose, and our resources in population and money are so enormous and our capacity for doing damage when once roused so great, than any enemy, or any two enemies combined, would be sure to get the worst of it. But you gentlemen would have us sacrifice our security and set ourselves on a career of foreign acquisition, colonial expansion, or whatever you want to call it."

"Surely you're aware of the latest racial science?" Schurz asked, referring to the abundance of theories on racial hierarchy masquerading as science.

"Of course," Castle responded. "It is our desire to enlarge the white portion of the Hawaiian population."

"Then you know nothing of race science," Schurz responded. "Your tropical climate precludes the white race from ever being the majority in Hawaii. Whites are biologically ill-suited to it. There are, in fact, projects afoot to organize a large-scale emigration of Negroes from our southern states to Hawaii because white men cannot work on the cane, rice, or coffee fields of Hawaii, while the climate would be congenial to the blacks. A transfer of a large part of our colored population would be beneficial to both countries."

"That is the last thing we want to do," Castle insisted.

"Is it? Behind this scheme, no doubt, is the thought that a substitution of American Negroes for Japanese and Chinese laborers in Hawaii would make the annexation of the islands less objectionable to the American people. Even if such a scheme could be affected, the essential fact would still remain: Hawaii is a country whose laboring force, that is, the bulk of whose population, will not be of the white race."

Castle was too confounded and dumfounded to respond. The editorialists, entirely pleased with themselves, moved on to shine the light of consternation elsewhere.

"Unbelievable," said Castle, shaking his head.

"But instructive," said Thurston.

"Instructive, how?" Castle was incredulous.

"I have completely miscalculated the protean quality of the race question."

"Come again?"

"Race prejudice can work more than one way in the annexation argument," Thurston explained. "I assumed, incorrectly, that we could turn American race prejudice to our advantage, expecting *their* paternalism toward colored races to make them sympathetic to *our* history with Hawaiian natives. But these men, and they represent many, have no interest in uplifting races they see as inferior—they simply want to keep them as far away as possible."

"Can we eat now?" asked Jonah.

Four tables put together in a square filled the dining room so all the guests could watch each other eat. Jonah was relieved to see his bosses seated next to society ladies who would presumably be less likely to attack them than the intellectual musketeers who had just spent the cocktail hour flaying them and their purpose in life. In a fleeting moment of honesty, Jonah had to admit to himself that while he rather enjoyed the spectacle of Castle getting bandied about so handily, Schurz's iron-clad assumptions about higher and lower races just made him angry. He wished Muanu could somehow have been here. He felt certain that she would have had some very interesting commentary.

As it happened, he was seated between the French ambassador, who ignored him in favor of the woman on his left, and the wife of someone whose name had already left his memory. *Can't let that happen again*, he chided himself, *you never know when you may need that information.* Making conversation was difficult because she seemed not to know anything at all about Washington, yet had a great deal to say about it. He was doing his best to follow her inane babble and ignore the way the lower half of her breasts were straining to escape her bodice to join the top half in the open air. *Do not stare at her bosom*, he told himself. *Just don't.* For one thing, it gave him a pang of loneliness for his dear Penelope, although their breasts were the only feature the two women had in common. For another, when he looked directly into her eyes he thought he may as well have been looking out the window.

"Tell me, Mr. Christian." Ah, a question! "Are the Hawaiian Islands at all close to the Sandwich Islands?"

"Very," Jonah answered.

"Oh, good. I knew it," she giggled. "How close are they?"

"They're actually one and the same."

"How on earth can the same place have two names?"

"When Captain Cook discovered the Islands he named them for his friend, the Earl of Sandwich, but of course the natives already had a name for their Islands."

"Did they? Imagine that!" she responded with genuine surprise.

Oh, what the hell, Jonah thought as allowed his gaze to drift southward until it came to rest in her décolletage. Of course at precisely that moment he felt Thurston's gaze upon him and he knew this would be his last Washington dinner party, which he did not regret in the least.

CHAPTER ELEVEN

The dinner party had been a disaster. The editorial trio that flayed the commissioners so savagely at the Townshend mansion were merely warming up for the editorials they were about to unleash on America. The ensuing articles from Harper's and The Nation were, collectively, an air-tight case in which all arguments for annexation seemed to suffocate.

Along with that loss of momentum, Jonah was once again banished from the capital salons and relegated to the underworld, as he had come to think of the below street-level taverns where he conducted so much of his evening business. The exception to his exile—thanks to a healthy dose of pleading—would be President Grover Cleveland's inaugural ball.

A fresh snowfall had discouraged attendance at Cleveland's inauguration earlier that day. Missing a speech was one thing, but it would take more than a little snow to keep the Democratic faithful away from all that food and booze. Attendance was in the thousands. Jonah arrived late after having put his work away unfinished, lying to himself that he would finish the article on which he was working after he stumbled home from the ball. The path from Pennsylvania Avenue to the Capitol was lighted by forty massive Union Illuminators, whose luminous power was vastly expanded as it reflected off of the new fallen snow, giving the city a glowing aura of white. Jonah reluctantly left the fairyland atmosphere of the avenue to turn up F Street toward the newly completed Pension

Building where the ball was already underway. Derisively known around Washington as General Meig's big red barn, for the man who built it, the mammoth edifice was a truly magnificent structure. The problem for the denizens of Washington, accustomed as they were to buildings that looked like big Greek wedding cakes, the façade of red bricks—over fifteen million of them—was aesthetically awkward. General Sherman, when asked what he thought about the building replied, "The worst part is, it's fireproof."

Once inside Jonah was in no particular to hurry to find his employers, which probably would have been impossible in any case. The throng had already gathered to overflow capacity, and intentionally finding anyone would be an impressive feat.

The place shimmered. This was the first government building to be constructed with electric wiring, and the place was brilliantly lit with massive electric chandeliers. Standing at the entrance of the great hall, Jonah looked past the eight Corinthian columns— the largest internal columns in the world, as it happened—to a fountain twenty-eight feet across in the center of the place. The lights played on the green tinted water and made rainbows in its mist, creating an atmosphere for the party quite unlike anything he had ever seen. Ringing the hall were balconies supported by Doric columns, which rose almost literally into the sky because the ceiling was lined with a series of skylights. This was part of the building's innovative ventilation system, which kept the air constantly moving, an essential feature when the place was crammed full of a few thousand overdressed dancing revelers. But the skylights had a more theatrical benefit as well—fireworks exploding above the building could be seen without leaving the arcade.

This was Cleveland's second inaugural, and his party planners seemed to have learned from their previous mistakes because there was an abundance of everything. Jonah had no sooner entered the arcade when someone placed the first of several drinks in his hand. Food was everywhere. A staff of more than two hundred busied themselves serving up 60,000 oysters, 150 gallons of lobster salad—

God that was good, thought Jonah as he washed down a mouthful of it with a gulp of champagne—10,000 chicken croquettes, 7,000 sandwiches of various types, 150 turkeys, and 300 gallons of chicken salad. A more modest crew handled untold hundreds of pounds of pâté de foie gras and the dessert of 1,300 quarts of ice cream. What, he had to ask himself, was Grover Cleveland, the erstwhile sheriff of Buffalo, doing serving people pâté de foie gras?

As the orchestra played a promenade, Jonah, emboldened by drink, asked a woman whose judgment was similarly impaired if she would care to dance. Moments later they were among the swarm of bodies on the arcade floor, dancing through the transfer of power. For the next hour or so Jonah danced and chatted, moving from one amiable group of revelers to another, meeting Cleveland supporters from all across America—all of them ready to party. After several dances with several different women, Jonah bumped into his employer on his way to get another glass of champagne.

"Jonah, so glad I found you. We have a table on the balcony just above us. Come."

Jonah looked longingly at all the women with whom he had yet to dance, and glumly turned to follow Thurston. They arrived at a table on the first balcony where Castle was standing with Godkin and Ogden and their wives, who were just taking their leave.

"Well," Godkin barked by way of conclusion, "I'll accept your argument that the revolution wasn't simply a 'job' by the sugar interests, but I think we'll have to continue to disagree about everything else."

"Understood, sir," said Castle, shaking his hand. He was obviously glad for the small victory. Handshakes and goodbyes all around, the journalists took their leave, and Thurston and Jonah took their seats.

"Well, Jonah," Castle turned his attention to the secretary. "You look like you've been having quite a time. Have you made any observations we can use?"

"Indeed," said Jonah, wiping the perspiration from his brow. "There are women here from all over the country—I've talked to as many as I could—and their fashion sense seems to have distinctly regional variations."

"Jonah?" Thurston was offering him a chance to shut up, but Jonah went right on.

"There's a real pattern to it. The East Coast ladies, running from Washington northward, wear their dresses cut with a very deep and square neckline, generously revealing as much of their breasts as could possibly be legal. As you move westward or southward the necklines become progressively and parsimoniously higher and V-shaped, providing barely a glimpse, until you get to those few from the Northwest, where the women are wearing high collars that keep their breasts a total mystery. I don't know how they breathe. Two noteworthy exceptions, however, are the ladies of San Francisco and New Orleans, who I think would prefer to get rid of the upper bodice entirely. Geographic anomalies, I suppose."

"Really, Thurston! Why did you saddle the Commission with this lascivious barbarian?" Castle looked toward the ceiling in exasperation.

Thurston ignored his partner and turned to Jonah. "I think Mr. Castle was asking if you had made any useful observations about the members of the incoming Cleveland administration. And do you, indeed, think of anything besides women's breasts?" Jonah began to seriously ponder the question, which was intended rhetorically, when Thurston asked another. "How long has it been since you've heard from Penelope?"

The question brought back the dark clouds Jonah had hoped to escape for the evening. "Over a week, actually. I don't know what's wrong. I don't think I wrote anything amiss. I'm sure it's nothing," he said with more conviction than he felt.

"Well, you were working earlier today," said Castle. "Perhaps you've learned something of our chances with the incoming administration, besides their wives' 'fashion sense.'"

"Fine," Jonah surrendered, seeing that these men were determined to turn this splendid party into nothing more than another night at work. "Cleveland doesn't seem to have any particular predisposition towards Hawaii, or American expansion in general. He is opposed to the Republican high tariffs, as you would expect of a Democrat, but that issue becomes moot if Hawaii becomes a U.S. territory anyway. Beyond that there just aren't any clues as to how he'll approach our treaty. His Secretary of State, on the other hand—"

"Walter Gresham?" Castle said. "A converted Republican, as I hear it."

"Yes. In fact he was nearly the Republican nominee for president a couple of times."

"So what's a thorough-going Republican like that doing in a Democratic administration?"

"It's complicated," Jonah said, looking around unsuccessfully for a drink. "Gresham, like Foster, was a charter Republican in 1856. These men were Republicans before Lincoln was. And like Foster, Gresham joined the Union Army the moment the Civil War began. But after the war Foster and Gresham gravitated toward different wings of the Republican Party. Both times Gresham ran for the Republican nomination for president, Foster was part of the movement that derailed him—quite publicly the second time."

"So, what you're saying is that we're going to ask Gresham to support a treaty written by the man who kept him from becoming president?"

"It could be stated that way," Jonah said, looking around and finally snagging a drink from a passing waiter. "But Gresham probably wouldn't like our treaty anyway. He's a strict constructionist, as they say."

"Strict constructionist?"

"Yes, he believes that if a power isn't specifically stated and clearly spelled out in the Constitution then it doesn't exist," Jonah explained. "Accordingly, he believes that the U.S. agreement with Germany and Britain for their combined sovereignty over Samoa constitutes an 'entangling alliance.'"

"Never mind that the agreement kept the three countries from going to war over the place?" asked Castle, incredulous.

"That's strict constructionism, sir."

"We made a huge mistake," Thurston said. "We bet everything on Foster's ability to get the treaty through the Senate before the Cleveland administration took office. Now he's gone, and we've got his political enemy to deal with."

"What else could we have done?" asked Castle.

"I'm not sure. Maybe nothing. But this is our situation and we need to make something of it." Thurston thought a moment. "Jonah, petition the State Department for a meeting with Gresham as soon as possible."

"Sure. First thing tomorrow," Jonah assured him, before he was distracted by the orchestra that had just begun a Strauss waltz. "This orchestra is very good. Are these U.S. Army musicians, really?"

"I have a program here," said Castle, adjusting his spectacles as he looked over the document. "Yes, 'U.S. Army Band and Orchestra.'"

"Who is the conductor?"

"Hmm... says here 'John Phillips Sousa.'"

"Never heard of him," Jonah said. "Still, they're awfully good."

Thurston, as usual, was in a hurry. Any momentum they may have enjoyed in the Senate was quickly dissipating, and if there was any chance at all of getting Walter Q. Gresham on board in favor of annexation, he wanted to find out as soon as possible. Accordingly, Jonah marched through the light snow to the State Department where he found a lot of people who did not seem to be exactly sure where they were going or what they were doing, but there was a lot of going and doing nonetheless. These new political appointees were finding their desks or offices and moving into them; it was not an inspirational scene. Jonah stopped one twentyish-looking fellow carrying a box full of papers and asked if he knew where he might find Secretary Gresham's appointment secretary. He could tell the young man wanted to answer his question, but it was hard for him to speak as he craned his head this way and that, as if to get his bearings.

"That's all right," Jonah told him. "I'll just keep looking." Just then he saw an older gentlemen walking toward him, dressed in what could be called the State Department uniform—goatee, gray pinstriped suit and vest, and watch chain stretched across his chest—who seemed to know exactly what he was about.

"Excuse me," Jonah stopped him. "I'm Jonah Christian, Secretary of the Hawaiian Commission. I'm looking for Secretary Gresham's appointment secretary."

"Oh, yes, I've met the commissioners, Messieurs Castle and Thurston, I believe," the man responded. He was friendlier than Jonah would have expected, but he had a disturbing habit of staring directly at the mouth of the person speaking to him.

"You have?"

"Yes, of course I have. I'm Alvey Adee, Second Assistant Secretary of State. Unlike nearly everyone else in the building, I'm not new here."

"Well, I'm certainly glad I ran into you," Jonah said, pumping Adee's hand. "I'm having a real time of it trying to get an appointment with the new Secretary of State."

"Well, he doesn't have an appointment secretary yet, so it's unlikely you'll find him. But don't worry, you have a treaty pending in the Senate; I assure you, Secretary Gresham will be speaking with you soon. We'll send a meeting request to you in the next couple of days."

"Thank you, that's excellent. Let me leave you a card with our address—"

"We know where you are," Adee said. Jonah looked askance at the Second Assistant Secretary, a little suspicious all of the sudden.

"As I said, you have a treaty pending in the United States Senate. You're not exactly anonymous personages in Washington."

"Oh," said Jonah, more than a little relieved. "I guess that makes sense."

"Good day, Mr. Christian," Adee said with a smile and a nod and he was on his way, an island of calm in striped pants amid a sea of anxious novices.

That job done, Jonah headed toward the Willard Hotel where he planned to loiter with a newspaper until he "accidentally" bumped into someone from the royal Hawaiian deputation. He did not expect that they would be happy to see him, or willing to speak with him, but he didn't have much choice but to have a crack at it. The royal commissioners were not a well-known commodity in Washington, and none of the contacts Jonah had made on congressional staffs and in the press seemed to have much more information about their progress or strategy than he did. There was general agreement that the royals were probably getting nowhere, but nobody knew any specifics. Jonah's typical skullduggery having failed him, he allowed that the direct approach might be reasonable.

He was about to cross the street to enter the hotel when he saw the royal commission's counselor, Paul Neumann, exit the building into the snowy street, dressed in brand new overcoat, hat, gloves and, scarf—Hawaiians rarely owned such items—heading toward the Capitol. Jonah followed a discreet distance behind, until Neumann ascended the Capitol steps, entered the building and stopped to get his bearings. Jonah would have an advantage following Neumann here—the Capitol itself was one of his favorite buildings in Washington. As Commission Secretary Jonah did not enjoy the same cachet there that his bosses did, but he spent a lot more time working there and consequently had a lot more friends on the congressional staffs, including a few congressmen and senators.

He casually followed the deposed Queen's lawyer around Congress as Neumann searched for a congressman or senator who might give him a moment to explain the Queen's position. It was sad, really; each conversation began well enough—politicians are always willing to shake a hand—but once it became clear that the devoted Mr. Neumann actually wanted something from them, and he wanted it on behalf of a deposed foreign monarch, the elected officials suddenly had very little time for the Queen's solicitor.

Jonah did his best to make it worse. At first he was furtive about his mission, making sure that Neumann was unaware of his shadow, but as the morning turned to late morning, and the pantomime of introduction, explanation, and rejection was repeated, Jonah ceased hiding himself. Worse, he started to comment aloud on Neumann's progress, or lack thereof, *to Neumann*. At one point Neumann grew so irritated at the way Jonah stood in plain sight while he tried to convince a senator to oppose the annexation treaty, that Neumann actually pointed Jonah out to the senator, exclaiming, "There's one of the pirates right there!" This proved to be a mistake. "Hey, that's Jonah Christian," the senator responded. "Hey, Jonah," the senator shouted, as Neumann turned pale. "Were you able to find any more of that Canadian bourbon?"

"Sure was, Senator. I'm sending a case of it to your office. Let me know when it gets there, will you?

"Will do, my boy. Will do." Then, turning back to Neumann, the senator asked, "Who are you, again?"

"No one, sir. I'm sorry to have bothered you."

"Good! Fine!" the senator said, evidently not having heard the actual words he said, then pumped his hand again, turned on his heel, and went on his way. Jonah observed this dehumanizing process with a certain amount of sympathy.

"Ouch. I think that interview was even shorter than the last, Neumann."

"Oh, shut up, Christian," the frustrated lawyer said. "I don't need criticism from Thurston's damn lapdog."

"Come now, Neumann, be nice. I'm just trying to help you," said Jonah, almost meaning it. "You're not going to get anywhere trying to buttonhole busy congressmen who are on their way to do something, anything, that's obviously more important to them than talking to you. You are, after all, the representative of a monarchy that no longer exists."

"If I wanted the advice of somebody's lackey—"

"Now, now. Let's not forget our manners. If you won't take my advice, at least take my food. Let me buy you lunch. We can swap information on our respective employers."

"I would no sooner sit down to a meal with the likes of you, than, than—" Neumann began to splutter.

"Neumann, look at yourself. You're accomplishing nothing here. I know this town and the people in it better than you. I promise to give you some information you can use. *C'mon*, you could use some food and drink. Admit it."

Tired and discouraged, Neumann relented. "As you like, Christian. Buy me a meal, but I'm not telling you anything."

An hour later they were in the restaurant of the Willard Hotel, drinking and laughing, and filling themselves on appetizers. Neumann, pounded the table as he tried to recover from his last guffaw, until finally he was able to speak. "What was that charming little name you called Thurston?"

"'Solipsistic prick.' But I mean it in a nice way," Jonah said, struggling unsuccessfully to keep a straight face.

"I always thought the man was simply frightening," Neumann admitted, wiping a tear of laughter from his face.

"That's exactly what he wants you to think. It surprises me how many people never get past that."

"He does execute revolutions at his whim—two of them so far, by my count—so a reasonable amount of fear is probably appropriate," the queen's counselor pointed out.

"Okay, I'll grant you that," Jonah conceded. "But it can't be too much of a treat working for the royals, either. I imagine they expect to be treated like, well, royalty."

"They can be a handful, that's for sure. They're so smart, so educated and worldly, but at times they can be so obstinately obtuse and unreasonable," Neumann mused. "It makes me want to go work at a quiet little law firm and forget all about them."

"You'll have to, soon enough," Jonah said, pointing out the obvious yet painful fact of Neumann's future. But he knew how to soften the blow. "Waiter," he caught the young man on his way past their table. "Two more, if you would." They had started with beer, but switched to whiskey a few rounds ago.

"Don't be so sure," Neumann responded. "What are you going to do if President Cleveland sees things differently than President Harrison, which he surely will? Suppose he tells Thurston to give the Queen her country back?"

"I... I don't know." Jonah had never considered this before. "I guess," he paused to think on it another moment. "Well, the Honolulu Rifles being no match for the U.S. Marines, I suppose President Dole—"

"*Provisional* President Dole," Neumann corrected him.

"Quite. I suppose the Provisional Government would have no choice but to do what Cleveland told them to do. If you all can convince him to tell Dole and the P.G.'s to step aside and reinstate the Queen, I don't really know what choice they'd have."

"That's my job. If I could get somebody to talk to me I might make some progress."

At that moment Jonah recognized a reporter friend of his, Henry Garrett, coming toward them. Jonah looked quickly at the table next to them, just behind Neumann, and Garrett understood that he should take his seat, keep his mouth shut, and eavesdrop.

"But which queen would they reinstate?" Jonah asked, a little louder than he needed to for Garrett's benefit.

"What do you mean, 'which queen'? There's only one."

"Not the way I hear it. There are a lot of people on your side who are not at all happy about the Queen's performance in this mess. They think that if she hadn't been so clumsy in the abrogation of the Bayonet Constitution, she'd still be in power. So while they want a queen, there's a lot of talk that maybe another queen would be a better choice. Or haven't you heard that the lovely Princess Ka'iulani is coming to town."

"She's *already* in town. She's here, at the Willard," he grumbled. "My job wasn't difficult enough to begin with."

"The Princess is making things difficult for you? But what is she doing here if you didn't want her here?"

"It's the influence of Theo Davies, her guardian. He's one of the 'Big Five' sugar magnates in Hawaii. I don't know what he wants, but he didn't consult us or the Queen. He just told the whole world, through the British press, that they were coming, which made it impossible for us to tell them not to, obviously."

"So, is Davies fighting for the monarchy, or simply for his own personal monarch?"

"No one knows, but we don't have any choice but to take advantage of her. She's already charmed the pants off the press. Those snotty scribblers are like putty in her hands as soon as they find out she doesn't wear a grass skirt and boil missionaries in a big black cauldron."

"'Snotty scribblers,' you say? Good one." Jonah wanted to make sure Garrett got that down in his notebook. "There is a third claimant to the throne as well, isn't there? I mean you have the Princess's cousin here with you."

"Koa?"

"Is that what you call him?"

"Prince David Kaw'nanakoa."

"Easy for you to say."

"Yes, I imagine if you had a name like that you'd find it easier to go by 'Koa' as well. The Queen sent him here with us. She trusts him."

"Sure, but if Princess Ka'iulani made a bid for the throne that would change everything. With the throne up for grabs, Koa would almost certainly take his chances, don't you think?"

"Definitely," Neumann agreed with a rueful look, as if he could see how complicated the hypothetical situation would be. "Koa was furious when the Queen named Ka'iulani heir to the thrown ahead of him. He's older, after all, and every bit as royal as she."

"So, many people would see his claim as the more legitimate one?" Jonah spoke as if the claim had already been made, and Neumann, enjoying the drinks that kept arriving, happily traipsed along behind the hypothetical logic of the conversation, perilously unaware that the *Washington Post*, in the person of their snotty scribbler Henry Garrett, was listening to every word of it.

"The funny thing is," Neumann slurred, "the cousins love each other."

"Romantically?" It just kept getting better.

"Yes! They've been an on-again, off-again item since she was a little girl. Just when everyone expects them to announce their engagement, it turns out they're no longer speaking to each other."

"Since she was a little girl, you say? Americans probably wouldn't understand a romantic relationship between a little girl and a cousin several years older than she, but this whole royal thing tends to escape them. Anyway, you're saying that you could have a situation with two lovers—from the same family—competing for the same throne?" Jonah tried to sum it up, lest Garrett miss a good angle.

"Can you imagine what my job would be like then?" Neumann shook his head and sipped his whisky.

"What does the Queen think of all this?"

"I don't know. I really don't. But she's back there in Honolulu, and the Princess is here, meeting with the President. So—"

"When is she meeting with the President?"

"Sunday night. The President and Mrs. Cleveland have invited her over to the White House for the evening—dinner and whatnot."

"I suppose they have to do that when a royal personage shows up," Jonah suggested.

"Yes, I suppose so. I can't get five minutes with a Senator, but the Princess shows up and the White House immediately invites her for dinner!"

Jonah spent a few minutes consoling the Queen's inebriated lawyer, then advised him to go up to his room for a nap. He collected the check and took his leave, stopping at the maître d's desk to pick up Garrett's check as well. He ducked back into the restaurant just long enough to exchange a discreet salute with the appreciative reporter, and made his way back to the Wormly, to sleep off his lunch and write up what he had learned, in a less speculative form than would appear the next day in the *Post*.

Thurston and Castle sat in their suite going over a file Jonah had prepared for them on Secretary Gresham when they heard someone or something bump into the door. This was followed by the sound of a small metal object banging against the doorknob and some guttural noises, possibly human, then another bump against the door. Castle approached the entry cautiously, his hand hovering over the doorknob, then pulled it open in one swift motion. Jonah, who had been crouched in front of the keyhole trying to insert his key into it, rolled forward into the room, down the three steps at the entry, until he came to rest in a heap on the carpeted floor.

"Good afternoon, gentlemen," came the muffled and slightly slurred words from somewhere beneath his overcoat.

"He's drunk!" Castle exclaimed. "Thurston, how much of this boorish behavior must we bear?"

Jonah would have preferred to remain as he was more or less indefinitely, but reluctantly pulled himself up to a sitting position before he tried to speak. "This evening's *Washington Post* will report that the Princess Ka...Ka... well, the Princess, is here to fight Prince David Kawanah...nah...nah... *Koa*, for the Queen's throne, although the old gal has yet to relinquish it to either of them." He cautiously rose to a standing position, took a moment to steady himself, adjusted his mouth as if there were some problem with it, then continued. "Never mind that the story is in reality no more than so much bullshit, by tomorrow morning all of Washington will be talking about royal infighting, romantic and incestuous intrigue, and general chaos among the Hawaiian competitors to a throne that no longer exists." He puffed out his chest proudly. "As for me, I believe I'll have a bath."

Castle and Thurston stared at him, mouths agape, as he ceremoniously saluted them and disappeared into the bathroom. As they turned toward each other the bathroom door opened again and Jonah stuck out his head and declared, "You're welcome," and slammed the door behind him.

The commissioners snatched up the afternoon's *Washington Post* and found the article on the front page, just below the fold. It was everything Jonah had promised. And by the time the papers arrived the following morning Garrett's story had inspired a reaction of successive pieces in every other paper. Never mind that the original story was based on a hypothetical discussion between two very drunk political operatives, it sent reporters from every paper after the royals and their representatives to give them a chance to confirm or deny Garrett's story. Naturally they denied every word of it, but the press tended to find what it was looking for, regardless of whether it actually existed. The buzz intensified when Koa told the *New York Times* that he did not believe the Princess's presence in Washington served any constructive purpose and she should return to England. That ill-advised comment extended the life cycle of the story by at least a few days.

When Jonah emerged from his room the next morning, refreshed from twelve hours of sleep, which must have begun in the bathtub— he had no memory of actually going to his bed, despite waking up there—he found two very happy commissioners enjoying their breakfast amid the morning papers.

"Come in, Jonah!" said Castle, strangely happy to see him. "I ordered you a plate of breakfast. Come and read the morning papers while you eat."

He did as he was told and enjoyed his ham and eggs with a collection of articles on the "Battle Royale"—a wild story of competition among various Hawaiian elites, some of whom he had never heard of, and who may in fact not have existed. The story, being less than a day old, could probably have used some fact-checking, but the editorial staffs obviously found that burdensome in the face of deadlines and cut-throat competition.

"More good news, perhaps," said Thurston, pointing to the morning's mail on the window sill. "We have received a summons from the State Department. You seem to have secured us a meeting with the Secretary of State for Monday the ninth."

"Really? The President and Mrs. Cleveland are having the Princess over for dinner on the eighth."

"How on earth do you know these things?" Castle asked with a mixture of exasperation and incredulity. Rather than answer, Jonah decided to stuff a forkful of ham in his mouth. After washing it down with a gulp of coffee he turned to Thurston and asked about the morning's mail.

"Do you mind if I have a look through the stack?"

"There's nothing from Penelope, I'm afraid," Thurston said, knowing what Jonah was looking for.

Jonah fell silent. He searched his memory for every line he had written her, quite unable to remember anything that might cause offense. Thurston, suffering a rare moment of bonhomies, could see that the secretary was deeply troubled and decided to buck him up a bit.

"Jonah, you know, planting this story was no small thing. In the past it's always seemed to me that you were just along for the ride—helpful, to be sure, and commendably resourceful, but this is the first time you've ever shown any initiative. I feel I need to point out that this move was ethically suspect, underhanded, and completely Machiavellian." He paused and then added, "I'm proud of you."

"Thank you?" Jonah responded, a little unsure if he had just received a compliment.

"Not at all. As I've said before, I think you're a natural lawyer. We'll have to see to that once the current business is done."

"Here, here," Castle said in agreement, without looking up from his newspaper. "If it were possible to teach him manners we could even bring him into our firm."

Jonah pointed at Castle and asked Thurston, "Does he not realize that I'm still in the room?"

"He doesn't care," Castle said, referring to himself in the third person.

With the wild coverage of the royals, the commissioners regained some of the momentum they had lost with the departure of the Harrison Administration. Jonah calculated the number of editorials on Hawaiian annexation, pro and con, and found a considerable majority in favor of welcoming the islands into the American orbit. The annexationists counted on these editorialists having some influence with Cleveland and his cabinet. And just as surely all the propaganda the commissioners had so assiduously distributed would have some effect. But on Sunday night when Jonah strolled past the White House he lingered there a few moments, wondering how the Princess was doing with the President. Would all his labor fall impotent before the power of this seventeen-year-old beauty? It was a damnably reasonable question.

"That's fine," Jonah responded when his superiors informed him Monday morning that he would not be joining them in their meeting with Secretary Gresham.

"It is?" Thurston asked. "I imagined you'd be disappointed."

"I am, I suppose, but I really want to get down to the Willard. I'm going to invite Neumann to breakfast with me there. He could still be a very useful contact if he hasn't figured out that I'm the one who planted that story, or rather manipulated him into planting it."

"You know," Castle said to Thurston, soto voce, "the boy is crafty. Before too long we could end up working for him," he indicated Jonah with a twitch of his brow.

"Fine with me," Thurston observed. "I didn't want this job, anyhow."

Jonah walked down to the Willard Hotel and left a note at the desk asking Neumann to join him in the restaurant. Jonah took a table where he could keep one eye on the lobby as he absently passed the time with coffee and a newspaper. After a while he saw Neumann walk through the lobby, but not toward the restaurant. Jonah briskly left to catch him on the sidewalk.

"Neumann, I thought we could have breakfast."

"Fuck you, Christian."

"I see you've learned the local dialect." *So much for keeping Neumann as a contact,* he thought.

"And I see you're a damn snake in the grass. I don't know how you got that story into the *Post,* but I've got a good mind to sue you."

"I didn't put anything anywhere. And if I were you I'd be talking to Koa about what he says to the *New York Times.*"

Neumann turned at Jonah, clearly feeling like he had the upper hand. "Koa doesn't matter. You and the rest of the damn P.G.'s don't matter. Cleveland matters, and that's all. He thinks the Princess is spectacular. His Secretary of State thinks P.G.'s are a bunch of bandits—

"Pirates," Jonah corrected him.

"As you like... In any case, he's going to withdraw your damn treaty and open an investigation."

"An investigation?" Jonah responded lamely.

"Correct! Once he gets the full story on what your damned little group of pirates did, you'll be receiving instructions from the United States government to reinstate the Queen."

"Can you prove this?" Jonah hoped he sounded genuinely skeptical, but he saw the truth of it in Neumann's anger.

"You'll see the proof of it soon enough."

'Soon enough,' was of course not soon enough. The earth was shifting beneath the Commission and Jonah needed to know what it meant—now. He bade farewell and good luck to Neumann, who responded by turning his back and stomping away. Jonah returned to the restaurant in the Willard and slumped in his chair where he found his paper and coffee, now cold, still at his table. He needed to move, but how? A lot of hard work and alcohol had been expended in vain.

Princess Ka'iulani and her lady-in-waiting, Mrs. Whatoff, who doubled as a chaperone, were seated at a booth across the restaurant and saw him come in. When Jonah finally noticed the Princess, she had put on her spectacles and was peering across the room at him. Jonah watched them over his paper. Mrs. Whatoff joined her in the stare; they looked his way and put their heads together, very obviously talking about him. It began to look like something approaching a disagreement, which never actually happens between royals and their minions, but the older woman was clearly advising the Princess against whatever it was she wanted to do. Finally, with a look of surrender, the dignified Mrs. Whatoff rose from their booth and crossed the room toward Jonah.

"Excuse me," the older woman asked, "You are one of the P.G.'s?"

"It's highly unlikely that you'd be standing here if I were not."

"Princess Ka'iulani," she said coldly, "has graciously invited you to her table."

"I'd be delighted," said Jonah. He did not wish to hear a seventeen-year-old girl gloat at his expense, even if she was a princess, but he thought it prudent to hear what she had to say. Besides, the Princess had an undeniable allure, which Jonah noticed when he saw her in New York and never quite forgot.

Jonah followed the woman across the restaurant and bowed appropriately before the Princess. She looked into his eyes with deep interest as he stood before her and introduced himself. There was no warmth in her expression, only curiosity, as if she sought information in his visage. After too many uncomfortable moments of silent examination, Jonah finally asked, "May I sit?" The Princess indicated the bench opposite her. He sat. She stared. A minute passed and Jonah had had enough.

"Good day, Princess. I hope you enjoy the rest of your stay in Washington."

"Sit" she ordered quietly.

"I am sorry, but I don't think so. There are limits to how long I can be expected to sit here under overt scrutiny."

"You do not look like a pirate, Jonah Christian."

"Thank you, your highness, I think. You do, on the other hand, look very much like a princess."

"You are cousin Muanu's paramour?"

"Was. I've been dismissed." This got Jonah's attention; Muanu was the last thing he expected to discuss with the Princess.

"Small wonder. She gave you love and you stole her country."

"Actually, I was but the amanuensis for the man who stole her country, but I did take excellent notes on the event." He rose to leave.

"I find your humor misplaced."

"My apologies, Your Majesty. I'm only trying to make the point that I can hardly be held responsible for the revolution that was executed by Hawaiians. I only work for them."

"Hawaiians?"

"Inasmuch as they were born and raised in Hawaii, yes. I always thought, as the Fourteenth Amendment states, that being born in America makes you an American. Thus it seems logical enough to my American brain that being born in Hawaii made one a Hawaiian."

The Princess stared at him for a long moment. "There is more to being a Hawaiian than simply being born on the islands."

266

"Indeed, I've learned that there was more to being Hawaiian than I could possibly comprehend," Jonah admitted. Sensing they might have temporarily reached some common ground, he sought to change the subject to what he really wanted to know. "I hear you spent the evening at the White House the other night. I hope you enjoyed it. I've never been there, myself."

The Princess relaxed a little with the change in subject. "Your President is a good man—and funny, too. We enjoyed ourselves, very much, thank you."

"Did he promise that he would return your country to you, as Neumann tells me?"

The Princess continued her habit of pausing and staring before answering her questioner. "You would not know this, but one does not discuss such things at a state dinner. This process may be a long one, but in the end Hawaii will be returned to the Hawaiians, and the P.G.'s will be lost to history." Her dark eyes went cold again. "Good day, Mr. Christian."

Jonah still knew nothing of the threatened investigation, but having spoken with the Princess, he actually found himself in sympathy with Neumann for having to work with royals on a daily basis. The encounter had proved a tactical waste of time; he had learned nothing of value, and he was not at all sure that she could have told him anything about the President's plans, or Neumann's insistence that there would be an investigation. It was clear—as Thurston had surmised from the start—that the Princess and the royal commissioners were not working in concert. The opposition was divided.

Jonah spent the rest of the morning and afternoon "dropping in" on friends at the newspapers and congressional offices casually trying to discover what they knew. It was a balancing act, trying to learn if they had any news without tipping them off to something they did not already know; the last thing he wanted to do was inadvertently plant a story about a possible investigation. He learned nothing. By the end of the afternoon all the effort had gotten him was a series of short visits and sore feet.

He returned to the hotel to check for messages, only to find that there were none. In a moment of inspiration he picked up the Canadian Bourbon he had illegally procured through a diplomatic pouch, and took a cab back to the Capitol with his case of alcohol bouncing on the seat beside him.

"Senator Morgan around?" Jonah asked, poking his head into the offices of the senior senator from Alabama.

"Hello, Jonah," came the response of his aide. "I'll ask him if he has a minute."

"Be sure to tell him what I'm carrying under my arm here," Jonah indicated the case of bourbon.

Moments later he was in Morgan's office. Jonah set his offering on the Senator's desk and with a slight smile said, "Compliments of the future great state of Hawaii."

"Thank you, my boy," said the Senator in his slow southern drawl. "Officially, I prefer Southern sour mash, but just between you and me, this is some of the smoothest sippin' stuff I've ever tasted." The Senator cocked an eyebrow and added, "I'm guessing that it is no coincidence that you chose this particular evening to call on me?" The old man obviously knew something. Jonah waited for him to continue. Instead, Morgan walked to the door and spoke to his aide. "Harley, I believe that the Hawaiian gentleman and I will have a 'social dinner' this evening. Make the arrangements, won't you?"

"I'm not actually Hawaiian, Senator," Jonah corrected him. But Morgan didn't care. He put his arm around Jonah's shoulder and said, "You didn't have plans for the evening, did you, son?" He continued without waiting for an answer. "You do not know it yet, but you're actually having a very bad day, my boy. And if you'll allow me, I'd like to provide you with a meal, some salve for your political wounds, and a little education about the Southern congressional caucus. I believe you're going to need all three."

"I have political wounds?"

"Grab one of those bottles, won't you, and we'll be on our way."

Moments later, bourbon in hand and a senator on his arm, Jonah was walking across the District of Columbia listening to the Southern narrative of post-Civil War redemption. Senator Morgan was part of a cadre of Southern congressmen known as "the Redeemers" for their devotion to the South's recovery after defeat in war and the humiliation of Northern occupation. The probationary period called "congressional reconstruction" seared a generation of Southern politicians. The story continued, block after block in a mild Washington evening, until they entered a luxuriously appointed house that was obviously some sort of social club. They were greeted at the door by a black man in a tuxedo who recognized Senator Morgan with a bow. He turned out to be the only man in the employ of this establishment.

A beautiful woman dressed in a breathtakingly immodest gown slunk up to Morgan familiarly. "Welcome, Senator." She took his overcoat, hat, and scarf. "Who's your friend?" she looked Jonah up and down as if she were measuring him for something. She noticed the bottle in Jonah's hand. "Why, Senator, you have always found the whiskey in my house to your liking in the past—did you really need to bring your own?" Her southern drawl matched the senator's exactly, which was probably no coincidence.

"It's a special fifth from my Hawaiian friend here, Mr. Jonah Christian."

"Well then," she said, slipping the bottle out of Jonah's hand. "I'll see that it makes it to your table. In the meantime, I'll have a couple glasses brought to you in the parlor." She took a few steps, stopped and turned back to them. "He certainly doesn't look Hawaiian."

The parlor was a large room with velvet couches and brocade settees arranged around small tables. The moneyed men of

Washington, and various moneyed passers-through, came here for cigars, brandy, and, not incidentally, carnal recreation. The room was, in most respects, just like any other gentleman's club, except that the servers were all vividly painted ladies in attire so provocative that they would certainly face arrest if they were so dressed in any other public establishment. Jonah admired the economical way the women served drinks, bending down to put their breasts into the recipient's direct line of sight, while simultaneously placing derrieres within inches of the face of the men at the adjacent table. Lovely as the maneuver was, it made it difficult to focus on the reprise of the Senator's narrative on Southern redemption, which seemed to have no end.

Once they had finished their drinks a comely young woman led them to a private dining room where they were served one of the best meals Jonah had encountered in Washington. As he munched on his steak, Morgan finally summed up his story. "You see, Jonah, the Southern politician doesn't care for acquiring foreign territory. He feels too much like his home has been treated like foreign territory—defeated and dominated by outsiders for too long. He wants the Southland developed, its economy repaired, its white children schooled, and its race problem solved."

"But you're a Southern congressman and you've always favored American expansion."

"And I'll see to it that the rest of the Southern delegation does as well, but it will take time, my boy, perhaps years. For now, they see American expansion as Yankee aggrandizement, and that will tend to make a Southern man's blood run cold."

"So it's true? The President is going to send an investigator to Hawaii?"

Morgan nodded. "James Blount. United States Representative from Georgia these last twenty years, and Chairman of the House Committee on Foreign Relations the last two. He chose not to run again this year. I believe he wanted a diplomatic post—looks like he got it."

"You mean he'll be the U.S. minister to Hawaii?"

"Yes, ambassador plenipotentiary. He'll be empowered to do pretty much whatever he wants on behalf of the United States government. Blount's a good man, and I won't speak ill of him," the senator stated firmly.

"But you think he may be bad for the provisional government?" Jonah continued to probe.

"It doesn't look good for you white Hawaiians. It surely does not. Those boys you work for look, sound, and act like something right out of Boston. A bunch of Yankees in charge of a bunch of coloreds. That won't set well with a gentleman veteran of the Confederate Army like Congressman Blount." Morgan shook his head slowly. "Now, myself, it seems to me that Hawaii would be an excellent place to send American Negroes, but I don't think Blount sees it that way. Most of my colleagues want to keep them in the South for labor."

Jonah could not quite believe what he just heard. He wanted to ask Morgan how he could possibly consider actually removing a population of millions. Even if he ignored the ethics of it, the logistics alone made the idea absurd on its face. He decided to stick to the topic at hand and press his case one last time. "The treaty has already gone to the Senate. You're the Foreign Affairs chairman there. Couldn't the Senate simply pass the treaty while Blount is in Hawaii?"

"Your treaty has been withdrawn." He stuck a bite of steak in his mouth and chewed while Jonah digested that piece of news. "I *told* you that you were having a bad day, son. I received a one-sentence message from the State Department this afternoon just before you got to my office. The thing is withdrawn and I can't hold a vote on a treaty I don't have."

"Well, thank you, sir. I appreciate you telling me this. If it's not too much to ask, do you think we could return to your office? I'd like to have a look at that message for myself, if I may, and collect any other details I can."

"Sure, son. I understand you need to nail this down, even though it won't make much difference. Once we're done with our, shall we say, *dessert*, we can head back to the Capitol."

"'Dessert' sir?"

Jonah was led down the hall to a room by a young woman wearing nothing but a bodice and bloomers. She closed the door behind them, dimmed the oil lamp slightly, then led him to the bed.

"What's your name?" Jonah asked awkwardly, as the girl slid off his vest and untied his tie.

"Tammy, unless you'd like to call me something else, sugar," came the sultry reply. She reached up to unbutton his shirt.

"Thank you, Tammy," he said as he gently held her hands to stop her from undoing any more of his buttons.

"You want to keep your clothes on? We can do it that way, sugar," she said, most accommodatingly as she stood back and unbuttoned her bodice and dropped it to the floor. Her qualifications for the job were obvious and alluring, but after a moment's gaping Jonah was able to find his voice.

"Please, Tammy, I really shouldn't be here."

"Sure you should, honey. Any friend of the Senator is a friend of ours."

"No, it's not that. I mean…," but in fact he was not at all sure what he meant, and the generous distractions swaying before his eyes did nothing to clear his head. "You are very lovely, but I have someone at home, I think."

"You're not sure, sugar?" She fiddled with the bloomer ties at her waist.

"Jonah. I wish you'd call me Jonah."

"I'll call you anything you want," she whispered in his ear, then placed little kisses on his neck while her hand slid slowly down his chest, over his stomach, and into his pants. Her touch was so gentle, so warm, and what he had been missing since he left Hawaii. He forced himself to step back from her, and holding her at arm's length he said, "Perhaps we could just talk?"

"Oh, sure, suga—I mean, Jonah. We do that here, too. Would you like me to put my top back on?"

"Uh, well, not necessarily." It did not seem reasonable to take fidelity too far, given that he was no longer sure he had someone to be faithful to. "I mean, I want you to be comfortable, naturally. If this is good for you, uh, I think—"

She smiled at his discomfiture, and sat on the bed. She patted the mattress next to her, and Jonah took his place. "Do you want to talk," she asked, then lowered her voice to something like a groan that left absolutely no room for misinterpretation, "or do you want to... *talk?*"

"Uh, the other one," Jonah stammered.

"All right, honey," she said, scooting back on the bed to a conversational distance. "Why don't you tell me about this girl of yours—it is a girl, isn't it?"

"Oh yes, very much so. I've known her for quite some time, but we only recently became romantically attached a day or so before I had to leave her to come here."

"Well, write her a letter, darlin'. A girl loves to receive romantic letters from her beau."

"I have—dozens of them." Suddenly his doubts began to spill out. "I started writing the day we left. It was wonderful for about a month, receiving a letter from her every day. But then they stopped, and I can't understand why."

Tammy began to look just the slightest bit bored. "Why, that's just terrible, honey." She pulled his head to her naked breasts and lay back on the bed. "You tell Tammy all about it."

He enjoyed the position for a moment, but it just felt entirely too good. With heroic restraint, he sat up again on the edge of the bed and continued. "If something had happened to her, my boss certainly would have heard about it, but we've heard nothing. I

273

don't know what I could have done to make her stop writing."

"I don't imagine you've done *anything*, darlin'. How old is this girl?"

"Seventeen."

She perked up a little. "Oh, sweetie pie, a seventeen-year-old girl doesn't know what she wants if what she wants is so far away. Oh my! You're here, she's there—where, exactly?"

"Hawaii," Jonah said, suddenly realizing how very far away it was.

"Hawaii!" Tammy exclaimed. "Way out there in the ocean? Oh, please, honey, that girl has found someone else to send her letters by now—perhaps French ones from someone who can deliver them personally."

Jonah's heart sank. His shoulders slumped while he sat silently in the semidarkness of the room. Tammy, an expert in such matters, sat up next to him and leaned her head on his shoulder and whispered, "Why don't you let Tammy make you feel better, honey?"

"Thanks, really, but no. I don't feel well," he said quite honestly. He had been through heartbreak before, and having heard Tammy's analysis of the situation, the pain returned. "I'm going to go back to the dining room to wait for the Senator." He stood up and looked down at the lovely prostitute. "I'm sure our time together has been taken care of. You can enjoy some rest. But if the Senator asks, would you please tell him that I made such passionate love to you that I have spoiled you for other men?"

"Sure, honey. Happy to oblige."

Jonah took one look at Castle and Thurston upon entering the suite and knew their meeting with the Secretary of State had not gone well.

"How was your meeting with Gresham?" he asked.

The two men glowered at him.

"That good, eh?"

"If our destiny is in the hands of that dark, vindictive little man," Castle said of the Secretary of State, "then we have no hope."

"Dark? Vindictive?" Jonah echoed. Evidently the grudge he was rumored to hold against his predecessor was inconveniently real.

"It was *not* an encouraging meeting," Thurston ameliorated Castle's interpretation somewhat.

"Not encouraging?" Castle roared. "The man treated us like beggars! It was as if he couldn't look at us without seeing John Foster's face. We were nothing but a waste of his time. He said almost nothing, just sat there behind his desk waiting for us to leave. He would not even deign to discuss the treaty. Well, the treaty is in the Senate and we've got the votes, so that nasty little man can go hang."

Jonah did not respond, and the two men noted his silence immediately.

"Jonah?" Thurston said cautiously. "What do you know?"

"The treaty has been withdrawn," Jonah said evenly. Castle and Thurston were thunderstruck. "I'm sorry," Jonah continued. "Senator Morgan just told me."

"Gresham! That patronizing son of a bitch!" Castle thundered. Jonah had never heard the man use that particular term before, and from Thurston's expression he could tell that his boss hadn't either. "He gave no indication that he would do any such thing. We were right there in his office! He might have said *something*."

"Jonah, are you sure?" Thurston was grasping at straws. Jonah handed him a piece of paper.

"Senator Morgan allowed me to copy this down from the original note. One sentence. That's all it takes, evidently."

"Well, goddamn," was all Thurston could think to say.

"It gets worse."

The two men looked incredulously at the young man.

"Gresham has appointed an investigator, Former Congressman James Blount. He's going to Honolulu."

"I know Blount," said Thurston. "I met him last year when I was here." Thurston went into silent calculation, as he always did when disaster struck. Castle, who saw no hope, sat in morose silence.

Jonah went to the cabinet and procured a bottle of brandy and three glasses. He placed a glass in front of each man. Castle looked at his glass, then Thurston, shrugged his shoulders and took a long sip from his glass. Then another. Thurston did the same, and a moment later Jonah refilled the glasses.

"I don't know where this leaves us," Castle said, shaking his gray head.

"Limbo," was Thurston's response. "There is nothing we can do until Blount finishes his investigation. Not here, in any case." He looked at Jonah. "Go to Honolulu. Get there before Blount if you can. Set things up for him. He's a Southern gentleman—a former slaveholder and Confederate officer—who is very unlikely to approve of colored people running a strategic island in the middle of the Pacific. We should be able to turn this man to our way of thinking."

"I'm not sure," Jonah said. "Senator Morgan schooled me on these Southern 'redeemers,' and American expansion is not their cup of bourbon, it seems."

"That does not matter," Thurston insisted. "We have come too far to lose everything because Walter Gresham holds a grudge against John Foster."

"Okay, I'll go to Honolulu immediately. What are you going to do?"

"Castle," Thurston turned to his colleague, ignoring Jonah's question. "Can you stay here through July?"

"I suppose. Why, where are you going?"

"I'm going to the World's Fair. Hawaii has an exhibition there and I'm going to use it to show the world that for the first time our island nation is in capable hands." Thurston's determination had returned; he was already strategizing the next phase of Hawaiian annexation. "Jonah, as soon as Blount concludes his investigation in Honolulu I want you to meet me in Chicago."

"Yes, sir," Jonah said. He was already planning how to take advantage of the opportunity to see Penelope face to face.

"We're not finished yet, gentleman," Thurston declared. "Not by a damn sight."

CHAPTER TWELVE

The reporter noticed that the briefest question asked of Lorrin Thurston received the most thorough and loquacious reply. When speaking of the proposed union between Hawaii and America, the man was nothing less than rhapsodic. Thurston rose and began to pace in the back office of the Hawaiian exhibit at the Chicago World's Fair, his voice clear and confident, expounding on the historical relationship between Hawaii and the United States, and not incidentally the obvious, self-evident, irrefutable logic of annexation. He must have answered every one of these questions a hundred times before, for a hundred different audiences. Yet, as a good lawyer, or salesman, he stated his case as if the commandment to join Hawaii with the United States was handed down on stone tablets.

"—But what about Congressman Blount's investigation?" She interrupted him just as he was about to launch into the "key" theory of Hawaii's strategic importance to the United States.

"Blount," Thurston began carefully, "that is *former* Congressman Blount, I'm sure will recommend annexation. I've met the man—a true southern gentleman. He has devoted himself to the cause of improving government and society in his native South; I simply can't imagine that he would prevent us from doing the same for our beloved islands."

"So you see the Provisional Government of Hawaii as fulfilling a role similar to that of the so-called 'Redeemers' in Congress, uplifting a benighted race?"

"Essentially, yes." He paused for a moment, searching for just the right words. He didn't want to seem condescending just because the reporter was a woman. "Consider the African exhibits here at the Exposition—I'm sure you've seen them. You can see the lower civilizations and more advanced tribes on display. It's as if Darwin's theory is laid out before our very eyes."

"I don't know," the reporter said, "All I saw were a bunch of colored people."

"That's the point, my dear. Look at them in their primitive environment and compare it to the utopian heights of Western civilization on display all around you at this fair—or any Western city."

"Yes, I suppose you're right, but they're just displays, Mr. Thurston."

"Please," Thurston continued. "Consider the case of my own homeland, Hawaii. We have been able to take colored savages and, through a rigorous process of instruction and example, uplift them to a point where they could live as civilized men and women—still childlike in many ways, but certainly no longer savage."

They were interrupted by a knock on the door, but the visitor barged in without awaiting invitation. Jonah Christian entered quickly without actually greeting Thurston, whom he had not seen in months. Carrying a leather valise in his left hand while digging into it with his right, he was obviously in a hurry to show Thurston whatever the bag contained and he rushed past the pretty reporter, quite unaware anyone else was in the room. "Thurston," he began without looking up. "You've got to read this."

Thurston put his hand on Jonah's arm to prevent him from pulling whatever it was from the valise. "Jonah, a moment, if you would." Jonah lifted his head and began to protest, but Thurston held up a hand to stop him. "First, welcome to Chicago—good to see you. Second, allow me to introduce you to Miss Lydia Burke, better known as L. C. Burke, of United Press International."

Jonah dropped both his jaw and his valise. His mind raced. What the hell was his ex-wife doing here? He was obviously not going to be able to form words for a while, so Lydia, who recovered her composure more quickly, helped him. "How do you do, Mr. Jones?" She rose and extended her hand in a gesture of journalistic professionalism.

Somewhere between his secretary's dumbstruck paralysis and the visiting reporter's knowledge of Jonah's name—albeit not his current name—Thurston deduced that these two were not unknown to each other.

"Tell me, Miss Burke; how long have you been in Chicago?" Thurston asked, probing as Jonah recovered his composure.

"Just a few months, actually," she responded, disengaging her hand from that of her still mute ex-husband.

"And where were you before that?" Thurston pressed.

"Is that important?" Lydia was suddenly aware that these were not merely questions, but rather a line of questioning.

"Are you, by any chance, from Seattle?"

"Yes, she is," Jonah finally found his voice.

"Your wife?"

"*Ex*-wife, yes."

"Ah!" Thurston's demeanor brightened immediately. "Any wife of Jonah's is a friend of mine, Miss Burke. I was truly impressed with the way your lawyers handled the annulment—absolutely seamless!"

"You must say that to all his wives," she said, somewhat relieved, if puzzled by the odd compliment.

"But tell me, my dear—are you still going to print the article, or was this just a ruse to see Jonah?"

"Jonah? You mean Christopher," Lydia corrected him.

"Well then…" Thurston began the sentence but allowed the words to hang in the air as he relished Jonah's agitated silence. If the young woman was unaware that Jonah had changed his name, she could not have known that he would be there. And just as obviously, Jonah had not expected to see Miss Burke. Thurston had never before seen the usually insouciant assistant so nonplussed. At last, he broke the silence. "Why don't you two go ahead and chat here in the office. I'll go out and mingle with the folks."

"Actually, sir," Jonah responded, "you and I ought to talk. Right now." He turned to his former wife, still not quite comprehending her presence in the room. "Lydia," he said with all the cold politeness he could muster. "Would you be so kind as to wait outside? This shouldn't take a minute."

"Of course," she said, still wondering why Thurston called him 'Jonah.' "I'll be outside enjoying your instructive exhibit."

Once she had left the room Thurston turned to Jonah and awaited an explanation. Given the way he shooed his ex-wife out of the room, Thurston reasoned that he must have been carrying quite a bomb in that valise. Jonah pulled out sixty hastily typed pages and set them on the desk. "Read this. Once you've finished I believe it would be wisest to burn it."

"What is it?" Thurston asked as he began to read, but the answer was obvious before he got through the first paragraph. "Blount's report! My God, Jonah, how did you get this?"

"This is just the most important fifty-pages of it—Blount's interpretation of the revolution and his recommendations. All told, it's almost a 1,500-page document."

"But how did you get these pages?"

Jonah paused for a moment before deciding how to answer this delicate question. The moment Jonah had learned that Blount had completed his report, he dispatched Willie Kaae to burglarize Blount's office in the dead of night. The ethically flexible Willie brought the pilfered report to the Annexation Commission office, where five loyal clerks helped Jonah type the most critical section, Blount's own analysis and conclusions. While Willie snuck the document back into the American investigator's office, Jonah packed up his copied sections and abandoned Hawaii on the first available ship to San Francisco. Jonah thought it unwise to share these duplicitous details with Thurston, so rather than answer the man's question he asked one of his own.

"Do you really want to know?"

It was Thurston's turn to pause. "No," he said, narrowing his eyes at Jonah. "No, I don't."

Jonah stood by while Thurston read the first few pages. As the contents became clear to him he dropped his hands in his lap and slumped in his chair, crestfallen. "For God's sake. This could have been written by the Queen herself."

"My thoughts, exactly. As you read on it doesn't get any better."

"He makes us look like mere tools of the American minister's freelance imperialism—or worse—common thieves! Has anyone else seen this yet?"

"No. Blount was still in Honolulu when I left, and would be for several days," Jonah reassured him. "The moment I secured these pages I packed a bag and headed to the wharf to book passage for San Francisco."

"Good. You'd better move on to Washington. We'll need to find a way to attack the report without attacking its author, at least not overtly. If we don't undermine his conclusions..." Thurston started pacing in front of the desk. After months away from politics, occupying himself with business in Chicago, he was back in the fight. "You have the advantage of knowing what is in this... this damned report," he said, waving his hand toward it as if it were emitting a foul smell. "Use that foreknowledge. Preemptively subvert as many of his points as you can. Start planting articles to that end—under my byline."

"I will, of course." He would have happily boarded a train that minute to avoid the woman who was waiting for him outside the door.

"Before you go out to meet your lovely former wife, I would like to clarify a couple things about your work in Honolulu," Thurston said sternly.

"I sent you regular reports," Jonah replied, thankful for the delay. He did not want to go out there.

"So you did, Jonah," Thurston said as he pulled the file containing

Jonah's correspondence from a valise he carried with him. "But there are also these other reports," he said, indicating the papers on his desk, "from other ministries. Evidently there was a great deal of concern about your activities?"

"I don't know why," Jonah tried to dismiss the question. "All I was doing was setting up a permanent home in the government for the Annexation Commission—as per your instructions. Compared to the methodology I used in Washington, I was positively angelic."

"Yes, that may be. But you do seem to have stepped on a quite a few toes."

"Toes, sir?" Distracted as he was, Jonah tried to appear interested. "How so?"

"Well, staffing was an issue, for one thing."

Jonah was taken aback. "We have an excellent staff. They work hard, and they're efficient as can be. Not only that, I've got them working with their counterparts at your newspaper, using the *Advertiser's* resources. We've produced some of the slickest propaganda for annexation, well—you've seen it. I've sent it all to you."

"Yes, yes, Jonah," Thurston tried to settle him down. "You've been doing excellent work, and the staff is obviously well-trained, but some of the ministers are concerned with the way you appropriated trained staff from the other ministries and, well the—how shall I put it?—tenor of the staff."

"Sir?"

"They're all women, Jonah. Young ones, pretty ones, from what I read here," Thurston tapped the file folder before him.

"I can hardly be held responsible for that," the secretary replied defensively. "I requested clerical personnel from the other ministries and all these girls showed up. 'Type writers and clerks' is what I asked for. I'm certain I never used the term 'pretty girl.'" Under his boss's cross-examination, Jonah felt suddenly guilty, but the fact that the women far outnumbered the men was actually to be expected. So many more women matriculated now, yet, as Thurston's informants demonstrated, the professions remained actively hostile to working women. Armed with fine educations and the best intentions, these women found almost nowhere to apply their newfound learning except missionary work and teaching. Laws of supply and demand being as they are, clerical work, once an all-male bastion, was quickly becoming a more feminine preserve.

Thurston redirected. "What was this baseball business?" He pulled another letter from the sheaf. "I read that you actually formed your," Thurston caught himself, "*our* staff, into a baseball team."

"I thought it would be good for morale," Jonah shrugged. And it was. Besides, it was softball."

"Softball?"

"Yes—larger, softer ball, smaller diamond, four outfielders. It's a better game for women, and they took to it right away."

"I heard."

"We formed a team—*The P.G.'s*—and found other teams to play at least once a week."

"And didn't anyone from the other ministries complain about seeing you and your young ladies practicing baseball, er, softball, on the grounds of the Aliiolani Hale?" Thurston was genuinely interested in how he accomplished this. "They were certainly complaining to me," he said, holding up a letter.

"No one complained," he insisted. "Come to think of it, I did notice a couple officials approaching me rather sternly one afternoon while I was practicing with the girls, but they saw something on the field that stopped them."

"And what might that have been?"

"President Dole."

"What the devil was President Dole doing on the field?"

"He helped me teach the girls to throw and catch, from time to time. He said it relaxed him."

Thurston had to think about that for a moment. He contemplated the image of President Dole, kindly in his formal black suit and long and flowing beard, taking a few moments out of his day to have a catch with a bunch of pretty young clerks. Only Jonah could make this happen.

"Well, as I hear it, these girls—"

"They weren't all girls, sir. I had two men on staff as well—Willie Kaae, in fact."

"Apparently, these girls were all quite devoted to you—working late into the evenings when asked. I don't suppose that sat well with your dear Penelope."

Jonah said nothing, but winced noticeably at the mention of Penelope's name.

"Jonah?" Thurston unexpectedly hit a nerve and he knew it. He had brought up the most miserable part of Jonah's miserable stay in Hawaii. The crushing disappointment had come early, and Jonah spent nearly every moment of the ensuing three months impatiently waiting for Congressman Blount to finish his report so he could get off the islands and never return. Thurston, unaware of this, pressed on. "Given your state of mind when we parted in Washington, I fully expected to meet you here in Chicago with Miss Tubbs on your arm as your latest wife."

"Yes, well, something unexpectedly came between us," Jonah observed quietly.

"Her father?"

"Her husband. And their baby," he paused, "but not in that order."

Thurston was momentarily mute as he attempted to make sense of Jonah's few words. "She was pregnant when you arrived?"

"—And married; the one event precipitating the other."

"My God, a minister's daughter? How could this happen?"

"The usual way, I suppose." In fact, beyond the mechanics of conceiving a child, Jonah knew exactly how Penelope had come to be pregnant. Once he had recovered from the devastating news, he arranged to see her alone. Penelope sheepishly explained that in those frantic days of revolution, he had left her initiation into sensual pleasure frustratingly incomplete. She was "in quite a state," as she put it. Consumed with a yearning she scarcely understood,

285

one that intensified as she watched Jonah sail off to sea, not knowing when, or if, he would return, she sought Muanu's advice. Jonah had rolled his eyes at the mention of the *pukua*'s name, knowing whatever came next could not be good. Still angry with Jonah for appropriating her country, the sorceress counseled Penelope to slake her lust with Jonah's good friend, her cousin Kalani. To Penelope's protestations of faithfulness to Jonah, Muanu assured her that a man like Jonah would prefer a knowledgeable wife—as proof of which Muanu offered her the lurid details of their own relationship. Trusting and innocent, Penelope accepted her advice and yielded; cousin Kalani was happy to help.

Muanu explained that the first time is rarely satisfying for a girl, so subsequent encounters ensued, each more satisfying than the last. Desire encouraged abandon, leading to recklessness, ultimately ending in pregnancy. The Reverend Tubbs, at first apoplectic at the news, was at least as concerned with his good name as he was for his daughter's virtue, and thus he reacted with pragmatic aplomb. Kalani was retroactively metamorphosed from a lazy laborer of a contemptuous race into "an old family friend—practically a member of the family already," who was married to his daughter with extreme haste. The Reverend Tubbs's discomfiture, however amusing, was hardly enough to ameliorate Jonah's heartbreak at discovering that, once again, the woman he loved was married to someone else.

"Ouch," Thurston winced. "Reverend Tubbs's own daughter? And you—your luck with women is, well, you just don't have any. Maybe you should avoid them for a while." He clapped the boy on the shoulder sympathetically.

"Good advice, sir. Meanwhile I'm going to go have a chat with one of my other mistakes. Maybe we'll go out into the crowds and see some of the fair together." Jonah attempted a wan smile. "Doubtless it's wiser that we keep as many witnesses around as possible."

"Either that or be sure to make it look like an accident." It was difficult to tell whether Thurston was kidding. "Nice chatting."

"Before I go out there," he pointed vaguely in the direction Lydia had gone, "what the hell is that woman doing here?" he asked, referring to his former wife.

"As I said, she's a reporter for the UPI. Came here to interview me." Thurston paused a moment, aware that Jonah was obviously reluctant to meet with the woman. "Jonah," Thurston lowered his voice, "reporters are good friends to have."

"Not this one, sir."

Jonah walked through the crowd looking for Lydia in the dark of the exhibit. It was a diorama representing the inside of the great Kilauea Volcano. Modest pyrotechnic displays and well-placed electric lights made it seem almost as if the ersatz volcano was bubbling to life. He saw Lydia standing off to the side of a group of spectators scribbling something in a notepad and he strode up her purposefully. He hoped to get this over with quickly.

"So," he began, "United Press International, eh? No wonder you never joined me in Hawaii."

Lydia stopped writing, which she had been doing not so much to take down useful information as to keep a mass of conflicting emotions in check. She was frightened, curious, and generally nervous about seeing her ex-husband again. She imagined he must hate her, and so far his demeanor did nothing to relieve her apprehension. She was also unbearably curious to know how and why "Christopher Jones" had become "Jonah Christian."

"Yes," she responded as casually as she could. "'UPI' we call it. It's good to see you, 'Jonah,' is it?"

"I'm sure you heard about my fall from grace. A change of identity seemed wise, under the circumstances." As he found himself making explanations to Lydia, of all people, he felt nothing but contempt for her and sought to end the reunion quickly. "I really don't believe we have anything to discuss."

"I don't blame you for being angry," she said calmly, hoping to avoid a public scene.

"Angry? I'm sure I'm not. Why would I be? After all, you merely married me under false pretenses, duped me into a missionary venture with the empty promise of connubial bliss, abandoned me to strangers, and then when I was far away and alone you spread magic lawyer dust over our unconsummated marriage and—poof—it disappeared as if it never existed at all. Why on earth would I be angry?"

"Look," she said, desperately seeking a truce, "could we possibly just spend a little time together today? We can discuss all of this in good time, but not now—*please*?"

"We don't need to discuss it at all. And I have no desire to spend any time with you, Lydia. I'd rather pay a visit to the dentist."

"Oh, Christopher—"

"Jonah!" He spoke more sharply than he intended to. Regaining his composure, he continued, "Christopher Jones is dead, and I'd prefer he stayed that way. And now Jonah Christian has only a day or two before he has to return to Washington. I'm going to see this fucking fair."

She was taken aback, but tried to ignore his shocking language; this was not the young man she had married. "Well, let me show you around, then," she began tentatively, "I know everything about this fair. I'm here working almost every day, and this press pass gets you anywhere you want to go." She flashed the cardstock with a golden "UPI" emblazoned below the word "Press."

He stood silently contemplating the offer for a long moment. His first impulse was to turn on his heel and walk away, but curiosity nagged at him. He would like to know, finally, the answer to several deep questions like 'Why?' 'What were you thinking?' and 'How could you?'

"You are my personal tour guide," he said flatly. "Lead on."

The Hawaiian exhibit was near the end of the Midway Plaisance, the mile-long, rectangular park that extended from Washington Park to the West and the great White City at Jackson Park on the banks of Lake Michigan. Walking down this vast avenue, every few steps they passed a new and exotic set of amusements.

"I think you'll like this," Lydia said, trying to sound cheerful. She directed him down a side street that seemed to open onto a page from the *Arabian Nights*. The open-air market bustled with activity, with sideshows here and there of jugglers, snake charmers—even a contortionist.

"What is this place?" Jonah asked, already too amused with the sight before his eyes he almost forgot how angry he was.

"You are in 'Little Egypt.' This lovely little nook of the fair is called Cairo Street. Just think of it as an open-air brothel." She peeked at his face out of the corner of her eyes.

"I beg your pardon?"

Lydia just smiled, boldly put her arm in his, and led him into a café. They made their way between the crowd of fairgoers in the Egyptian café and found a table with two open spots. They sat on pillows, the table being no more than fifteen inches off the ground; in the middle of the table sat a hookah pipe with hoses dangling here and there, like a great smoking spider. Several men—there were very few female guests in the café—were taking long pulls from the hoses of the pipe, inhaling the Turkish tobacco, blowing smoke rings at the veiled women with bare midriffs and plunging halters that did not so much cover their breasts as thrust them outward for display.

"This place is *fantastic*," Jonah said.

"Just wait," Lydia responded, indicating with a nod of her head the stage at the front of the café. One of the waitresses put down her tray and ascended the stage. The lights in the room lowered while two colored spotlights shone on the woman, making her dark skin seem to glow. Her body began to undulate in rhythm to the beating of drums and the melody of a wind instrument Jonah had never heard before, like a clarinet, yet different, with a far-away sound. It seemed as if the musicians controlled this woman's muscles, causing her to thrust and gyrate this way and that in long, sensual motions. Jonah could not help but think of the righteous indignation with which the Hawaiian Protestants had cast vitriol on the hula dance, which was all innocence compared to what he was witnessing now. The music and the dancer increased their speed and intensity, and her slow motions now became frenetic—her hips shaking with incredible speed in time with the drummers' rapid roll as the performance seemed to be approaching climax.

"My God," he whispered, spellbound, "this is…,this is *carnal*."

"As I said," she leaned and breathed in his ear, rather closer than she needed to, "think of it as an open-air brothel. They don't perform the ultimate service here, but that's easy enough to come by in the rest of Chicago."

"Thanks for the tip," Jonah said absently, not taking his eyes off the performance in front of him. As Lydia watched him, transfixed by the nearly naked woman on the stage, she could only puzzle over the predilections alleged in that long-ago cable from Reverend Steele.

They emerged from the café and turned east toward Jackson Park. Jonah noticed a number of beer gardens. He wanted to stop at one to get the taste of that hookah pipe out of his mouth, but Lydia kept him moving from one exhibit to another, leaving the decadent Midway behind.

"What is that?" Jonah asked, pointing to a tent advertising "Moving Pictures."

"Oh, you'll like that. It will appeal to your love of gadgetry."

"What love of gadgetry?" Jonah responded, not at all aware that he had any such interest.

"Have you forgotten how you stayed cooped up in your room for days after you spent an entire summer's earnings to purchase a typewriting machine?" Indeed, he remembered it well, but what he remembered most about it was how stubbornly unimpressed Lydia was when he showed her the different platens that came with it, which enabled him to select from four different typefaces, almost like a typesetter. She never understood what he found so fascinating.

"So, how do they make the pictures move?" he wondered aloud.

"I haven't a clue, but they do—you'll see," she said, waving her press pass to the door attendant as she blithely ignored those who had to wait their turn. The queue was long, even though admission was twenty-five cents—two and a half day's wages for one of the fair's laborers. Lydia and Jonah found a place to sit on one of the rows of backless benches in the darkened tent. He found the demonstration unnerving; he had expected to see a series of pictures, as he had before, taken in sequence and run together so as to create the illusion of movement. What he saw, however, was no illusion—it was *actual* movement, like a ghost dancing on the wall. And such a ghost! A young woman danced the seven veils, removing one after the other as her body gyrated in much the same way as the woman he had seen an hour earlier on Cairo Street. Jonah looked behind him and saw a device called a Cinamatograph, essentially a lamp with a track in front of it which pulled film quickly past the light and projected a moving image on the wall. *Amazing.*

"Lydia, they could show an entire play with this device," Jonah marveled.

"Don't be silly—who would want to see a play in these flat images when you can see live human beings perform it right in front of you?"

"I suppose you're right. Although this particular subject matter is probably better suited to moving pictures."

"A woman taking her clothes off?" Lydia laughed. "Why, have all the burlesque theaters closed down?"

Once back in the light of the Midway, again heading east to the main fairgrounds, Jonah noticed an African exhibition tent, with real Africans and their plainly exposed dark breasts. Aside from noticing that they were the only ones at the fair dressed for the heat, it occurred to him that this had been a far racier affair than he would have expected, if he had indeed expected anything.

"You like the African exhibit?" Lydia asked, more than a little amused.

"I'm surprised by it, actually—along with every other lascivious pleasure I've witnessed on this little tour. Why aren't the leading moral authorities of the city down here setting their torches to the Midway?"

"They would be if they hadn't approved all these exhibits."

"They *agreed* to this?"

"Not happily, but yes. Originally the 'moral authorities' opposed all of it. The Board of Lady Managers, or some such, were part of the planning of the fair—designated by Congress, no less. They advised that the fair allow no dancing, no alcohol, and that it should close on Sundays to observe the Sabbath. But in the end they sanctioned this exotic exposition of vice—as long as it is presented in dark skin, which gives it an anthropological flare."

"More *National Geographic* than burlesque?"

"Exactly."

"So far, in spite of the 'Lady Managers,'" Jonah ticked the attractions off on his fingers, "I've seen plenty of dancing; the place is awash in beer, happily; and I'm assuming that if I stay through Sunday I'd enjoy a lovely Sabbath at the fair."

"Quite so. The Midway is all carnival and vice. Over there," she pointed to the east, "in Jackson Park is the magnificent White City— the central fairgrounds, where they chart the future of civilization. So you see, the White City makes their statement, but Midway makes their money."

"I'll bet that's a money-maker," Jonah said, pointing to the crown jewel of the Midway: George Ferris's magnificent wheel.

"Oh, yes indeed," Lydia agreed. "Since its first day it's been by far the most popular—and profitable—attraction at the fair, although the committee was very slow to sanction the thing."

"Well, looking at it, I'm not sure I blame them," Jonah admitted. "It looks as if one good strong wind would knock it over." They both looked at it dubiously; it looked like a massive human tragedy waiting to happen. It was so huge—260 feet high—and any reasonable person could see that the thin ribbons of steel between the wheel and its axle could not possibly be adequate to the task of supporting its thirty-six hanging cars, each of which was large enough to accommodate sixty passengers.

"Let's ride it," said Jonah.

"All right, then. It's a good way to get a bird's-eye-view of the fair. 260 feet is higher than you think it is."

The closer they got to the wheel the larger it became. The passenger cars in particular, which looked like little match boxes from a distance, were more like railway cars—30 feet long, 13 feet wide, enclosed with glass and wire mesh. A uniformed conductor manned the door of every car. Ferris's company was determined that "no crank or hysterical woman is going to commit suicide by jumping out of one of our cars." The ride itself took twenty minutes; one revolution was spent in loading the cars, after which the passengers were treated to a single uninterrupted revolution to view the grandeur of the fair from the Olympian heights of the great wheel. As they ascended into the sky Jonah looked down at the White City beyond the Midway and was struck by the amount of water running through the place.

"I'd say fair 'grounds' is something of a misnomer," Jonah said as he surveyed the spectacle below them. "Look at those canals, and the big lagoon there—and that reflecting pool over there," he pointed at all the waterways running through the White City, leading to Lake Michigan just beyond the fair's gigantic walls.

"They help move people around," she explained. "Remember, this fair covers nearly 700 acres. There are water taxis and there's also an electric railroad that runs around the perimeter... Come to think of it, I don't think it's the water that distinguishes this fair so much as it is the electricity. Wait 'til tonight, you'll see lights everywhere. It's quite something to behold."

"Uh-huh," Jonah grunted, as he looked out over the spectacle before him. He felt like he had a God's-eye view of the world.

More than the simple immensity of the place, the vast, white buildings harmonized with the watery landscape to exemplify the absolute mastery of man over space. The buildings themselves, so incomprehensibly large, were crafted with such precision, with the cornices of each building at exactly the same height, pillars opposite pillars, all surrounding a symmetrical Grand Basin—a reflecting pool that balanced the majestic heights of the surrounding structures with the illusion of depth. Electrically powered fountains in the basin shot elegant plumes of water sixty feet into the air, all the more ethereal for the colored lights directed toward their mist. The immediate effect on the visitor was overwhelming, and tears were a common response.

"I hardly know what to say," Jonah admitted, a little breathless. "It seems so vast. Look at these waterways—they go on forever! And so do the buildings. They're so... substantial. Surely this is not merely a fairground—they have actually constructed a permanent city."

"You're babbling." She smiled gently, pleased at his reaction.

"I'm sorry."

"Don't be. I've noticed that the two most common responses to a person's first sight of the White City are complete opposites: dumbstruck awe and babbling."

"This will stand longer than Rome."

"If by that you mean it will soon be ruins, then you're quite right."

"What are you talking about? Just look at these buildings—marble everywhere."

"Staff."

"Excuse me?"

"It's not marble; it's called 'staff.' It's like plaster or that stuff you smear on buildings..."

"Stucco?"

"That's it—only smoother. Then they painted it all white. They actually sprayed the paint on, in a new process."

"Sprayed the paint?" Jonah tried to picture how that would work.

"Wood? Stucco? But wooden buildings this large should collapse on themselves."

"The whole thing is a skeleton of wood, reinforced with iron, covered with white-painted staff." She rocked back on her heels, feeling quite knowledgeable as she revealed for Jonah the mysteries of the fair.

"And after a few Chicago winters..." Jonah paused to imagine these illusory structures, deflated by a Midwestern freeze. "They'll be leaky, misshapen, ruined," he said sadly.

"They'll either tear them down or burn them when the time comes," Lydia said. "The White City is indeed an illusion."

"Or a dream," Jonah corrected her.

"Yes," Lydia agreed. "But at some point you do have to wake from your dreams."

They spent the next few hours walking through the majestic, if fraudulent buildings, seeing so many grand exhibitions of this, that, and those, that after a while he felt like he was floating through a land of make-believe. They rode one of the electric launches through the great basin to a canal that led to a lagoon; he was astounded that it made no noise as it propelled them across the water. They walked through gardens of Occidental and Oriental origin, and rested their legs at a relaxing Japanese public house before returning to the launch and riding back to the Court of Honor. The two sought shelter from the late afternoon sun in the Manufacturers and Liberal Arts Building—the largest of them all. He thought back to the great hall in which he had celebrated President Cleveland's inaugural; dozens of them would have fit in this building, and dozens more stacked in layers on top of each other. Fair promoters claimed that all of the Czar's armies could assemble here and still have room to march. But rather than armies, the hall was filled with some 70,000 exhibits, and taking them all in was impossible, and the effort to do so, exhausting. It was time to leave this hall and find a comfortable place to sit and eat.

As they sat at the outdoor restaurant among the gleaming white buildings and colossal white columns of the White City, it disturbed Jonah to think that these structures—clearly designed to announce by their size and brilliance the emergence of the American nation—were not as substantial as they seemed. It seemed an ill omen. Still, the atmosphere was electric, transporting its visitors to a vision of the American future, a better place than they had ever been, perhaps. Every turn of every corner stirred the imagination. Lydia began to share this dizzying feeling that this place belonged to a new map, in a better place, where all the rules were suspended and the future was a place of infinite possibility. And it was in this spirit that she looked at her lost husband as if she had never seen him before, trying to comprehend that they had once been joined, however briefly.

"Why are you looking at me like that?" he asked uncomfortably.

She was caught unawares, found out, and recovered awkwardly. "I'm not looking at you, really, but the big white columns behind you. They're enormous, don't you think?"

"Yes, quite large." He turned back to look for a waiter. "Let's have a drink."

"A drink?" She tried to appear aghast. "What do you take me for, a dance hall girl?"

"Nothing so exalted as that," he assured her. "You're a reporter, and the ones I have known drink a good deal. But don't worry, I won't order the reporter's usual drink, whisky. Wine will do."

"I'll have none, thank you."

"As you wish." He turned his attention to their surroundings. They sat on the great portico of terraced ersatz marble. The booths with high rounded backs surrounded it in a great semicircle that opened on the lower end to the walkway along the man-made lake. It was magnificent, and he would have stayed there happily all afternoon without a word, but silence felt more awkward to the estranged couple than stilted conversation. The waiter brought wine and bread, and they began to chat almost like old friends, save for the fact that he could not completely dispel an idle fantasy about plunging a knife into her.

"Where is your employer, Mr. Thurston?" Lydia inquired politely, when what she meant was, *How much longer can we spend together?*

"I don't know. He has business here at the fair. He seems to have business everywhere."

"When will you be going back to Hawaii?"

Why is she asking that? he wondered. "I don't know. Maybe never," he said without explanation.

"Surely you're not going back to Seattle? I mean, you couldn't, could you?"

"The prodigal sodomite returns? No, I couldn't."

She turned her eyes up toward him with a look that seemed to say, *well, you brought it up, not me.* He stared at her unapologetically, then waved the waiter over. "Refill this carafe and bring the lady a glass, if you please."

"I don't drink, Jonah."

"There's no such thing as a reporter who doesn't drink. If you want to discuss this you're going to join me in a glass of wine. I have some questions of my own, in any case."

"For me?" She tried to sound innocent. She looked at the half glass of wine he had poured for her and decided to dispense with all pretense. She tossed it back and set down the empty glass to be refilled.

"Uh, yes," he said and he refilled her glass, a bit unnerved by her bravado. "You were married again, as I hear it. By what contrivance did you make this fellow disappear?"

She took the glass and sipped slowly this time. "That was cruel."

"You're calling *me* cruel?" he shot back.

"All right," she said, not yet ready to explore her own admitted sins. She indicated that her glass was empty again. "He was a successful merchant seaman who became a shipping magnate. He needed a wife to complete the tableau of respectability so he could swindle everyone who ever supped at our table. He—Warren—left me several months after we were married."

"That seems brief even for you. But then the two of you didn't have the advantages of distance that we enjoyed." Jonah was determined to see her wince. "I read about the swindle, by the way. Crafty fellow. At least the bastard had a chance to consummate *his* marriage before absconding with his millions."

Lydia did not immediately respond to the barb, and her silence told a tale of its own. He read her carefully, squinting through his incredulity.

"Oh, Lydia. You can't be serious. You didn't? Not even once?" He had always imagined her standoffishness would end in the marriage bed. She had been cold with him, certainly, but he never took her for the kind of woman who thought of love-making strictly as a means of conception. "Why on earth not, Lydia? For God's sake, couldn't you offer another human being a little bit of... warmth, of affection, even after you got the poor fool to marry you?"

"Lower your voice," she said, looking around at the other patrons, none of whom had noticed them at all. "Well, we might have, once."

"You're not sure?"

"It was all very awkward. He obviously didn't want to and when we finally did, I didn't know what to do anyway, except, you know, very generally. If he knew what to do he wasn't willing to guide me. It just didn't seem to work very well," and her voice trailed off as her story wound down.

"You had to ask for it? I can't imagine." His incredulity passed, he was enjoying this immensely. "He married you because he needed a wife and he left you because he couldn't stand having one. I guess that leaves you twice married and still chaste, or nearly so."

"It seems I have a habit of finding men who don't much care for women." It was her turn to stick the knife in.

"You can't mean me! I did everything you asked, and would have continued through the wedding night had you not dispatched me to *Polynesia*."

"Hmm, yes," she said, more comfortable with the subject turning back to Jonah. "This has always puzzled me. You were always so aggressively amorous, improperly so to be plain about it. Then I

298

hear that you've taken up with some native boy."

"Really? I'd never heard that version of it, myself," he said impassively. He had long ago accepted that beyond dispensing with the inconvenient 'Christopher Jones,' there was nothing he could do about what other people might say or think. "Tell me about it. What outlandish tales of buggery have you heard?"

"Nothing terribly specific, thank God." She took another sip of Bordeaux, which tasted no more pungent than water after the third glass. "All I had was a telegram from Reverend Steele. It was cryptic—I don't think he was willing to put any evidence of your crime on paper."

"Generous man," he said without rancor. "What did it say?"

"See for yourself." To his amazement she dug into her bag and produced the document. Evidently she carried it with her and he wondered what that meant. He unfolded the weary piece of paper and read it.

"Yes, very cryptic," he agreed. "But you're not so well versed in scripture as to know Leviticus 18:22. Did you look it up or ask someone's help with this?"

"I asked Warren. He knew it."

"The seaman? He was a biblical scholar?"

"No, but he knew this passage." They both let that hang in the air for a moment without responding to it. She resumed in a softer voice. "I don't want to speculate about Warren. If it were possible I wouldn't give him another thought. He will get his punishment."

"Marriage wasn't enough?" That one stung her, and he instantly regretted saying it. "By all means, let's forget about Warren." He changed the subject. "You obviously heard rumors about me, at the church I suppose."

"Yes. Evidently word went through the entire missionary world that one of their very own was a...," she dramatically lowered her voice before continuing, "a sodomite."

"You know, I'm not even sure what that word means," he said, truly perplexed. "Does it refer to one who commits a specific act with men, or is it a more general impropriety in sexual matters?"

"Well, I certainly don't know. What did you do?"

"I thought you didn't want to know."

She ignored that and reminded him, again in a hushed voice, that any number of people consider him guilty of the serious crime of homosexuality. "But someone said a woman was involved. Is that true? Does this mean you're still interested in women?"

"Muanu," he said.

"I don't speak Hawaiian, Jonah." She thought he might be cursing at her in that savage tongue.

"Her name, it's Muanu. She is a person, with a name, with a history, a family, feelings, and emotions—almost like a real human being."

"So you did, you had sss—," she caught herself. "You had *relations* with this native woman?"

"Passionately. Repeatedly," he confirmed. "It was the most," he searched for the right word. "It was the most *complete* experience I've ever had."

She contemplated that for a moment—a complete experience. *Tantalizing concept*, she thought, but not quite comprehensible without actually having done it herself, so she turned to the one remaining dirty little detail. "And the boy?" she asked.

"Kalani. Her cousin. He is a man, actually. I have no idea how he got involved in this. He was there when we were caught, *in flagrante*, if you like. I was tired and drunk, and she seduced me, bless her. In the darkness and confusion of it all, Kalani had, well," now he was struggling to explain it, not quite understanding it himself. "He sort of helped her, I suppose. Just as I began to understand that he was actually still there, the door of her hut opened, and all I could see was a lamplight, behind which, I gather, were the Steeles and a few scandalized members of the church family I was staying with." He could smile now at the absurdity of the moment, and Lydia surprised herself by laughing. Her guffaw was at his expense, but he nonetheless leaned back in his chair and saw levity in it for the first time. The tragedy and distance between them evaporated for a moment. He reached across the table and took her small hand in his. She did not draw it away, as she had so many times in the past, but curled her fingers gently into his palm. "Let's go," he said.

"Where to, Mr. Christian?" She pretended not to know.

He stood and assisted her with her chair, all but ignoring the question. "You were once my wife, you know."

As they walked into the hotel she floated a few of his better phrases along the river of alcohol in her brain. The acerbic push of *twice married, still chaste*, mingled with the gentle challenge of his obviously warm memories of the native woman. "What did you call it, Jonah, 'a complete experience'?"

"I'll do my best, Lydia."

He was as good as his word. Lydia was to be the beneficiary of Muanu's graduate course in human kindness, the milk of which would be poured out upon her liberally in the coming hours. Arm in arm, like any other couple, they ascended the elevator to his fourth-floor room, nearly directly above the portico. Once there they gazed out on the pure white city, protected from view by the semi-darkness of the room. He kissed her, caressed her, and over the course of the following half hour stripped her down to her linen bodice. Kneeling behind her he gently moved his hands over her skin, up above her waist, then down over her thighs. Swaying slowly, she remained in emotional anticipation, always wanting what was next, and what was after that. Then in the moist heat in which she had lost herself, everything fell into place and their bed became a world unto itself where only the two of them existed.

Eventually the sun went down and electric lights of many colors flickered to life, seeming to dance on the lake beneath them. They lay together on the bed watching those lights shimmer on the water, she with her head in the soft nook between his shoulder and his chest as she languidly allowed her fingers to wander about his body, first here, then there. His left arm encircled her body until it ended with his hand cupped around her left breast. He absently fingered her nipple, which seemed to send her hips slowly, but purposefully into motion against his thigh. Further penetration was out of the question as too painful, but the two of them found alternatives, naturally enough, then let gravity pull them back to their favorite position of repose, he on his back, she on her side, her head rose and fell with the rhythm of his breath.

"You said you're not going back to Hawaii. Why not?"

"A number of reasons; foremost among them is that I've got work to do in Washington."

"But that isn't the only reason—is it that native girl?"

"No. Not directly anyway. There was another girl, Penelope. I thought we were in love, but she married Kalani—"

"The native boy? But... Oh, this is confusing!"

"It is complicated, I'll grant you. People are complicated. We can talk about this another time," he said, putting an end to the discussion. "Anyway, I've lost my taste for the place."

She thought for a long moment, searching for the right way to offer her idea. She propped herself up on one elbow to face him. "You know, after I interviewed Jane Addams at Hull House, I thought seriously of turning away from journalism and joining the settlement house movement—you know, helping immigrants become Americans."

"You, a social worker?"

"I know, it does seem a bit farfetched. I'm about sick to death of this settlement house business—nothing but a bunch of stinking immigrants, really—and covering this fair isn't much better. Anyway, it didn't last long, but it got me thinking that I didn't have to stay here in Chicago, hiding from my life in Seattle as a twice-married church mouse. I have a job that is, well, portable." She took a breath and plunged forward with her idea. "I was thinking that I might ask for a transfer to Washington. In fact, if my employer knew I had an inside source on the Hawaiian Commission, there wouldn't be any doubt about me getting the transfer."

302

"Well, I don't know, Lydia. I'm hardly in a position to make an honest woman of you," he said, obviously lukewarm about the notion.

"Hardly," she agreed. She was not quite sure what she expected. Nor did she know how they would ever get beyond a shared past that was built mostly on deceit and manipulation. As nice as the afternoon had been, she still was not at all sure what was so monumental about sex. Lovely as it was, she was certain she could live without it if she had to. It was like a nice place to visit, but she knew she would never be like Jonah, always plagued by his desire for women.

"You're rather deep in thought, my dear," Jonah interrupted her reverie.

"Sorry." She made an effort to brighten her voice. "I was just thinking that I'll go ahead and request that transfer to Washington. I'll be busy when I get there, and so will you, obviously. We probably won't have time to see each other. But I would like to see you again, or," she chose her words carefully, "maybe even occasionally."

"Are you proposing an arrangement?" Jonah asked, amused at this latest turn of her conniving nature.

"I am proposing nothing. My reputation is faring little better than yours, although at least I'm still on the right side of the law."

"Yes, but you know what they say about career women."

"What, that they spend their afternoons with sodomite missionaries in their hotel rooms?"

"Something like that."

CHAPTER THIRTEEN

Fifteen hundred pages? the president thought to himself as he looked at the massive bound report on his desk. He had expected something that could be called a "brief." The State Department had sent the President a copy from the Government Printing Office as soon as it was properly bound three days earlier. Grover Cleveland had taken one look at it and his heart sank; he had opened his desk drawer and dropped it in, where it had remained until this moment. Now, in anticipation of a cabinet meeting on the weighty tome's contents, he hefted it out and let it fall on his desk. What a resounding thud fifteen hundred pages make!

The President fumed as he fingered his mustache. *Just what in the hell was Blount thinking?* he wondered. *A report—a little report—that's all I asked for, and he returns with eight pounds of paper, all of it covered with ink. My God, it would take the better part of a week to read this thing—perhaps longer. I've got a country to run, for God's sake! I sent that damn Georgian there to write up a little report telling me what he thought, and he sends me a record of everyone's thoughts—everyone's thoughts since the first volcano.*

Fifteen hundred pages. Jesus!

"Mr. President?" a quizzical aide interrupted his silent diatribe. "The Cabinet is waiting for you."

"Hmmph," the President acknowledged, sort of. He opened the desk drawer, swatted the report into it, and listened for the rewarding *thump* as it landed. He slammed the drawer shut and ambled to the Cabinet room.

At 5'11" and over 250 pounds, Grover Cleveland was a difficult presence to ignore even had he not been president of the United States. As he lumbered into the room all eight Cabinet officers rose and waited for him to take his seat.

"Gentleman," the President saluted his Cabinet with a genuine smile. He could be gruff, and even deadly—as Sheriff of Buffalo he insisted on pulling the lever that executed condemned prisoners with his own hand, mostly because he thought it unfair to drop such a weighty duty on an underling. He was, nevertheless, a good fellow. People liked him. Whether you were in the White House receiving line with a drink in your hand, or on a scaffold with a rope around your neck, you knew where you stood with Grover Cleveland.

"Now then," the president looked around the table, "I believe we're going to discuss this Hawaiian business, isn't that right Mr. Secretary?" He asked the question of the man sitting to his right, Secretary of State Gresham, although nearly everyone else in the room could answer to the title "Mr. Secretary" as well.

"Yes, Mr. President," responded Gresham, whom the President informally called "Judge," as a tip of the hat to his years on the bench. He might have called him "General" as so many others did, but alluding to Gresham's service for the Union Army was not good politics in a Democratic party so full of veterans of the Confederacy. Worse yet, until a few months earlier Gresham was a Republican. "Mr. President, I would defer for the moment," the Judge graciously offered, "to the Secretary of Agriculture, whom I believe has some pressing business."

The President, who accepted Gresham's judgment in nearly all things, merely directed his attention to Julius Sterling Morton—an Agricultural secretary who actually knew something about farming, something of a rarity.

"The Congress, Mr. President, has reported out a bill to relieve the drought-stricken farmers of Texas. It has been a hard year for them—their crops are completely destroyed by the lack of rain—

and this money will allow the Department to distribute seed grain to them to facilitate a recovery in the coming planting season."

"How much?"

"Sir?" The Secretary had not expected the question.

"How much money? I'm just curious."

"Ten thousand dollars, sir. The figure is based on estimates written by the Texas congressional delegation."

"Hmm," the President thought briefly of finding a way to do this gently, but none being readily apparent, he pushed ahead as he did with most things: directly. "I'm going to veto this bill, Mr. Morton," the President said evenly. The Secretary was silently shocked, but knew better than to protest. "Federal aid in such cases," Cleveland continued, "encourages the expectation of paternal care on the part of the government and weakens the sturdiness of our national character." The Agricultural Secretary sat still, not knowing quite what to say, wondering what in hell the Agriculture Department was supposed to do if not help American farmers. Morton said nothing. Having dispensed with this little bit of unpleasantness, the President turned back toward Gresham. "Now, this Hawaiian business, Judge?"

"Thank you, Mr. President," said the Honorable Walter Quintin Gresham, two-time Republican candidate for president of the United States, now serving as the Secretary of State for twice Democratic President Grover Cleveland. It was a curious selection, but there was simply no one in America whom Cleveland trusted more to keep American foreign affairs on the path of constitutional prudence than Gresham. "We have," Gresham continued, "the report of our special minister to Hawaii, the former Congressman James Blount. I trust you have had a chance to look it over, Mr. President?"

Cleveland saw no reason to express his opinion on what a stupid idea it was to explode a simple directive into a fifteen-hundred page elaboration of Hawaii's place in world history since the creation of the earth, so he simply answered, "No."

"Fine, Mr. President. Since the rest of the Cabinet has also not had a chance to see copies of the report, allow me to summarize,"

Gresham smiled benignly, turning his attention to the rest of the table. "Blount analyzed the situation much as the President had expected...," this turn of phrase caught the President slightly unawares, as he had, in fact, expected nothing. Only two months into his presidency, Cleveland truly had no preconceived notions about the Hawaiian treaty, he simply did not wish to support a treaty he did not understand. On the advice of his Secretary of State, Cleveland had withdrawn the treaty from the Senate and sent Blount to Hawaii to report on what exactly had happened there. Nonetheless, Cleveland sat silent as Gresham gave his boss credit for omniscience.

Gresham continued. "They have no popular support—none— and consequently they depend on American military support for their survival." He turned to a dog-eared page about sixty pages into the volume and said, "Allow me to read Blount's conclusion." Cleveland's eyes widened in surprise. *The conclusion is at the beginning of the report?*

Gresham read, "The present Government can only rest on the use of military force, possessed of most of the arms in the islands, with a small white population to draw from to strengthen it. Ultimately, it will fall without fail. It may preserve its existence for a year or two, but not longer."

It took fifteen hundred pages to say that? The President was more disgusted than before with the excessive size of the report. Gresham was not quite sure to make of the President's dyspeptic expression, but soldiered on. "Having finished his task—and finished it well—Mr. Blount has resigned his position as ambassador plenipotentiary. I dispatched his replacement some weeks ago," he continued a little uneasily, as the President scowled at the report in front of him. "Albert Willis is now representing us in Honolulu and awaits instructions."

"Who else has seen this report?" the President asked.

"No one," answered Gresham. "But some of the conclusions may be common knowledge in Hawaii. I have spoken with the

P.G.'s new ambassador to Washington, a Mr. Thurston. You would think Thurston had a copy of this report on his desk the way he anticipates Blount's arguments. He offers me veiled threats that if the United States does not offer Hawaii protection, they will simply seek it elsewhere."

"And what do you propose, Judge?" the President asked.

Gresham closed the report with a snap. "I believe you should reinstate the Queen, Mr. President. A great wrong has been committed against this woman. If you direct President Dole of the provisional government to step down, he will no doubt do so."

The rest of the Cabinet waited their turn. Attorney General Richard Olney shifted uncomfortably in his chair when he heard Gresham's sweeping conclusions, but he said nothing. The Secretary of the Navy, Hilary Herbert, also sat through Gresham's analysis uneasily, but he was disinclined to silence. The former Confederate colonel, whose military career ended with a bullet at the Battle of the Wilderness in 1864, had spent his subsequent political career trying to convince the Democratic Party to enlarge both the size and capabilities of the U.S. Navy, first as an Alabama congressman and now as Naval Secretary. He had already lost one war and had no interest in repeating the experience; the idea of owning Pearl Harbor and its commanding position, mid-Pacific, struck him as damned handy.

"Excuse me, Mr. Secretary," Herbert said slowly, in his thick Southern drawl. "I consider myself a friend of the honorable Congressman Blount. Indeed, we fought for the same Cause." (For Confederate veterans, their "Cause" would always be spelled with a capital "C.") "I know him to be a brave and trustworthy man. But I would ask if perhaps we are elevating our concerns regarding the Queen above strategic considerations, specifically naval considerations, of greater moment to the security of these United States."

Gresham, who fought as a general on the opposite side of the Civil War from Secretary Herbert, was always slightly irritated with statements that began with a recitation of one's bona fides as a traitor to the United States. He looked at the barely reconstructed

Confederate, then turned to the President, pointedly addressing his response to Cleveland, who fought for neither side during the Civil War—and was the first man to hold the presidency since the war ended who had not participated in it.

"Should not the great wrong done to a feeble but independent state by an abuse of the authority of the United States be undone by restoring the legitimate government?" Gresham asked. "Anything short of that will not, I respectfully submit, satisfy the demands of Justice." Then, turning to Secretary Herbert to offer his estimation of his strategic considerations, he continued, "Can the United States consistently insist that other nations respect the independence of Hawaii while not respecting it themselves? Our Government was the first to recognize the independence of the Islands and as such it ought to be the last to acquire sovereignty over them by force and fraud."

The two Cabinet secretaries stared at each other a long moment, each of them secretly desiring he could don his old uniform and settle this with a pistol. Rank, however, has its privileges, and Walter Gresham had won this argument before it began. As Secretary of State, his was the preeminent voice in American foreign policy. Besides, he was in the Cabinet because the President wanted him there, while Herbert was there because the Redeemers forced Cleveland to take him. Rescuing the Polynesian damsel in distress, Queen Lilioulokalani, was about to become official U.S. policy.

Lydia Burke wondered why the young Justice Department lawyer, Hector Symington, could not seem to answer a question without leaning three-quarters of the way across the table toward her. *Was this some sort of lawyerly technique to make people uncomfortable?* she wondered. If so, it certainly worked. Of course when he reached across the table to hold her hand his behavior lost any lawyerly attributes.

"My notes," Lydia said.

"Beg pardon?" said a confused young Mr. Symington.

"I can't write my notes," she said as she tried to extricate her hand. "Perhaps you can pitch woo later if you're still feeling amorous, Mr. Symington, but at the moment I'd like to write some notes so I might remember what you say." She batted her eyelashes so as not to lose his attention.

"Call me Hector," he said, giving her hand a gentle squeeze before he released it.

"Earlier at the Justice Department you said something about, let's see, how did you put it?…" She searched her notes for a moment. "Ah yes, you referred to the Secretary of State's Hawaiian policy as 'the diplomacy of the knight errant,' isn't that correct—*Hector*?" She felt his shoe rubbing against her calf beneath the table. She generally chose to meet with sources in public cafes like this one to avoid precisely this type of behavior. A pretty, young, evidently single female meeting a government official behind the closed door of his office was always more of an adventure than she wanted, and she found that men were more apt to behave themselves in public places.

"Hector?" she prompted him. Evidently rubbing her calf with his toe and discussing foreign policy at the same time were beyond him.

"Oh, yes, 'diplomacy of the knight errant.' That was a good one, wasn't it?"

Obviously one to laugh at his own jokes, she thought. "Yes, very witty. What did you mean by it?"

"I wouldn't want to be quoted, Lydia—may I call you 'Lydia'?"

"Certainly, if you wish." She craned her neck down to bring her face level with his gaze. It never ceased to amaze her how men absently allowed their gaze to drop from her face to her modest, corset-crushed breasts, hidden as they were behind a shirtwaist suit that went all the way up to her throat. If she were a particularly large-breasted woman, she mused, men might not ever remember her face. He took the hint and his eyes snapped up. "Thank you,"

310

she continued. "Please consider yourself an 'unnamed source.' Now, what did you mean by the term 'knight errant'?"

"Well," Hector looked down at the table for a moment, adjusting his round, wire-rimmed glasses and showing Lydia the perfectly straight part in his well-oiled hair. "We don't have anything to do with diplomacy, per se, at the Justice Department. But as a Cabinet officer, the Attorney General is free to contribute his views on any policy the President is contemplating."

"And your boss, Attorney General Olney, is not happy with something?"

"Well, no, not one bit, actually." His attention had begun to wander again.

"I'm up here, Hector," Lydia prompted him to elevate his gaze again.

"Oh, yes, well it's just that Mr. Olney believes that trying to restore the Queen is going to create more problems than it will solve."

"Really?" Lydia asked, a little too eagerly.

"Well, yes. Say, why is a pretty girl like you so interested in this?"

Lydia did not answer. She tore off a piece of note paper and wrote down the address of Jonah's hotel and a suite number. She handed it to Hector as she stood up to leave. "Can you meet me there at 7:00 this evening?"

The young attorney mouthed the words 'Wormly Hotel' as he read the note, hungrily looking Lydia up and down. He nodded his assent, but no words came from his mouth as he contemplated his good fortune.

"Good. I'll see you there." And with that she briskly walked out of the café leaving behind a very confused and excited young Justice Department attorney.

* * *

After a particularly well-spent afternoon concluded with several moments of clenching intensity and a few desperate gasps, Lydia gave Jonah a peck on the cheek, slid out from underneath him, and got out of his bed. As she padded naked across the room to the water closet she said, "Get dressed. He'll be here in a half hour."

It never ceased to amaze Jonah how quickly she switched moods. One moment they would be two intertwined bodies, writhing in ecstasy; the next it would simply be over. The deed done, she would have other things to do, and off she would go to do them. No dénouement, no unnecessary affection. At least, Jonah consoled himself, he could still enjoy the splendid view of her naked body as she fumbled with her clothing.

"How did you meet this fellow, anyway?"

"Jealous?"

"Sure, why not?" he replied casually. Their relationship was not entirely a physical one, but neither was it a romantic one. He found her, as he always had, so painfully pretty, and she found him comfortable and familiar. Each appealed to the other on a very basic level, which from time to time led to some very basic behavior. The fact that they had once been married, at least on paper, facilitated a certain sexual abandon between them. Afterwards, always, their mutual irritation inched its way back into their consciousness, adding a "yes, but..." quality to his view of her, and a "hmm, I just don't see it" quality to her view of him. Momentary lust balanced by mutual dissatisfaction was hardly the basis for a lasting relationship, but last it had; in some strange way, their friendship seemed to endure. After years of unsatisfactory courtship, a laughable botch of a marriage, and a year of broken hearts and personal failure, each had landed upright, and in proximity to the other. Life was not at all what either of them had wanted or anticipated, but neither was it entirely bad. They had their jobs, and when life in the capital proved too cold and calculating to endure, each had the other to turn to for comfort and support, if only briefly.

"I'll do my best to keep my possessiveness in check while you explain to me how some functionary in the Justice Department can possibly be helpful with policy in the State Department."

"Sarcasm will get you nowhere, Jonah," she said as she did battle with the thousand-and-one hooks and buttons on her whalebone corset. "Besides, if anyone around here should be worried, it's me. I've seen you getting on the trolley out to Kensington with that bunch of pretty young ladies you refer to as your 'staff.' And don't think I haven't noticed the way they look at you, either."

"We go out to Kensington to play softball. They're really quite good," he assured her. "How *do* they look at me?"

"Let's just say it's a far more friendly look than the one they reserve for me, that lady journalist who steals you away from them anytime I choose to waltz into the office. They look as if they'd like to take their baseball bats to my head."

"Sorry. I'll reassure them that you're far more pleasant than you seem. Now, please tell me about this Symington."

"He has the ear of the Attorney General. He may have said that just to impress me, but I saw them together at the Justice Department and they seem to have a genuine rapport, almost familiarity—if anyone actually has that with Richard Olney. The Attorney General seems as stiff and impersonal as a block of wood. Dammit!" She was sick and tired of all the buttons. "Remember that thing we saw in the men's trousers in that one display at the fair—you know, it replaced the buttons."

"The zipper?"

"Yes, that's it. Why can't they put something like that on a woman's corset?" she complained.

"Because then men wouldn't be able to enjoy watching you dress for ten minutes."

"You could help, you know."

"What fun would that be? Besides, I'm better at helping you *undress*." He slid his feet to the floor; she stepped between his knees and he began to fumble with the tiny fasteners. "Anyway, thanks for pointing the gentleman my way. It will be useful to talk with someone close to the Cabinet; the Cleveland Administration has treated us like lepers. I thought that might change after Thurston became ambassador, but it hasn't. Gresham simply hates him—me, too. I should see if he's got a daughter I can seduce, just to get even with him."

"The sacrifices you make for your career!"

"There you go—all done!" He gave her bottom an affectionate pat after finishing the final clasp of the demonic garment.

"Where is Thurston, anyway?"

"New York. He's doing another round with the magazine editors up there. I think he feels like he's got to do something, even if it isn't working."

Once the corset was fastened, the rest of her toilette was quickly completed. Lydia leaned toward the mirror on the wall making some final adjustments to her hair and giving her cheeks a pinch. "There," she said, saucily. "Not bad for a girl who's just been through an afternoon rut."

"Again, charming."

She was about to defend her choice of words when they heard a knock on the door. Jonah had already pulled on his pants and shirt, and was stepping into his boots, when they heard another knock.

"That's Hector—finish up!" Lydia said, giving herself one last look in the mirror.

"He sounds eager," Jonah said, as he escorted her into the sitting room of the suite. She turned back to make sure the bedroom door was closed, then took a seat in the chair opposite the couch while Jonah answered the door. He found a well-dressed, severely coiffed young man about his own age standing in the corridor with a bouquet of flowers, a bottle of wine, and a painfully disappointed expression.

"There must be some mistake," Hector stammered, looking at the piece of note paper Lydia had given him earlier. "I'm looking for

Lydia Burke?"

"No mistake," Jonah assured him. "Come right this way." He led him into the sitting room where Lydia was prettily perched on her little chair.

"Are those for me?" Lydia said at the sight of the flowers.

"Well, uh…" Hector responded uncertainly, looking first at Lydia, then at Jonah.

"A lovely gesture," Jonah said, "I'll just put these in water," taking the blooms from Symington. "Oh, where are my manners? I'm Jonah Christian, part of the Hawaiian delegation here. Lydia and I are old friends."

"Old *friends*?" Hector asked hopefully.

"Just friends," Jonah assured him, offering a little wink Lydia could not see. Hector immediately brightened. "And allow me to open this." Jonah took the wine from his grasp. "I think it's late enough in the day for a drink."

"Indeed," Hector agreed, as a disconcerting smile crept across his lips.

Jonah returned to the sitting room with an open bottle and three glasses and poured everyone a drink. The first glass was accompanied by small talk about work in the Justice Department and Symington's first job as a clerk in Richard Olney's law firm in Massachusetts. What set the young man's tongue to wagging was a simple question Jonah asked about their travails as Democrats in solidly Republican New England.

"Oh, my God! You just can't imagine it. My boss has had the bloody shirt waved in his face constantly since the war ended. That's…let me see—"

"28 years ago," Jonah helped.

"Yes, I think so."

"The 'bloody shirt'?" Lydia asked.

"Yes, you know, the Civil War. All the Republicans, except for those who didn't, trotted off to volunteer for the Army of the Potomac, to fight the rebels, save the Union, and so on. As if there weren't any

Democrats fighting for the Union."

"Did Olney fight?" Lydia asked.

"Well, no, of course not. He thought it was a damned waste of time and treasure..." and Hector was off. For the next sixty minutes he fulminated and fumed about the despotism of the bloody shirt, the figurative garment of sacrifice that metaphorically adorned Civil War veterans who ran for office. As Jonah opened a second bottle of wine, Hector railed in his nasal Boston accent against the injustice: his brilliant boss—with degrees from Brown University and Harvard Law School, and more clear-sighted intelligence than the entire Republican Party of Massachusetts—still had to defend himself in one election after another against charges that he was somehow a traitor. And finally, after twenty-eight years—twenty-eight years!— the nation had a chief executive that was himself without a record of Civil War service and a man with his boss's vast intelligence could be considered for high office. Aside from being a damned nuisance, he evidently found this business of stained metaphors to be downright unfair. He was about to launch into another story of another slander against New England Democrats, when he noticed Lydia's unsuccessful attempt to stifle a yawn. "Oh, I do go on, don't I?"

"Fascinating stuff, Hector," Jonah assured him. "I had no idea. Really. But, as I hear it, the Attorney General is not at all comfortable with Gresham's approach to Hawaii?"

"Oh, well, that's all confidential government dealings. I shouldn't talk about it."

"I just want you to know I think I can help you."

"Help me? How?" Hector was unaware that he needed help, except in getting rid of Jonah.

"I was in Honolulu at the same time Blount was, and I know he made some serious mistakes. Consequently he has produced a grievously flawed report, and any policy derived from it could result in serious embarrassment for all parties."

"Flawed? How? What sort of embarrassment?" Hector narrowed

his eyes at Jonah. He could see that Hector was interested, but skeptical.

"The information he has is based entirely on partisan sources—disgruntled, embittered sources, like the Queen's supporters." Jonah began to warm to the topic. "They've lost their access to the royal coffers and they're furious, and they painted a distorted picture for Blount about the power and effectiveness of the provisional government."

"You mean the *powerlessness* of the provisional government, don't you?" Hector replied with a snort.

"That's Blount's first mistake, which is my point, exactly." Jonah sensed he had Symington hooked. "U.S. troops were withdrawn from Hawaii and sent back to the *Boston* while I was there. If the Queen's partisans really thought the P.G.s were so weak, wouldn't they have moved against them by now?"

"Go on," said the newly curious young lawyer.

"Blount neglected to speak to the men who actually executed the revolution—motivated, determined men who will not sit idly by while their revolution is overturned." He hoped the implication of violence was clear.

"If the report is undependable, what do you suggest?"

"That depends on what Gresham has in mind. You must tell me, Hector."

"Yes, Hector," Lydia chimed in, placing a hand on his knee. "Your words will not leave this room." She still hadn't decided whether she would actually keep that particular promise.

"All right," Hector succumbed. "What I said to you off-handedly at the Justice Department, Lydia—about the diplomacy of the knight errant—that's Gresham's approach. Even before he read Blount's report, he saw the Queen as a damsel in distress, and thus the United States would have to rescue her. I mean, that's the form of the policy, what it adds up to, though not necessarily his motivation."

"What *does* motivate him?" Jonah asked. "Is it Gresham's hatred for Harrison and Foster? I know they cost him the presidency, at least once, maybe twice."

"I don't know. That's definitely part of it, but he also just hates the idea of the U.S. involving itself in overseas affairs in any capacity. The Secretary of State is the strictest of strict constructionists; if a certain federal power isn't specifically written into the Constitution, he doesn't believe it exists. Ironically, his dogmatic perception of the situation might well end up putting troops back on the ground to reinstate the Queen—direct involvement. Well, Olney just doesn't believe strict constructionism is realistic, *especially* if it means you end up using American power to place a monarch on the throne. I mean, we're a democracy, for goodness' sake!"

"And you have Olney's ear?" Jonah asked hopefully.

"Yes, I do. Well, I mean, as much as anybody does. He's a very smart man, and he won't accept any counsel he disagrees with—not from me or anybody else."

Jonah pounced. "Here's what I suggest: You write up a memorandum—put something on paper—something that will convince your boss to make an effort to soften Gresham's policy. You can help your boss prevent Cleveland from moving too precipitously. This could work out very well for you."

"For me? Well, if your information is correct, I suppose you're right about that." He thought a moment, looking uncertain. "I'll get to work on it tomorrow when I have a clear head."

"Perhaps," Jonah said, "I could jot a few ideas down for you. Why don't you and Lydia sit and chat a bit while I disappear into my study for a few minutes?"

"That's an excellent idea," Hector said, that disconcerting smile returning to his face. Lydia smiled painfully and looked at Jonah with daggers in her eyes.

* * *

Olney was deeply appreciative of the memorandum his aide had left on his desk with the accompanying handwritten note, which read, *Mr. Attorney General, the legal implications of our Hawaii policy have been much on my mind, as I know they have been on yours, and I wanted to share my thoughts in a confidential way. I hope you do not think me presumptuous—Hector.* The boy had worked for him since he was barely a teenager, yet he still addressed him as "Mr. Attorney General." The memo's specifics were very helpful; they put flesh on the bones of his own misgivings about Gresham's policy and offered ameliorative amendments to it that he believed he could persuade both Gresham and the President to accept. He called the Secretary of State immediately and proposed a meeting. But before he left for the State Department he penned a little note to Hector suggesting he come over to dinner and that he would be welcome to bring a guest. He figured dinner at the Attorney General's house might be a good way for the young fellow to attract a date.

Later that afternoon in the Secretary of State's office Gresham and Olney enjoyed a glass of soda water—neither man was a drinker— and some small talk before Gresham got down to cases.

"You think we need to amend our approach to these bandits in the Hawaiian government?"

"I think the course you proposed in Cabinet was both sound and wise," which was not at all what he thought of Gresham's policy— naïve and counterproductive, perhaps, but sound and wise? Not so much. "But in my judgment," Olney continued carefully, "the honor of the United States is hardly less concerned in securing justice and fair play for the Provisional Government, which the United States Minister had helped into the saddle, than in the restoring to power of the Queen's Government."

"You're concerned with justice for the Provisional Government? But they're pirates."

"Yes, of course you're right, but they're *our* pirates. It must ever be remembered that the Stevens government is *our* government; that is, it was set up by *our* Minister with the aid of our naval and military forces and was accorded the protection of *our* flag. Whatever the views of this Administration, its predecessor, for all practical purposes, sanctioned everything Minister Stevens took upon himself to do. Under such circumstances, to permit damage to the men who were Stevens' instruments—to permit the Queen to hang or banish them, or otherwise punish them for their connection with the Stevens Government, would, it seems to me, be grossly unjust and unwise. Ignoring such actions would bring the government of the United States into great discredit both at home and abroad."

"You believe the Queen would pursue vengeance?" This had clearly never occurred to Gresham.

"I would like a guarantee that she would not."

"Agreed," said the Secretary of State, clearly disturbed by the realization that, as Olney pointed out, this Hawaiian situation could become damned awkward.

Olney pressed his case. "And we need to consider the possibility that President Dole and his government might refuse to step down."

"Now that, my dear counselor, would not be a problem. Blount assures us that the Dole government is as weak as a kitten. The *Boston* is still in Pearl Harbor and can affect any sort of policy we determine."

"I'm sure you're right, Mr. Secretary, but the consequences of being wrong could be deadly and embarrassing." Olney decided to double down. "Also, there are constitutional issues at stake."

"Constitutional issues?"

"Yes. If we remove the Provisional Government by force to reinstate the Queen, we will have, in effect, declared war on a foreign government, which is Congress's constitutional prerogative, not the President's." Strict construction and a narrow interpretation of federal power—now Olney was speaking Gresham's language.

"I see your point, counselor. What do you suggest?"

Olney paused a moment. He did not want to seem too well prepared, or make Gresham suspect his policy was being supplanted. "Ahem, well, first, we should try to restore the Queen by diplomatic means. Second, if peaceful restoration doesn't work, let us not use force without the consent of Congress—we ought to secure from the Queen full power to negotiate for her restoration on terms the Congress finds practicable, that is, we should not allow her to dictate terms. Among such terms and conditions must be, I think, full pardon and amnesty for all those connected with the Stevens Government who might otherwise be charged with treason."

"Yes, we can't accept any bloodshed. My God." Gresham blanched, contemplating some of the more grisly consequences that could arise from intervention. "Counselor, I think your amendments are wise. And, frankly, I'm more than a little relieved that you thought of them. Such safeguards could spare us considerable embarrassment should violence erupt in Hawaii. I'll forward these to the President and advise our man in Hawaii to approach the Queen and Dole once President Cleveland agrees."

Olney returned to his offices that night, reassured that his government would take a more cautious course in the unpredictable affairs of the Polynesians. His assistant's memo helped save the U.S. government from humiliation, and Olney silently took more than a little credit for mentoring Symington into the insightful diplomat's aide he had become. Now he would have to see about getting young Mr. Symington over to dinner in appreciation for his Hawaiian rescue. He wondered if the awkward young man would be able to convince a girl to join him.

CHAPTER FOURTEEN

Lydia finally won the argument over who should do the endless row of corset buttons. Jonah admitted that it was only right given that he derived so much benefit from taking it off in the first place. As he sat behind her doing one button after another, he wondered how she ever managed to do this by herself. He took a moment to rub his finger up and down the nape of her neck, which she permitted, but when he took a moment to kiss it she let him know that this intimate interlude had well and truly concluded.

"Jonah, stop it. You'll make me late."

"Sorry, Miss Burke. Lost my head." He paused a moment to rub the soreness out of the bones around his mouth. "You know, Lydia, when you buck like that it hurts my jaw."

"You've got your nerve. Jonah, when you place your face beneath a girl like that you've got to expect her to move around a bit."

"Fair enough, I suppose," he conceded, still rubbing his abused face. "Where are you going tonight?"

"Hector is taking me to dinner at Olney's house."

"Again? This sounds serious."

"He wants it to be. The other day he asked if he could kiss me."

"Ooh, this *is* serious. What did you say?"

"I told him I would consider it," she said as she squeezed a breast into the unfriendly confines of her corset. "I wouldn't want him to think I was some sort of floozy."

"Certainly not. You know, at this point, it might not be

unreasonable to let the fellow have a little kiss." The best part of her toilette complete, he stopped watching and began to dress.

"That's fine advice to offer your wife," Lydia said, and an edge crept into her voice.

"*Ex*-wife."

She shuddered. "Oh, I just can't bring myself to do it. Something about him… I know it's the fashion, but that greasy hair tonic he uses—I just hate it. It smells like something that should attract flies. And I'm afraid my hand would slip right off his head if I touched it."

"Ah, true love."

"And that Boston accent—it does violence to my ears."

"Okay, so I don't have to worry about Hector stealing you away from me."

She turned to look him in the eyes. "I'm not yours to steal, as you so often remind me."

"You wound me deeply, but I'll recover. Has Hector heard anything from their man Willis in Hawaii?"

"No, but I'm sure he'll let us know as soon as he does. Willis's orders were sent over four weeks ago, so they should hear something soon."

"Damn!" It was obvious to the Attorney General and the Secretary of State that the President was not happy. When he followed the first "damn" with three more of them, finally concluding with an emphatic "God dammit!" it was clear that he was not pleased with the latest message from their representative in Honolulu. "Those were the Queen's exact words?" the President asked.

"Well, I'm afraid so, Mr. President, or words to that effect, anyway." Walter Gresham hoped to avoid repeating Queen Lilioukalani's exact words. In fact, he wanted very much at that moment to slump into a chair and sulk, but as the President was standing—pacing, actually—sitting down was not an option for anyone else in the room.

"Read it to me, verbatim," the President commanded.

Albert Willis had drafted this missive, reporting on his rather disastrous interview with the Queen, in which she autocratically dashed the Cleveland Administration's fondest hopes for an uncomplicated undoing of the Hawaiian Revolution. Gresham picked the letter up off the table in front of him and put his reading glasses on. "Would you like me to start at the beginning or go to the critical passage?"

"I want the Queen's words."

"Yes, sir. According to Willis, when he asked the Queen if she could guarantee an amnesty for the revolutionaries in the event that the U.S. restored her throne, 'she hesitated a moment and then slowly and calmly answered'—I'm quoting directly here—'There are certain laws of my government by which I shall abide. My decision would be, as the law directs, that such persons should be beheaded and their property confiscated by the government.' End quote." Gresham looked up to see the color rising in Cleveland's round cheeks.

"Oh, Christ! Beheaded? She wants to cut their damn heads off?"

"That is the generally accepted meaning of the term, Mr. President."

"Well it's not the generally accepted policy of the United States! Jesus. We can't allow this to happen. If we restore her to power and she starts chopping white people's heads off, well, we... we just can't let that happen."

"Would you like to hear the rest, Mr. President?" Gresham asked.

"Summarize, if you would," the President answered glumly. Done pacing, he slumped into his chair.

"Willis believes that the Queen would not be satisfied with mere restoration, that she would not find the status quo ante acceptable. He believes, if restored, she will end constitutional government in Hawaii."

"Why?" the President asked; his voice had gone from angry to plaintive.

"The Queen told him, and I'm quoting here," he said, adjusting his spectacles, "'These people,' that is, Thurston and his cronies, 'were the cause of the revolution of 1887.' That was the event that produced the constitutional monarchy—sort of a British-style parliamentary system," he said as an aside. "Willis writes that she has concluded, 'There will never be any peace while they are here.' He followed with his own analysis: 'I feel satisfied that, in the event of a restoration, there will be a concerted movement for the overthrow of constitutional government and the restoration of absolute monarchical dominion.'"

"She aspires to be a despot?" the President asked weakly.

Gresham looked at Olney before he continued, as if to make sure he had some support. "It gets worse, Mr. President."

"Worse? How could it possibly get worse?"

"Willis *was* able to convince the Queen to soften her stance, at least verbally, and so he informed the Dole Government that they would be asked to step aside."

"Well?"

"Dole declined."

"You mean he refused!" the President thundered.

"Yes, sir. May I quote?"

"Please," the President said with a wan wave of his hand.

"President Dole wrote to Willis: 'If American forces illegally assisted the revolutionaries in the establishment of the Provisional Government, that Government cannot be held responsible for the military's wrong-doing. There is no precedent in international law for the theory that malfeasance on the part of American troops has conferred upon the United States authority over the internal affairs of this government. Should it be true that the American government has made itself beholden to the Hawaiian Queen, that is also not a matter for me to discuss, except to submit that, if such be the case, it is a matter for the American government and her to settle.'"

The President was dumbstruck. The so-called president of a no-account little group of islands had just told the President of the

United States, in effect, to take a hike. The President turned to Olney, the legal expert in the room. "Is this true, this business about there being no basis in international law for our authority in Hawaii?"

"I know of no such precedent, I'm afraid," said Olney, who was silently thanking God and Gresham they had not simply blundered ahead and restored the Queen. "And, clearly, if we try to displace Dole's government by force, they will be disposed to fight. It could get very, very messy—Blount's assessment notwithstanding."

President Cleveland took a deep breath. "So this little upstart can tell us to mind our own business?"

"Well," Gresham started hesitantly, "given the Queen's threats, that might not be a bad policy."

"But how?" demanded the President. "We can't just wash our hands of the islands. Everybody in Washington knows we sent Blount there, and that we have his report. We must make policy and execute it."

"Mr. President," Gresham interrupted, "while it is true that the President must *execute* policy, it is Congress's prerogative to *make* policy. It *can* be left to that body."

"Go on," a newly curious president prompted.

"We can simply defer to Congress."

"We can?"

"Yes, we can."

Jonah was in the new offices of the Hawaiian embassy on Connecticut Avenue. No one in Washington recognized it as the Hawaiian embassy, but Thurston had rented the house, and the first floor was filled with desks and telephones and even a few of the young ladies Jonah had hired to work on the Annexation Commission back in Honolulu. He was gratified to see that they had brought their bats and gloves with them. It was November, but he saw no reason they could not play softball until the snow started to fall.

"Did you see this, Mr. Ambassador?" Jonah interrupted Thurston's work with a copy of the *Washington Post*.

"See what?" Thurston grumbled.

"This statement from President Cleveland. It's a 6,000-word message in which he washes his hands of us."

"Well, you predicted that was coming, did you not?"

"Yes, but I didn't think he'd be so verbose about it."

"What does he say?"

"The usual. That Minister Stevens created you and President Dole out of whole cloth. You, like Stevens' Frankenstein's monster, have complicated U.S. diplomacy immeasurably. But here's a new wrinkle: He is sending the Blount report and a sheaf of other documents to the Capitol and recommending the subject to 'the extended powers and wide discretion of Congress.'"

"In other words," Thurston concluded, "we are now Congress's problem and he is well rid of us."

"That's what it sounds like to me."

"Then it sounds to me like you'll be spending most of your days on the Capitol Hill."

Jonah knew that protest was futile. "You're too good to me, Mr. Ambassador."

The lower house of Congress dealt with the President's request in five days. The House of Representatives was in a hurry to get started on the coming lollapalooza over the coinage of silver at a ratio of sixteen-to-one with gold. It was a monetary argument sure to put the average American to sleep, but to "sound money" gold bugs who opposed it, and to farmers and silver miners who wanted to inflate depressed prices, it was a life-or-death struggle. In any case, the House acted quickly, returning some hastily written weasel words vaguely supportive of Cleveland's Hawaiian policy—a neat trick, considering that Cleveland no longer had a Hawaiian policy. This made congressional support for the non-policy difficult to interpret.

"They seem to have said nothing at all, which, I suppose, is a good thing?" Thurston was grasping.

"I think so," Jonah tentatively agreed. Thurston gave him the familiar sidelong glance that told him he had better explain further. "Okay, here's my best guess. The Democratic House of Representatives, in order to get to work on more important things—silver and gold, to be precise—has voted a resolution to affirm the Hawaii policy of the Democratic President. The only problem with said affirmation is that the President doesn't actually have a Hawaii policy to affirm, and was actually asking Congress to give him one, which means...," Jonah threw up his hands, "well, I don't know what it means."

"It means that they want to talk about money, not Hawaii," grumbled Thurston.

"Yes, but Cleveland remains free to do as he chooses, like say, send in the troops to depose the P.G.'s. There is nothing in this resolution that says he can't."

Thurston chewed on that for a moment. "All right," he began, "Cleveland and Congress may have no idea what they're doing, so let us be clear about what we want and how to get it." He leaned back in his chair and rubbed his temples for a few moments while he formulated an outline in his mind. "It appears that annexation is—for now—a dead letter. Gresham hates everyone who wrote the treaty and the very idea of overseas expansion, so as long as he is alive, annexation is dead."

"So, if Hawaii's goal is no longer annexation to the United States, what is it?" asked Jonah.

"I think that President Dole decided that for everyone in his response to Cleveland. Hawaii is—for now, at least—an independent republic."

"I suppose he did. Say, did Dole consult you on that?"

"No, I don't think he talked to anyone about it. I think that he was so offended by the notion that the President of the United States assumed that he could simply instruct him to step down that he immediately sat down and penned a reply telling him where he could stick it, in a lawyerly way, of course. And, for what it's worth, I think it was brilliant.

"The Republic of Hawaii," Jonah repeated. "Has a nice ring." Returning to the subject at hand, "Then our goal is...?"

"To prevent our republic from returning to monarchy—and keep President Dole's head attached to his neck. As this debate moves from the House to the Senate, our goal must be to achieve recognition of Hawaii as an independent republic, or at least get them to prohibit reinstating the Queen."

"Okay, then," Jonah said. He looked out at the staff outside Thurston's office, glad to have a clear direction again. "I'll get the propaganda machine rolling."

"Hey, Jonah, how long did the House debate the resolution before they passed it?" Thurston asked him before he got out the door.

"Five days, but that was just because they were in a hurry to dispense with it—and us. The Senate shouldn't take much longer, though. It's a much smaller body, with fewer tongues to wag. We can hope they'll be done within a week or two."

Five months later Jonah found himself sitting in the visitors' gallery of the Senate, listening to yet another senator emphatically declare for or against American expansion, or the restoration of the Queen, or the value of Hawaii as a naval asset, or this, or that, and on and on. The members of the House of Representatives may have been in a hurry to move on from the Polynesian peccadillo to address the country's failing economy, but the Senate—sometimes referred to as a millionaire's club (despite the fact that only a few of them were actually millionaires)—felt no such compulsion. What irked Jonah about the interminable pace of the debate was that he clearly remembered a dinner party the previous March at which each and every issue relevant to Hawaii had been debated far more expediently. He recalled William Castle flailing away at the arguments of the three-headed monster of Godkin, Ogden, and Schurz, without much effect, but having witnessed the Senate's approach, Castle was rising in his estimation.

The process of musing aloud on the Senate floor was predictably endless. Unlike the House of Representatives, the Senate is a club in which the members jealously guard their prerogatives, foremost among which, evidently, is the right to talk any subject to death. (The House, on the other hand, mindful of the politician's tendency to blather, has rules to control such things.) The Senate—the upper house—would never subject themselves to rules that would shut their mouths. And so...five months passed.

While the Senate droned on, Jonah knew that if anything happened in Hawaii, U.S. Marines, not U.S. Senators, would decide the issue. Given Cleveland Administration antipathy to the P.G.'s, such a turn of events could be disastrous. While the Senate debated, the Queen's partisans were plotting counterrevolution. The lid could blow off the cauldron of Hawaiian politics at any time.

"Why on earth won't they move on this?" Thurston roared.

Jonah sat opposite his desk and looked impassively at his frustrated boss. They had been stuck in this situation for months and neither had any idea how to break the logjam. "I don't know," Jonah admitted. "They all want to dispense with the Hawaii issue, but they can't figure out how to do it. There have now been three government reports written on the revolution, not to mention thousands of articles and editorials advocating for or against annexation. And there are other, larger issues."

"Such as?"

"You know, the larger implications of the change in traditional policy—abandoning the Washington Doctrine against entangling alliances, and all that."

"I know, I know," Thurston said with an impatient wave of his hand. "These fossilized troglodytes in the Senate are scared to death that acquiring Hawaii will instantly transform the United States into an imperial power."

"You have to admit that it would be a departure," Jonah pointed out.

"But the issues they're discussing don't even matter anymore," Thurston insisted. "The Senate continues to debate the revolution and annexation, yet the revolution is an accomplished fact and we're no longer asking for annexation."

They were interrupted by a tap on the door.

Melissa popped her head in, smiled at Jonah, then turned to Thurston and said, "Miss Burke is here to see you, Mr. Ambassador." Jonah couldn't help but notice the hard edge that came to Melissa's otherwise sweet voice when she said *Miss Burke*. She stepped aside and allowed Lydia to pass by.

Lydia smiled at Melissa and thanked her with exaggerated gratitude. "Oh, look Melissa, Mr. Christian is here as well. It's always good to see Mr. Christian, don't you agree, Melissa?"

Melissa closed the door without answering.

"I hope that girl doesn't keep her baseball bat close to her desk or I might be in danger the next time I come."

"To what do we owe the pleasure?" Jonah changed the subject.

"I think I have an opportunity to help you gentlemen, that is, if Jonah isn't in a hurry to take the girls out to softball practice."

"What sort of opportunity?" Thurston asked.

"Jonah may have told you, I have a friend in the Justice Department, and I've had several opportunities to speak with the Attorney General informally lately."

"Several?" Jonah asked. Evidently Hector was bringing her along to Olney family gatherings regularly. Lydia ignored the question.

"The Justice Department would like nothing more than for Hawaii to go away," she reported.

"Justice?" Thurston asked. "What do they have to do with it? Foreign relations is the province of the State Department and that bastard—excuse me—Gresham."

"Yes, of course," Lydia continued, "but Justice is particularly pressed right now with thousands of strikers taking up arms and setting fires in Chicago, and that man Coxey marching on Washington with his 'army' of unemployed men. All of that seems a lot more pressing than Hawaii. And yet, there it is, occupying the Senate daily, keeping useful legislation off the docket."

"I couldn't agree more," said Thurston. "But what would you have us do about it?"

"Yes," Jonah chimed in. He was curious why she brought this to the office instead of mentioning it the previous evening when they were together. "We have been cajoling every senator who will listen to us that they would all do well to simply drop it and leave Hawaii alone, but they're all hell-bent on discussing the larger doctrinal issues—discussing them to death, as it happens."

"Oh, Jonah—'doctrinal issues'?" Lidia was amused. "You sound like you're back in seminary. Well, what do you want?"

"We want them to resolve to respect the independence of Hawaii and promise not to reinstate the Queen."

"Then write the resolution for them."

"I would love to write such a resolution, but that won't do us a lot of good given that neither Ambassador Thurston nor I are United States Senators!"

Thurston found it more informative, not to mention amusing, to observe this conversation rather than participate in it.

"You don't have to be a Senator, Jonah—you just have to have a Senator submit it."

"But none of them want a resolution pledging non-interference. They're all bound up over the President's 6,000-word message, which has them divided between annexation or reinstating the Queen—you know, whether America should be the imperialist or the knight errant."

"But what if your resolution found its way to a Senator who was desperately looking for a way out?"

Thurston and Jonah looked at each other, then at Lydia.

"You know such a Senator?" Thurston asked skeptically.

"No, but my friend in the Justice Department does. He won't tell me who it is. But he says if he were to provide this unnamed Senator a workable resolution, as long as there was nothing to suggest that it came from the Hawaiian legation—they really don't like you fellows—he might be able to persuade the Senator to submit it for a vote."

"Why doesn't Olney just call in a favor or two and do this himself?" Thurston asked.

"Olney doesn't know about this. Hector is just trying to save his boss some grief."

"Hector?" Thurston was confused.

"Her friend in the Justice Department," Jonah informed him. "Nice young man: good legal mind, unfortunate hair."

"Justice," Lydia continued, giving Jonah a sidelong look, "really wishes Cleveland would have just left the treaty in the Senate and allowed Blount to go quietly into retirement. But State won't tell Congress what to do, and if Justice were caught lobbying on a foreign policy issue it could cause great embarrassment for the Administration, and awkwardness between State and Justice. In short, it has to be done discreetly."

Thurston was convinced. "All right, then!" he declared, "If your young man wants a resolution, we shall give him one. Jonah," he said, standing up so he could pace, as was his wont when dictating. "Fetch your typewriter." Turning to Lydia, he said, "Miss Burke, I am very glad you decided to stop by this afternoon."

"Well," said Lydia, a little self-satisfied after bestowing this ray of sunshine on the Hawaiian legation, "you gentlemen seem to have your hands full, so I'll be on my way." And with that she sashayed out of the office, pausing briefly to offer Melissa a little wink and a smile on her way out.

In Thurston's office Jonah sat poised behind a typewriter while Thurston paraded back and forth. After a few false starts, some edits and one rewrite, they produced the mystery Senator's resolution: Resolved, *that of right it belongs wholly to the people of the Hawaiian Islands to establish and maintain their own form of government and domestic polity; that the United States ought in no wise to interfere therewith, and that any intervention in the political affairs of these islands by any other government will be regarded as an act unfriendly to the United States.*

"It's unequivocal and non-interfering," Jonah said, nodding his head approvingly at the document.

"That should do it," said Thurston, though still not quite sure about it. "It promises us that Cleveland won't interfere with us, but reassures the American people that Hawaii won't seek to become a protectorate of Britain, without naming her of course."

"Now, if it will just meet the approval of Hector's unnamed legislator."

Later that evening, passionately celebrating the events of the day, Lydia pulled her mouth from Jonah's to say between gasps, "Oh, I… umh, I delivered that resolution to… uh,"

"Hector?" Jonah supplied helpfully.

"Yes!"

"Thank…you," Jonah replied. It used to irritate him that she insisted on talking about whatever crossed her mind during sex, but he had gotten used to it, or at least learned to live with it. It was, he rationalized, better than not having sex at all. Besides, when she finally went silent for a few moments he always knew why, and he found that gratifying. Afterward, she rolled over and pulled up the covers. Unlike her usual quick exit, tonight she was in no apparent hurry to jump out of the bed.

"You must have finally given Hector that kiss," Jonah ventured.

"No," Lydia said, tossing the covers off her naked body, deciding it was just too warm in the room. "I just told him I'm not that kind of girl and he accepted it. He seems satisfied to have someone to accompany him to dinner at the Olney's."

Jonah absently stroked her breast as her phrase echoed in his brain, *not that kind of girl*. "Did he tell you who the Senator is—the one who will submit the resolution for our deliverance?"

"Turpie, I think it was. Indiana Democrat."

"Excellent," Jonah concluded. He did not know him, but he knew of him. "David Turpie—he's well-respected. I think we've got a shot at getting this thing passed."

"What time is it?" she asked.

"Nine-thirty."

"Oh, I've got to go! If I'm not back at my boarding house by ten o'clock that old busy-body will lock me out and start telling UPI I'm a fallen woman."

A little less than a week later Lydia found Jonah sitting anxiously in the visitors' gallery of the Senate awaiting a roll-call vote on Senator Turpie's resolution pledging the United States to keep its mitts off of Hawaii—for the moment. He sat poised with a notepad on his knees and a roster of senators in alphabetical order. He saw Thurston standing among the editorial heavyweights from New York, who had come down for the vote. Thurston glanced Jonah's way, and Jonah held up his roster and pencil, as if to say, *I'm ready, I'm counting*. Thurston nodded his approval and turned back to his guests.

The magic number of "yeas" was forty-five, if all the Senators voted, which was unlikely. Jonah estimated that they could probably carry the resolution with as few as forty votes in favor, if there were a several abstentions, as he suspected there would be. The problem was, since Turpie had submitted the resolution everything had moved so quickly that Jonah had not had the time to canvass and get a rough estimate of how the vote would go. It was as if the whole Senate had been trying to feel their way out of a pitch black room, and once Turpie's resolution opened the door to the light beyond, they all rushed toward it. At least that's what Jonah hoped would happen.

The presiding senator, President Pro Tempore John Sherman, took up his gavel and banged the proceedings to order, then ordered the clerk to read the resolution. Senator Sherman thanked the clerk, and began the roll call. "Senator Aldrich?"

"Yea."

"Senator Allen?"

"Abstain."

"Senator Bacon?"

"Yea, Mr. President…"

Jonah stood with Lydia on the steps of the Capitol in the warm sun of a lovely April afternoon. They were waiting for Thurston to detach himself from the journalists who crowded around him to get his reaction to the vote, but he was making no effort to escape them. As the journalists dispersed they were replaced by other members of the Washington power structure, all of them anxious to congratulate Thurston, or ask him what exactly the resolution actually meant to Hawaii's provisional government.

"I don't think he's coming," Lydia said.

"That's fine. I've seen enough of him in the past few months." Jonah looked relieved.

"Let me see that piece of paper again, please." She reached into his breast pocket and removed the folded Senate roster. She read Jonah's vote tabulation at the bottom and smiled as she looked up at him. "Fifty-five yeas, zero nays, and thirty abstentions. Mr. Christian, I'd say you have yourselves a unanimous vote, after a fashion."

"By the numbers. Thanks for the help."

"My pleasure. I thought you were working too hard."

"How 'bout dinner? The Republic of Hawaii owes you a meal, at least."

"I'd like to, but I'm meeting Hector. He wanted to celebrate as well. You fellows have been a real headache for him and he's glad to be rid of you, frankly."

"I had no idea we were regarded so fondly."

She put her arm through his and started walking up Pennsylvania Avenue toward UPI's office across from the White House. "You've spent the last year and a half trying to establish Hawaii's status one way or another. Well, that's done. What are you going to do next?"

"Thurston wants me to go back to Hawaii—be his man in the Foreign Ministry—but I'm not going to do it. I can't go back there."

"Why ever not?"

"Sick of it," he said without elaborating.

"All right then, are you going to stay here?"

"Well, I've been thinking about it. I have established relationships with nearly every reporter and news organization between here and New York—some of them more intimate than others," he smiled at Lydia. "I don't want to sit in an office anymore. I think I'd like to see more of the world, but I'd like somebody like the *New York World* or *The Times* to pay for it."

"But do you actually know how to be a journalist?"

"Having been at the center of a story for the last year or so, it seems to me that most of you just make it all up anyway. I can do that."

As they approached her office they noticed Hector loitering outside. Lydia slipped her arm out of Jonah's just as he turned toward them with a quizzical smile.

"I think he's probably more interested in seeing you than me," Jonah volunteered. "I'll be on my way then."

"Wait. Don't go. I'm sure he would like to hear about the vote from you." She began to sense that the relationship they had enjoyed the last few months was coming to an end, and she was not ready to let him go just yet.

"I'll be around a while longer. I'll see you around." And with that he took his leave and headed back to the embassy to see if he could scare up a game of softball.

EPILOGUE

Havana, Cuba, four years later.

He was not sure if the pounding he heard was at the door or in his head. Jonah opened his eyes carefully, not wanting to risk letting in too much light all at once. Happily, the dawn was only just breaking, and there was little light to assault his throbbing brain. It was not so dim as to allow him to overlook the cascading black hair of the woman sleeping next to him, however. *Who could she be?* he wondered. Then came the pounding again—yes, it was at the door. It was followed by a voice this time.

"Come on, Christian—get out of bed. You'll want to see this." It was Stephen Crane, fellow journalist, here in Cuba to cover the War with Spain. Evidently he had not yet gone to bed.

"Go away," Jonah ordered, knowing Crane would do no such thing. Crane opened the door and let himself in. He tossed a ragged newspaper at Jonah's chest and strained to get a better look at the woman in bed next to him.

"Who's that?"

"I don't know. Last thing I remember you were buying drink in the cantina downstairs...." Jonah brushed the woman's hair back for a better look.

"I'm sure she was prettier last night, old man," Crane offered helpfully.

"What's this?" Jonah regarded the newspaper through half-closed eyes.

"You ought to recognize it, Christian; it's your paper, *The New York World?*"

"So you thought you'd wake me up in the middle of the night to show it to me? Thanks."

"Have you read that little article there about Hawaii? I know how hard you worked on that—I thought you'd want to see it."

"Hawaii?" Jonah sat up suddenly on the edge of the bed. "Light that lamp, will you?"

While Crane crashed around the darkened room, searching for a lamp, Jonah squinted to read the type. He looked at the date, July 6, 1898—a week ago. By joint resolution, submitted by President McKinley, the House and the Senate had voted to annex Hawaii as a territory of the United States.

"What the hell?" Jonah demanded angrily, tossing the newspaper at Crane. The woman in the bed rolled over, revealing her dark breasts as she stretched luxuriously, still evidently very much asleep. Crane looked her way and gave an approving nod.

"Pay attention, Crane," said Jonah as he pulled a cover over the woman.

"Sorry, but she does look better from this angle."

"Are you telling me that after I spent eighteen months doing everything imaginable to get a treaty through the U.S. Senate and getting nowhere, no matter how much propaganda I wrote, drinks I bought, bribes I paid—you're telling me that McKinley casually mentions he'd like to have Hawaii and it's a done deal?"

"Evidently the islands are on the way to the Philippines. A convenient stop, as it were, for ships and troops," Crane pointed out.

"Yes," Jonah said, adjusting his bedmates legs so he could slump against the wall. "I suppose it is."

Crane picked up the paper and started to read, seemingly oblivious to the fact that he and his colleague were sitting on a bed with a naked woman. "Crane?" Jonah interrupted him. "Would you please get out of here? I seem to have poisoned myself and your

340

news has made it worse. I'd like to sleep it off, if you don't mind. I have a terrible headache."

"Which one, Hawaii, Guam, the Philippines? It seems to me the headaches have just begun." He blew out the lamp and closed the door behind him, leaving Jonah to his headache.

9004404R0

Made in the USA
Charleston, SC
02 August 2011